Praise for Debby Holt's *The Ex-Wife's Survival Guide*

'Thoroughly enjoyable . . . Had me smiling from start to finish' ERICA JAMES

'I absolutely loved this book. It is as funny as it's wise and I couldn't put it down' KATIE FFORDE

'A wickedly comical read' *Heat*

'A marvellous read' *Mail on Sunday*

'An acutely observed comedy of manners in a small English village, this book will make you smile' *My Weekly*

'A deliciously funny, gently ironic novel, Jane Austen-like in its elegance and playfulness . . . touching romantic comedy that finishes on such a wonderfully liberating note that you want to stand and cheer. Bravo! Encore!' *Australian Women's Weekly*

Also by Debby Holt

THE EX-WIFE'S SURVIVAL GUIDE

Debby Holt lives in Bath with her husband and whichever of their five children are around at the time. Debby is the author of *The Ex-Wife's Survival Guide*. This is her second novel.

Annie May's Black Book

Debby Holt

POCKET
BOOKS

LONDON • NEW YORK • SYDNEY • TORONTO

First published in Great Britain by Pocket Books, 2007
An imprint of Simon & Schuster UK Ltd
A CBS COMPANY

This edition published 2009 for Index Books Ltd

1 3 5 7 9 10 8 6 4 2

Simon & Schuster UK Ltd
1st Floor
222 Gray's Inn Road
London WC1X 8HB

www.simonsays.co.uk

Simon & Schuster Australia
Sydney

A CIP catalogue record for this book is available from the British Library

ISBN 978-1-84739-820-8

Typeset by Rowland Phototypesetting Ltd
Bury St Edmunds, Suffolk
Printed and bound in Great Britain by
CPI Cox & Wyman, Reading, Berkshire

For my sister, Fiona,
who could never be in anyone's black book.

Thanks, as always, to my Fromesbury friends for great advice; to Louise Whitehead and Michelle Sheppard for giving me my very own black books; to David Holt for endless support; to my excellent agent, Teresa Chris and the brilliant people at Simon & Schuster, especially Kate Lyall Grant and Tara Wigley. Finally, very special thanks to my son, Charlie, for giving me the idea.

In her Black Book, Annie has recorded the name and offence of everyone who has ever done her wrong. The greatest transgressor of them all was the man who jilted her seventeen years ago.

Now, he's moving into a house round the corner.

Entries From Annie May's
Black Book

15 October 1974
Miss Baker for telling me how to blow my nose and not believing when I still couldn't do it.

6 February 1977
David Llewellyn for saying my landscape painting looked like a pig's trough and then making honking noises every time he saw me.

10 May 1979
Carol Anderson for telling everyone I thought necking meant kissing on the neck.

8 March, 1980
Helen Owen for telling Miss Morrish she heard me swearing when she knew we were only swapping words and anyway I didn't pronounce it properly.

5 March 1982
Janet Elliot for telling Nigel my bra was stuffed with tissues.

8 March 1983

Mr Cawthorne for telling me I was the stupidest girl he'd ever met.

2 January 1984

My cousin Peter for introducing me to his friend as his country cousin and making me feel like one by talking only about his London buddies who I didn't know and who I certainly don't want to know because they all sound horrible.

6 June 1985

Alison Parker for telling Lucy she'd be very attractive if her bottom was smaller.

9 October 1985

Lizzie Gatehouse for telling Nigel, Gary and Paul that I'd told everyone at school that they fancied me. So now they won't speak to me and I shall never speak to Lizzie.

3 November 1986

Angus Trent for telling me he loved me and kissing me passionately at Lucy's party and neglecting to tell me he was emigrating to Australia the very next day.

6 January 1987

Harriet Murray for listening with crocodile sympathy while Lucy told her that the only time Peter Elton paid any attention to her was when he went to bed with her and Harriet again for going off and sleeping with Peter that very night.

12 April 1987
Peter Elton for 'borrowing' my cigarettes and never buying any of his own.

6 June 1987
Andrea Johns for staying in my flat for fourteen weeks and never paying rent or housekeeping and giving me a thank-you present that was a belt that turned out to be one she'd bought for herself and hadn't liked and anyway it was too big for me.

3 September 1987
Jenny Edwards for trying to lure Ben away from me. (Not that she ever had a chance.)

CHAPTER ONE

Black Book Entry, 8 February: Mr Cawthorne for coming round the day before my wedding and trying to make us all feel guilty for not inviting him.

Lily was the last person in whom Annie would normally confide the state of her soul. Lily and souls did not go together. Annie sometimes wondered if Lily *had* a soul. Nevertheless, tonight, on the eve of her wedding, back in the bosom of her family, sitting in her bedroom with its fading Duran Duran posters still on the wall, Annie felt compelled to articulate her thoughts.

'It's difficult to explain,' she said, 'but I feel so different, I feel like I'm rolling on a blanket of love. I love everyone. I hope I always feel like this.'

'I hope so too,' said Lily, expertly rifling the contents of Annie's wardrobe. 'I don't suppose you feel like giving me your brown velvet jacket?'

'No,' said Annie. Of course Lily didn't understand. Lily could never understand. Annie sat down at her dressing table and reached for her Nearly Nude nail varnish.

Annie had discovered the meaning of life. Lily couldn't understand that either. Annie had discovered the meaning of life a few months ago. To be precise, she had discovered the meaning of life at half past two on 27 December.

At twenty-nine minutes past two on 27 December, she sat at her desk in her bedroom. Supposedly writing thank-you letters, she was in fact picking over the bones of her break-up with Ben six weeks earlier. At half past two, she heard the sound of crunching gravel outside. Looking through the window, she saw Ben walking up the drive. She raced out of her room, along the corridor, down the stairs, through the hall and out into his arms and he whispered, 'Marry me. Marry me at once.'

That moment, that memory, sat in a little box in the corner of her mind and every time she opened it, whether she was in her Hammersmith flat trying to make her shower work, or on the underground, stuck in a carriage with at least fifty-five too many passengers, or at work trying to deal with ten different queries all at once, she would open the box and a thousand tiny sparks of joy would fly out, rearranging the atoms, making her see that life was good.

Love was the meaning of life. Love changed everything. Without love, she could go to work, revel in the fact that she was at least a small part of the august institution that was the BBC, look forward to the day when she could stop being a secretary and start being a Drama Production Assistant and then, possibly, a producer.

Without love, it was still possible to enjoy seeing her friends, coming home to her family, going on holiday to France. Without love, she could do all these things and almost manage to ignore the shapeless blur of confused discontent that had been with her for as long as she could remember. But now that, somehow, she had won the love of the most charming, sensitive, funny man on the planet, love gave her life a structure and a purpose. Ben had taken her smudgy, chameleon-like existence and given it dignity and depth. She had spent her life with her face pressed to the window, watching the party through the glass and knowing there was a way in if only she could find it. Ben had opened the door and ushered her in and there she was, warm and safe for evermore.

Her entire life before Ben comprised a kaleidoscope of memories: her childish longing to be an actress, her fierce quarrels with Lily, her doomed attempts to emulate Josephine's academic successes, her numerous infatuations with boys whose attractions turned to dust as soon as they reciprocated her feelings, her joy at joining the BBC, her excitement at leaving home and renting a flat with friends. Everything in her life seemed to form a backdrop to this moment. This would be the last time she would sit in her old bedroom trying to do something while her sister tried to stop her doing it.

Lily, her younger sister by eighteen months, was going to be her bridesmaid. Annie had not been terribly enthusiastic about sharing the limelight with a sister who had the ego of Madonna and the looks of Kim Basinger but had felt unable to disappoint her mother's blithe confidence in her sisterly good nature.

Having finished with the wardrobe, Lily was now studying herself in front of the full-length mirror. 'Do you like my hair?' she asked. She had been to the hairdresser's that afternoon.

'Do you think I should have had another inch taken off? Annie, you do have to look at me!'

Annie who was trying to paint her left thumb with the nail polish glanced fleetingly at her sister. 'I don't know why you bother to ask me,' she said. 'You know very well you think you look perfect.'

'Yes,' agreed Lily, 'but I want to know if *you* think so too.' Their mother always maintained that Lily's honesty was commendable but Annie reckoned that there was a fine line between honesty and complacency and that Lily had crossed that line from the time she had learnt to speak.

'It pains me to say this,' Annie confessed, 'but you do look rather good. I like the fringe.'

She jumped as her bedroom door swerved violently against the bookcase and the newest member of the family, her one-year-old nephew, Sidney, waddled in. Sidney had what her parents liked to call a 'precocious intellect'; this observation seemed to be based solely on the fact that he repeated the last word of anything that was said to him. 'Hello, Sidney!' Annie said. 'What have you got in your hand?'

This was not a sensible question to ask since she could see what he had in his hand; he had a plastic yellow duck which he obligingly tottered forward to give her, thus causing her to smudge the nail polish. 'Oh Sidney!' she exclaimed, reaching for a tissue. 'Do you know what you are? You are a naughty little devil!'

One of Sidney's more endearing characteristics was the pleasure he took in everything anyone said to him. 'Dev-il! Dev-il!' he chortled.

Annie's mother, Rosemary, bustling into the room with the

8

air of someone who had forgotten what she wanted to say, smiled at the sight of her grandson. 'Hello, Sidney! What are you doing? Are you helping Annie to do her nails?' Neither of these questions was sensible either since it was quite clear what Sidney was doing; he was hitting Annie's knees with his bottom and he was not helping Annie with her nails. Showing less than precocious understanding, he tried to retrieve his yellow duck, knocking over Annie's nail varnish in the process.

'Annie . . .' Rosemary's voice trailed away as she tried to recall what she was doing here. She caught sight of her reflection in the mirror and absently patted her newly permed hair. Her face cleared. 'Annie! I meant to tell you that Mr Cawthorne dropped by with a wedding present for you and I must say it's a very nice wedding present! It's a garden spade and I felt *so* embarrassed that we hadn't invited him and I was just wondering if we couldn't . . .'

Annie reached out for another tissue. 'I'm sorry,' she said in a voice that made it clear she wasn't sorry at all, 'I am not inviting a man who told me I was the stupidest girl he had ever taught!'

'You just said you loved everybody,' Lily said.

'I love everybody except Mr Cawthorne.'

'Oh really, Annie!' Rosemary protested. 'He's so fond of you! And you used to be fond of *him* too! He tutored you in maths for six years! I must say, it's quite . . . *disconcerting* . . . the way you take against people! And you have to admit, you *were* very stupid at maths.'

'I know I was stupid at maths. I was even more stupid at maths after Mr Cawthorne *told* me I was stupid at maths.'

'You're about to get married!' Rosemary remonstrated. 'It's the happiest day of your life! It's time to put away grudges and show some Christian charity!'

'I have done,' Annie said. 'I let you invite Cousin Peter. That's quite enough Christian charity for me.'

'Has anyone seen Sidney?' Josephine's bump appeared in the doorway, closely followed by Josephine. Josephine was Annie's older and extremely pregnant sister. She and Lily had very similar features and it was difficult to say why the youngest sister was stunning and the oldest was not. Josephine's dark blonde hair was tied back in a utilitarian ponytail while Lily's unfettered, shining locks were enhanced by Harmony's Heavenly Blonde Rinse. Both girls had extravagantly long eyelashes and exquisite bow-shaped mouths, but everything about Lily seemed to sing, 'Aren't I gorgeous?' whereas Josephine looked as if she was permanently worried, probably because she was. If she wasn't worrying about the unfairness of Third World poverty or the iniquity of Mrs Thatcher, she was bemoaning the probable fate of Sidney's generation in a world of nuclear weapons and unregulated pollution. She was also very short-sighted and did not spot her son until he jumped up and down, screeching 'Mummee!' and jogging Annie's arm in the process, just as she had finished applying Nearly Nude for the third time.

'Oh Sidney!' Josephine said. 'I've unpacked your pyjamas and now your bath's getting cold!' Her attention was diverted by the bridal gown hanging from the curtain rail. 'So this is the dress!' she said.

'What do you think?' Annie asked.

'It's very nice,' Josephine said, 'though I still can't see

why you wasted money on a new dress. You could have had mine.'

'No offence,' Lily said, 'but there is no one in the world who would want to borrow your wedding dress.'

This was true. Josephine had bought her dress from her friend's sister who had started a business called Bridal Gowns for Ever After. Her friend's sister had had the intriguing idea of making wedding gowns that could be used *ever after* as sheets. It would have been an even better idea if the wedding dresses had looked a little more like dresses and a little less like sheets. Not surprisingly, Josephine's friend's sister had only ever sold one wedding dress.

'It was a lovely wedding dress, wasn't it, Sidney?' Josephine said, asking the one person in the room who was in no position to reply. 'Are you going to have a bath before bedtime? Shall we ask Granny to help?'

'I *would* like to!' said Rosemary wistfully. 'I really ought to rearrange the wedding presents but it's like trying to finish a jigsaw puzzle without all the pieces. I can't manage to fit them all into the dining room and I know Jean Farnleigh-Anderson will be furious if I don't display every one of her Wedgwood Florentine soup bowls. I still have boxes of stuff all over the floor.'

'I'll do it for you,' Lily said. 'No offence, Mother, but you haven't the first idea about presentation and it is something I'm particularly good at. And I do like playing with the wedding presents. I can't wait to get married. I shall make the biggest and most expensive present list in the world. I shall go and live at Harrods for a week!'

'I wish I could believe you were joking,' said Josephine

sorrowfully. 'I really do wish that.' She hoisted Sidney onto her hip. 'Shall we go and have our bath now, Sidney? Shall Granny come too?'

Granny smiled happily. 'I think Granny will! Granny wants to make some big bubbles! Say goodnight to Auntie Annie! Say goodnight to Auntie Lily!'

The two aunts raised their right hands and waved dutifully. 'Goodnight, Sidney!' They watched their nephew being borne away like a young pharaoh with his adoring handmaidens.

'If I weren't such a well-adjusted teenager,' Lily observed, 'I might be upset that our mother bestows so much attention upon Sidney.'

'You're only a teenager for another few months,' Annie pointed out. 'And, anyway, what about *me*? Do you remember when Ben and I were trying to tell everyone we were engaged? Sidney had chosen that precise moment to take his first steps. He won hands down.'

'You do realize,' mused Lily, 'that when you and Ben have children, Josephine will expect you to use all of Sidney's home-made baby clothes? How many children are you going to have?'

'Ben wants two,' Annie said. 'I'd like five.'

'I'd like three girls who will look just like me and we'll all be invited to model for soap adverts.' Lily glanced at the mirror one last time and went to the door. 'I'm off to sort out your wedding presents. Remember we're having the champagne at eight.'

'I'll be there.'

'Your hair looks nice,' Lily said. 'You'll make a very pretty bride.'

12

Lily's compliments were very rare and therefore doubly precious. Annie smiled. 'Thank you!'

'That's all right. All's well that ends well.'

'Love conquers everything.'

Lily grinned and walked out. Their maternal grandmother had a habit of talking in clichés and ever since they were little and the two younger sisters had been told once too often that little birds in their nest should agree, they had competed with each other to reach for the appropriate cliché whenever possible. But actually, Annie thought, clichés were there for a reason and love *did* conquer everything.

With her bedroom now blissfully empty, Annie applied herself diligently to her nails. Tomorrow afternoon, she would be Mrs Seymour. Tomorrow evening she and Ben would be drinking champagne in a little hotel near Gatwick and after that they would be in Corfu. Two weeks later, they would be living in Pixie Cottage and travelling to work together every morning. One day they would live in a house with a pond or a river at the bottom of the garden – Annie had always wanted to live near water – and they would have lots of children and a dog and drink wine on the terrace. Her life lay before her like a glittering beach.

She caught sight of her reflection in the mirror. She, like Lily, had been to the hairdresser's that afternoon and her brown hair, normally an undisciplined tangle of curls, was sleek and shiny like the coat of a racing horse. She might not have the bone structure of her sisters, she certainly didn't possess Josephine's brains or Lily's beauty but she had a trim figure, bright eyes and what she now knew was an alluring nose. Ben said it was her nose that had first attracted him. He said he loved the way it went straight down and then changed its mind at the last minute. Scrutinizing her nose now, Annie couldn't quite understand why this particular part of her anatomy was so spectacular but she was happy to take Ben's word for it. She was happy to take Ben's word for anything.

She went downstairs at eight, her newly painted fingernails splayed out like fish fins. Her father was on the phone in the hall. David May was almost always on the phone, either in the hall, or in the study where he had had two phone lines installed, or in the garden where he had one cunningly concealed in the rhododendron bush. This evening there was, as he had explained to Annie earlier when she wanted to call Ben, a crisis at work. David had a crisis at least once a fortnight but Annie knew very well that the latest crisis was always the worst; there was no point in even thinking of trying to use the phone for herself. Now her father stood in front of the hall mirror, smoothing back his hair while he talked earnestly into the mouthpiece. 'No, no, this is unacceptable, Harold, quite unacceptable. Write me another draft and get back to me . . . no, not tonight, I've at least six other branch managers ringing later this evening . . . That's right, old boy, ring in the morning. Any time will do as long as it's before half past one . . . No, it must be before half past one. My daughter's getting married and I have to be there. Good man! And by the way, Harold, how's the diet going? How many pounds have you lost? Not bad, Harold, but you need to lose another stone. A fat manager is an unproductive manager. Quite so! Good chap!'

Josephine's husband, Clement, was also in the hall, getting champagne glasses from the drinks cabinet, his brow vaguely furrowed. As a committed socialist, Clement felt compelled to disapprove of the autocratic manner in which his father-in-law ran his company. Clement had suggested that by adopting a more egalitarian and inclusive attitude towards his employees, they would be less inclined to revolt. David had received the suggestion with great enthusiasm and had immediately decided to offer his employees shares in the company, the only proviso being that they waive their rights to join a union. He told Clement he was a genius. After this, Clement had felt unequal to the task of converting his father-in-law and now he merely gave Annie a weary little smile.

David put down the phone and smiled at his daughter. 'Hello, darling! All ready for the big day? I've just got one more call to make . . .'

Rosemary's voice, unusually decisive, floated down the stairs. 'David, don't even think of picking up that receiver! Your daughter is getting married tomorrow and it's time for drinks.'

Lily, emerging from the kitchen with a bottle of champagne in one hand, grabbed her father's arm with the other. 'Come along, Daddy,' she said firmly. 'I've been waiting for this all day!'

Annie was ushered towards the best armchair and her family stood around her while Clement poured out the champagne.

'David?' Rosemary looked at her husband expectantly. 'Aren't you going to make a toast?'

'Oh! Absolutely!' David cleared his throat and blinked rapidly, a sure sign of serious thought. 'Well, Annie,' he said, 'here we all are to toast your future happiness! I have one splendid son-in-law in Clement–' he raised his glass towards

Clement who responded by nervously tugging his beard – 'who has given me a brilliant little grandson in Sidney.'

'Josephine gave him to you too,' murmured Lily.

'Shush, Lily,' Rosemary said.

'And I know,' continued David serenely, 'that Ben will be a splendid son-in-law too.' He paused. 'I would just like to give you one piece of advice if I may, Annie . . .'

'Keep it short,' Lily said. 'I'd like to drink my champagne before the bubbles go.'

'Shush, Lily,' Rosemary repeated.

'One *short* piece of advice. I have sometimes felt, Annie, that you reminded me of those fishermen who fish for the thrill of the pursuit; that having captured your victims, you tend to lose interest and throw them back, half-dead, into the water.'

'Annie hasn't left anyone half-dead,' Lily protested, 'and she's never fished in her life.'

'I am talking metaphorically,' David said, 'and if I may pursue the analogy, I would advise you to appreciate that Ben is like a golden salmon. Treasure him, be wary of any urge to throw him back into the water, cosset him as I have cosseted your mother—'

'Excuse me,' said Josephine, 'but you have *never* cosseted Mum.'

'That is true,' David conceded. 'I wish it wasn't, but it is. However, I have always *cherished* her and she has always cherished me.'

'David, if we don't drink our champagne soon, supper will be at midnight,' Rosemary said. 'Can you please get to the point.'

'In conclusion, then, Annie,' said David, 'what I am trying to say is—'

'Try not to go off Ben too quickly,' Lily translated helpfully, 'and if you do, you can pass him on to me.'

'In conclusion, then, Annie,' corrected David, 'we all love you very much and look forward to you loving and being loved by your husband!' He raised his glass high. 'To Annie and Ben!'

Annie looked at them all. She looked at her kind, patient, loving mother; her crazy, infuriating, wonderfully unique father; her sweet-natured, hopelessly idealistic older sister; her gentle brother-in-law; and her beautiful, maddening, hard-headed younger sister. She loved them all. She loved Ben. She was utterly, perfectly, completely happy.

At one o'clock the next day, Annie proceeded carefully down the stairs with Lily holding up the end of her veil behind her.

Rosemary, waiting in the hall, wearing her pink suit and new hat, clapped her hands together. 'Oh Annie,' she breathed, 'you look beautiful!'

For the fifteenth time that day, the telephone rang. From the study, David's voice could be heard clearly. 'David May here.'

'I shall give David one minute,' Rosemary exploded. 'And then I shall disconnect the phone. We shall have to go soon. Annie, don't let him ring anyone once we've gone or we'll be waiting at the church for ever. How do you feel, darling? You hardly ate any lunch . . .'

'I was too excited,' Annie said. 'I feel fine. I feel wonderful!'

Josephine came slowly down the stairs, holding the hand

of Sidney who looked unusually tidy and angelic in a little sailor suit that Rosemary had bought him. Behind them came Clement, holding a bag of toys in one hand and tugging at his tie with the other. Josephine smiled at Annie. 'You look lovely!' she said. 'You make me want to cry!'

'No one can cry,' Rosemary warned, 'or I shall start and I don't want to powder my face again. Now, I'm really going . . .' She stopped as David's voice could be heard booming out of the study.

'That is UNACCEPTABLE!' he roared. 'That is wholly UNACCEPTABLE!' A moment later, he came storming into the hall. He stopped abruptly when he saw his family and thrust his hair back with his hands.

'For goodness sake, David—' Rosemary began and then paused as she saw his face. 'David? David, are you all right?'

David frowned and took a deep breath. Then he went up to Annie and took her hands. 'Darling,' he said, 'I want you to be very brave . . .'

Annie felt a fierce contraction of terror. 'Is it Ben?' she breathed. 'What's happened to Ben?'

'The thing is,' David said, 'I don't know what's happened to Ben. No one knows what's happened to Ben. That was his mother on the phone. He went off suddenly last night to see a pal and said he'd be back in the morning. He didn't come back. Why the woman didn't ring us earlier I can't think. Anyway, he finally rang her ten minutes ago and said he's not coming back. He's done a runner. He's gone, vanished, disappeared. He's a bounder and a rat and I hope he has to roll stones up every hill in hell like that chap Sisyphus. Darling Annie, I am so, so sorry. The man's a total idiot and you are a beautiful, beautiful girl who is far too good for him.'

There was a long, stunned silence. No one moved. It was as if everyone had frozen. Then Lily cleared her throat. 'No offence,' she said, 'but does this mean Annie has to give back her wedding presents?'

Entries From Annie May's
Black Book

9 February 1988
BEN SEYMOUR FOR EVERYTHING FOR EVER.

17 June 1988
God for making me realize that he doesn't exist and that if he does exist he's not paying any attention.

21 September 1988
The three couples in Abbeville who spend every available moment indulging in Public Displays of Affection.

12 March 1989
Armand Duvalier for telling me I was a frigid, neurotic English girl. (Why do men always think uninterested girls are frigid when girls assume uninterested boys are not only uninterested but are probably quite right to be so?)

16 June 1989

The spotty man on the ferry back to England who displayed such witty originality when he told me I ought to try smiling in case the wind changed.

8 March 1990

My tutor who watched me trying to give a practice lesson to the nastiest group of children I've ever met and telling me afterwards that I should try to remember that teaching should be FUN.

6 May 1990

Angus Dredge for assuming I would sleep with him just because he bought me dinner.

10 August 1990

Lucy for giving her husband a TWO MINUTE tongue-kiss in front of me when he was forty-five minutes late for the dinner at which I was the sole guest and which tasted of charcoal.

15 September 1990

Mr Wyngarde for suggesting I shouldn't wear such a short skirt when teaching boys.

16 September 1990

Tyler Jones for wolf-whistling me in front of Mr Wyngarde.

20 February 1991
Mrs Abbott for asking me not to play my Leonard Cohen music after half past ten.

17 May 1991
Jeremy Davies for being insulting and aggressive when drunk and for thinking it doesn't matter so long as he says sorry when he's sober.

20 June 1991
Cousin Vanessa for asking me if I found it difficult to be the only unmarried sister now.

11 October 1991
Mrs Forrest for asking me not to play my Leonard Cohen music after half past nine.

22 July 1992
8F for being impossible to teach.

18 December 1992
Simon Francis for not telling me he'd met someone else and for thinking I'd care.

7 February 1993
Wendy Freeman for borrowing my new dress, worn only once, and for spilling red wine down it and washing it in the washing machine and then giving it back to me as if nothing had happened and only confessing when said dress proved to be fit only for a malnourished runner bean.

12 July 1994

Sam Crewe's father for telling me at parents' evening that if I ever had children of my own, I'd understand why he felt it necessary to make his son do two hours' extra homework every evening.

15 July 1995

Sally Williams's mother for not bothering to come to see her daughter act her socks off in the end-of-year school play.

16 April 1997

The man who spent an hour telling me about his near-suicidal depression and concluded by saying that one more disappointment would tip him over the edge and by the way would I sleep with him. I could hear him telling another woman about his near-suicidal depression half an hour later.

12 February 1998

Jessica Brown for sitting in the staffroom and massaging her pregnant tummy while telling me how sorry she was to hear that Robbie had left me.

1 June 1998

Cherry White for ignoring me ever since I joined the school and suddenly discovering she likes me when she wants to buy my flat at a knock-down price.

12 September 2000

Henry Bertram for being a prat.

5 March 2002

Sidney's friend Robert for stealing Sidney's first girlfriend.

21 October 2003

Clement for being weak and selfish and sanctimonious and going off with his supposedly saintly girlfriend to save the children in Africa while leaving his own son and daughter back home in Herne Hill.

7 March 2004

The two women who came to my door at a crucial moment during The West Wing in order to ask me if I wanted to let God into my home. (When I told them I didn't, they told me I'd go to hell and when I said I wouldn't want to live in a heaven with a God who could happily send people like me to hell, they said God would be very sad about sending me and I said in that case why didn't he just keep me in heaven and then I remembered The West Wing and swore, so now I'm definitely facing eternal damnation.)

20 November 2004

Xanthe Miller for talking ad nauseam about her daughter's school reports and then telling me how lucky I was not to have children.

CHAPTER TWO

Black Book Entry, 12 April: Me for being utterly inept at terminating relationships.

On balance, with two glaring exceptions, Annie preferred being dumped to dumping. Virtuous self-pity was a far easier bedfellow than the sticky residue of guilt that always clung like chewing gum long after the termination had been carried out.

She had planned tonight's dispatch carefully. The occasion, a drink after work, would be short and therefore easy to manage. The time, half past six, was perfect since Annie had, as Derek knew, a drama lesson to give at eight, thus avoiding any danger of having to stay on and chomp one's way through a plate of pasta while trying to make breaking-up seem like an exciting new life path. The location, All Bar One, was a particularly clever choice, Annie thought, since Derek would be surrounded by loads of pretty young girls in their twenties and might begin to realize that he was better off without a woman who was three years off forty.

She arrived at six twenty-nine and spotted Derek immediately. He was sitting, checking his mobile, at a corner table on which stood two full glasses of white wine and a bowl of crisps. He was, as always, beautifully dressed in a grey suit, pale blue shirt and lilac tie. He had the right sort of head for his close-cropped haircut. The first time Annie had seen him, she'd thought he looked like a Roman general, a sensitive but macho general like Russell Crowe in *Gladiator*, not a creepy, deeply twisted Roman general like Laurence Olivier in *Spartacus*.

At a nearby table, two attractive women, both blonde, both impeccably groomed, sat chatting and laughing. They kept throwing their heads back and every time they did so, their eyes drifted carelessly towards Derek, willing him to look their way. Annie quite understood. She felt a moment's doubt: did she really want to say goodbye to five feet, ten inches of masculine beauty? Then she saw him glance across at the door. His eyes lit up when he saw her. Annie squared her shoulders and walked across to him.

'Derek!' she said. 'No matter how early I am, you always arrive before me!'

He stood up and kissed her cheek. 'I hate to keep a lady waiting,' he said. 'I've bought you a Pinot Grigio. Is that all right for you?'

'Lovely!' Annie sat down. He was so thoughtful. He was such a gentleman. She was such a cow. She took a sip of her drink and murmured, 'Wonderful,' gathering her resources about her. 'This is wonderful.'

Derek leant forward. 'I'm glad you wanted to meet up tonight,' he said. 'I wanted to talk to you about my mother. It's her seventieth birthday in three weeks and there's going to be a big family party throughout the weekend. My mother wants you to come. Is that all right?'

Oh God. She could feel the blood rising to her face. She must do it now, right now, before she lost her courage. 'Derek, the thing is . . .' She hesitated for a moment and then, making herself look directly into his kind, eager eyes, ploughed on heavily. 'I wanted to see you tonight because I felt that . . . I feel that . . . well, what I think is that we've had a great time together in the last few months. I've so enjoyed being with you and I have this conviction . . . this very firm conviction . . . that now is the time to call things a day before things go wrong and while things are so right, before we get into the niggling, being irritated with each other stage which would be such a tragedy since we are such good friends if you know what I mean. I think it is so much better if we stop going out together while we're such good friends so that we can go on being good friends which I really want us to be. The trouble is that—'

'Wait a moment, please.' Derek was sitting ramrod straight now, his complexion as pale as Annie's was red. Annie could see the wounded bewilderment in his eyes and felt her soul shrink.

Derek plaited his fingers together and stared at her. 'Are you trying to tell me you don't want to see me any more?'

'It's not that I don't want to see you any more, it's that—'

'Annie, could you do me the courtesy of being straight with me? Are you saying you don't want to see me any more?'

Annie bit her lip miserably. 'Yes,' she murmured. 'In the way you mean. Not in the way I mean. If you know what I mean.' She was handling this terribly. Even to her own ears, her prevarications and excuses sounded pathetic and feeble and clearly mendacious. She should have taken a deep breath and told him the plain, unvarnished, unadulterated, pure, simple, honest-to-God truth:

Derek, do you remember you came to my flat for supper two weeks ago and we'd both had exhausting days at work and after supper we switched on the television and watched The Wedding Singer? *And do you remember at the end of the film, Adam Sandler sings this really soppy song to Drew Barrymore about wanting to grow old with her? Well, I looked at you and I was about to make a pretending-to-be-sick gesture and you looked at me and you took my hand and you had the same soppy smile that Adam Sandler had and I thought, oh God, Derek's become a Triffid. Goodbye to fun, enjoyable sex, hello to deep, meaningful sex. Goodbye to my-home-is-my-castle and hello to Derek expecting to see me every evening and talking about moving in together. And, Derek, I'm really sorry, because if you hadn't become a Triffid, I would have gone on seeing you for ever because you're fun and you're attractive and you're interesting but, now you're a Triffid, you've ruined it all because I don't want to see you every night of the week, I don't want to see anyone every night of the week and I don't want to share my kitchen, my bathroom and my bedroom and I know that makes me sound selfish, Derek, but that's because I am selfish. Derek, I recognize I'm selfish and if I'm absolutely truthful, I have no desire to stop being selfish.*

That was what she should have said.

'Are you worried about the time?' Derek asked abruptly.

'What?' Involuntarily, Annie looked at her watch. 'No, don't worry. The new pupil isn't coming round until eight.'

'No, I mean, are you worried about the – you know, your biological whatever it is. Do you want children? I mean, if that's what you want . . .'

'Good heavens, no!' Annie shook her head fervently. 'My biological thingy is quite happy to make do with my niece and my nephews. It's nothing like that. In fact, it's quite the reverse. I'm no good at things like that. I mean I don't want to be committed to anybody, whether it's children or boyfriends. I like my own company, I like my flat, I like my independence. You and I . . . We were beginning to get serious and I don't want to be serious about anyone. If I wanted to be serious about anyone, then you would be the perfect choice because you're nice and you're kind and you're attractive . . .'

'Do you have any idea how patronizing you sound?'

'I'm sorry.' Annie bit her lip again. 'I didn't mean to be. I thought I was telling the truth.'

'Have you met someone else? Is that it?'

'Of course I haven't! It's just that I'm not interested in the . . . the love thing. I think falling in love is . . . silly.'

'Silly?' Derek gave one of those laughs that are totally devoid of any mirth. At the next table, the two blonde women had dropped all pretence of not listening.

'Silly?' Derek said again. 'Have you ever *been* in love?'

'Yes. I didn't like it. It's . . . silly.'

Derek raised his hands in the air and then let them drop back to the table. 'You ought to see a therapist. You are seriously mixed-up.'

'You're probably right.'

'I mean, I don't understand any of this. We've got on so well together. We have great sex . . . Haven't we had great sex?'

'We've had very great sex,' Annie assured him earnestly.

'We like the same things, we get on with each other's friends and now you want to finish it because we might get serious? That's what happens when a relationship works, Annie, it gets serious. Things get better or they get worse, one thing they never do is stand still. And now you're telling me you'd rather go back to your lonely little flat and make yourself meals for one every night? I don't buy it. I just don't buy it. Sorry.'

There was another long silence. Annie took a crisp and then wished she hadn't because it was impossible to eat a crisp quietly. 'I don't know what else to say,' she murmured. 'Except, I hope we can be friends.'

'Well, sorry, Annie, we can't be friends. My friends are people I respect and understand and I don't understand you and I certainly can't respect you. I think you're weird, screwed-up, emotionally stunted and actually–' he pushed back his chair and stood up to go – 'I really have no interest in seeing you again.'

Annie watched him stride out into the street. It helped that he'd been angry. The memory of an angry Derek was easier to manage than the memory of a sad Derek. With any luck, he'd soon persuade himself that he'd had a narrow escape. She felt a slight surge of indignation and seized upon it eagerly. What Derek was really saying was that any woman who preferred to be on her own than to be with Derek must be mad. Fine. She was quite happy to be mad in that case.

At the next table, the two women were talking in hushed voices and giggling. She knew they were talking about her. They were probably wondering what on earth a hunk like Derek was doing with someone like her. Fine. She didn't care. They were typical Bath women, she thought viciously: well-heeled after lucrative divorces, in Bath for the schools and perpetually on the lookout for the next rich husband. If they saw Derek again, they'd be circling him like piranha fish. Annie finished her wine and rose from the table. As she walked out, one of the women gave her a sweet and clearly sympathetic smile, making Annie feel even more wretched. It had come to a pretty pass when blonde, beautiful, well-dressed women turned out to be nice people as well. Her anger, deprived of an apparently easy target, redoubled its strength and hurled itself back at her.

As she walked home, she maintained a fast and furious pace, with her eyes fixed like gimlets on the pavement. In the seven years she had lived in Bath, she had never failed to gain pleasure from the generous proportions of Great Pulteney Street with its long borders of grand and gracious Georgian terraces. Tonight, she noticed nothing. She had handled the entire Derek affair with unparalleled clumsiness. There had been signs long before *The Wedding Singer* that Derek and she had different expectations from each other. As long ago as New Year's Eve he had suggested they should go on holiday together in the summer and he had said more than once that he'd like to meet her family. She should have known, she should have seen, she was stupid, stupid, stupid!

She raised her eyes in time to catch the amused glances of a couple of teenage girls as they passed her. She realized she had been muttering to herself. Great. She was already turning into a demented old lady. She was too old to cope with this sort of trauma any more. In future, she would lay the ground rules straight away, make quite clear that she was only interested in no-strings relationships. Alternatively, of course, she could simply resign herself to celibacy. In fact, given the dearth of attractive middle-aged men in Bath and the legions of stunning women, she would probably have no choice *but* to resign herself to celibacy. Perhaps she should take up running instead.

She crossed the road, unlocked the front door and went up the stairs to her flat. Once inside, she threw her bag on the floor and collapsed onto her sofa. She threw off her shoes, wriggled her toes and stretched her legs and arms. It was good to be home.

The first time she had seen the apartment, she had known she wanted it. Lily came with her on her second visit and Annie pointed out its high ceilings and its large sash windows that flooded the rooms with light. 'And look at this,' she said proudly, pointing to the two great doors that separated the bedroom from the sitting and dining area. 'They're called wedding doors. All Georgian houses have them. Aren't they wonderful?' Lily pointed out that the kitchen and the bathroom were tiny, the carpets were stained and threadbare and the wallpaper looked like it had a skin disease. None of this mattered to Annie. She made an offer that day.

As soon as she moved in, she set to work. She stripped the walls, pulled out the carpets and scrubbed every inch of the place, removing what seemed like centuries of dirt and dust. She painted the walls a pale yellow and the woodwork white. She sanded and lacquered the floors and replaced the harsh central lights with muted lamps. Her two big extravagances were her vast double bed and her long, cream sofa. She kept the wedding doors open so that she could see them both and so that she had the benefit of light from both windows. When she sat on her sofa, as she did now, she could look out to her left and see the trees of Henrietta Park and she could look out to her right and see the honey-coloured Georgian terraces on the other side of the street.

She sat back against the cushions and let the peace of her home work its magic. Derek would be all right. He'd soon find someone else. And when she thought about it, it really was a bit rich of him to call her emotionally stunted simply because she didn't feel she could fall in love with him. All right, he was entitled to feel angry, but not *that* angry. She sighed. She had no time to dwell on him now. She stood up and went to the kitchen where she made herself a toasted sandwich and poured herself a glass of water in order to counteract the effects of the hastily gulped Pinot Grigio. Her new pupil would be here soon.

Annie had started giving private drama lessons a few years ago in an effort to help chip away at her gargantuan mortgage. The income she received was far too modest to make any impact but she soon found the money was of secondary importance. She loved the intimacy of the one-to-one sessions. After a hectic day at school, teaching classes of over thirty, it was a delight to spend forty minutes with one highly motivated student. And there was always the seductive possibility that she might just find the Meryl Streep of tomorrow.

The buzzer sounded on the dot of eight. Annie lifted the door phone, said, 'I won't be a moment!' and went downstairs to open the front door.

A young girl stood on the doorstep. She was clutching the ends of her sleeves in her fingers and her right foot tapped the ground. Twin curtains of dark hair obliterated most of her face. 'Miss May?' she asked.

'That's me!' Annie smiled. 'Do call me Annie. You must be Bella Partridge! I'm sorry you had to wait. I do have a switch that's supposed to unlock the door but it's never worked! Come on up!'

The girl nodded nervously. 'I hope I'm not too early.'

'Bang on time!' said Annie cheerfully. She had expected someone with more confidence. Bella had rung and fixed the class for herself, saying she was a friend of Abby. She had sounded decisive and focused. Annie had assumed she'd be like Abby who was a terrifyingly self-assured, articulate teenager with a tiny skirt and the legs to go with it. This girl was very different. Apart from the fact that she was dressed in tracksuit bottoms and an oversized sweatshirt, she looked as if she might run away any moment.

Annie led her into the flat and waved a hand at the sofa. 'Have you come far or do you live in Bath?'

'I live up Lansdown. I walked.'

'Good for you!' Annie took a seat and looked encouragingly at Bella. 'I presume Abby told you about the sort of things we do. She's preparing for her LAMDA exam at the moment. And then there's the Mid-Somerset Festival. I have a couple of students who want to try for the National Youth Theatre. Is there anything in particular you want to do?'

The girl perched on the edge of the sofa. She reminded Annie of a frightened bird. She had pulled her sleeves over her hands again and was twisting the ends together. 'Well,' she said softly, 'you'll probably think this is silly . . '

'I'm pretty sure I won't,' Annie promised.

Bella coiled a lock of hair round her index finger and stared fixedly at her scuffed grey trainers. 'I want to be an actress!'

Her eyes flickered momentarily towards Annie. 'I know it's stupid. I know I don't look right and my drama teacher thinks I'm rubbish. Abby and Martha always get the main parts in school plays and I know I'm not pretty and my voice is wrong and I never know what to do with my hands and I'm too short and—'

'Wait a moment,' Annie said. 'Stop there, stop right there!' She folded her arms in front of her and sighed. 'You've more or less informed me that you're unattractive and you can't act. What on earth are you doing here?'

The girl blinked miserably. 'I'm not sure,' she whispered.

'Nor am I,' said Annie. 'Because if *you* don't have any confidence in yourself, why should anyone else? At the very least, you need to be able to look as if you're confident. So I tell you what, Bella Partridge, I want you to give the performance of your life right now. I want you to pretend that I am a hard-nosed old cow. I know that must be difficult to imagine . . .' She waited for Bella to give a laugh or at least a smile but Bella merely nodded earnestly meaning that she either had no sense of humour or she thought that Annie *was* a hard-nosed old cow. 'You are trying to tell me why I, the world's most influential agent, should take you on. You are acting the part of a Bella Partridge who has no doubt, no doubt at all, that she can be a star. Start when you're ready!'

Bella sat, mute, a picture of misery. This was not going to work. Annie cursed herself silently. She had handled this all wrong. First, Derek and now this poor, blameless teenager. Well done, Annie.

Suddenly the girl pushed back her sleeves, sat up very straight and stared directly at Annie. She pushed her hair back behind her ears, revealing an oval-shaped face and big, brown eyes. 'My name is Bella Partridge,' she said. 'I'm seventeen and I want to be an actress. I want to be a *great* actress. I am good. I am very, very good. I have a face you don't forget. I have dark hair and dark eyebrows and they stand out in photographs. I'm short, but short is good because I won't dwarf all the short male actors. There are lots of tall, thin, blonde, pretty girls but there aren't many people who look like me and who can act like me and I *can* act. I really can!' Her eyes were shining now and her chin was up, defiant, unafraid. Annie felt like cheering.

'Bella,' she said, 'you were terrific! I'd hire you on the spot!'

'Would you?' Bella's mouth twisted slightly. It was almost a smile.

'Yes, and for your information, I've never heard such tosh about your being plain. Lecture Number One: you are not plain. You are not beautiful either. Neither is Judi Dench nor Kate Winslet but they act so well that when they want to look beautiful they make you believe they are beautiful. Look at Dame Edith Evans or Wendy Hiller . . .'

'Who are they?' Bella asked.

'They're dead,' Annie admitted, 'but before they were dead they were terrific actresses who were not nearly as pretty as you are. The point is, if you want to star in *Hollyoaks* or the latest teen movie, you might have a problem because, as you so sensibly pointed out, you don't look like the five million other teenagers who all look pretty and bland and predictable. If you want a proper career and you have the talent, you might have a chance.'

Bella pulled at a small copper ring on the little finger of

her left hand. 'I want a career,' she said slowly, 'but Miss May—'

'Annie. Call me Annie. So here comes Lecture Number Two. Out of every thousand people who go into acting, perhaps one will achieve a reasonable amount of success. The statistics are appalling and you need to develop the hide of an armadillo because rejections will rain down upon you and life will be hell. End of lecture. Let's see how you cope with more immediate hurdles. Do you know *Oleanna?*'

'I'm not sure . . .'

'Never mind. All you need to know is that Oleanna has gone to see her tutor because he's given her a low mark for her essay and she wants to find out why. She is not hugely bright and she's very unsure of herself but she's also very obstinate – rather a terrifying combination. Read this page through and then see what you can make of it.'

Bella took the script eagerly. Annie sat back. As always when confronted by a student with promise, she felt a surge of adrenalin. For a moment, Derek's face – hurt, baffled and angry – came before her and she blinked and looked out towards the window. Then Bella coughed and Annie turned back and waited for the performance to begin.

It was probably not a good idea to watch the harrowing drama of two Afghan refugees trying to get from Pakistan to England. Programmes about impoverished people always made Annie feel guilty for not giving more to charity, guilty again for being preoccupied with her own far more trivial problems and guilty yet again for *continuing* to be preoccupied with her trivial problems.

If she'd been sensible she would have gone straight to bed after her lesson with Bella Partridge. It had helped to diminish, or at least diffuse, the depression she felt over Derek. She liked Bella. The girl took herself far too seriously and was even more self-absorbed than most girls of her age but she had integrity and determination and was clearly talented. It would be good to build up her self-confidence and watch her grow.

She had just started to clean her teeth when the telephone rang. Hastily, she rinsed out her mouth and rushed to her bedroom.

'You aren't asleep, are you?' It was Lily. Of course it was Lily. Who else would ring at ten to eleven? Only Lily saved her phone calls for bedtime.

'No,' said Annie, adding pointedly, 'I was doing my teeth.'

'I've been talking to Josephine,' said Lily. 'I told her we were both very disappointed not to be invited to her wedding—'

'I wasn't disappointed,' Annie protested. 'She never wanted a big do the first time around. I'm glad she didn't let the second get hijacked.'

'Anyway, I told her that the very least she could do was to bring Mark down to stay and that otherwise we'd never forgive her—'

'What do you mean "*we*"?' Talking to Lily was like trying to interrupt a speaking clock.

'After all, we've only met him a few times. So I suggested they come down at the end of May, it's the last weekend of the month. You can come and stay then, can't you?'

'I think that's all right, it's the start of half-term—'

'Good, you won't have to hurry back on Sunday. I'll ring

Josephine now and confirm it. Will you come down in time for lunch on the Saturday? I want you to look at Luke's story in the afternoon. They're running a short-story competition at school and he's written a lovely one about a dragon. The trouble is he's gone rather over the top in places: his dragon is always farting and the villain's death is unspeakably gory. He's written three paragraphs about quivering intestines oozing on the ground and I don't think intestines *would* ooze, do you? Of course he won't listen to *me*, so I need you to persuade him to tone things down a bit. His teacher will think he's been watching *Reservoir Dogs* or something. Oh, and by the way, why don't you bring Derek? We're longing to meet him.'

'That might be difficult,' Annie said. 'I broke up with him a few hours ago.'

'Oh Annie, you didn't! What *is* it with you? You can't afford to throw away good men like Derek.'

'You've never *met* Derek!'

'I hate to say this, Annie, but you're getting to the age where good available men are few and far between. You hadn't had a boyfriend for at least two years when you met Derek—'

'One year, it was one year—'

'And now you get rid of Derek before we've even had a chance to look at him. Why? Do you *want* to be alone for the rest of your life? And don't tell me you do because I don't believe it. I know you don't like talking about the past and I've always respected that but I have to say—'

'Lily,' Annie said, 'I have to go. My mobile's going. No offence.' She slammed the phone down and returned to the bathroom where she vented her anger on her complexion, rubbing cleansing milk and then toning lotion into her skin with such venom that her face soon resembled a tomato. She picked up her toothbrush for the second time, only to be interrupted yet again by the phone.

'Annie?' It was Josephine. 'You're not asleep, are you?'

'No,' said Annie, climbing into her bed and sitting against the pillows, 'I've been talking to Lily.'

'Of course you have. So have I. I just wanted to make sure that you weren't really cross about the wedding. We didn't invite anyone and—'

'Josephine, you *know* I understand. I think you were very sensible. How *are* you?'

'I'm getting fat! Mark is a wonderful cook. Sidney and Beattie can't believe their luck! Mark made a wonderful broccoli dish yesterday and Sidney had two helpings! Sidney *never* eats broccoli!'

'How *is* Sidney? Will he and Beattie come with you to Lily's? I haven't seen them for ages.'

'I'm sure they'll come.' Josephine hesitated. 'Lily told me you'd broken up with your boyfriend. I'm so sorry. Are you all right about it?'

'I'm fine.'

'Good. That's very good. Had you quarrelled about something? Because sometimes all you need to do is sit down together and talk quietly and listen to each other and it's funny how things can fall into place.'

'We hadn't quarrelled,' Annie said. 'He was getting too serious.'

'I see,' said Josephine who plainly didn't. 'Did you feel he

40

was cramping you? Was he expecting you to cook for him all the time? Because sometimes all you have to say—'

'Derek is quite aware of my limited culinary skills. He's cooked for me more than I've cooked for him. He's a very nice man. He just spoilt things by getting serious.'

'Really?' There was another pause. 'Have I told you about my friend, Helena? She's a lovely woman and an amazingly perceptive therapist—'

'I don't need a therapist,' Annie said.

'No, of course not.'

'Actually,' Annie said, 'I have to go. My mobile is going. Tell Mark I'm looking forward to seeing him soon!' She stormed back to the bathroom, took up her toothbrush and exerted the same punishment on her teeth as she had done earlier on her skin. Finally, she returned to her bedroom, mashed her face with night cream and climbed into bed.

Annie was aware that many families had their weak links or their scapegoats, individuals who became the focus of generalized concern or pity, whose inadequacies had the great benefit of making everyone else feel correspondingly superior. She was also aware that in the years since the wedding fiasco, she had been relegated to this particular role. It didn't matter how successful she was. She could write a book and win the Booker Prize, she could enter politics and become Secretary of State for Education, she could take up acting and win an Oscar; her family would still treat her with the same combination of impatience and pity. It was apparent that the only passport to real success was to marry someone, however tedious, and provide an already over-populated planet with more human beings. Annie wasn't sure what was the more irritating, the fact that the family thought she should marry and have children or the fact that the family thought that, 'deep down', *she* wanted to marry and have children. She knew her parents and her siblings were convinced that she'd never got over Ben's desertion. They didn't understand that the only reason she didn't want to talk about Ben was because she didn't want to waste her breath on such a low-life, treacherous specimen of humanity.

She switched out the light and threw the duvet over her head. It annoyed her that they all thought she was still locked in the past. All right, she'd been very upset and she was the first person to admit she'd taken a long time to get back her equilibrium, but after a few years she'd been fine; in fact she remembered thinking on what would have been her tenth wedding anniversary that she was absolutely fine. She'd be a pretty sad person if she wasn't. 'And I am not,' Annie hissed into the darkness, 'a sad person.'

CHAPTER THREE

Black Book Entry, 30 April: Jake and Henry for being patronizing and pleased with themselves for NO REASON.

Annie's friends proved to be far more understanding than her sisters. Frances did express regret at Annie's decision, probably because she had introduced Derek to Annie in the first place; however, she was philosophical about his dispatch, saying everyone knew it would take a combination of Brad Pitt and Tom Cruise to make Annie turn sentimental. Hannah, ecstatically in love with her new boyfriend, her first since her husband's untimely death five years earlier, told Annie she'd been very sensible: 'You didn't love him: end of story!' Best of all was Grace who had seen the writing on the wall for some time now. 'Do you remember when you came to supper and you drank too much and you started going on about the government's transport policy and Derek sat there nodding at you as if you were the wisest person he'd ever met? He didn't even smile when you said the government ought to invest in electric helicopters, he just kept nodding. Do you want some more coffee?'

It was over a fortnight since the Derek evening and Grace and Annie were enjoying a protracted post-mortem. Annie had met Grace five years ago when they had been the only people to attend a course on creative writing. Their teacher, an elderly gentleman called Mr Bucket, wore a tweed jacket and a rather grubby jersey and was accompanied by his very young wife who had maintained the same sort of adoring smile that Nancy Reagan used to direct to President Reagan. Mr Bucket had spent the first ten minutes reading and then re-reading and then re-reading again the opening paragraphs of *Lolita*, conferring on each word the same momentous intonation. Eventually he had put the book down and asked his pupils what was the first requirement in writing a novel. After they had failed to provide the correct answer, he stared at them wisely and delivered the one word, 'Chapters'. This seemed to divest him of any further inspiration or energy and, after a long silence, Grace asked him rather desperately what were his favourite novels. He did have one he liked, he said, it was about a parrot and a boat; unfortunately he couldn't remember the title. It was at this point that Annie stood up having just remembered that she should be somewhere else on Wednesday evenings and so would have to leave right away. Grace also sprang up, having remembered exactly the same thing. The smile on the young Mrs Bucket's face abruptly disappeared and she insisted they both pay the fee for one lesson. Once out of the building, the two women had fled to the nearest bar and collapsed into hysteria. They had been great friends ever since, their relationship cemented by the fact that they lived within ten minutes' walk of each other.

Grace lived with her husband and children on Bathwick

Hill in a Georgian doll's house of perfect symmetry. The house suited its chatelaine. Grace's features were of equally pleasing proportions and her hair, usually swept back into an elegant chignon, was the very colour of the Bath stone walls. On the left of the front door was the big square study and on the right was the big, square sitting room. On the first floor there was Henry and Grace's bedroom on the left and on the right was Chloe's, currently empty since Chloe was in her first year at Manchester. On the second floor were the two bedrooms belonging to seventeen-year-old Jake and fifteen-year-old Fizzie. Annie's favourite room was the kitchen which comprised the entire lower ground floor and included two squashy sofas, a large red Aga and a vast old pine table around which they were currently sitting.

'Have one more cup!' pleaded Grace. 'I haven't told you my brilliant idea yet. I want to hold a ball for the Refugee Council! What do you think?'

Fizzie, exposing an impossibly flat stomach between black hipster trousers and a tiny white T-shirt, wandered into the kitchen and helped herself to an apple. 'Are we going to have lunch soon?' she asked. 'When *is* lunch?'

'When your father gets back from his golf,' Grace said, filling Annie's cup with the last of the coffee. 'I was just telling Annie about the ball idea.'

'There are too many balls in Bath,' Fizzie said, tossing back her hair. 'And it's not as if you know anything about how to organize one. Mum, I'm meeting Cassie in town at two and I need some money to get my trainers. You said you'd pay for them as I'll use them for games, remember?' She took a bite of her apple and nodded at Annie, 'Hi, Annie.'

'Hi, Fizzie,' said Annie. She sipped her coffee during the ensuing financial negotiations between mother and daughter and allowed her mind to wander. Why did pretty girls constantly toss their hair back even when there weren't any good-looking boys around? Was it something that had developed into the equivalent of a facial tic or was it because the gleaming locks kept getting in the eyes? In which case why didn't they devise a hairstyle that was less time-consuming?

'Annie,' Grace said, 'about my ball. What do you think?'

Jake, who had just walked in and made straight for the fridge, answered for her. 'It's a crap idea,' he said. 'Hi, Annie.'

'Hi, Jake,' Annie said. 'Why is it a crap idea?'

Jake was a tall, good-looking boy who spent a great deal of time and energy in protecting his reputation as Bath's most devastatingly successful Pied Piper. Girls rang and texted and emailed him all the time. His hair was carefully highlighted and artfully dishevelled. He had developed a nonchalant approach and a way of narrowing his eyes and swallowing his words that was the envy of his friends. Annie had always tried very hard to like him.

'It's Bath's answer to everything,' he said, pulling out a large piece of Cheddar and a jar of pickle. 'It's just an excuse for loads of middle-class women with too much time on their hands to buy new dresses and get new haircuts. The charity angle is irrelevant. The whole idea stinks.' He cut a piece of the Cheddar and spread it with a precariously big dollop of pickle. 'Mum, can I have next month's allowance now?'

'I thought I'd already given it to you,' Grace said, 'and anyway the charity angle isn't irrelevant.'

'The Refugee Council!' scorned Jake. 'There aren't any

refugees in Bath! What do Bath women know about refugees?'

'That's why I thought we should hold a ball,' said his mother. 'And I wish you wouldn't talk with your mouth full. Everyone talks about asylum seekers flooding our country. People seem to forget what asylum actually means. Asylum is about saving lives not reducing numbers. What do you think, Annie? Is it a good idea?'

Annie, who had hated the only ball she had ever been to and had thus far managed to avoid going to any in all the time she'd lived here, found herself, as so often in the company of Jake, taking a position she had not meant to. 'I think it's a great idea,' she said. 'It will generate lots of publicity and money for a very good charity. If we took your view, Jake, we wouldn't support Amnesty or Oxfam because there aren't any political prisoners or starving children hanging around the Roman Baths. So, go for it, I say, and in fact,' she added heroically, 'I'm looking forward to it already.'

'It won't come to anything,' Jake said through a mouthful of cheese. 'Mum's projects never do.'

Annie, sensing an imminent outbreak of bile emerging from her vocal chords, pushed back her chair and stood up. 'I must go,' she said, 'I've been here far too long. Goodbye Fizzie, goodbye Jake.'

Grace led the way up the stairs. 'By the way, do you think you'll be free on the last Saturday in May? We have Henry's sister staying.' She opened the front door. 'Why don't you come to supper?'

Outside, Henry was unloading his golf clubs from his four-by-four. 'Hell-o, Annie!' he said, adopting the heartily avuncular tone he used towards all of Grace's single friends.

'How are *you*? Filling your pupils' minds with the wonder of Shakespeare, I hope?'

'I'm *very* well, thank you,' said Annie, not quite unconsciously adopting the same intonation. 'How are *you*? Filling your patients with lots of Botox?'

'Very funny!' said Henry. Henry had a lucrative dental practice in Bath and had recently inaugurated a range of non-surgical beauty treatments.

'I've just invited Annie to supper when your sister comes,' said Grace.

'Thanks but I can't,' said Annie. 'I'm going to stay with Lily for a weekend in the country.'

'That's nice,' said Henry. 'Any chance of some lunch, Gracie? I'm starving!'

Annie made her farewells and set off down the hill, playing through in her mind all the things she would have liked to tell Jake a few minutes earlier.

The next few weeks at school were hectic, with the SATs exams looming like a thundercloud over everyone. It was at this time of year, when she brought back huge piles of homework and practice papers for marking, that she wondered if she should cut down her private drama pupils. On the other hand, hearing girls like Abby and Bella breathe life into Chekhov and Ibsen provided a blissful release from correcting worksheets on the correct use of the apostrophe.

It was bliss to finally pack away the last exam paper and look forward to an entire week off work. On Saturday morning, she loaded her small case and a bottle of wine into her car and set off. Lily's house was in deepest Somerset, surrounded by hills and fields and hedges full of cow parsley. It always took an age to get there since one had to drive through winding, narrow lanes in which at least one tractor would always be trundling at about one mile an hour. The house was a great, sprawling mass of stone with a long, generous, gravel drive.

Today, a yellow sports car was parked bang in the middle and it took Annie a good few minutes to manoeuvre her car into a position in which it would not block the vehicle. No sooner had she disembarked than she heard her name being called. She looked up and saw her sister leaning out of the bedroom window.

'Thank goodness you're here,' Lily hissed. 'I'm showing a lady from the *Telegraph* round the house. Luke's in the dining room. Will you tell him to stop banging on about Milly?' Her head disappeared before Annie could say anything.

Pausing only to admire the two tubs of lavender, one on either side of the front door, Annie went into the house. Every time she came here, she felt as if she were entering Aladdin's cave. Every corner and every cranny had something that was eye-catching, be it a life-size papier-mâché Dalmatian or a piece of Cornish pottery or a weird and wonderful plant. The dining room was the largest room in the house. It was attached to the kitchen by means of a soaring arch but whereas the kitchen was purely utilitarian, housing twin sinks, an American fridge freezer, an electric oven and some cupboards, the dining room was a work of art. At one end stood an inky-blue Aga, its depth of colour enhanced by the surrounding pale blue and white Victorian tiles. Lily had found them in a reclamation centre. Lily was always finding bargains in reclamation centres. The other end of the room was dominated by a huge painting of two opulent red poppies and, below it, a long, antique sideboard on which Lily had set photographs of Luke and Gabriel, a multi-coloured bowl of fruit, three creamy white church candles and an enormous vase of lilies. In the middle of the room there was a refectory table that could seat twenty people with ease. Behind one side of the table was a seven-foot dresser almost completely covered in Bridgewater mugs and plates. On the other side were the three tall, gracious windows that gave the place its sense of light and which helped the Venetian chandelier to spread its fractured light around the room.

The place was, like Lily herself, a combination of elegance and fun. Josephine always said it was like stepping into a glossy magazine, which was hardly surprising since the glories of Lily's house had been displayed in most of them. Lily had no formal training but she knew how to combine colours and she had a knack of arranging furniture and effects into harmonious order. Sometimes Annie was tempted to copy Lily's style and fill her own rather spartan home with more colour and clutter but she knew she didn't have the talent or the money to replicate Lily's magic.

Another characteristic of Lily's house was its tidiness. It was always tidy. Lily had help in the considerable shape of Mrs Perkins, but even so it was no mean achievement to keep the place so immaculate in the face of an amiable but clumsy husband and two young boys.

The older of the two, Luke, was currently lying spread-eagled on the floor beside the prostrate form of Milly, the family Labrador. When Luke saw Annie, he jumped up and ran into her arms with the customary extravagance of emotion that made her love him.

Annie returned his embrace warmly. 'Luke!' she said. 'You look so smart!'

Luke made a face. 'We had to have our photos taken for the paper. I wanted Milly to be in them but Mum wouldn't let her. Mum,' he added darkly, 'has ruined her life!'

'Really?' Annie stared at Milly. Milly's tail slapped the polished floorboards feebly. 'She looks very tired. I'm sure she doesn't care about being photographed.'

'Mum says she's convalescing but Mum said she'd be all right by breakfast and she wasn't and Mum said she'd be back to normal in no time and she isn't. Mum made her have an operation yesterday and now she will never have babies.'

'I'm sure she'll be all right.' Annie went over to Milly and knelt down beside her. 'I mean, look at her. She has a lovely, shiny coat, her nose is wet. She's fine!'

Milly raised her head a fraction of an inch and then laid it down again. If Annie hadn't known better, she might have thought Milly was playing to the gallery. 'Where's Gabriel? And William?'

'Gabriel wanted to show the lady his bedroom himself. Dad went off to play tennis when the lady arrived. I don't think he wanted to be photographed.'

Annie grinned. 'I think you're probably right.' She stood up as Lily came in, followed by an unusually neat Gabriel and a plumply pretty blonde in a grey trouser suit.

'Annie!' cried Lily in a tone of delighted surprise. 'How lovely to see you!' She turned to the blonde. 'This is my sister.

She teaches English and Drama in a state school.' The last two words were uttered in a significant whisper.

'How wonderful,' breathed the blonde, gazing at Annie with the wide-eyed respect of one who's not certain whether she's in front of a saint or a fool.

'Annie, this is Flora Mackenzie,' said Lily. 'She's doing an article on me for the *Telegraph* magazine.'

'I think your sister's a genius,' Flora told Annie. 'The entire house *works*, do you know what I mean? I love everything: the subtle, muted colours in the sitting room, the gloriously extravagant hangings in the spare room . . . The place positively exudes serenity and family harmony!'

Lily allowed herself a modest smile. 'People do seem to relax here,' she said. 'Would you like some more coffee, Flora?'

'No, thanks! If I have another cup I'll want another of your delicious home-made biscuits and that would play hell with my diet. I've had a wonderful morning.' She smiled at Luke. 'You have a very clever mother!' she said merrily.

Luke shook his head sorrowfully. 'Milly will never have children,' he said.

'Lucky Milly,' Lily murmured before gazing earnestly at Luke. 'Dogs aren't like humans, darling. Remember when Milly's mother came to visit? She wasn't interested in Milly at all. In fact, she was very irritated by Milly. Not like human mothers at all. Anyway, I'm sure Flora doesn't want to hear about Milly's operation!'

Luke turned to Flora. 'Do you have a dog?' he asked.

'Unfortunately for me, I don't,' Flora said. 'Well, I really should be going. I'll be in touch very soon.' She smiled at Luke. 'Don't worry about your dog. He'll be fine!'

'She,' Luke said. 'Milly is a she.'

'Of course she is!' Flora checked her watch. 'Heavens, I must go!'

'I'll see you out,' Lily said, ushering her visitor towards the front door.

Annie turned to Gabriel. 'I like your trousers,' she said. 'Very dashing!'

'A man on a motorbike came and took masses of photos of us,' Gabriel told her. 'I had to smile up at Mum like this!' His eyes opened wide and his mouth pulled away from his teeth in an expression of demented panic. Annie couldn't wait to see the photos.

Lily swept back in and put her hands on her hips. 'Well, thank you, boys, thank you very much! Thank you, Luke, for monopolizing the photographer!' She turned to Annie. 'It turned out the man loved animals. Luke had him thinking Milly was a case for the RSPCA. I bet he's taken horrible photos of me. And Gabriel, did you have to show Flora that painting you did of Jesus with his intestines hanging out? Why are you two so obsessed with intestines? She probably thinks you're crazy. Come to think of it, she's probably right. Now you can go and watch thirty minutes television in the playroom while I have a quiet chat with Annie and recover my composure. And Luke, if you even mention Milly once more today, I will be very, very angry.'

'But—'

'I mean it! Go! Go now!'

The boys, knowing their mother, went. Lily put a finger to her lips, listened to the clatter of shoes on the polished floorboards in the hall and made a dash for the middle drawer of the dresser. 'Thank God!' she said, taking out her cigarettes and lighter. 'I've been wanting one all morning! I thought Luke would never shut up about Milly and then Josephine rang up . . . Oh God, I must tell you about Josephine . . . and then . . .' She lit a cigarette and inhaled deeply. 'I am so glad it's all over! Do you want some coffee? There's loads in the pot.'

'Yes, please,' said Annie, 'along with one of your delicious home-made biscuits.'

Lily grinned. 'Thank heavens for the WI stall! They're very good!'

'So tell me,' Annie said. 'How did you get the *Telegraph* interested? I'm impressed!'

'They did a piece a few months ago on women who work at home. They fixed on some hatchet-faced novelist whose sitting room looked like a home for woodlice. So I wrote to Flora and enclosed the *Country Living* article. I thought it would be good publicity – you know, look at Lily's perfect family in her perfect house and let her do the same to your family and house, and then William slopes off to the tennis club and the boys start acting like they're auditioning for the *Omen IV*.' She thrust her cigarette under the table as Gabriel appeared in the doorway. 'I thought I told you to stay in the playroom for half an hour,' she said. 'What do you want?'

'Luke says can he have some crisps because we're hungry.'

'No, you can't,' said Lily. 'Between you, you've eaten most of the biscuits. Now go away!'

Gabriel's eyes narrowed. 'You're smoking a cigarette! I can see the smoke!'

'Gabriel!' said Lily. 'Go away!'

Gabriel duly went, making one last parting shot from the hall, 'I can smell it too!'

Lily withdrew her hand from under the table and had one last puff before taking the evidence to the sink. 'Sidney's coming but not Beattie. She has a party. And guess what? Mark's daughter is coming to live with them!'

'That's nice!'

'No, Annie, it is not nice. You sound just like Josephine. They've only just got married and already the serpent is coming to invade their Eden. She's hardly going to love Josephine, is she? At the very least Josephine should give herself some time to adjust to Mark before she takes on his daughter as well.'

'What about Mark? He's had to adjust to Sidney and Beattie.'

'That's different. Mark is living in their house. I tell you, I have bad feelings about this, very bad feelings.'

On the other side of the room, Milly raised her head and whimpered.

'Would you believe it?' Lily demanded. 'That ruddy dog thinks we're talking about *her*!'

Milly's tail began to wag, slowly at first and then with increasing fervour. Like Lazarus rising from the dead, she stood up on legs that were suddenly firm and padded out into the hall. The reason for this miracle could be heard banging the door behind him and greeting Milly with enthusiasm. 'Hello, old girl, how are *you*? Who's my brave girl? Who's my brave, brave girl?'

'That dog,' Lily announced, 'is a con artist.'

William entered the dining room like the West Wind. 'Annie, my darling, how lovely to see you! Give me a hug! This is a treat!'

Annie rose and responded to his embrace with equal warmth. William had dark Byronic curls and a very un-Byronic body. Despite his father-in-law's best efforts, his girth remained as generous as his character. He had murmured to Annie during his wedding reception that he was the luckiest man on earth. 'I can't understand what Lily sees in me,' he'd said. 'It's a mystery!' The fact that it was a mystery only to William – everyone knew he had a huge private income as well as a rare ability to make money in the city – merely increased her affection for him.

'Do you know something?' William said. 'This is your first visit since Christmas! And you live only an hour away! Not good enough, Annie, we want to see you more often!'

'It's lovely to be here,' said Annie. 'How was tennis?'

'Good fun! I play with my mate, Freddy, who's even fatter than me! We lumber around like two hippos on tranquillizers! I only took it up to keep your father quiet but it didn't work. He sent me a pedometer last week and keeps ringing up to see how many steps I do. He says I should do at least ten thousand a day! Ten thousand! Lily, my love, was the newspaper lady nice to you?'

'Very nice,' said Lily, 'and very unimpressed that you'd slipped away. You can make it up to me by taking the boys out this afternoon so I can cook in peace. Josephine will be here at six.'

'Absolutely! We're going to look for that wild cat! Have you heard about this, Annie? Some wild cat's been seen twice recently. We're going to track him down! You'll come, won't you?'

'I'd love to,' said Annie, 'unless Lily wants me to help in the kitchen.'

'Last time you helped me in the kitchen,' Lily said, 'you burnt my best saucepan. You're nearly as bad as Josephine. You can go with William. But I want you to look at Luke's story first.'

Annie duly spent a half-hour with Luke after lunch and managed to persuade him to ditch a couple of farting references and also the eye-gouging paragraph. The rest of the afternoon was spent on the hills with William and the boys. They failed to find the wild cat but did stumble across a very nice tea room where William ordered cream teas for all. By the time they returned home, it was nearer seven than six and the green Volkswagen in the drive showed that the latest guests had arrived.

Marriage to Mark clearly suited Josephine. Her thin frame, almost skeletal since Clement's departure, had at last gained some welcome covering. She and Clement had never been a tactile couple and it was good to see Josephine respond with a shy, almost coquettish smile, every time Mark touched her hand or her arm. Mark was short and balding, with cheerful brown eyes that disappeared when he smiled. Annie decided that she liked him very much, not least for the way he kept deferring to Sidney ... 'Sidney knows how to record programmes!' he said. 'All these years I've been trying and failing to record programmes and Sidney can do it in a second.' ... Sidney, who had suffered hugely from his parents' divorce and who had the added disadvantage of having a terrifyingly confident younger sister, responded with a shy smile that made Annie want to cheer.

At the end of Lily's excellent meal (garlic mushrooms, fish pie and fruit cobbler), William finished his wine and beamed at Sidney. 'Now, Sidney, you have a choice. You can either continue to enjoy your family's excellent conversation for the next two hours or you can watch my latest DVD. I bought it last week: *The Magnificent Seven*. Wonderful film, the best Western ever made. What would you like to do?'

Sidney grinned. 'The best Western ever made, I think.'

'Good lad!' approved William. 'I'll help you put it on, shall I?'

Lily watched William follow Sidney out. 'That's the last we'll see of William,' she said. She fixed Josephine and Mark with a purposeful stare. 'Now, tell me about Cressida. Is she really coming to live with you?'

'She is,' Mark said. 'The family will be complete at last!'

'But why,' asked Lily, 'is she coming? Doesn't she want to stay with her mother any more?'

'Amanda's having a few problems with her new boyfriend,' Josephine said. 'She thinks it might be easier to sort them out if Cressida lives with us.'

'Really?' said Lily. 'If Amanda ever does sort out her problems, will Cressida go back to her?'

Josephine shrugged. 'That's up to Cressida. Obviously, we hope she'll want to stay with us.'

'Really?' said Lily again. 'I'd have thought you—'

'Josephine,' interrupted Annie, 'I'm going to stay with

Mum and Dad for a few days at the end of term and I wondered if I could come on and stay with you for a couple of days afterwards. It would be early August, I suppose . . .'

'Of course you can,' said Josephine. 'Let me know the dates as soon as you've worked them out. We went to stay with the parents last weekend. Mum's trying to get Dad interested in the local Save our Post Office campaign. Anything to stop him ringing poor Harold and telling him how to run the company . . .'

The conversation meandered pleasantly from parents to children to work and some of Josephine's more colourful patients. It was only after Josephine and Mark had retired to bed on the grounds that Josephine had been on call throughout the previous night that Lily turned to Annie. 'Why did you stop me going on about Cressida? I was just about to give them some very good advice.'

'They don't need it,' said Annie. 'Or at least, they don't *want* it and people never pay heed to advice they don't want. It's great to see Josephine looking so happy. And you never know: Cressida might be very nice.'

'She's thirteen,' Lily said. 'Has there ever been a thirteen-year-old who's nice?'

'Probably not but let them at least enjoy their happiness while they can. Lord knows, married couples don't stay happy for very long.'

'You're such a cynic,' Lily said, reaching for a cigarette.

'I'm a realist. I observe and draw conclusions. Most of the wives I know are either bullied by their husbands or bored by their husbands.'

'Yes, and I bet you ignore all those happy wives who don't

fit your particular mindset. You let yourself be completely de-railed by one bad experience—'

'I didn't.'

'You did, you know you did. You quit a promising career at the BBC and exiled yourself to France for a year and then you buried yourself in darkest Cornwall for ages and then when you finally met a really nice man who wanted to marry you, you cut him out—'

'You're the one with the wonky mindset. You seem to forget that Robbie left *me*. And he never actually asked me to marry him. You're only going on like this because you're cross with me for breaking up with Derek before you could check him over.'

'All right,' said Lily, 'tell me why you left him. Tell me *really* why you left him.'

'All right,' said Annie, pouring herself some more wine and then settling back in her chair. 'Have you ever seen *The Wedding Singer*?'

CHAPTER FOUR

Black Book Entry, 7 June: Miss Bickery who should be made to choke on a hundred gingerbread men.

In the years following the non-marriage, Annie had met a variety of men and none of them had been very important. Robbie should have been one of the least important. The entire Robbie episode was a crazy mistake.

It had happened when she was living and teaching in Cornwall. Her best friend there was Deirdre who taught geography. Deirdre had recently fallen for a shy and strait-laced electrician called Phil and was throwing a party in order to display her suitability as a future spouse. The only fly in the ointment was the return to Falmouth of her brother who would have to be invited and who had a tendency to behave erratically and would thus alert Phil to the dangers of linking his life to a woman with a dodgy gene pool.

Over coffee in the staffroom, Deirdre relayed her anxieties to Annie. 'Robbie's my brother and I love him dearly, but he's quite hopeless. He's lived in more places and started more jobs than I've had hot dinners. He's also . . . and I'm telling you this because I like you and because you're young and attractive . . . he is also sexually incontinent. He's thirty years old and still shows no sign of wanting to settle down.'

'Well, I'm thirty and *I* still have no desire to settle down,' Annie pointed out. 'However, I appreciate the warning. Why's he come to Falmouth? Does he want to be near to you?'

Deirdre let out a sarcastic crack of laughter. 'You must be joking! No, he's a friend of Travis Scott, the man who owns the pottery shop near the post office. Travis had the chance to go to India for a few months and asked Robbie if he'd like to look after his shop and his flat while he was away. Robbie came down two weeks ago. I told him he could come to my party as long as he behaved. You'll like him. He's very charming. Just don't fall in love with him.'

'I won't,' Annie promised. In retrospect, Deirdre's well-meaning advice dulled Annie's normally acute antennae. Having been forewarned, she was so sure she was far too sensible to fall in love with anyone, least of all Deirdre's reprobate brother, that she never stopped to see what was happening.

Robbie was indeed very charming and since Annie was the only available female at Deirdre's party (there were two others but one had a tummy upset and wasn't looking her best and the other got drunk very quickly and kept rushing to the bathroom), he did of course make a beeline for her. At the end of the party, he invited her back to his flat above the pottery shop and Annie, slightly tipsily, agreed. He took her straight upstairs into the bedroom where he proceeded to undress her with tantalizing slowness. Annie discovered that

Robbie was an expert at taking his time. When he finally rolled away from her, he said, 'I enjoyed that.'

Annie stretched limbs that felt drugged with pleasure. 'So did I.'

In the darkness, Robbie chuckled. 'We sound like two old people who've just had a good meal.'

Annie grinned. 'I *feel* like I've had a good meal.'

Robbie said, 'Would you like to have sex with me next week? I could throw in a good meal as well.'

'Thank you,' said Annie. 'That would be very nice.'

Robbie turned back towards her, kissed her briefly but efficiently on the mouth and then rolled away again. 'Good-night, then.'

And so it had started. Annie felt she was quite safe. She knew what Robbie was like. She had no expectations.

At supper, the week after, they found out a little more about each other. Robbie learnt that after qualifying to teach English and drama, Annie had found a job in Falmouth and was still with the same school five years later. Annie learnt that Robbie wrote music and had once nearly had a song chosen to be the United Kingdom's Eurovision Song Contest entry. They both learnt that they had found it difficult in the last few days to think about anything other than having sex with each other and they both decided that a whole week's abstinence was too great for them to bear.

The next time they met, Robbie discovered that Annie couldn't cook and Annie discovered that Robbie could rustle up an excellent tomato sauce. They discovered that they had both loved the Narnian Chronicles as children and that they both had sisters who didn't understand them. Annie asked

Robbie what he was going to do when Travis returned from India and Robbie said he didn't know. Then they went to bed and Annie told herself it was liberating to be in a relationship in which both partners had such limited expectations.

Two weeks later, Robbie told her he did know what he was going to do, he was going to go to Australia. 'A mate of mine works in the music industry out in Sydney. He's wangled me a job. I thought I'd give it a go.' He looked at Annie and smiled. 'Why don't you come too?'

She had laughed of course, told him he was mad. She had a good job in Falmouth, nice friends, her own flat at last after the years of unsatisfactory lodgings. Why on earth would she give all that up to go away with a man who would probably tire of both her and Australia within a year?

'I might tire of Australia,' Robbie said, 'I wouldn't tire of you. It's just an idea. Think about it.'

To her amazement, she did think about it. She thought about it very seriously. Eventually, she decided it was too big a risk. She told Robbie it had all happened too quickly. She asked him to write to her and give her time to think about it more carefully.

Two months after he left, she got a postcard of the Sydney Opera House. He wrote on the back: *Sorry, Annie, I'm no good at sexual abstinence. Have met a lady who now seems to be pregnant. Sorry. Love, Robbie.*

The day she got the postcard was the tenth anniversary of her non-marriage to Ben. That night she lay in bed and cried. She tried to console herself with the thought that at least her unhappiness over Robbie's exit from her life had shown she was definitely over Ben.

The irony was that her reasons for not going to Australia – her friends, her job and her flat – all became as important as dust once Robbie had gone. She handed in her notice, sold her flat, got a new job and moved to Bath.

Annie stayed with Lily until Monday and then went up to Norwich to spend a few days with an old schoolfriend. She spent the rest of the half-term catching up on her marking, repainting her kitchen window frame and going window-shopping. She felt refreshed and invigorated by her week off. So, obviously, did Bella who actually laughed when Annie opened the door and said at once, 'Don't you dare call me Miss May!'

'Hello, *Annie!*' Bella said obediently. 'I've got something really important to tell you.'

'In that case,' Annie said, 'we'd better not waste any time.'

Bella said no more until she entered the flat and then she fixed Annie with an intense stare. 'We're going to do *Romeo and Juliet* at school!' she said. 'It's happening in November and Miss Appleby, our drama teacher, is holding auditions next week. I've put my name down for Juliet and it's very, very, very important that I get it. My dad wants me to go to university next year, straight after my A Levels, but I thought if I had a gap year, I could apply to drama school and if I get in, he'll see I'm good and he'll let me go, I mean it's stupid me going to university, I don't want to study anything at university and getting Juliet would be brilliant, it would be perfect, Dad would see me in it and he'd know I could act.' Bella bit her lip. 'To be honest, he's not interested in my acting, I can't make him see how much it means to me.

I really need to get the part. Would it be all right if we go over my audition piece? Would that be all right?'

'Certainly,' Annie said, 'but slow down! We have lots of time! And as for your father, don't you think you're being a little unfair? He must be quite interested: he's paying for your lessons with me, after all.'

'No, he's not,' said Bella. 'I am. I do a Saturday job to pay for them.'

'Oh,' said Annie, feeling immediately guilty for charging so much. 'Well let's take a look. Do you have the play with you?'

'There are two speeches,' Bella said, pulling a dog-eared text out of her bag. 'There's one long speech and one short one. Shall I read them both?'

'Let's hear the short one first,' Annie said.

Bella opened her script, found the right page and took a deep breath. When she finished reading, she looked anxiously at Annie. 'You didn't think I was any good, did you?'

'You were fine. You read too fast, I couldn't hear everything you said. Just listen to those last few lines again:

> *"Come, night! Come, Romeo! Come, thou day in night!*
> *For thou wilt lie upon the wings of night,*
> *Whiter than new snow on a raven's back.*
> *Come, gentle night; come, loving, black-brow'd night,*
> *Give me my Romeo: and when he shall die,*
> *Take him and cut him out in little stars,*
> *And he will make the face of heaven so fine*
> *That all the world will be in love with night,*
> *And pay no worship to the garish sun."*

'Wonderful, aren't they? They tell you all you need to know about being in love and, believe me, Juliet is definitely in love. You need to project that urgency! Being in love,' Annie said, warming to her theme, 'is a kind of madness. It affects her physically: her heart beats faster every time she thinks of Romeo, let alone when she actually sees him. Being in love distorts everything, she sees nothing clearly. She cares only about Romeo, he is her reason for living and every minute she doesn't see him is a minute wasted. Her heart aches and her body yearns. Being in love is,' Annie concluded, 'an exhausting condition!'

'It doesn't sound much fun,' Bella observed doubtfully.

'It isn't,' Annie said. 'It's hell. When Juliet cries, "Come, night, come, Romeo!" she wants him like a lost man in the desert wants a bottle of water. She *has* to have him and soon. And when she says, "Come, thou day in night," she means it! She thinks Romeo does light up her life, without him everything is dark. Think of everything you ever wanted, feel all that longing and then double it because at this moment, Juliet is a woman obsessed, she is a woman consumed with love and she wants Romeo far more than you want this part.'

'In that case,' said Bella, 'she wants him so much she could die!'

'Exactly!' said Annie. 'And that is what she ends up doing. She dies because life without Romeo is worse than death. I told you she's mad. All women in love are. Now read that passage through to yourself and think about what I've said. Then you can stand up and try it again.'

It was almost painful to watch Bella fix her eyes on the page with such intensity. She didn't stir, not even when the phone rang. Annie went to her bedroom, picked up the handset, listened to a woman tell her that she'd won a free holiday. Annie explained that she could never go on holiday because she could never find anyone to take care of her twelve Alsatians, then she put the handset down and returned to her armchair.

Bella looked up. 'I'm ready,' she said.

This time she was good. She was very, very good. 'Bella,' Annie said, 'if you perform like that when you do the audition, your teacher will be mad if she doesn't give you the part! You've got it perfectly: the longing, the yearning, the obsession! You were great! You made me really think you were in love! *Are* you in love?'

The enthusiasm drained from Bella's face. She blushed and shook her head.

'Sensible girl,' Annie said briskly.

'Last term,' Bella confessed, 'our form mistress, Miss Bickery, got married. She asked me and three others to sing at her wedding and afterwards she gave us all presents to say thank you. My present was a gingerbread man. Miss Bickery said it was a substitute to make up for the fact that I was the only one who didn't have a boyfriend.'

'How unbelievably crass!' Annie thundered. 'I cannot believe that in the twenty-first century there still exists a female teacher who can imply that in order to be happy you have to have a boyfriend! How utterly pathetic!'

'My friend Amy says she's in love,' Bella said. 'She says it's wonderful. She says she feels drunk the whole time!'

'She's right,' said Annie. 'You do. Just remind your friend to expect a hell of a hangover afterwards.'

Every summer, Frances and Ted threw a small party and tonight's promised to be just as good as its predecessors. The usual suspects were there: Grace and Henry of course, who had given Annie a lift; Hannah, looking radiant, with her boyfriend, Archie. Then there was Carla who was recently divorced and drinking too much. A particular friend of Hannah and Frances, Carla was known for her unintentionally tactless comments which most people found amusing and endearing and which Annie found tedious and irritating. In her cattier moments, Annie wondered how unintentional her unintentionally tactless observations really were. Finally there was Edward, a short man with a large nose and an optimistic nature who had at various times tried to attract Annie and who was now doing his best to flirt with Carla. His wife had left him ten years ago and he had been looking for a replacement ever since.

Frances and Ted lived in an old house in Claverton, a small, pretty village with spectacular views over the Limpley Stoke Valley. Their garden was a tribute to Frances's genius, an oasis of old English roses, lupins and daisies with a gently rolling lawn, a boules pitch surrounded by shrubs of rosemary and a few gnarled apple trees.

It was one of those perfect early summer evenings, warm and mild, with a hint of bonfire smoke in the air. The guests had gathered round the garden table outside the conservatory. Annie and Frances had wandered over to the climbing roses that grew against the stone wall. Frances was complaining about her daughter's university education. 'It's such a con,' she said. 'Alice has five hours of teaching a week and the rest of the time she has nothing at all. Grace says Chloe is just the same though at least she has *six* hours a week so the professors at Manchester must be working very hard. Alice is taking out huge loans for five hours' education a week. Five hours! It's no wonder all the students turn to drink and drugs. There's nothing else for them to do. I mean, Annie, you're a teacher. What sort of education is that? They all work their socks off, taking endless exams and then go to these seats of so-called higher learning and watch reality programmes about stupid celebrities fornicating with pigs.'

'Really?' asked Annie. 'When was that one on? Why did no one tell me?'

'You know what I mean. Of course, Josh can't wait to go and spend three years doing nothing! Do you know, I suggested Alice read *Middlemarch* at Easter and she asked me what Middlemarch *was*? And she's supposed to be studying English literature!'

Ted, always an assiduous host, bore down on them with a bottle. 'Rather a nice Chardonnay,' he said. 'See what you think.'

Annie, who was an If-It's-Alcohol-I'll-Drink-It sort of woman, took a decorous sip. 'Lovely!' she pronounced. 'Your wine is always lovely.'

'Did Frances tell you what Josh did last week?' Ted asked gloomily. Josh was their younger child, a blond bombshell of seventeen who always made Annie wistfully aware of her encroaching middle age. 'He'd been clubbing with his friends and they all came home and he decided to make some mulled wine for them. I mean only Josh would decide to make some mulled wine in June. He rooted around for a bottle of plonk and found one hidden in the larder. Frances and I came down in the morning to find a foul-smelling saucepan and an empty bottle of the Chateau Lafitte my father gave me for my fortieth birthday. I tell you, I was nearly sick. I actually had to go to the lavatory, I felt so sick. I feel sick now just telling you about it . . .' He shook his head and then paused as the sound of the doorbell could be heard. 'Ah!' he said. 'That will be our last guest! Very exciting this, a new friend of mine, Annie. He's quite a celebrity, you'll have heard of him and,' he looked significantly at Annie, 'he's single!'

Annie glanced enquiringly at Frances. 'Since when did Ted start mixing with celebrities?'

'He met him on the train last week. He's been very secretive about him. All he'll say is that I'll recognize him when I see him. It's probably one of the rugby players. Ted's a fanatical follower of Bath Rugby. He obviously thinks *you* might like him. In his usual, subtle way, I suspect he's trying to set you up.'

'And why would Ted think a gorgeous young rugby player would want to meet me?' Annie paused. 'This is where you're supposed to say a gorgeous young rugby player would be thrilled to meet me.'

'He might like older women,' Frances suggested. She stiffened suddenly and her face craned forward like a dog on the scent of a fox. 'Here comes our rugby champion and he is definitely not a rugby champion! He's not tall enough and he's too old, though I must say he *is* rather gorgeous. Actually,

71

he does look familiar. Now where have I seen him before? Annie, have a look!'

Annie, not wishing to appear too curious, bent down to brush away an imaginary fly, then straightened and turned slightly in order to catch a glimpse of the non-rugby champion. The man had smooth sandy-coloured hair, electric-blue eyes and a smile that ignited a dimple on either side of his mouth. Annie's heart lurched like an electrocuted rabbit. She saw him laugh at something Ted said and her glass fell on to the grass with a dull thud, splashes of Chardonnay littering her dress and her legs.

It was Ben.

CHAPTER FIVE

Black Book Entry, 11 June: Ben Seymour for climbing out of whatever sewer he's been living in and coming HERE.

Ben had recognized her. She could see he had recognized her. She barely had time to pick up her glass, reassure Frances she was fine and dust the lingering drops of wine from her dress before he and Ted were standing in front of her.

'Annie!' Ted laughed. 'You *are* a dark horse! Ben says he knows you! It certainly is a small world! This is always happening in Bath, everyone seems to know everyone else!'

Annie's mouth was very dry. She hoped Ben hadn't noticed she'd dropped her glass. 'Hello, Ben,' she said faintly.

Frances, who had been staring quite blatantly at him, crowed triumphantly, 'I know who you are! You're the new man on the local news! I watch you on television!' She glanced indignantly at Annie. 'You must have seen him on the local news. Why didn't you tell me you knew him?'

'I don't watch the local news,' Annie murmured.

'Well, you ought to, it's very interesting.' She reached out to shake Ben's hand. 'I'm Frances. It's very nice to have you here.'

'It's very kind of you to invite me,' Ben said. 'You have a beautiful garden.'

'Thank you. Have you come far? Do you live locally?'

'I'm living in Bristol at the moment. I'm hoping to move to Bath soon.'

'You'll love Bath,' Frances assured him. 'Won't he love Bath, Annie?'

'I think,' Annie said stiffly, 'Bristol might suit him better. Bristol is very nice.'

'You hate Bristol!' Frances said. 'You never go to Bristol!'

'Only because I get lost whenever I do go. I think Ben would like it.'

'I tend to get lost there too,' said Ben. 'It's nice to see you again, Annie. Is your husband here?'

'Annie doesn't have a husband!' Frances said. 'Unless that's something else she hasn't mentioned. Have you ever had a husband, Annie?'

'No,' said Annie.

'I was told you had a husband,' Ben said.

He was as shocked as she was. They were both floundering, both trying to put simple, sensible sentences together and both failing dismally. For once, she was grateful for the arrival of Carla who swept down on them with the energy of one who has just found a new project. 'I had to come and say hello to Ben!' She grasped both his hands in hers. 'Hello! It is so good to meet you! I saw you on TV only last night. You handled that interview with the man whose wife smashed his railway set so tactfully! Although I do think that in the interests of balance, you should have interviewed the wife as well. I mean, he had taken over the entire sitting room, it must have been very difficult for her . . .'

'Excuse me,' Annie murmured. She slipped away and walked purposefully towards the conservatory. She was hailed by Edward, who was apparently eating his way through the entire bowl of cheese straws, and called lightly, 'I'll be right back!'

She went into the conservatory and then through to the kitchen and then the hall. She pulled open the large oak front door, shut it carefully behind her and stepped out onto the narrow stone pavement. She took three very deep breaths, exhaling slowly each time. Her one instinctive thought had been to escape but she didn't have her car here and doing a two-mile walk in her strap-on sandals would be a nightmare. On the other hand, anything would be better than staying at the party and pretending to be normal. She took a few steps and then paused, frozen with indecision. Walking out on the party was just like sticking up a neon sign with the words 'Annie's gone mad' emblazoned on it. Worse, Ben would assume she'd left the party because of him and she didn't want him to think she'd do anything because of him. She had to go back. She couldn't bear to go back but she would have to. She retraced her steps and went back to the front door. She looked at it helplessly. If she rang the doorbell, Ted or Frances would open it and ask her quite reasonably what she was doing on the pavement. Perhaps she could say she had heard a dog fight or a scream and had gone to investigate. Perhaps she could say she had seen a butterfly trapped in the hall, had opened the door to let it out, had guided it towards the field and had then returned to find the door had blown shut in the wind. Except there was no wind. This was ridiculous, she couldn't stay out here on the doorstep all night. It was beginning to get cold and Annie's little grey cardigan was only marginally less flimsy than her pink, floral frock.

She was still standing, concocting ever more incredible scenarios when the cavalry arrived in the shape of Josh on his bicycle. Josh seemed unsurprised by the sight of Annie shivering on the doorstep. He pulled out his keys and said, 'Hi, Annie! How are you?'

'Very well, thank you,' Annie said gratefully. She followed him through to the kitchen where Frances was putting the finishing touches to her meal.

'There you are, Josh,' she said. 'Can you take the plates through? I meant to do a seating plan but I forgot so people will just have to sit where they like. Annie, come and tell me about Ben! How do you know him? Have you known him long? Was he a very good friend?'

'I haven't seen him for years,' Annie said. Was it paranoia that made her think Frances's last question was pregnant with significance? In a moment of panic she offered a diversion. 'He . . . he used to go out with Josephine.'

'Josephine? She's the very clever sister, isn't she? The one who's a consultant? How fascinating! How long did they go out for?'

Annie was saved for the second time that evening by the reappearance of Josh who was fast becoming her favourite teenager. 'I'm going to have a shower,' he said, 'and then I'm off. Have a good evening.'

'Thank you, darling. Just go and call everyone in first, will you?'

'I'll do that!' Annie said quickly and went out into the garden before Frances could ask any more questions. Outside, Ben and Archie were talking as if they were old friends. Annie swallowed and called out with a severity she had not intended, 'Supper is ready now!' She went back in and kept herself busy ferrying dishes until she had checked that Ben was safely ensconced between Carla and Grace.

She ended up sitting between Ted and Edward and spent the first course listening to Ted give her a detailed description of the last rugby match he had seen. She had never felt less hungry in her life and when Frances put a huge plate of curry in front of her, she glanced at it with something akin to despair. Edward put a hand on her arm and whispered, 'I hear you're an old friend of the TV man. What's he like?'

'I haven't seen him in years,' Annie said.

'Just because he's on the telly, everyone thinks he's wonderful,' Edward muttered. He bit into a poppadom. 'I mean, when the chips are down, what's he got that I haven't?' He shook the crumbs of poppadom from his shirt and raised his napkin to his streaming face. 'I love curry,' he said. 'Trouble is it always makes me sweat.' He looked hopefully at Annie. 'A woman once told me excessive perspiration was a sign of excessive manliness. Do you think that's true?'

'I think it probably is,' Annie said. She stole a glance at Ben. He was listening intently to Grace. Annie wondered what they were talking about. She looked at her plate again and knew she couldn't eat a thing.

She was trapped in a nightmare. One part of her could listen with seemingly rapt concentration to Ted's rambling stories, encourage Edward to swap plates and tease him about his gargantuan appetite, help Frances make coffee and congratulate her on her meal. Another part of her was aware through every moment of the endless dinner that Ben Seymour was sitting only a few feet away, enjoying the fawning attention of her closest friends.

By the time he was on his second cup of coffee and his third glass of pudding wine, Edward was feeling less belligerent towards the newcomer. 'So tell me, Ben,' he called across the table, 'do you like being famous?'

'You're very kind!' Ben laughed. 'I would hardly say I'm famous!'

'You are famous round here!' Carla said. 'I think I'd like to be famous. Don't you love having so many people being interested in you? You could do a Ben Seymour Opens His Heart to the *Bath Chronicle* and it would be a sell-out!'

'I can safely say,' said Ben fervently, 'that I would rather amputate my little finger than open my heart to the *Bath Chronicle*. I can't think of anything more humiliating than to be seen as someone who wants to open his heart to the *Bath Chronicle*!'

'I do agree,' said Hannah. 'I read an article last week by some journalist about his failing marriage and he started talking about his difficulties with premature ejaculation and I thought to myself I do not need to know about this!'

Archie, sitting opposite her, grinned affectionately. 'I bet you read it all the way through though!'

'Yes, I did, and then a couple of days later I read an article by the journalist's wife and she was going on about her husband's sexual difficulties and I realized he probably wrote his article because he knew she was going to write *her* article. If I were him, I'd never talk to her again. Some things can never be forgotten!'

Carla poured herself some more wine. 'You're beginning to sound like Annie.'

'Why?' asked Ben. 'Is that what Annie says?'

Carla put her elbows on the table and just missed knocking over her glass. 'Annie,' she said, 'has a black book in which she records the name and offence of everyone who's ever crossed her path and done her wrong. Once you're in it you can never get out! We're all terrified of finding ourselves in it! Isn't that true, Annie?'

'No!' said Annie. 'Of course it's not. I used to keep one long ago just for fun! Everyone has an imaginary black book. We all remember the people and the things we will never forgive.'

Carla smirked. 'It's just that your list is longer than most!'

'Annie's right,' said Grace. 'You never forget some things. The day Chloe left her first school – I was moving her, she was being bullied – she was given a box of chocolates by the one person in the class who'd been nice to her. Chloe was so thrilled. And then two of the girls took it and ate the sweets themselves. I see one of those girls in town still and I can never bring myself to even nod at her.'

'For all you know,' Ben said, 'that girl might have spent years feeling guilty about taking those sweets. People can change.'

'I don't think so,' Grace said. 'She's very fat now. She's obviously been stealing sweets for years.' She glanced across at her husband. 'Henry, we must go. We have your mother coming to lunch tomorrow and I need all my wits about me. Annie, do you want to stay or are you coming back with us?'

'I'll come with you.' Annie stood up, aware that Ben half-rose before returning to his seat. She wished they could leave this second but it seemed to take interminable minutes for Henry to arrange something with one person, say goodbye to another, remember he'd left some gloves here the time before. Even when they were safely in the car, Annie couldn't escape from Ben. Henry went on for ages about him and then Grace said she thought he was lovely, so polite, so easy to talk to.

'I feel rather bad now,' Grace mused. 'I realize I did nothing but talk about myself to him. We didn't talk about him at all. He seemed really interested.'

'Of course he would,' Henry said. 'He spends his life being paid to ask questions and look interested.'

'Henry! Are you saying he wasn't really interested!'

'I'm sure he was, my darling. But he strikes me as quite a dark horse. He's not the sort of bloke who enjoys talking about himself. I heard both Ted and Carla ask him why he'd moved down here and both times he changed the subject. He did it very deftly but I could see that's what he was doing. You used to be friends with him, Annie. Did you know him well?'

'Not really.' Annie leant forward as they progressed into Bathwick Hill. 'Henry, please don't bother to take me home. It's a ten-minute walk from your house and I'd like the fresh air.'

'If you're sure,' Henry said, pulling to a stop outside his house. 'It is a lovely night.'

'It is,' agreed Annie. She climbed out of the car and waved cheerfully. 'Thank you for the lift! See you soon!'

She started crying before she reached the post box. It was the shock of course. He had hardly aged at all. A few laughter lines, a little more stocky, that was all. He still looked like he found everyone he talked to incredibly interesting, he still had to constantly push his hair back from his face, he still had that smile that made those dimples appear. Why couldn't he have lost his hair, got fat, developed a nervous tic, acquired a problem with perspiration like Edward, grown a spot on the end of his nose? She had given up everything in order to take herself out of his world and now here he was, barging into the world she had created for herself, being charming and sweet and likeable and looking like he'd never known a sleepless night in his life. And what was that he'd said about people changing? Had that been some sort of coded message, some sort of preparation so that he could later divest himself of his guilt, make himself feel better and take over her friends without having to worry about her? Not that he looked like someone who was beset by guilt.

She let herself into her flat and went over to the window to close the curtains. She knew why she was crying. She was crying because the sight of Ben had made her see that the great edifice she had built on the ruins of her non-marriage was far more fragile than she had thought. She hoped very much he would show the courtesy and the sensitivity to stay in Bristol and keep away from her territory. She hoped he wouldn't try to speak to her, explain himself, apologize. If that happened, if she let that happen, then the whole dark, despairing ugliness would come back and wash everything away. Her only solution lay in keeping her dislike and her anger pure and untainted, like a bulwark against the darkness that threatened her citadel.

She went through to her bedroom and pulled out the Black Book from under her bed. She did not feel the slightest bit guilty about denying its existence earlier. She had, after all, told Carla, Frances and Hannah about it in confidence during an extremely jolly girls' night out and it was quite wrong of Carla to talk about it to the entire dinner table. Besides, Annie thought, she had not been entirely mendacious. She rarely wrote in it these days. She certainly didn't write in it every day.

She rifled through the pages until she found the ones she was looking for. She read them carefully and her face hardened. Then she picked up her pen.

CHAPTER SIX

Black Book Entry, 21 June: Miss Appleby for purporting to be a drama teacher and being unable to recognize genuine talent when it stares her in the face.

Annie awoke late the next morning, having slept badly that night. She felt sluggish, exhausted and depressed, for all of which Ben Seymour was directly responsible. Usually, she loved Sundays. Sometimes she would walk into town, buy the papers, have a lazy brunch at the tapas bar in Bartlett Street, walk round the shops, come back and have some tea. Today, the thought of a long, empty day in Bath was anathema to her, particularly since the man who had ruined her life was living a mere sixteen miles away.

Escape seemed the only option and she knew just where to go. The first day back at school after half-term, Geoffrey Godlom, one of the more combustible teachers on the staff, had told Annie about the perfect day he'd had a few days earlier. 'I was in a foul mood,' he said – not an uncommon state of mind for Geoffrey – 'and Marjorie and I had planned to go off for the day, take a picnic to the seaside. Then Marjorie's appalling mother rang and said she was far too ill to make herself any lunch. The woman's a total fraud, she'll outlive us all, but off Marjorie trotted, leaving me on my own. So I took myself off to Stourhead and I walked around the gardens and sat on the edge of the lake. And I felt like . . . Well, you know when you fill a car with petrol? Well, I felt my spirit filled with peace. Surrounded by all that beauty, I stopped worrying about my son's divorce, I stopped worrying about the chronic stupidity of the entire Year Eight. I even stopped thinking about my wretched mother-in-law. I felt replenished and refreshed. You should try it.'

Annie had been very impressed by Geoffrey's unaccustomed eloquence and it seemed to her that if Stourhead could locate and replenish Geoffrey's inner spirituality, it could certainly do the same for her.

Arriving at the entrance building, she paid for her ticket and read all the information displayed on the walls. She read that Sir Henry Hoare, crushed by the early demise of first one and then another wife, had assuaged his grief by creating the gardens. His heir was his grandson, Sir Richard Colt Hoare. After *his* young wife died, he too turned to the estate for comfort. He never married again. Annie had glanced at the pictures of the grieving widowers before she had realized their sad history and looking at them again, she thought she could detect a lonely nobility in their features and a brave determination to create something positive from their tragedies.

At least they could preserve their early love in aspic, untainted by the grim reality of ageing spouses. Not for them

the boredom of once-fresh anecdotes or the growing understanding that what had once seemed sweet innocence was in
fact dull stupidity. If Ben had died, instead of jilting her,
she would undoubtedly have mourned him for the rest of her
life. So she was lucky. She had found out what he was really
like. It was just a pity that he was still so attractive. Not that
that counted for anything.

She was not going to think about Ben. She was going
to concentrate on Nature and on Man's Creativity and on
Beauty and on Wonder. She was going to inject her mind with
exalted thoughts and immunize it from the Anti-Christ
currently living in Bristol. She stepped out onto the path and
strolled down to the gardens.

And they *were* beautiful. The lake was smooth and opaque
with sunlight tickling the surface. In front of her, a young
couple walked with their small son toddling between them.
The mother called out gaily, 'Look, Heathcliffe! There's a
swan! Can you see?'

The little boy stopped. 'Chicken!' he said.

The father laughed fondly. 'Clever boy! It does look a little
like a chicken!'

It didn't look anything like a chicken. Annie overtook them
quickly and walked on, past an elderly couple squabbling
amicably about the identity of one of the larger trees, past
two women talking earnestly – 'He said, "I don't like your
steak and kidney pie and what's more, I never liked your steak
and kidney pie,"' – then past a young man taking photographs. Finally, she spotted a bench on the edge of the lake
and sat down.

Two swans glided effortlessly on the water. Nearby, a

mother duck paddled, busily shepherding her young babies, occasionally dipping her head in the water. The trees gently swayed in the breeze, their leaves softly whispering to one another.

Why had Ben come to Bristol? He was a London man, he had always loved London. How had he met Ted? And why had everyone been so easily gulled by his 'I'm not really famous' act? And why was she letting herself think about him? Look at the silver birches on the other side of the lake, Annie. Absorb the beauty of the colours, marvel at the foresight and the planning of all the different trees and shrubs.

Heathcliffe and his parents had caught up with her. Annie watched them meander down to the edge of the water.

'Look, Heathcliffe!' said the mother. 'There are two swans now!'

'Chickens!' screeched Heathcliffe and walloped his mother's leg with an angry fist.

'Heathcliffe!' said his mother reproachfully. 'That isn't very kind!'

Heathcliffe's father spoke soothingly. 'I think Heathcliffe is finding it difficult to cope with the thought of—' he nodded significantly at the woman's stomach – 'future productions. I think he is trying to articulate his anger and his fear. He doesn't understand, so he's venting his frustrations on you. He's a confused little boy.'

Annie thought it far more likely that Heathcliffe was simply a nasty little thug. Either that, or he was trying to express his wholly justified rage at being saddled with such an appalling name. She stood up and moved away. Between them, Ben Seymour and Heathcliffe had sabotaged any chance of her inner spirituality emerging from wherever it was supposed to lurk.

When she got home her answerphone was twinkling expectantly. Annie checked: four messages. She pulled out a pen and note pad from her bag and flicked the switch.

– Hello, Annie. This is your mother. I hope you are well. We haven't heard from you for quite a while so I thought I should check and make sure you are all right. Ring us when you have the time. Goodbye. –

Rosemary had never learnt to be at ease with answerphones. She always sounded very stiff and stilted, as if she wasn't sure if anyone was listening. Annie felt a twist of guilt. Behind every word her mother had uttered there was an unspoken dismay at the crumbling of yet another romantic possibility and an anxiety about Annie's state of mind. Which was why Annie had not rung her since her break-up with Derek. She would ring this evening and, if she felt strong enough, bring up the subject and assure her mother she had never been happier.

– Annie, it's Hannah! Last night was fun, wasn't it? Archie thought your friend Ben was very nice. Carla got more and more drunk after you left. We gave her a lift home and Archie was terrified she'd throw up. Anyway, Annie, can you come to supper on the twenty-fifth? Archie said he hardly talked to you and you haven't been over here for ages. Loved your dress by the way! Ring soon! –

When Annie had first met her, Hannah was painfully thin with deep, dark eyes that looked utterly lost. Jasper had died the year before in a motorway collision, leaving Hannah with her six-year-old twins, Eliza and Rose. She told Annie she did her translating work at night; it was better than lying in bed, raging at Jasper for leaving them.

Annie had seen the way Archie looked at Hannah and she had seen the transformation he had wrought. Archie was all right. It was very satisfying to hear Hannah's voice bubbling with gaiety and confidence and Annie felt a rush of affection for Archie. She could even forgive him for his lapse of taste where Ben was concerned.

– Annie, it's Ben. I think we should talk. Can I take you out for dinner or at least a drink? You can reach me on my mobile any time at . . . –

Annie pressed the delete button at once. How *dare* he? How dare he ring up and say in that peremptory way, 'I think we should talk'! How could he think that she would want to spend any time with him at all? What did he expect would happen? What did he plan to say? *Annie, I know I walked out on you thirty seconds before the wedding but, hey, that's all water under the bridge, let's be friends!* And what did he expect *her* to say? *Hey, that's all right, Ben, we all make mistakes and after all you were very young and of course I'd love to be friends, especially now you're a local newsreader!* Amazing! Incredible! Unforgivable!

– Annie, it's Ben again. I'm sorry if I sounded a bit short on the phone, I think I'm a bit shell-shocked. I got the feeling last night that you weren't totally thrilled to see me. Of course I could be wrong and it could be that you genuinely believe I'd be happier in Bristol than in Bath. If so, then thank you for the advice. I would really like to see you. We do have a lot to talk about, don't you think? At any rate, I certainly have a lot to talk about. Please meet me, Annie. In case you deleted my last message, my number is . . . –

Annie deleted the message. So he had the feeling she didn't want to see him? Ten marks for perspicacity, Ben! So he had a lot to talk to her about? I bet you do, Ben! Do you really think I want to hear your weasel words and pathetic attempts to salve your rotten conscience? Rot in hell, Ben!

He rang again on Tuesday. Annie had stayed late at school in an effort to tackle her display boards which had displayed all the excitement of limp lettuce in recent weeks. When she finally came home, the answerphone was flashing.

– Hi, Annie. I haven't heard from you so I reckon there are four possible explanations. One, your answerphone is not working, in which case you should get it mended. Two, you haven't yet listened to your messages. Three, you don't want to answer your messages, or at least you don't want to answer *my* messages. Four, you might have deleted all your messages by mistake and might be wanting to ring but can't, because you deleted my number. So, let me give it to you again . . . –

Annie was about to delete his message but her finger hovered and then froze over the button. If she went on deleting his messages, he might continue to think she was dying to ring him. This thought revolted her so much that she immediately replayed his message and scribbled down his number. Then she took a deep breath and punched the digits with fury.

'Now, look here, Ben . . .'

Ben's recorded voice, brisk and buoyant, stopped her in her tracks. 'Hello, I'm afraid I'm not here at the moment but if you leave your name and number I will get back to you as soon as possible.'

Annie gripped the phone. 'This is Annie May. My machine is not broken, I have heard all your messages and I do not want to talk to you, I do not want to listen to you, I do not want to see you. Ever, ever, ever. I find you loathsome, repellent and disgusting . . .' She paused and then finished a little lamely, 'Goodbye, then.'

That was it. She'd finished it. If he had a tenth of the sensitivity of most people, he would never see her again.

Fate, or rather Waitrose, ensured he did. Early Friday evening, Annie walked down to the supermarket to get food for her supper. Having selected the night's menu (ham, potato salad and a yogurt), she joined the queue at the basket-only check-out. She stood, staring at the back of the woman in front of her, noting idly that her dyed hair failed to conceal that her natural colour was grey.

Behind Annie, a voice called her name. She turned, as did the woman with badly dyed hair. There had to be an etiquette, Annie thought, for speaking to a person to whom you have recently told that you do not wish to speak. Probably the correct etiquette was to say something like 'Bugger off.'

Annie, aware of the dyed-hair woman's interest, said stiffly, 'Hello.'

'How are you?' Ben asked.

'I'm very well.' Annie wished the hair woman would stop looking at them. It was almost as if she anticipated some cataclysmic explosion. Annie picked a random polite question from out of the ether. 'How are your parents?'

'They're very well.'

'Good.' Annie shifted her basket to her other hand. 'Do they still live in that lovely house in Wimbledon?'

'My mother does. My father lives in Brighton. How are *your* parents? Do they still live in *their* lovely house?'

Annie regarded him with suspicion. If he hadn't just effectively told her his parents were divorced or at least separated she might have suspected him of making fun of her painful attempts to retain a level of social decorum. 'They moved into Pixie Cottage,' she said. For a moment her eyes met his.

Reluctantly, the hair woman turned her back on them in order to pay for her purchases.

'I got your message,' Ben said.

'That's good,' Annie said. 'I'm so glad.'

'Shall I give you my card?' Ben suggested. 'In case you change your mind?'

'I won't,' Annie snapped and then, aware of the cashier's startled glance, gave an unconvincing smile. She put her basket on the counter and took out her wallet. Ben put his basket next to her own.

'It is very nice to see you,' Ben said.

Annie gave him a look that she hoped would speak volumes, collected her groceries and walked out of the shop as fast as she could. She thought about the things she had seen in his basket: two Chicken Kievs, a strawberry trifle, a bottle of Chardonnay. She wondered who would be eating with him tonight. Not that she cared.

On Tuesday evening, Bella arrived for her lesson, as always, on the dot of eight. In answer to Annie's unspoken query, she opened her mouth, her face puckered and she burst into tears.

Annie went to her at once and put her arm round her. 'Bella! Bella, please don't cry! Bella?'

Bella's shoulders heaved and in between sobs, she gasped out, 'Sorry! I'm so sorry! I'm so stupid!'

Annie, patting her shoulder awkwardly, kept murmuring, 'It's all right, it's all right.'

At last, when Bella blew her nose fiercely, Annie said, 'I think we both need a cup of tea! What do you say?'

Bella nodded dolefully. 'Thank you. I'm so sorry!'

'Stop saying sorry!' Annie gave Bella a last bracing pat. 'If you want to wash your face, go through to my bedroom and you'll find the bathroom on the right.'

Bella joined her in the kitchen after a few minutes. Her face was shiny and her eyes were swollen. 'I'm sorry,' she said. 'I didn't mean to cry. I'm not sure I should come here any more. I don't think there's any point.' Her lips compressed and she swallowed very hard. 'Actually, there doesn't seem much point to anything at the moment.'

Annie lifted the tea bags from the mugs and threw them in the bin. 'A long time ago,' she said, 'when I was only a few years older than you are now, I felt just like this. I know exactly how you feel. I promise you I know how you feel. At night I was so unhappy I couldn't sleep. And then I made myself think of the place in the world I loved the most. And I made myself try to remember every aspect of that place, every corner, every shop, every road. And it helped, it really did. Tell me your favourite place in the universe.'

'Well,' Bella began, biting her lip and trying valiantly to participate in Annie's remedy for heartache, 'I have two favourite places. A friend of my mother lives in Blackheath. She has a funny address: Westward Ho, Dartmouth Row! She has a lovely house right near the heath and when I stay I have the room at the top of the house and above the bed there's a framed photo of Audrey Hepburn in *Breakfast at Tiffany's* because that's my favourite film.'

'I like that film too. What's your other favourite place?'

'In Scotland. My great-grandmother lives in a little cottage near Oban and it's on the edge of the loch and she doesn't have a telephone and half the time the electricity doesn't work but it's the most beautiful place in the world.'

'My favourite place was in France,' Annie said, 'near a town called Abbeville. I had a pen-friend there and we became very good friends. When I was really unhappy I went over there. Now what you must do, whenever you feel like crying, is think about Scotland or Dartmouth Row, concentrate on them, imagine you're there, remember how happy you are when you're there. Will you try it?'

Bella swallowed hard and nodded.

'Good. Now do you feel able to tell me what happened? You don't have to if you don't want to.'

Bella gave a long, exhausted sigh. 'I didn't get the part,' she said. 'I did my best and I didn't get the part. Miss Appleby said I was very good but she said Martha looked more like Juliet than I did.'

'I see,' said Annie. 'I didn't know Miss Appleby was on such close terms with Juliet. Does she have a photo?'

'She gave me the part of the nurse.'

'That's a big part,' Annie said brightly. 'That's a very good part. You can have lots of fun with that part. For what it's worth, I think Miss Appleby is mad not to give you Juliet but it's not the end of the world. It's a school play. It's one play.'

Bella bit her lip. 'It is the end of the world,' she said flatly. 'I'm not interested in boys and clothes and clubbing. I'm only interested in acting. If I can't act I might as well not live! I wanted to be Juliet so much, I tried so hard, I really did try!'

'There will be other plays . . .'

'But this was the play that counted! My dad won't even consider drama school. Getting Juliet was the only way I had to show him . . . Now he'll make me go to university.'

'I'm sure he won't *make* you! No one can make you do anything! But actually, Bella, university can be a very good training ground for actors. If you go to one with a good drama society, you can join that and do lots of acting. You'll probably end up going to the Edinburgh Festival!'

'I don't want to go to university.'

Annie opened a packet of chocolate digestives and passed them to Bella. She wanted to tell her that life would go on, bringing new opportunities, lancing her unhappiness. She remembered the scorn with which she had treated her mother's attempts to give her similar advice after Ben had left her. 'What about your mother?' she asked gently. 'What does she think?'

'She thinks I should do what I want to do. But Dad won't listen to her.' Bella took out the remains of her tissue and blew her nose again. 'My mum is an actress.'

'Really? So that's where you get your talent from!'

'She was in a television serial once,' Bella said. 'before I was born. It was called *End of the Road*. She played a beautiful woman who has to choose between a failed boxer and a rich politician and she chooses the politician and it turns out he killed her sister.'

'I remember it!' Annie cried. 'I remember it very well. The last episode was on my fourteenth birthday and my grandmother rang to wish me happy birthday and I told her I'd ring her after the programme and my mother was very cross with me! But it was so romantic. I can still remember the boxer killing the politician in self-defence and he has this scar down his face which is supposed to make him ugly but actually it was very sexy and the girl – your mother – kisses the scar and tells him she loves him! Great stuff! I thought she was so beautiful!'

'Thank you,' said Bella. 'I'll tell her.' She sighed wistfully. '*She* went to drama school.'

'It can be overrated,' Annie said. 'I had a cousin who went to one in Kent and she said all the students were horribly pleased with themselves and full of their own self-importance. I can think of loads of successful actors who didn't go . . .'

'I probably wouldn't get in anyway,' Bella said. She looked small and defeated and crushed. Her misery was absurd of course and one day she'd probably look back and laugh. Annie didn't feel like laughing. Annie felt like murdering Miss Appleby. 'Bella,' she said, 'you can act. Whether you end up going to drama school or university or the Job Centre doesn't matter. You can act.'

Bella attempted a smile. 'You're very kind.'

'I'm not in the habit of telling people they have talent if they don't. Now listen to me. I have a proposition to put before you. For the time being, I'll give you a fifty per cent discount on every lesson. I want to put you in for the LAMDA exam.

No messing, we'll go straight for the Gold. If you get honours you go back to paying me the full whack again. If you only get merit or even distinction, you not only start paying me the full amount again, you also have to help me repaint my kitchen. Well? Is it a deal?'

'I can't,' Bella said. 'It's not right.'

'It's a bet,' said Annie. 'It's only for a few months. You don't need to tell anyone else about it. I like having a little flutter occasionally. I should also tell you that only three of my students have ever got honours, though quite a few have had distinction. So you'll probably end up painting my kitchen. What do you say?'

Bella looked doubtfully at Annie. 'Well . . .'

'Of course if you don't think you're up to it,' Annie said kindly, 'I quite understand. Perhaps you should just give up, take up some other interest. I've got a book on knitting somewhere . . .'

Bella gave a reluctant smile. 'I don't want to knit,' she said.

'Good.' Annie extended her hand. 'Deal?'

Bella nodded. 'Deal.'

As soon as Bella left, Annie went back to the kitchen. She opened the fridge, regarded the pepperoni pizza without enthusiasm and took out the half-full bottle of Chardonnay instead. She poured herself a glass of wine. She had the feeling that she had just done something very stupid. On the plus side, she had cheered Bella up and given her a new challenge on which to focus and she had also assuaged her own distaste for taking Bella's Saturday money. On the minus side, if Bella ever told Abby about the cut-price lessons, Abby would quite reasonably want to pay the same. Also, if Bella didn't get honours, she'd end up being just as miserable as she was about not getting Juliet.

Annie took another sip of wine. She had been stupid and impulsive. The phone went and Annie, still fretting about Bella, went through to the bedroom. 'Yes?' she said absently. 'Who's speaking please?'

'It's Ben. Am I speaking to an answerphone?'

Annie contemplated putting the phone down. 'What do you want?' she asked.

'I was thinking you might have changed your mind about talking to me,' Ben said. 'And I thought that if you had, it might be a good idea to ring.'

'Listen,' said Annie. 'Shall I tell you what I will do if I see you again?'

'What?' asked Ben hopefully.

'I shall be sick,' Annie said slowly. 'I shall be very, very sick!' She slammed the phone down and went through to the kitchen to cook the pizza. She had recovered her appetite.

It was one of those days when the sun and the sky conspired together to pull people from their houses. It was a day for spontaneity, a day for picnics in the park, strolls by the seaside, climbing up very small hills. Unfortunately for Annie, she had been spontaneous a few days earlier when she had rashly promised her Year Seven sets that she would mark their biography projects over the weekend.

Having spent the entire day going through them (Sample: *Charles Dickens was a man who rote a book called Oliver Twist about a boy who ate two much*), she felt she deserved the forthcoming evening with Archie and Hannah.

Hannah lived in Widcombe in a strangely Gothic cottage close to the canal. It was a long walk but Annie had been deprived of sunlight all day and she had no intention of taking her car. She closed her last project at half past six (Sample: *J. K. Rowling bought a cup of coffee in a café and wrote Harry Potter and then went home*), and emerged from her front door an hour or so later to find that the sun was still shining.

Annie was in a very good mood. She knew she looked her best with her newly washed hair and her grey linen dress and the little pink cardigan. She walked past a woman who was struggling to fill a bag with her dog's excrement and felt lucky not to have a dog. She saw a fat man on a green long boat. He was loudly berating his wife for dropping a rope in the water and Annie felt she was very lucky not to be married to him. She felt lucky to be living in Bath, lucky to have a good friend like Hannah, lucky to have marked all her biography projects. The only blot on her interior landscape was Ben and she felt she had effectively prevented him from becoming more than a distantly menacing blur.

Hannah's door was opened by one of the twins. Try as she might, Annie could never tell one from the other. Both girls had long hair which they wore in plaits, both had exquisite manners and neither had as yet succumbed to pre-pubescent ennui. Annie took a gamble and said, 'Hi, Rose!'

'I'm Eliza,' Eliza said without rancour. 'Rosie is outside. I've been decorating the trifle. *And* I made a fruit salad! You're to go through to the garden,' she added. 'We'll be out in a moment.'

Annie, slightly daunted by such extensive preparations for what she had thought was to be a simple supper, meekly went on through to the garden where she met a hive of activity. Frances was buttering bread, Grace was cutting smoked salmon and Ted and Henry were playing boules with Rose.

'We nearly sent out a search party to find you,' Frances confessed. 'Hannah said we couldn't start drinking until you got here!'

'Annie!' Hannah came out, holding a tray of glasses in front of her. She put the tray on the table and called out, 'Finish the game now! It's champagne time!'

Archie appeared with two bottles of champagne. Behind Archie came Eliza with a bowl of crisps. Behind Eliza came one last person, swathed in a large maroon apron. Annie stared. Ben caught her eye but didn't say anything. Then he reached into his pocket, took out a brown paper bag and, with a face devoid of expression, offered it to her without saying a word.

CHAPTER SEVEN

Black Book Entry, 25 June: Ben Seymour for being an arrogant, amoral, immoral, obtuse, unimaginative, conceited charlatan.

Bang! The cork erupted from Archie's fingers. Champagne was quickly poured into glasses, handed out to the waiting guests and, in at least one instance, raised surreptitiously to the lips for a guilty but definitely medicinal gulp.

Hannah clapped her hands. 'Quiet, please! Archie and I have an announcement to make.' Her face broke into a broad smile. 'I have done Archie the very great honour of agreeing to be his wife!'

Amidst the clamour of exclamations, one of the twins clapped her hands. 'I would just like to say,' she said proudly, 'that Rose and I gave Archie our permission to ask Mummy and we said he could and we are both going to be brides-maids and Archie says I can make a speech at the wedding and—'

'Eliza!' Rose shouted. 'The bubbles are going and I want to drink my champagne!'

Annie's vision blurred and she blinked furiously. She knew that Ben was looking at her and she swallowed before raising her glass. 'To Hannah and Archie!' she cried. 'And to Rose and Eliza!'

'To Hannah and Archie! To Rose and Eliza!' There were claps and hurrahs and laughter and everyone drank.

As long as she kept talking, kept smiling, kept concentrating on the happy couple, she would be all right. She went up to Hannah and hugged her. 'When's the big day?' she asked. 'And will I have to wear a hat?'

'No hats!' Hannah promised. 'We think it will be in December. Archie's son will be back from Venice by then.'

'How did Archie propose?' Frances asked. 'Did he get down on his knee?'

'Much better than that,' said Hannah. 'He made me dinner and his neighbour's father came in and played the violin.'

'That was nearly a disaster,' Archie said. 'He was only supposed to play for a few minutes but he got carried away and we sat there like prunes while I felt all my courage slipping away. Luckily, my neighbour came round and dragged him away and I asked Hannah quickly before I lost my nerve.'

'It was lovely!' Hannah said. 'Archie, pour some more champagne. I'll be back in a minute.'

'Can I help?' asked Ben.

'Certainly not, you've done more than enough! I've only got to serve out.'

'I'll help you,' said Annie. She followed Hannah through to the kitchen and hugged her again. 'Hannah, I'm so pleased for you. Archie looks ecstatic!'

'I am so lucky,' Hannah said.

'Luck has nothing to do with it. You deserve to be happy! Now how can I help?'

'Could you grate the Gruyère for the soup? I've only got to chop the parsley and then I'm ready.'

'I thought this was to be a simple supper!'

'It is really. Ben did the main course. He is such a star!'

Annie strove to purge all traces of poison from her voice. 'He seems to be quite at home here.'

'He and Archie got talking at Frances's do. They discovered they both love cycling. Archie suggested they meet up on Saturday mornings. So today they went to Bradford-on-Avon and Archie told Ben about tonight. He told him I was in a state because I'd burnt the casserole. Serves me right for trying to be too well organized. I made it yesterday afternoon, put it in the bottom of the Aga and forgot all about it! Ben said he'd cook us something. He wanted to slip away before you all came but I wouldn't hear of it. I had to bully him into staying.'

'I'm sure you didn't have to bully him very hard.'

'I do like him. He told Archie you met at the BBC. I didn't know you used to work there. Why did you change to teaching?'

'I suppose I got bored. Is that enough cheese?'

'Great! Tell everyone to come through. I've got a seating plan somewhere.'

There was a ghastly inevitability about Hannah's seating plan. Annie found herself between Archie and Ben. Archie was busy helping Hannah serve out the soup. Annie sat with a Still Life expression on her face until she heard Ben clear his throat.

She looked at him coldly. 'Did you want to say something?' she asked.

'Nothing at all.'

Annie took out her napkin and set it on her lap with a flourish. 'I didn't expect to see you here,' she murmured.

'I didn't intend to be here,' Ben replied. His mouth twitched slightly. 'Please don't look at me like that.'

'I'll try not to look at you at all,' Annie murmured icily. She turned to Archie who had sat down at last and began interrogating him about his son's gap year. She learnt that Angus was his only child and that he was good-looking, clever and, in the eyes of his prejudiced father, destined for a brilliant career as an architect.

By the end of the first course, Annie began to relax. Two glasses of very good Rioja had certainly helped but of far more importance was the realization that this was an evening of genuine celebration with her very best friends and she was not going to let the presence of Ben spoil the occasion.

She did feel a tinge of irritation when Ben produced his slow-cooked lamb and everyone reacted as if he was the new Jamie Oliver. It was even more irritating to discover that the lamb was very good indeed. Annie knew that if she had to listen to Ben modestly disclaiming his culinary genius one more time, her stress levels would soar, so she changed the subject. 'Did anyone see that programme on the hundred best film stars?' she asked. 'It was so ridiculous. Cary Grant was at number twelve, Gary Cooper was at number eight and Ewan McGregor was at number three! And then they had Al Pacino at number one! Ewan McGregor shouldn't even be in the top twenty, let alone the top ten and Al Pacino definitely shouldn't be number one.'

'Al Pacino's brilliant,' Frances said. 'He was terrific in *The Godfather.*'

'Yes, he was,' Annie conceded. 'But he usually overacts. Cary Grant should be number one.'

'No, he shouldn't,' Ben said.

'I beg your pardon?' Annie said with awful politeness.

'Gary Cooper should be number one. He has more gravitas than Cary Grant. Can you imagine Cary Grant playing the sheriff in *High Noon?*'

'Actually,' Annie said, 'Gary Cooper played a marshal not a sheriff.'

'Ben's right,' said Henry, unwittingly adding fuel to the fire that had broken out in a corner of Annie's brain. '*High Noon* is the best Western in the world.'

'Of course he isn't right,' Annie said crossly. 'Have you seen *Suspicion*? Have you seen *Bringing Up Baby*? Have you seen *Charade*?'

Henry poured himself some more wine. 'I've seen *North By Northwest.*'

'Well, if you haven't seen the others, you're in no position to judge.'

Ted grinned. 'I know you're the resident film buff, Annie, but I must say *High Noon* is terrific.'

'I've seen them all,' Ben said. 'I still say Gary Cooper is the better actor.'

'That doesn't surprise me.'

'Really?' Ben turned and rested his arm on the back of Annie's chair. 'Why doesn't it surprise you?'

'Well,' Annie said, sitting up very straight and resisting the urge to push Ben's arm away. 'Gary Cooper portrays the sort of noble, modest hero that most men would like to resemble. In fact he's never anything *but* noble and modest. Cary Grant can do sweet and charming or sexy and sophisticated better than anyone but he's not afraid to tackle darker roles either. He's far more *honest* than Gary Cooper. His men are far more complex. In *Notorious*, he plays a man who blackmails Ingrid Bergman into sleeping with a Nazi sympathizer. Can you imagine Gary Cooper doing something like that? And then in *Suspicion* he is utterly convincing as a man who is apparently trying to murder his wife.' Annie stared coolly at Ben. 'I'd say Cary Grant gives a far truer idea of what men are really like.'

'That's a bit harsh,' Ted protested. 'Most of us don't go round murdering our wives. I don't know anyone who's murdered his wife.'

'Gary Cooper is versatile,' Ben insisted. 'He can do sweet and simple in *Mr Deeds Goes To Town*. That's the complete opposite of *High Noon*. And anyway, I seem to remember you liked *High Noon*. I'm sure you said it was the best Western you'd ever seen.'

'Ah, that was probably before she became the deeply twisted woman we know and love today!' chuckled Henry. 'What Annie needs is the love of a good man!'

'There goes the traditional cry of all deluded males,' Frances scoffed. 'You can't accept that not every woman wants to spend her life ironing your shirts and washing your underwear.'

'I don't see anything wrong with that,' commented Henry. 'I go off to work every day so that Gracie can stay home and relax. She'd probably be very bored if she didn't have to iron my shirts.'

'I iron my own shirts,' said Ted.

'Which is why,' said Frances, 'I'm married to you and not to Henry!'

'What is *your* favourite film?' Ben asked Grace.

'*Pollyanna*,' said Grace.

Henry said, 'That's my Gracie!' with an indulgent laugh that made Annie want to hit him.

'I always loved *Pollyanna*!' Ben said.

For the first time that evening, Annie felt a slight grudging approval.

'Really?' asked Grace.

'Yes,' said Ben. 'I always fancied Hayley Mills.'

Annie raised her eyebrows and mentally drew a line through the approval rating.

By half past eleven, Annie had had enough. The shock she had felt when Ben had referred to their past still reverberated. For once she felt isolated from her married friends. All of them had drunk too much. Henry had ordered a cab for midnight for him and Grace. Frances and Ted were being collected by a neighbour who was at a working dinner in the Ring O' Bells.

'I must go,' she said, standing up. 'It's been a lovely evening!'

Ben stood up too. 'It's time I went as well. Can I give you a lift, Annie?'

'I think I'll walk,' Annie said. 'I'll go back along the canal.'

'Nonsense!' said Archie, struggling to his feet. 'I'm not

having you walk along in the dark. I'll walk you home.'

'Don't be silly!' Annie protested. 'I've done it loads of times. Archie, please sit down!'

'I am not,' Archie said firmly, 'letting you walk home on your own!'

'In that case,' Annie said, accepting the inevitable, 'I will accept Ben's kind offer.'

She had planned to go her own way as soon as she got to the door but Hannah and Archie insisted on waving them both off and so Annie was forced to get into Ben's car.

As they turned in to Widcombe Hill, Ben said politely, 'Where do you live?'

Annie hesitated.

'I promise I won't stalk your home once I know where it is,' Ben said.

'I live in Great Pulteney Street.'

'Annie,' Ben said, 'I'm sorry I said that about *High Noon*. It just slipped out. I remember us watching it at your house and—'

'I would be grateful,' Annie said, 'if you would try to exorcize from your mind everything that happened to us in the past. It is the only way – the *only* way by which I can continue to be polite to you.'

'It's not that easy, Annie. I can't just forget that I know you liked *High Noon*.'

'Stop banging on about *High Noon*! Let me tell you the alternative. The alternative is that I tell all my friends that I'd rather they didn't see you again because I'm trying to forget that once upon a time you walked out on me about half an hour before our wedding was due to start!'

'Annie, I could never forget that and I really think we have to talk about it.'

'No. We don't! We don't at all and by the way, you turn left at the roundabout.'

'I know. Annie, I just want to—'

'I don't care what you want. You forfeited your rights to have any wants a long time ago. You can stop here. I live opposite.'

'I need to explain to you—'

'To hell with your needs! All you *need* to know is that however many excuses you have, whatever they are, and believe me I've thought of them all: terminal diseases, other women, weird heredity issues – whatever they are, nothing, absolutely nothing, can ever excuse what you did to me that day. You also *need* to know that the only way I can live with your very unwelcome presence in my locality is if I censor every memory of the past. I'm happy with my life. It took me a long time to be happy and I'm not prepared to let you dig up the past all over again and spoil the life I made for myself. I am quite prepared to acknowledge you as a person I once knew and didn't care much for. I can live with that. You have no right, no right at all, to ease your conscience by explaining why it was once so necessary for you to humiliate me in the way you did. I'm the victim here, not you, so you do what I say and you do not refer to the past ever again. Do you understand?'

'Yes, I do, but—'

'No buts! You can go cycling with Archie, you can cook meals for Hannah, you can be as sweet and smarmy as you like, but you can't pretend to an understanding with me that isn't there.' She opened the door. 'Thank you for the lift.'

'It's a pleasure. Annie?'

'What?'

'Do you really think Cary Grant is better than Gary Cooper?'

'Oh for heaven's sake!' Annie said and walked across the road. She unlocked the door and turned round. 'Of course he's better!' she yelled before slamming the door behind her.

Just how quickly Ben had inveigled himself into Annie's circle was shown a few days later when Annie dropped in on Grace in order to return a book.

Grace opened the door and hauled Annie in. 'Coffee?'

'I have been dreaming of coffee all the way up Bathwick Hill!' Annie confessed. 'It's so steep! No wonder you're so healthy! It gets me every time!'

Ben was sitting in Henry's chair. He had picked up the paper and looked as if he owned the place. 'Hello, Annie,' he said.

'Hello.' Annie wondered fleetingly if she could quickly remember a pressing engagement and realized she couldn't. 'What are you doing here?'

'We were talking about my Refugee Ball,' Grace said. 'Ben thinks he might be able to give it some publicity on the telly. I keep getting facts and figures and there's so much to *say*! Did you know that Africa and Asia between them host over sixty per cent of the world's refugees? Europe looks after just twenty-five per cent! Did you know that?'

'No,' Annie admitted. 'I didn't.'

'Well, it's true. Ben thinks he might be able to do a feature on the subject a few weeks before the ball. Do you want black or white?'

'Very black,' Annie said. 'Do you know where you're going to have it yet?'

Grace pushed the biscuit tin towards Annie. 'Hopefully in the Assembly Rooms. They're so beautiful and there'd be room for a disco and for a live band and there's a big bar where people can talk . . . Good morning, Jake!'

Jake shuffled into the kitchen with all the energy of a bewildered zombie. His hair stood up in thick tufts, very different to the delicately constructed spikes that usually adorned his head. His skin was pale and his eyes were blood-shot. He wore a grey T-shirt and tartan pyjama bottoms. 'Morning!' he said to no one in particular and made for the dresser where he extracted both cereal and bowl.

Grace regarded him with some severity. 'Jake, I don't mind you having your friends back in the early hours of the morning, I don't even mind you giving them pizzas and beers. I do mind that you don't clear anything away after you. The kitchen stinks of tobacco and heaven knows what. Is it too much to ask you to ask your friends to go in the garden when they want to clog up their lungs and their brains?'

'Sorry,' Jake muttered, pouring what seemed like the entire carton of Coco Pops into his bowl.

'And come and say hello to Ben. You haven't met him before.'

'Hello, Ben,' Jake said, reaching for the milk.

'You might have seen Ben on television,' said Grace proudly. 'He's on the local news!'

'Are you?' Jake brought his brimming bowl over to the table. 'I'm thinking of going into television.'

'That's interesting.' Ben folded the paper. 'Which area do you want to go into?'

'I'm not sure yet,' Jake said in a voice that seemed to imply that any number of television moguls were beating a path to his door. 'I wouldn't mind being a reporter actually. I wouldn't want to get bogged down in local television though.' He took a huge mouthful of Coco Pops and then realized belatedly he might have been a little tactless. 'I don't mean that local television is rubbish. I mean . . .'

'That's all right,' said Ben equably. 'I know exactly what you mean. I can quite understand you'd have higher ambitions.'

Grace looked enquiringly at Ben. 'What did you do before you came to Bristol? Have you always been on television?'

'Pretty much,' Ben said. 'I used to work on the London news.'

'Wow!' Jake's spoon hovered near his mouth. 'Why did you leave?'

'Oh . . .' Ben gave a careless shrug. 'I suppose I got tired of London. I thought it would be nice to see some green fields and rolling hills.'

He was lying. Apart from the fact that Annie was quite certain that Ben wouldn't go near a field or a rolling hill unless he was paid to, she knew he was lying. She looked at him curiously. Aware of her scrutiny, his eyes met hers and she looked away quickly.

'I can't wait to leave Bath,' Jake said. 'It's so provincial.

You don't live in Bath if you want to make a difference to society.'

'I love Bath,' said Grace.

'Yeah, Mum, but you don't do anything.'

'I don't think that's quite true,' Ben said mildly. 'She spends one morning a week looking after a child with cystic fibrosis so the mother can have a short break. She takes an elderly neighbour out to tea every fortnight. She writes letters for Amnesty International, she's organizing a ball to raise funds for the Refugee Council, she's doing a French degree with the Open University and she cooks and cleans for her family. Oh yes, she also helps special needs children with their reading at the local primary school. That's right, isn't it, Grace?'

Grace gave a startled laugh. 'I must have told you my entire life history! How very embarrassing . . .'

'But I suppose,' Ben conceded graciously, 'that apart from all that, she doesn't do anything.'

Jake's face went a dull red. Annie almost felt sorry for him. 'I didn't mean that Mum doesn't *do* anything,' he mumbled. He picked up his empty bowl and spoon and took them to the sink. 'I simply mean she doesn't have a career, that's all.'

'She doesn't have time for a career!' Annie protested. 'I suppose you'd think it better if she were some company lawyer, helping millionaires to offload sheds of money on to the Canary Isles or wherever it is they siphon it to?'

Jake rubbed his eyes and blinked. 'I wasn't saying . . . I didn't mean . . . I'm going back to bed.' He gave a careless wave and slouched out of the kitchen, pausing only to say, 'People don't send money to the Canary Isles anyway.'

112

'Ben, I'm mortified!' said Grace. 'I had no idea I told you all that! How very boring for you! You must think I'm such a big-head!'

'You didn't bore me in the least and I don't think you've ever bragged about anything in your life. You ought to start.'

Grace smiled. 'Poor Jake! He's only had a few hours' sleep!'

'Poor Jake,' said Annie, without any attempt at conviction. 'I suppose children never appreciate their parents until they grow up. Lily always says she never knew how wonderful Mum was until she had her boys.'

'Lily has sons?' Ben laughed. 'I can't imagine her as a mother!'

'Of course! I keep forgetting you two know each other.' Grace rested her chin on her hands, fully primed for an inquisition. 'Frances says you used to go out with one of Annie's sisters. Which one was it?'

'Josephine,' said Annie.

'Lily,' said Ben.

'Really?' Grace frowned. 'You went out with *both* of them?' She looked at Annie for corroboration. So did Ben.

'Well,' Annie said slowly and thought rapidly, 'Lily didn't really count. He went out with Josephine for a few months but he only went out with Lily for a fortnight. Lily got bored of him.'

'I can't think why!' Grace gazed reproachfully at Annie. 'I don't think Ben's boring at all!'

Ben gave a sad little smile. 'Thank you,' he said.

Annie's eyes narrowed. 'I don't think Ben minded very much,' she said airily. 'I think he was just playing around!'

'I did try to give that impression afterwards,' Ben sighed

heavily. 'I felt pretty bad. What's that song called? Do you know the one I mean? Something like "The Tears of a Clown". Well, that was me: laughing on the outside and crying on the inside.'

Annie shot him a disgusted glance. 'What utter rot!' she muttered.

Grace, always a sucker for a hard-luck story, shook her head vigorously. 'It isn't rot, I know exactly what Ben means. I remember when Henry broke up with me, I pretended I didn't care at all. I pretended so well that he got quite miffed and ended up asking me out again and the rest is history!'

'Well!' said Annie briskly. 'I can't sit around and discuss Ben's very crowded love life, fun though it is! Thanks for the coffee!'

'I'll come with you,' Ben said. 'I've got my car at Sydney Buildings.'

As soon as they were outside the front door, Ben said, 'I can't believe you said that!'

'Said what?'

'Did you have to tell Grace and Frances I went out with Josephine? I was always terrified of Josephine. We would never ever have gone out together!'

'Certainly *she* would never have gone out with *you*! Frances asked me how I knew you and I panicked. I said the first thing that came into my head. And anyway, you only went out with her for a few months.'

'That's all right, then. Except, if you recall, Josephine was married to Clement before I'd even met you.'

'No one will know that. And why did *you* say you were going out with Lily?'

'Because I didn't think you'd be stupid enough to say I was going out with Josephine. Lily was a far more obvious choice than Josephine. It wasn't very gallant of you to say she got bored of me. After a fortnight?'

Annie sniffed. 'I think that's highly likely.'

'This is all getting terribly complicated,' Ben said. 'I didn't know I'd had relationships with either of your sisters. I told Archie I'd met you at the BBC.'

'Oh for heaven's sake,' Annie said crossly, 'why did you say that?'

'Probably,' said Ben gently, 'because I did meet you at the BBC.'

Annie sighed. 'This is getting absurd.'

'I agree,' Ben said. 'We need to coordinate our stories and come up with a foolproof history in the event of future questions. What's your nearest restaurant?'

'It's French,' said Annie, 'and it's very expensive.'

'That's all right, we need only have one course. That will be quite enough time to sort things out.'

'I am not having dinner with you. And by the way, we've reached Sydney Buildings. Why did you park your car at Sydney Buildings?'

'I've bought a house there.'

'You've bought a house in Sydney Buildings!'

'Yes, that's right, I've bought a house in Sydney Buildings. Do you want to see it?'

'I can't believe you bought a house in Sydney Buildings. You'll be virtually round the corner from my house! Why did you buy a house here?'

'I could hardly ring up the estate agent and say, sorry, I've changed my mind because there's a woman who lives in Great Pulteney Street who's very keen that I live as far away from her as possible.'

'I don't see why not! Why are you moving here anyway? You should be living in Bristol or somewhere just outside Bristol.'

'I fell in love with the house. The garden goes right down to the canal. Come and see!'

Annie had always loved the houses in Sydney Buildings. Curiosity conquered pride. She said stiffly, 'I'll have a quick look.'

'Good, it's just a few minutes' walk.'

'Ben,' Annie said, 'how did you get all that information out of Grace?'

Ben shrugged. 'I tend to prefer to ask questions than to give answers. I got the impression that she isn't used to talking about herself. I like her. I wish she had more confidence.'

Annie didn't respond. She was guiltily aware that in Grace's company, she usually spent far more time talking about her affairs than she did listening to Grace talking about her own. She silently vowed to be different in future. It was both chastening and infuriating that Ben had found out more about her friend in one evening than she had done in years.

'Right,' said Ben. 'Here we are.' They were standing in front of a small detached house with olive-white walls and a pale green door. Ben took out some keys and opened the door.

Inside, the walls were painted a very bright orange. 'Not too good if you have a hangover!' Annie said.

'Terrible, aren't they? The whole house is painted that

colour. I'm not moving in for another six weeks; I'm going
to let the builders get to work first. Come and see the sitting
room.'

He led her into a large room with long windows and a
stone fireplace. She could see the garden, a tangle of shrubs
and rose bushes and a lawn covered with daisies. And there,
at the bottom, glittering like a mirage, was the canal. A long
red narrow boat glided silently by.

She swallowed and said, 'It's very nice.'

'Do you want to see downstairs? The kitchen's not up to
much but—'

'No. I have to go. It's very nice.' She turned and made for
the door.

'Annie,' Ben said, 'about dinner. I mean it. We really
need to meet. We can't keep giving different stories to your
friends.'

'I break up in three weeks,' Annie said. 'I'm up to my ears
in end-of-term plays, I can't go anywhere.'

'When do you break up?'

'Twentieth of July but—'

'Let's meet on the twenty-first, then. At the French
restaurant. Where is it?'

'In Argyll Street but—'

'I'll meet you there, then, at eight o'clock on the twenty-
first.'

'All right, all right. Goodbye, then.'

She walked away without looking back. '*One day,*' *she had
promised Ben,* '*we'll have a house with water at the bottom of the
garden. It can be the sea or a river or a canal or a stream but
there has to be water!*' Did he remember that? No, of course he

didn't and neither should she. The only reason she had agreed to have dinner with him was because it was the only way to get out of that house as quickly as possible. From the moment she'd walked through the door to the moment she'd seen the shining water she had experienced a gut-wrenching desire to live there.

She had a heap of homework waiting to be marked but in her present state of mind she could summon no enthusiasm for Year Seven's comprehension exercises. Instead of walking back down Bathwick Hill, she crossed the road, rejoined the canal and marched briskly towards Bathampton.

She was angry. She was angry with Ben and she was angry with herself. Too late, she knew she had never appreciated the life she had made for herself. Her family's attitude had influenced her more than she had thought. If she was absolutely honest, she had always thought she was living a second-best life and that having failed in love she had settled for the life of a single woman. Too late, she could see now that in fact her life had been a good one. She was like Thomas Hardy who had taken his first wife for granted. After her death, he spent the rest of his life mourning her, even though he married again. (What a fun husband he must have been.)

Annie side-stepped two cyclists and walked on. Would she really have swapped her life for those of her early friends who had followed the conventional path? Would she wish to be Lucy who, two children on, could barely disguise the fact that her husband's every utterance bored her to distraction? And what about Wendy Freeman who had abandoned her husband and children for a man who turned out to be a violent alcoholic?

Annie had chosen a life without love. She had proved that self-esteem was not contingent on a man in her life. She had a steady job, she had developed a group of loyal drama pupils in Bath, acquired a pleasant home and some good friends. What was infuriating was that it was only when Ben arrived and threw a boulder into her pleasant little pond that she appreciated what a very nice pond it was. And now he'd muddied the waters.

She glanced at her watch and decided to go home. It was time to get a grip and remind herself again and again if necessary that she had been content before Ben and would be content again. She would go to dinner with him. She would keep the conversation business-like and focused. They would construct a plausible tale that would satisfy her friends, preferably something involving both sisters dumping him in the most humiliating circumstances possible. And then she wouldn't see him any more.

CHAPTER EIGHT

Black Book Entry, 12 July: Harriet for breaking Sidney's heart with dough balls.

Sidney rang and asked without any preamble or greeting, if Annie would like him to come and stay with her.

Annie, a little taken aback by the question, assured him that she would. 'I can hardly hear you,' she told him. 'Do you have a cold? What's happened to your voice?'

'Do you want me to come and stay with you tomorrow?' Sidney asked. He still sounded as if he was lying under a thick blanket.

'Tomorrow? Sidney, you do know I'm still at school? I suppose you are too, aren't you?'

'I've finished my A Levels, so I don't have to go back. Would you like me to come tomorrow?'

'All right, Sidney, that would be very nice, if you don't mind me not being around during the day . . .'

'Will you ring Mum and tell her you're inviting me? Don't say I rang! Will you ring her right away?'

'All right, but Sidney . . .'

Sidney had rung off.

Annie pondered the implications of the conversation with her nephew, sighed and rang her sister's number. 'Josephine!' she said with an energy she was far from feeling. 'How are you?'

'I'm very well. A little tired. One of my patients went into labour last night and there were complications. It was all right in the end though. A very beautiful little girl.'

'And I suppose you were back at work today. I don't know how you do it.'

'It's my job. How about you? I hope you're still coming to see us next month?'

'You bet! It's early August, isn't it? I know you're going to France in the middle of the month. You must be looking forward to that!'

'Yes. Yes, I am. I'm looking forward to it very much.'

Josephine didn't sound as if she was looking forward to it. Something wasn't right but Annie didn't like to probe. She had always been able to say anything to Lily, mainly because it was impossible to insult or upset her. Josephine was and always would be the brilliant, oldest sister and any conversation with her was filtered through a layer of younger sibling awe on Annie's part and Josephine's own natural reserve.

'I was just thinking,' Annie said carelessly, 'that it would be lovely to have Sidney to stay. I could take him round the art galleries. Would he like to come, do you think? Would he like to come soon? In fact,' she added slowly, sounding as if she had just thought of this brilliant idea, 'why doesn't he come tomorrow?'

'Tomorrow?' Josephine sounded a little perplexed by her

sister's enthusiasm. 'That's very kind of you. Are you *sure* you want him? Aren't you still at school? Surely, you haven't broken up yet?'

'No, I haven't,' Annie admitted, 'but I thought that Sidney . . . I thought that Sidney might like to help me with the Shakespeare play we're doing at school. He's so good at English!'

'He's not that good at English,' Josephine said doubtfully. 'He only got C in his A/S exam and he gave it up right after that.'

'Yes, but he'll be very useful in all sorts of ways,' Annie said, praying that Josephine wouldn't ask her to elaborate. 'And I'd love to see him.'

'I have no idea what he's got planned for this week. I'll go and get him. Hang on!'

Annie did and within a few moments heard Sidney ask politely, 'Hello, Annie, how are you?'

'I'm very well, Sidney. I suddenly had this inexplicable urge to ring and ask if you'd like to come and stay with me tomorrow.'

'Let me think . . . I'm not sure what I'm doing . . .'

'Well, in that case,' Annie said with some asperity, 'feel free to stay at home!'

'I've remembered,' Sidney said hastily. 'I'm not doing anything! You want me to come tomorrow? I'll get a train. I can walk to your flat. You needn't collect me.'

'That's very good of you.'

'No worries. I'll see you tomorrow. Here's Mum.'

'Annie? It's very kind of you to have Sidney. I do hope he'll be helpful.'

'I'm sure he will be. How's Beattie? Did her exams go well?'

'They always have done in the past. She seems pretty confident. She's working in Oxford Street at the moment and she's out every night. We hardly see her. You know Beattie!'

'And how's Mark? Is he well?'

'Very well. And we have Cressida living with us now!'

'Of course! Has she settled in?'

'Oh yes.'

'Good!' Something was definitely not good. 'Well!' said Annie heartily. 'I look forward to seeing Sidney! Goodbye now!'

Sidney rang her just after she'd got back from work to tell her he had missed his train and would be there in an hour. Annie accepted this news without surprise. Sidney and public transport had always had a problematic relationship. She had never known anyone who had missed more trains than Sidney and every time he went on a train he always left something behind when he got off it.

She applied her muscles to the futon armchair and made a bed up for him behind the sofa in the sitting room. Then she peeled the potatoes and prepared the beans, feeling as she always did when she prepared real vegetables as opposed to frozen ones, smug and domesticated.

By the time Sidney arrived, Annie had burnt the beans but the beefburgers were fine and so was the potato apart from the lumps. They sat at the kitchen bar and Annie raised her glass. 'Here's to you, Sidney!' she said. 'And now I want to know what all this is about. I mean it's lovely to see you but I'd prefer not to have to invent spurious reasons as to why it's essential that you come and see me right now, this minute.'

Sidney sighed. 'I'm sorry,' he said. 'I was desperate.'

'Clearly! Why?'

'Cressida!' The word was articulated with a venom that Annie had never heard before in the voice of her mild-mannered nephew.

'You don't get on with her?'

'Huh!' Sidney said bitterly. 'She's evil!'

'She's a child!'

'So were the children in *The Midwich Cuckoos.*'

'I seem to remember they were aliens.'

'I'm beginning to think Cressida is too. When Mark's around, she's all sweet and polite but when he's not there, she's horrific. She's made up all sorts of excuses as to why she can't come to France with us and now she's persuaded Mark to stay behind with her and Mum's upset but because she's so anxious to make Cressida feel at home she hasn't said anything.'

'Your mum is a saint,' Annie said, 'and—'

'And Cressida's a devil. She spies on me the whole time. I met a girl at Easter and she lives in Bath and—'

'And I'm beginning to see why you want to visit me!'

'And anyway last week, Mum and Mark had some friends to supper and I was in my room with Olly . . . You remember Olly?'

'He's the friend you went to Cornwall with last year.'

'Yes. And Cressida walks in and we'd been talking about Harriet, this girl in Bath. And Cressida walks in and says, "Have you got your V-plates yet, Sidney?"'

'Sorry,' Annie said, 'you've lost me.'

124

'V-plates!' Sidney repeated impatiently. 'Virginity plates! L-plates! Learner driver plates! You know?'

'I didn't,' Annie said apologetically. 'I'm obviously out of touch. What did you say to her?'

'I told her to go away. And then a bit later, Olly and I were having a spliff and—'

'Oh Sidney, you weren't!'

'Don't *you* start! Then Cressida came in and wanted to have some and so I told her to go away again and a bit later Mum came in and was all sad and shocked and it turned out that Cressida had interrupted their dinner to tell them she was a little worried because there was a funny smell coming from my bedroom. When Mum came up, Cressida stood behind her and smiled like this . . .' Here, Sidney rolled his eyes and wriggled his eyebrows and bared his teeth. 'I think she is seriously possessed.'

'Yes, but Sidney, you shouldn't be smoking joints or whatever it is you call it these days. There is so much information coming out now about possible long-term depression and other side effects and you know what happened to my friend's brother, Ian.'

'Yes, I do know what happened to Ian.'

'He smoked marijuana and cannabis and all that sort of stuff and he went very, very weird. I mean he went really weird. He thought people were injecting his bedroom walls with arsenic; in fact I think he thought his *mother* was trying to poison him and now ten years later, he is—'

'Still in a psychiatric ward. I know, Annie, you've told me this story hundreds of times . . .'

'It's not a story, it's true!'

'I know and I hardly ever smoke anything! If you had to live with Cressida, even you would turn to drugs! And now Mum is convinced I'm a drug addict and Cressida keeps spying on me. I hate being at home, I hate it. I won't go home until my job starts!'

'Oh.' Annie blinked. 'Does that mean I'm privileged to have your company for some time yet?'

'Ten days at most. Is that all right?'

'It's just about bearable,' Annie assured him. 'I hope you won't get bored. But of course you won't, I'd forgotten there's the lovely girl from Bath to see!'

'I met her at Easter,' Sidney said. 'We've been texting each other. I'm meeting her tomorrow. She is called,' he added reverentially, 'Harriet.'

'So you said,' Annie responded, adding politely, 'It's a very nice name.'

'It is,' Sidney agreed. 'You'd like her. She's so confident and funny and sparkling. She's special. And she is beautiful!'

Annie swept all the lumps of potato to one side of her plate and stood up. 'I'm sure she is,' she said. She hoped fervently that Harriet was looking forward to tomorrow with as much enthusiasm as Sidney.

Annie could tell as soon as she came home that her wish had not been fulfilled. Sidney was sitting on the sofa, slumped in front of Ben Seymour who was giving an impression of a deeply sensitive, caring interviewer, nodding his head sympathetically while a twenty-stone man told him his life had been ruined by the theft of his ten garden gnomes.

Annie put down her school satchel and her bag of groceries

and marched over to the television. She terminated Ben and looked enquiringly at her nephew. 'What happened?'

Sidney shrugged and made a brave attempt at a smile. 'I met her at Pizza Express,' he said. 'She arrived with her boyfriend.'

'Oh Sidney!'

'She brought along her best friend as well and I don't think she liked me too much either. They all had more money than me. They all ordered extra side dishes with their pizzas and they all had loads of dough balls. I said I wasn't that hungry and I could tell they didn't believe me. I didn't have any dough balls.' He looked forlornly at Annie. 'I really wanted them too.'

'Oh Sidney!'

'Harriet's best friend offered me one of hers and I took it and then it dropped to the floor, so I picked it up and ate it and I could see they thought I was being really gross. I don't think,' Sidney concluded, 'I will ever eat a dough ball again.'

'Sidney, I'm so sorry.'

'They invited me to a party tonight and I said I was already going out and I could tell they didn't believe me.'

'Well, I think Harriet sounds extremely unpleasant,' said Annie hotly. 'She should have told you she had a boyfriend! And why didn't *she* give you one of her dough balls? She sounds very greedy.' Annie sniffed. 'I bet she'll be fat as anything in a few years.'

Sidney gave a faint smile. 'You sound just like Grandfather!'

'Nonsense!' Annie picked up her shopping bag and cast a

glance at the contents. 'Oh dear! I'm sorry, Sidney, I've bought us pizzas for supper!'

'That's all right,' said Sidney. 'I like pizzas.'

'I tell you what!' Annie said. 'Why don't you come to school with me tomorrow? You can help me with the class from hell. You might find it interesting.'

'All right,' Sidney said, with an understandable lack of enthusiasm. He had imagined a long, romantic interlude with the girl of his dreams. Watching thirteen-year-old adolescents stumbling over Shakespearean pentameters was not quite in the same league.

'She's not worthy of you!' Annie told him. 'I'll get supper ready. I have a pupil arriving at eight and after that we'll watch some telly and forget the stupid girl. I never liked the name Harriet anyway.'

She couldn't bear to see Sidney looking so upset. If Harriet was to wander in now, she would cheerfully thump her. The trouble with Sidney was that he was sweet-natured, honest, open, gentle and kind and none of these qualities were attractive to teenage girls. Teenage girls liked boys like Jake. Teenage girls preferred deviousness, self-absorption and arrogance. Sidney didn't stand a chance.

Bella arrived just as the phone began to ring. Annie had only time to introduce her to her nephew before flying into the bedroom and picking up the receiver. A polite voice on the other end explained that if she signed up with his company she could have free evening and weekend calls and it would only take a minute to sort out.

Annie, having received a horrendous telephone bill only three days earlier, said she was interested and knew almost at once that she had made a big mistake. The man proceeded to ask her for her mother's maiden name, the name of her mother's dog, the address of her previous home, the address of her present home and what seemed like a thousand and one details of her bank account. Too late, she said that she was after all quite happy with her present system. The polite man then passed her on to another polite man who also wanted to learn about her mother's maiden name and dog.

When Annie finally emerged from her bedroom, with her sanity barely intact, she found Bella and Sidney chatting like old friends.

'I hate my name,' Sidney was saying. 'My parents called Beattie and me after some politicians they liked.'

'They weren't really politicians,' Annie said. 'They were the founders of the Fabian Society: Sidney and Beatrice Webb. Beatrice was very beautiful.'

'I bet Sidney wasn't,' Sidney said gloomily.

'Apparently,' Annie said, 'he looked like a frog. Bella, I'm so sorry to have kept you waiting!'

'That's all right,' said Bella. 'I've enjoyed talking to Sidney.'

She really was a nice girl. Annie said warmly, 'I'll give you an extra ten minutes at the end. Sidney, what are you going to do now? Do you want to take the television into my bedroom?'

'I'm not bothered,' said Sidney. 'I'll go and read my book.' He went over to the futon, picked up his bag and gave a wave to Bella. 'It was nice to meet you,' he said. He gave a rueful smile. 'I'm sorry if I went on about myself too much!'

'Abby and I are going to the cinema tomorrow,' Bella said. 'I don't have to be back at school for another week. If you've nothing else to do, you're very welcome to join us.'

'Great!' said Sidney, who had obviously forgotten his aunt's exciting invitation to come with her to school the next day.

The next day, Annie shot out of school as soon as the final bell rang. She had two end-of-term lessons that evening and wanted to get back for a restorative cup of tea first.

Sidney was still out when she got back. He had put her post on the desk and on top of it had scribbled a note: *Don't worry about cooking my supper. I'm not sure when I'll be back.*

She needn't bother with the sausages, then. She went through to the kitchen, put on the kettle and thought about her forthcoming lessons.

The first was at five. For the last three years, she had been teaching two boys together, both of whom were off to university in the autumn and both of whom she would probably have fallen for twenty years earlier. As it was, she felt almost maternal towards them. She had watched them grow from spotty, self-conscious children into gorgeous, self-confident young men and she knew she would miss them.

At six, Amber arrived. Amber was a fourteen-year-old with all the prima donna characteristics of a great star and with, as yet, none of the talent. Amber wanted Annie to help her with her audition piece for a summer concert run by her youth club. After hearing Amber screech 'I'm just a Girl Who Can't Say No', three times in swift and brutal succession, Annie's carefully controlled expression of polite attention was beginning to test her facial muscles.

As soon as Amber left, Annie went back into the kitchen and poured herself a large glass of wine. She went back to her desk and reached for her post. There was a small parcel with her name and address written in felt tip in large capital letters.

Inside was a biography of Gary Cooper and a note on top: *Thought this might interest you. See you on the 21st. Love, Ben.*

Annie picked up the book and hurled it into the bin by the end of Sidney's bed. The ringing of the phone made her jump and she walked purposefully to her bedroom. If it was Ben, she would tell him she'd had second thoughts about the dinner and she would definitely not thank him for the book.

In fact, it was her mother who had already had her evening sherry and was in a loquacious mood. 'I am so looking forward to seeing you, darling! We've had a small calamity here and your presence will be extremely welcome! Your father is not an easy man to live with at the moment. He organized a meeting for last night in the village hall. You know, he's leading a campaign here to save our local post office? So he went off to the village hall and he insisted on leaping onto the stage instead of using the steps like everyone else. So then he broke his ankle and now he's stuck at home and he's being quite impossible. He's on the phone the whole time and he's started bothering poor Harold again. I keep telling him, "David, you retired three years ago, you must let Harold do things *his* way now," but he won't listen and now he's got this idea that he might stand for parliament as a single-issue candidate. I told him, "David, you can't stand for parliament, you're seventy-seven for goodness sake," and so then he went on about Gladstone being Prime Minister at eighty-five and I said that Gladstone used to invite prostitutes home for tea; it didn't follow that he had to do the same. You must talk to him when you come down, darling, you must talk some sense into him.'

'He's never listened to me before,' Annie said. 'I don't see why he'd listen now.'

'And then half an hour ago, I rang Josephine for advice about David's ankle and I got her stepdaughter. So I said it was lovely to talk to her and I hoped she'd come and see us soon, now she was part of the family, and she just said, "I don't think so." So then I didn't know what to say so I asked to speak to Josephine and Cressida said she didn't know where she was. And then she rang off without even saying goodbye! And then, five minutes later, Josephine rang and said she'd been in the kitchen and hadn't got to the phone in time. Did Cressida not *know* that Josephine was in the kitchen? I have to tell you, I think Cressida is a very odd little girl.'

'I think you're right,' Annie said, 'although she's not that little. She's thirteen. There are at least twenty-eight thirteen-year-olds in my school who are currently making my hair go grey. Sidney doesn't like Cressida. You know he's staying with me at the moment? He's not here right now or I'd pass him on to you.'

'Dear Sidney! Do give him my love! Tell him to come and stay with us soon. David would love to play Scrabble with him. Hang on a moment, darling . . . David sends his love to you! I'm going to have to go, your father wants his supper! See you soon, darling!'

Annie put the phone down and went through to the kitchen. She was about to make a sandwich when she heard Sidney come in. 'Hi!' she called. 'I've just been on the phone to your gran! She sends her love.'

Sidney entered the kitchen, sat down at the breakfast bar and beamed. 'Good old Granny!' he said.

Annie smiled. 'You look as if you've had a nice time.'

'I did. I told Bella all about Harriet. She was great.'

'Really?'

'I don't mean like that! I mean she's nice. I like her family too. I went back with Bella after the film and had tea with them. Bella said she'd take me to the Roman Baths tomorrow.'

'Wouldn't you rather help me with my Year Seven bottom set?' Annie asked. 'I was so looking forward to your help!' She laughed at Sidney's crestfallen expression. 'I was joking, Sidney! I'm making myself something to eat. I suppose you don't want anything.'

'I only had a bit of pasta,' Sidney said. 'What are you cooking?'

'Sausages and chips?'

'Great!' said Sidney. He looked at the bread which Annie had just taken out. 'I'll have a piece of bread while I'm waiting.'

Having Sidney to stay was an education. Annie had no idea how Sidney could eat so much, so often. Mothers of eighteen-year-old boys must spend their whole time buying and preparing food and then buying some more.

Later that evening, Annie got into bed, thought for a moment and got out of bed. She put on her dressing gown, walked through to the sitting room, smiled at Sidney, who was reading a book in his bed behind the sofa and took the Gary Cooper biography out of the waste-paper bin. She was aware that Sidney was staring at her with unabashed curiosity. Since she could think of no suitable explanation for her behaviour, she simply smiled again and returned to her bedroom.

CHAPTER NINE

Black Book Entry, **20** *July: The green-haired boy who bashed up William.*

The end of the summer term, always the most longed-for day of the year, had finally come to pass. As always at this time, Annie was too tired to celebrate. Sidney was out, so she was able to have a simple supper of bread and cheese and retire to bed.

She was awoken by the phone and groped for the receiver. 'Hello?' she mumbled. She opened one eye and looked at the clock.

'Annie, is that you?'

'Who else could it be? Lily, do you realize it's ten past twelve?'

'Something's happened. William's in hospital. He was in London. He's been attacked or mugged or something. They've just operated on him. I want to go up first thing in the morning but I don't want to take the boys. A friend of mine had said she'd come over for the night as soon as her husband got home but he's been delayed. Could you come down and look after them for a couple of days, just until I sort something out? I'd ask Mum and Dad but Dad's broken his ankle and—'

Annie sat up. 'I'll pack a few things and come down right now. I've got Sidney with me. Can I bring him too?'

'Of course, the boys would love to see him.'

'I'll be with you as soon as I can.' Annie rubbed her eyes. 'William is going to be all right, isn't he?'

There was a long pause. 'I don't know,' said Lily.

Lily's hair was tied back and her face was shiny and scrubbed. Devoid of make-up, she looked like a young girl again, despite the elegant silk kimono she wore over her nightdress. Milly greeted the guests with enthusiasm. She had positioned herself in front of her mistress and now Lily pushed her out of the way and opened the door wide. 'Sidney, you must be tired. Would you like some cocoa or do you want to go straight to bed?'

Sidney glanced fleetingly at his aunts. 'I'll go to bed. Lily, I'm so sorry. Is William . . .'

'We'll know more tomorrow,' Lily said. 'You're in the room at the top, the one with the railway set all over the floor. I've put a towel on your bed.'

'Thanks.' Sidney scratched his head, tried and failed to think of anything useful to say, scratched his head again and bade his aunts goodnight before retreating gratefully up the stairs.

Lily turned to Annie. 'I've made a list for you. Come on through, it's on the table. Luke has a tennis lesson tomorrow, he'll show you how to get there. Gabriel's going to spend the afternoon with his friend Julian. Julian's mother will pick him up and she said she'll bring him back as well. The plumber's coming over in the afternoon to mend the shower next to Sidney's room. It won't turn off property. All of this is on the list. As for food, I did a shop only this morning and you'll find loads of stuff in the freezer. Feel free to take anything you want. I'll show you how to use the dishwasher and the washing machine.'

'Lily,' Annie protested gently, 'I know how to use them. I'll be fine. What time are you leaving tomorrow?'

'At six, so . . .'

'So you should go to bed at once, it's half past one.'

'I'm going to make a cup of tea to take up with me. Do you want one?'

'Yes, all right. Why don't I make it?'

'No, sit down, it won't take me a second. The kettle's boiled once already.' Lily went to the fridge and took out a jug of milk. 'William rang me just before he left the office. He said he couldn't leave London before Friday. He was very excited because he'd bought a vase for his mother's birthday. She was supposed to be staying with us this weekend. She always comes here for her birthday. He said it was a big blue and white spotted vase; it sounds terrible, William has atrocious taste. I told him he should take a taxi back to the flat if he was carrying a great sodding vase but of course William walks everywhere now because of that stupid pedometer Dad gave him. So he was walking back and this skinny, green-haired boy came up to him—'

'Somebody saw what happened?'

'A little old lady watched the whole thing from her sitting-room window. She probably saved William's life. She saw the boy go up to him, she said they talked and then the boy hit William and he fell.'

'But William's a big man. Didn't he try to fight back?'

'According to the little old lady, he was too busy hanging on to his stupid vase. The lady rang the police and saw the boy run away. William was carted off to hospital but the boy had taken his wallet and mobile so they couldn't identify him. Later on, the lady remembered she'd seen the boy throw something down the stairwell and they found his electronic diary.' Lily took the kettle off the Aga and poured the boiling water into two bone china mugs. 'They took William to the Accident and Emergency unit and they said he had a serious head injury. So then they took him to another hospital where they have a specialist neurological unit and they operated on him at once.' She poured out the milk and handed Annie her tea. 'Have I put enough milk in for you?'

'That's fine. How is William now?'

'I don't know.' Lily threw the tea bags into the bin and picked up her mug. 'I must go to bed. I'll try to sort things out as soon as I can. Go to bed, Milly, good girl! Basket!' She waited until Milly had padded to her bed by the Aga. 'Are you all right to look after everyone here for a few days?'

'As long as you like.' Annie stood up and followed Lily through to the hall. 'I'm sure William will be all right,' she said earnestly. 'He's strong as an ox.'

Lily nodded. 'I'll give you a ring tomorrow.' She watched Annie pick up her overnight bag. 'Is that all you brought?'

'It's enough,' Annie said. 'I'm not intending to go to any Hunt Balls while I'm here.'

Lily smiled. 'When have you ever been to a Hunt Ball?' She

mounted the stairs slowly, one hand holding her tea, the other resting on the banister. 'If you want any more clothes, you can borrow mine. Don't put any of my Cashmeres in the washing machine.'

'I have no intention of wearing any of your Cashmeres.'

'I've told you all about Milly's food on the list but Gabriel will feed her if you ask. If you can manage it, she'd love a good walk at some point in the day. Her lead's hanging up in the cloakroom.'

'Lily,' Annie said, 'don't worry about Milly. Go to bed.'

'Right. Goodnight, then.'

Annie walked into her bedroom and sat down on the big double bed. She glanced around at her surroundings. The walls were painted a pale yellow, the carpet was light blue and Lily had made cushions in a matching colour for the window seats. The extravagantly long curtains had been dipped in tea to enhance the old-fashioned look of the room. To Annie, it seemed to hark back to a distant, probably mythical age of gentle courtesy, moral certainties, a time when family was everything and society was safe. In such a room it seemed ridiculous that William had been attacked by a green-haired boy and only saved from a lonely death in the gutter because of the sharp eyes and wits of a little old woman. Annie thought of William trying to save his mother's vase from harm. A lump came to her throat. She hoped William, and the vase, were all right.

Lily was woken the next morning by Gabriel, who sat on her bed and asked her if she was awake, and by Milly, who licked each of her fingers with gentle efficiency.

'Luke's still asleep,' Gabriel said.

'Lucky Luke,' Annie muttered, opening one eye.

'I thought Mummy's friend Elsbeth was looking after us.'

'Elsbeth couldn't make it so I'm here instead.'

'Milly's very hungry,' Gabriel noted reprovingly. 'Do you want me to give her her breakfast?'

'That,' Annie said, trying to remove her right hand from Milly's tongue, 'would be very kind.'

'Mum's gone,' Gabriel said. 'Dad's in hospital.'

'I know.'

'I wanted to go with Mum but she said I couldn't.'

'You wouldn't be able to talk to William,' Annie explained. 'He's asleep.'

'He's not asleep,' Gabriel corrected her. 'He's unconscious.'

'Yes,' Annie agreed. Gabriel's unblinking gaze and impassive expression could unnerve her at the best of times but this morning she felt as if she was under a particularly hot spotlight. She should have asked Lily how much the boys knew about William's condition.

'I'm going to Julian's house this afternoon,' Gabriel said. 'We're going to play HeroQuest.' He got off the bed and walked to the door. 'I've had some cereal,' he said, 'but I'll have some proper breakfast when you come down. Then we can walk Milly if you like.' He called to Milly who turned at once and followed Gabriel down the stairs.

Annie got out of bed and went to the window. Beyond the house and the huge herbaceous border, there was a field and, at the bottom, Lily's nearest neighbour, a farmer – she could almost hear Lily correcting her – 'an *organic* farmer'. Up in the cloudless sky, a solitary plane left a thin white line in its wake. Downstairs, Milly was having her breakfast, Gabriel was planning his game of HeroQuest and somewhere in a London hospital, William was fighting for his life.

By the time Annie and Gabriel returned from walking Milly, both Luke and Sidney were up and dressed and shovelling cereal into their mouths. Luke, like his brother, seemed relatively unconcerned about the state of his father. He was more anxious about the possible cancellation of their holiday in Italy. 'We're supposed to be going next week,' he said, 'with Amabel and her family. Do you know Amabel?'

Annie had a vague memory of leather boots and a husky voice. 'I think so,' she said.

'We're hiring a big house with a tennis court and a pool and Dad said he'd take us to Perugia. You can go to an underground car park and go up to the ground on an escalator and you can see all these old ruins as you go up and it's really cool. Do you think Dad will be well enough to go?'

'I'm not sure he will be,' Annie said cautiously, 'but I'm sure Lily will work something out.' She looked from him to Sidney. 'What about a game of croquet? I'm going to make some soup for lunch and then I'll join you.'

'You have to take me to tennis at half past eleven,' Luke reminded her.

Annie smiled confidently. 'I'll have made the soup by then.' It was important, she felt, to make home-made food for the boys. It was what they were used to.

She only just made the deadline. The phone went twice in the next twenty minutes, both callers issuing dinner invitations to Lily. To both, Annie gave a brief account of William's attack. After that, there was a ten-minute lull and then the phone didn't stop ringing as what seemed like scores of friends and neighbours rang to find out about William and to express their dismay. It was clear that William and Lily who lived in rural isolation had a far busier social life than Annie.

Annie had thrown the last of the chopped potatoes and carrots into the sizzling butter when the phone went again.

'Hello,' said a high-pitched voice. 'This is Felix here. I'm William's godson. Is he going to get better soon?'

'I'm sure he will,' said Annie.

'Will you tell him that last time we played The Really Nasty Horse-Racing Game, I cheated? Tell him I only cheated because he cheated when he played croquet. I saw him move his ball. Will you tell him I'll make a card for him?'

'I will make sure,' Annie promised, 'that he gets your message.' She put the phone down, tore off a piece of kitchen paper from the roll on the wrought-iron holder and blew her nose. She then wasted a couple of minutes looking for a wooden spoon which she found in a hand-painted jar labelled 'Wooden Spoons'. She turned her attention back to the soup. The vegetables were glued to the bottom of the saucepan in a dark embrace.

Sidney came in and flopped onto a chair. 'I'm knackered!' he said. 'I play one game of croquet and I win and so Luke demands I play another and I win that and now he wants another. He's just like Grandfather. He's so competitive it's ridiculous. He won't give up until he wins.'

'There's an easy solution. Let him win!'

'I can't do that!' Sidney was appalled. 'I can't let a twelve-year-old beat me!' He stretched his arms out in front of him. 'Doesn't Luke have a tennis lesson to go to?'

'Oh Lord!' Annie glanced at the clock and shoved the glowering vegetables to one side. 'Tell him we're going right away!'

By the end of the day, Annie was exhausted. She had taken Milly for two walks, she had taken Luke to and collected him from his tennis lesson, she had met Gabriel's hyper-active friend Julian and his formidably glamorous mother. She had felt her heart rise into her mouth when she had spotted both boys hanging from the branch of the oak tree, while she was talking to the formidably glamorous mother. She had made tea for the plumber and pretended to understand his involved explanation of the top-floor shower's deficiencies. She had made a very thick soup, in which generous doses of seasoning had failed to disguise the charcoal-like aroma. She had fielded numerous phone calls. Sidney had been terrific, playing end-less games of croquet, extracting boys from trees, throwing balls to Milly. But Sidney was going home tomorrow.

Lily rang at seven and asked if everything was all right.

'Absolutely fine!' Annie assured her, adopting the tones of an overenthusiastic games teacher. 'The boys have been great. You've had thousands of phone calls and I've written down all the names. Your plumber came and I think he's mended the shower but he might have to come back again to fix something onto something else. I made a horrible soup and your boys were very polite and ate it all up.'

Lily gave a laugh. 'They'd eat anything!'

'How's William?'

'He looks terrible. His face has gone a weird dark colour, he has tubes everywhere and there's a bolt sticking out of his head. He's still unconscious. No one at the hospital seems prepared to say whether he's going to make it or not.'

'Oh Lily!' Annie felt a stab of fear. 'I'm so sorry!'

'I've sorted out the boys. Amabel has been a star. You know we're supposed to be going to Italy on Tuesday? I'll come back home on Monday and get them packed. Amabel says she'll pick them up on Tuesday morning. Are you all right to stay on until Monday?'

'Of course I am.'

'They've found the green-haired boy. His mother rang the police and he's made a full confession. Apparently he's had mental health problems for years. He says he didn't mean to hurt William, he just needed a fix and had to get some money.'

'So that's all right, then,' said Annie. 'I'd give him a fix all right.' She took a deep breath. Righteous anger was the last thing Lily needed. 'Shall I get the boys for you? They're longing to talk to you.'

'Thanks. I'll speak to you tomorrow.'

Luke and Gabriel were in the playroom, glued to a game of Worms in front of the computer. Annie handed Luke the phone and returned to the kitchen. She couldn't bear to think of William, good, kind William, lying unconscious in a hospital bed. She switched on the radio. Two men were having a very impassioned discussion on the importance of Renaissance art. She switched the radio off.

Supper was a subdued affair. Luke was torn between relief that he was still going to Italy and a barely understood guilt that he *was* relieved. Gabriel wanted to go and see his father and couldn't understand why Lily wouldn't let him.

'He's unconscious,' Annie pointed out. 'You couldn't talk to him.'

'I don't care,' Gabriel muttered. 'I want to see the bolt sticking out of his head. Mummy says he looks like Frankenstein's monster.'

Luke subjected his brother to a look of withering scorn. 'You are so gross!' he said. 'Dad's very ill and all you want to do is see the bolt sticking out of his head!'

Gabriel reddened. 'I don't *just* want to see the bolt!'

'Of course you don't,' Annie soothed. 'I think we should play Monopoly after supper. Of course, none of you has a chance of winning because I never lose!'

'You will tonight!' Gabriel promised.

'No, I won't.' Annie stood up to clear the plates when she suddenly froze. 'Oh my God! Luke, what have you done with the phone?'

'It's in the playroom. Why?'

'I'm meant to be having dinner with someone. I'll be right back!' Annie pushed back her chair, ran out of the room and into the playroom, then back to the dining room to grab her bag and then back again to the playroom.

Ben answered at once. He must have had the phone right by him.

'How long have you been waiting for me?' Annie asked breathlessly.

'Half an hour.' Ben sounded quite calm. 'How are you, Annie?'

'I haven't stood you up,' Annie said quickly, 'but I can't come.'

'I see,' said Ben, who patently didn't.

'I've only just remembered I should be with you. Lily rang at midnight. William, that's her husband, has been mugged in London. He's very badly hurt. So I came down to look after the boys and now I've just remembered. I'm sorry.'

'How is he?'

'I don't know.' Annie swallowed. 'The doctors seem to be hedging their bets.' She swallowed again. She mustn't cry, she mustn't let the boys see her crying. She said briskly, 'I hope you haven't been too bored in the restaurant.'

'I've had a very nice glass of wine and I've been reading.'

'You brought a book to the restaurant? Why did you bring a book with you?'

'I thought,' Ben said apologetically, 'you might be late.'

'I am *never* late,' Annie retorted, 'unless I am unavoidably detained. What are you reading?'

'*The Idiot*,' said Ben, 'by Dostoyevsky.'

'How very appropriate. How far have you got with it?'

'Not very far,' Ben confessed. 'I read it for ten minutes and then I switched to a Stephen King novel.'

'You brought *two* books with you? How late did you think I was going to be?'

'I am trying to educate myself: hence the Dostoyevsky. The trouble is I find I can only read him for ten minutes before I start to fall asleep. That's why I brought the Stephen King with me.'

'I see.'

'Also,' Ben admitted, 'I wasn't sure you'd come.'

'Just because *you* have a history of breaking important engagements doesn't mean that I do!'

'I'm glad you thought our dinner was important,' Ben said sweetly and then, possibly realizing that he was pushing his luck, proceeded swiftly with a question. 'What are *you* reading at the moment?'

'Not the Gary Cooper book you gave me.'

'I didn't think you were,' said Ben sadly.

'Although,' conceded Annie graciously, 'I might do later. In fact I'm reading a very interesting book about the essential differences between men and women. Its basic theme is that men are systemizers while women are empathizers and that autism is a symptom of extreme maleness. Males are no good at empathy.'

'Aren't we?' asked Ben. 'I never realized that.'

'Well, you wouldn't,' said Annie, 'because you're no good at it. Especially you. Now I must go and finish my supper.'

'What are you eating?'

'Spaghetti Bolognese. It's one of Lily's sauces from her freezer. I made a soup today. It was horrible. The boys were very sweet. They had second helpings.'

'They'll probably eat anything,' said Ben, unconsciously imitating Lily.

'Thank you for the vote of confidence. I'm going now.'

'If there's anything I can do . . .'

'I cannot imagine anything you could do for me. Goodbye.' Annie put down the phone. She no longer felt like crying. There was something about insulting Ben that was very uplifting.

Afterwards, she kept asking herself why she'd said yes. Was it because she'd spent one day at the seaside, watching the boys fighting each other like puppies in the water? Was it because she'd spent another day heating pizzas, playing games, aware that her nephews' increasingly fractious behaviour was the external manifestation of a fear they dared not articulate? On Friday evening they both spoke to Lily and then Gabriel went to bed and came down after twenty minutes with suspiciously swollen eyelids. The three of them had huddled on the sofa together, watching *Shrek* on the DVD player.

Ben had rung the next morning and offered to come over on Sunday and cook a proper roast lunch. She hadn't even hesitated. She'd accepted his suggestion without a thought.

He arrived the following day with a basket full of chicken and vegetables and bread and ice cream. He told the boys they were giving Annie some time off from the cooking. He got Gabriel topping and tailing the beans. He showed Luke how to chop onions. Afterwards they sat down and ate and Luke told Ben about the villa in Italy and Gabriel imitated the voice of Amabel's youngest daughter, Olivia. Annie said he shouldn't make fun of someone's speech impediment. Luke said that Oliva enjoyed pulling Milly's tail, so Ben said she deserved to have her speech impediment made fun of. Annie secretly agreed with this but felt duty bound to point out that Ben's sense of morality was extremely shaky.

At the end of the meal, Annie said they were all exempt from the washing-up. Ben went to the playroom with the boys while Annie cleared away. When she had finished, she went through and found them all sitting cross-legged in a line. All three had their heads slightly slanted to the left. All three were manically flicking switches on their consoles. For a moment,

Annie could imagine what her life might have been like if Ben had decided to go to the church seventeen years ago. She turned on her heel and went back to the kitchen.

CHAPTER TEN

Black Book Entry, 26 July: Ben Seymour for making it impossible for me not to think about him.

Annie's father had bought Pixie Cottage a week after Josephine and Clement announced their engagement. He said he had bought it as a future retirement home for himself and Rosemary. They would move there, he said, when they got old and frail. The whole family knew that David could never contemplate a time when he *would* be old and frail. He had bought it for Clement and Josephine. He was particularly pleased that it was only a five-minute walk from Beech Hurst. In an unguarded moment, he admitted to Lily that he would eventually like to buy all of his daughters a house in the village. Then, he said, he would be able to pop in at any time, night or day, to offer advice and support.

Neither Clement nor Josephine had been very excited at the prospect of such close attention and anyway, as Josephine pointed out, the demands of their medical careers necessitated close proximity to the London hospitals. David had let the cottage out to short-term tenants until Ben and Annie got engaged, when he immediately suggested it as a first home for them.

Ben, a committed Londoner, had been uncertain but Annie's enthusiasm for it had won the day. She had always loved the little cottage, with its woodland garden and generous bay window. When Annie's wedding plans had disintegrated, David had let it again. Lily had always said she had no intention of ever living there. When Lily and William bought their big house in Somerset, Lily made it clear she was more than happy to host all family gatherings in future. Appalled, though not surprised, by Lily's tactlessness, her sisters assured their mother they would always want to spend their Christmases at Beech Hurst. Rosemary said she hoped they wouldn't be too upset but she was very happy to let Lily organize Christmas and had long wanted to move to Pixie. Since Mr Harrington had retired, she had found it increasingly difficult to manage such a big garden on her own and her attempts to interest David in anything other than the croquet lawn had led nowhere. David, having first checked that the garden at Pixie Cottage was big enough for croquet, had been happy to support her.

Annie had thought she would find it painful to visit her parents in the place which should have been her first home with Ben, and it was true that on her first visit, she had felt a lump rise to her throat when she opened the little white gate. But once she had gone inside, she felt better. Rosemary had stamped her own personality on the place, making it almost a miniature replica of the old family home. The ancient Vermeer print hung above the mantelpiece, framed photos of her children and grandchildren covered the wall by the stairs. She had altered the green and pink curtains and had bought a couple of new cushions for the sofa and chairs.

Annie had long been impervious to any hypothetical memories of a blissful married life with Ben. In the last few years, she had made enough visits to be confident that she had exorcized her ghosts. So now, when she parked her car in the slip road outside the cottage and saw the silver birch in the corner of the garden – one wedding present that hadn't been returned – she was surprised by a sudden shiver of memory. She stayed in the car, trying to compose herself. Yesterday, she had stood in the doorway of Lily's house, thanking Ben a little formally for the lunch he had given her and the boys. He had said, 'You look so tried,' and had made it sound like a compliment.

The truth was that she was in a Catch 22 situation. She was unable to dwell on Ben's past monstrosities because that would bring up a past that had taken her years to bury. The only way, therefore, that she could deal with him was to regard him as an unpleasant acquaintance. The least he could do was to *be* unpleasant. When he behaved like he had done yesterday and when he smiled at her like he had done yesterday, her only defence was to remind herself that he had filled more pages of her Black Book than any other person in her whole life. Yet she could not allow herself to concentrate on his crime because then she found herself wanting to hear an explanation from him. Since no explanation could absolve him of his guilt for the years of misery he had subjected her to and since any explanation could only revive painful memories, she could only stamp on any thought of Ben as soon as it rose to the surface of her mind.

Unfortunately she seemed to be doing an awful lot of stamping lately.

Someone was tapping at her window. Annie turned her head and saw her mother staring quizzically at her. 'Hello, darling!' Rosemary said. 'Were you planning to come in and have some lunch with us or did you want to stay out here?'

Inside, there were enticing smells of newly baked bread and Rosemary's pea soup. David sat in his armchair, his long legs stretched out in front of him, one hand smoothing his hair, the other holding the phone into which he barked instructions. His dog, Harnish, a King Charles Cavalier spaniel who loved David almost as much as David loved him, lay on his lap and raised a sleepy head at Annie's arrival. David nodded at Annie and said, 'I have to go, Stephen. Ring me tomorrow if you get a response!' He switched off the phone and beamed at his daughter. 'Annie! Come and give your poor old father a kiss!'

'You look neither poor nor old!' Annie assured him. This was true. David looked much younger than his seventy-seven years. He was as slim as ever, he had lost none of his hair and his clear, grey eyes sparkled with animation. In fact, Annie thought, watching her mother's trim figure disappear into the small kitchen at the back, if she looked half as good as either of her parents in thirty years' time she would be very pleased with herself.

At lunch, the talk was mainly of William and Lily. 'How do you think she looks?' Rosemary asked. 'She must be frantic with worry.'

'Lily's amazing,' Annie said. 'She got home about ten last

night and still managed to look great. She'd spent most of the day at the hospital. You know the doctors are going to operate again?'

Rosemary nodded. 'Lily rang me yesterday afternoon. I don't know how she bears it. She says they still have no idea if he's going to make it or not. The consultant said it's possible he'll never come out of his coma. I feel so helpless. I wish there was something we could *do*!'

'Lily is formidably efficient,' Annie assured her. 'She has everything organized for the next couple of weeks at least. The boys are going to Italy with her friends, she's already been on to the school about the possibility of their being weekly boarders next term. Milly's going into kennels for a fortnight and when the boys get back, Luke's godfather is going to stay for a bit.'

'As soon as my blessed ankle is better,' David said, 'we'll have Milly down here. I told Lily that Hamish would love to have her with us. Also, I want to go up to London and have a word with William.'

'Dad,' Annie said, 'he's unconscious.'

'That doesn't mean anything,' David said confidently. 'Did I ever tell you about the riding accident I had when I was a boy? My mother said the doctors thought it was all over for me. She told me she sat by my bed and told me to pull myself together. And, of course, I did! You never know what people can understand. I have a strong feeling I could get through to William.'

Annie and Rosemary exchanged glances. David's mother had been a woman with dogmatic views on just about everything, but in the area of mental and physical health her ideas were particularly idiosyncratic. She always maintained that she had sorted out her son's nervous collapse in his early twenties by taking him to Ireland and feeding him on nothing but porridge for a week. She was convinced she could forecast the sex of any unborn baby and it was true that she had had a fifty per cent success rate. She also believed that central heating was an enemy of longevity and had kept her own home in a state of near Arctic conditions. Since she had lived to the ripe old age of ninety-eight, it was possible she had been on to something and David had often suggested they should follow her example. Rosemary refused to consider the idea. She would rather be warm and die at eighty, she said, than be cold and die at ninety.

'The trouble with William,' David said, 'is he's too fat. None of this would have happened if he'd been in better condition.'

'Don't you dare say that to Lily,' said Annie.

'Really, darling, I do have *some* tact,' David said, ignoring the raised eyebrows of his womenfolk. 'The point is if William had been fit, he could have run away or even thumped his attacker.'

'He was holding a vase!' Rosemary said patiently. 'As I understand it, the mugger hit him in the stomach, William tripped and fell and hit his head on the pavement. If William had only let go of the vase ... But then it must be very difficult to think clearly when someone with green hair jumps out on one. And I don't suppose the man with green hair was thinking clearly either because otherwise he might have realized that green hair is difficult to forget. The police picked him up almost immediately.'

'That was because his mother turned him in,' Annie said. 'He confessed.'

'Poor woman,' Rosemary said. 'I often wonder what Mrs Hitler must have thought of her son.'

'She died when Hitler was eighteen,' David said. 'He might have been different if she'd lived.'

'I doubt it,' Rosemary said. 'I don't seem to have any influence over my children.' She sighed and gave a sideways glance at Annie. 'How is life in Bath, darling? Have you been to any good parties lately?'

Have I met any nice men who will take pity on my unmarried state and make an honest woman of me? 'Not really. My friend Grace is organizing a ball. It's going to be very grand. I think she's booking the Assembly Rooms.'

'You should join a gym,' David said. 'Harold's daughter met her husband at a gym. And she's not a pretty woman. She's fat. Mind you, Harold says the husband is too.'

'I don't want to go to the gym and I don't want a husband either!' Annie said waspishly. She finished her soup and changed the subject pointedly. 'This bread is wonderful! There is nothing like home-made bread!'

Rosemary smiled. 'I got the recipe from George. Do you remember George? He lives in Forest Drive. He's David's campaign partner! Anyway, he's taken up cooking in the last few years and he's very good at it. This recipe uses cheese.'

'Talking about George,' David said, 'he's coming round this afternoon for a briefing.'

Rosemary passed the tomato pickle over to Annie. 'George and David,' she explained, 'have been collecting signatures for a petition against post office closures. A group of them are going to Downing Street tomorrow to hand in the petition.'

'I wish I could go,' said David. 'Damn stupid ankle! George is going to represent me.'

'I have to do the church flowers,' Rosemary announced. 'I'm doing them with Marjorie Cawthorne. There's a funeral tomorrow. Would you like to come and help us, Annie?'

'I was hoping Annie would take Hamish for a walk,' said David.

Annie had no wish to exchange pleasantries with the terrifying Marjorie Cawthorne who had never forgiven Annie for not inviting her and her husband to her wedding. She said she thought she would enjoy walking Hamish.

After lunch, she set out with Hamish and walked down to Beech Hurst. The old wooden gate had been replaced by grandiose wrought-iron ones with a voice box contraption on the side. A security camera had been fixed to the beech tree. Annie walked on quickly. She took Hamish up past the farm and finally stopped by the oak tree on the edge of the field. This had always been her favourite place. She used to come here and do her A Level revision, memorizing large chunks of *Othello*.

She took off her cardigan and sat down in the mossy clearing. Hamish, possibly the laziest dog in the world, settled happily on her lap. This, Annie could almost hear him saying, was his kind of walk. Annie raised her face to the sun for a moment and then feasted her eyes on the familiar view. The only sound she could hear was the gentle humming of a bee. She watched it pottering around the cow parsley, sampling odd blossoms like an elderly woman at a wine-tasting. At the bottom of the field, an old man in a Panama hat cycled along the lane, past the Duck and Drake.

The last time she had been in the Duck and Drake was with Ben. They were in the Duck and Drake because Ben wanted to have a row with her and he didn't want a row in the family home. They had come down from London for the weekend and David had asked them if they'd like to go with him and Rosemary and Lily to Gozo the following summer. It was, he told them, a very unspoilt island, next to Malta. But the reason why he wanted to go there was because it was the island on which Calypso had lured Odysseus away from his quest to seek out his home and his wife, Penelope.

Annie had said, without a thought, that of course she and Ben would go; it was her easy assumption of Ben's acquiescence that had led to the row. 'The point is,' Ben said, 'you didn't think to consult me first. How did you know I would want to go?'

'How could you *not* want to go?' Annie had countered. 'Blue sea, big beaches, great hotel! Are you telling me you *don't* want to go?'

'I don't know what I'll be doing next year. I don't know what *we'll* be doing next year.'

'What does that mean?'

'It doesn't mean anything. I'm just saying I don't like to plan things too far in advance. We might not even be together next year!'

'Are you planning to leave me in the near future?'

'I'm just saying that you're twenty, I'm twenty-four. It's ridiculous for us to start acting like some old married couple.'

'I thought I was acting like someone in a serious relationship.'

'There's a difference between being serious and planning a detailed itinerary for the next few years.'

'Actually, the holiday would be in ten months.'

'You know what I mean.'

'If you feel like that, perhaps we should just separate now.'

'Perhaps we should.'

Annie could remember it like it was yesterday. She stretched out on the mossy ground. Hamish grumbled a little and rearranged his limbs so that he could rest his chin on her leg. Annie put her hands behind her head and shut her eyes. It was true that she and Ben had been absurdly young. Had she pushed him too far? Had she frightened him off?

No, she hadn't. It was Ben, after all, who came back to her, not her to him. It was Ben who had come back to her and urged her to marry him. Had he merely asked her because he had thought he would lose her if he didn't?

She sat up abruptly, evincing a muttered reproach from Hamish. Stop it, she told herself, stop it right now or you'll be charging round to Ben's house, demanding to know the truth as soon as you get back to Bath. She knew what would happen then. It would be like pulling a thread, unpicking a few stitches and then watching a carefully crafted dress fall apart in front of her. *None of this matters any more!* She stood up and shook off the small spikes of grass that stuck to her skirt. 'Come on, Hamish!' she said. 'It's time to go home!'

Lily rang on Tuesday evening. Annie and David were playing an increasingly fractious game of Scrabble. Rosemary cast a reproving stare in their direction and fled upstairs with the phone.

'Excuse me,' Annie said. 'What is V-A-D-I-S?'

'Vadis as in quo vadis,' said David.

'You can't use vadis. That's Latin. We are playing English Scrabble.'

'Yes you can. It's entered the English language. People use it all the time. "Quo vadis?" they'll say and I'll reply, "I'm off to the shops," or "I'm taking Hamish for a walk."'

Annie gave him a withering look. 'In my entire life, not one of my friends has ever said to me, "Hi, Annie, quo vadis?"'

'I'm afraid that just goes to show what an uneducated bunch of people you surround yourself with. My friends never stop saying it.'

'Oh really,' Annie said crossly, 'it's quite impossible to have a sensible game with you.' She frowned and applied herself to her letters.

'Annie,' David said after what seemed like only a few seconds, 'I'm afraid I'm going to have to put the timer on. You're way over time.'

Sixty seconds later, the timer went off. 'I'm afraid . . .' David began.

'I know! I'm ready!' Annie added five letters to the V from vadis.

'Verily?' exclaimed David. 'You can't use verily! It's archaic!'

'Nonsense,' said Annie. 'My friends are always using verily. "Verily, Annie, you look radiantly beautiful." It's in the dictionary if you don't believe me. I'm sure it is.'

David shifted in his chair, muttered under his breath and began to rearrange his letters:

Annie was about to put the timer on when Rosemary came downstairs. 'Annie!' she said. 'Lily wants a word.'

Annie took the phone and pushed her chair back. 'Hi, Lily! Did the boys get off to Italy today?'

'I delivered them to Amabel and they arrived safely a couple of hours ago.' Lily's voice sounded flat and tired. 'Thank you for looking after them.'

'They were very easy to look after. How's William?'

'No change. They're operating on Thursday. Annie?'

'Yes?'

'The boys said a nice man called Ben came and gave you all lunch on Sunday. That was very decent of him! Who is he? A new boyfriend?'

'No.' Annie stood up and moved away from the table.

'Well, who is he?'

Annie glanced at her father and then walked quickly up the stairs. 'It's Ben Seymour,' she muttered.

'What?' Lily sounded as if she'd jumped into a huge tub of freezing water. 'Ben Seymour? *The* Ben Seymour?'

'Unfortunately, I don't know any others.'

'But why? How? Annie, what on earth is going on?'

'Nothing is going on. He has a job in Bristol now and he's bought a house in Bath. I met him at a friend's house. When he heard I was coming down to look after your boys, he offered to make a meal for us. That's all.'

'That's all! For seventeen years, no one in the family dares to mention his name in your presence and suddenly he's dropping in to cook you a cosy lunch? A very good, cosy lunch it was too, according to the boys. How come you're talking to him? How come you haven't torn him into a thousand tiny pieces?'

'It's complicated,' Annie said. 'I'm sure you're too tired to hear all this now.'

'I'm suddenly feeling very wide awake! I repeat: how come you're talking to him?'

'It's difficult,' Annie said slowly. 'He's met my friends, they like him, they invite him to things. They don't know what he did and I don't want to tell them. So in public, at least, I have to be polite to him. I've told him I don't want to have anything at all to do with him.'

'I see. So did he force his way into my house, brandishing his leg of beef?'

'It was chicken.'

'Did he force his way in, brandishing his chicken, then?'

'Not exactly.' Annie paused and tried to work out how she could explain the inexplicable. 'I'm not a brilliant cook—'

'That's the understatement of the year.'

'I was running out of things to cook. Ben rang and offered to make a real Sunday lunch. I was tired and . . .' Annie paused again. 'I thought the boys would appreciate a proper meal,' she finished. It sounded lame even to her.

'I can't believe this! So what has he got to say for himself? Why did he miss the wedding?'

Annie fell back onto her pillows and put a hand over her eyes. 'I don't know.'

'You don't know! Why don't you know?'

Annie swallowed. She tried hard to remember that Lily must be in a very fragile emotional state and that to tell her

162

that none of this was her business was not an option. Since the news about Ben had resulted in Lily suddenly sounding exactly like the bullying, self-opinionated Lily of old, this was not easy.

Annie removed her hand from her eyes. 'I haven't asked him.'

'WHY NOT?'

'Because I didn't want to! Nothing he can say will change what happened! I don't want to go over all those things again. I spent years thinking about them! I spent years teaching myself to stop thinking about them! I am fed up with the past! Which is why,' Annie added with great deliberation, 'I don't like talking to you or anyone else about him.'

'So you're honestly telling me it has never crossed your mind to ask him why he jilted you? You can honestly say to me you can look him in the eye and talk to him and not once feel like saying, all right, you bastard, why did you jilt me? Because if you are honestly saying that to me, then I'm sorry, I think you're lying ... Annie? Annie, are you still there?'

'Yes, and you've just used an oxymoron.'

'Don't try and fob me off with all that fancy English stuff. Answer me!'

Annie sighed. 'I have had the odd moment when I've been tempted to cross-question him under a single spotlight but I know ... I know that if I did find out, it would be like ripping off a plaster and plunging a knife into the wound.'

'On the other hand, you might find that if you *did* rip off the plaster, there would just be a sweet little scar that had healed up nicely and then you wouldn't want to plunge any old knife in. And in fact, why would anyone want to plunge a knife into a wound anyway?'

'Lily,' Annie said, 'I'm finding your argument very difficult to follow and I really don't want to talk about it any more. Did you know I'm going to stay with Josephine on Thursday?'

'I don't suppose,' Lily said, 'you could come and stay with me instead?'

Annie sat up. 'Oh Lily, of course! William's having his operation on Thursday! I'll go straight to the hospital.'

'William's mother is coming up next week. You could go and see Josephine then.'

'All right. I'll ring tomorrow and get directions.'

'I'm sorry I've gone on about Ben.'

It was so extraordinary to receive an apology from Lily that Annie felt quite overwhelmed. 'That's all right,' she said.

'It's so much more fun to talk about your weird attitude to him than it is to talk about William.'

'Glad to be of service,' said Annie stiffly. 'Goodbye, Lily.'

Downstairs, David was adding up the scores. 'I'm afraid,' he said nonchalantly, 'I have a seven-letter word and I've finished all my letters which I think you'll find means I'm the winner.'

Annie made straight for the table and scrutinized the board. 'Cordovan?' she demanded. 'There's no such word as cordovan.'

David gave a patronizing smile. 'You must have heard of cordovan,' he said.

'No, I haven't. What does it mean?'

'Goatskin leather,' David informed her, 'originally from Cordoba in Spain.'

'Rubbish!' Annie said. She reached for the dictionary and

rifled through the pages. '*Cordovan*,' she read out, '*goatskin leather, originally from Cordoba in Spain.*' Her eyes narrowed. 'You found this in the dictionary!'

'I don't know how you can say that,' David said. 'You must try not to be a bad loser, darling. It's only a game.'

Annie was reading her book when she heard the anticipated knock at the door. Rosemary appeared in her soft pink dressing gown. 'I thought you might like a cup of tea,' she said.

It did not escape Annie's notice that her mother had brought her own cup of tea in with her as well. Rosemary came and sat down on the edge of the bed. 'Lily told me,' she said carefully, 'that a friend of yours drove over to make lunch for you and the boys. That was very kind.'

'Yes.' Annie took a sip of tea. She knew very well that if she didn't tell her mother about Ben, then Lily certainly would. She took a deep breath and explained in as expressionless a voice as she could manage, exactly why Ben Seymour had made lunch for her a couple of days ago.

When she had finished, Rosemary stared into her tea. 'You know,' she murmured, 'I always felt bad about lying to him. Do you remember how he kept ringing us when you were abroad? He always sounded so anxious to get you and then when I told him you'd married a Frenchman, I felt horribly uncomfortable.'

'I don't know why. We're talking here about a man who callously left me virtually at the altar. And anyway you only lied because I told you to.'

'Yes, but it was wrong. It wasn't true and it felt wrong. Perhaps I should have simply told him where you were and—'

Debby Holt

'And I would never have spoken to you again! He had no right to keep pestering you with phone calls. He had no right to demand anything of any of us!'

'But he sounded so upset!'

'Then he shouldn't have gone off and left me and one hundred and eighty-five guests, should he? Don't you dare feel sorry for him just because he made a Sunday roast for me and the boys! Telling him I was married was the best thing you could have done because it left me alone so I could get over him in peace.'

'But now he's come back.'

'He hasn't come back to *me*. He's turned up in Bath, where I happen to live. He stopped meaning anything to me the day he left me. Don't feel guilty about Ben. Don't waste a moment of your time even thinking about him. I don't.'

'Right,' said Rosemary. 'I expect you're right.' She stood up and went to the door. 'If the subject ever comes up, though,' she said, 'you might tell him I'm sorry I lied.'

Later, Annie lay, sleepless, in bed. *Don't waste a moment of your time even thinking about him.* She should never have let him come down to Lily's house. She remembered the expert way in which he had cajoled the boys into helping him in the kitchen. She remembered the gentle manner in which he had taken his leave of her.

She switched on the light. This was *stupid*. She got out of bed and went over to her travelling bag. Like a drowning man reaching for a life-jacket, she took the Black Book from under her clothes. It was her talisman and her shield and it would keep her safe.

166

CHAPTER ELEVEN

Black Book Entry, 29 July: Ben Seymour for taking up residence in my head.

William's flat was in Chelsea, opposite the Embankment, in what had once been a fashionable hotel and was now a collection of thirty apartments. Fortunately for Annie, who found London's traffic congestion charges impossible to understand and who was very much aware of the ubiquity of the capital's traffic wardens, they had their own car park.

The last time Annie had been here was over fifteen years ago, at a time when William was pursuing Lily with the single-mindedness of an Exocet missile. Then, the flat had been a typically shambolic bachelor pad. On the sitting-room floor there had been a large, threadbare rug over which William had tripped at least twice. Annie could remember candle stumps jammed onto saucers, videos scattered around the floor, a lopsided brown leather armchair, random mugs with fungi growing inside them and a kitchen with rows of baked beans.

Remembering Lily's instructions, Annie bent down to

retrieve the key from the base of the cheese plant in the terracotta pot outside William's flat and let herself in. She would never have recognized the place. Instead of the perilous rug, there was now wall-to-wall carpeting of the palest blue. The previously curtainless window was framed by long satin drapes that extended languorously across at least five inches of carpet. There were plush chairs and a sofa in dove-grey, a black-stemmed lamp on either end of the mantelpiece and a huge mirror between them. A thin sliver of a television stood in one corner and a collection of DVDs was neatly arranged on shelves behind it.

Annie wandered through to the kitchen and gazed admiringly at the brushed-steel fitted units, built-in appliances and work surfaces. There was not a tin of baked beans in sight, in fact there wasn't much of anything in sight. Annie couldn't believe that William kept the flat like this and suspected that Lily had been at work. The kitchen's sleek sophistication was interrupted only by a framed photograph of the boys taken at a time when their teeth were all over the place. Gabriel was giving a gap-toothed grin while Luke looked as if he was about to explain why he hadn't meant to break Lily's latest best vase. Annie wondered when it had been taken: over a year ago at least since she could remember Luke having his brace fitted last summer. It would be nice to take the photo to William in hospital when he regained consciousness; if he regained consciousness.

There was a note from Lily on the table: *I made a fish pie this morning. If I'm not back by eight, put it in the oven for thirty minutes and then eat. There is salad in the fridge and a bottle of wine for you to open and drink. Lily.*

Lily was possibly making the pie while William's operation was going on. Annie found such resilience in the face of the horrific turn of events awe-inspiring and just a little chilling.

Lily got in at a quarter to nine, scolded Annie for not eating without her, told her to put the pie in the oven and disappeared to the bathroom to have a shower. When she reappeared fifteen minutes later in jeans and a white linen shirt, Annie silently handed her a glass of wine.

Lily sat down on the end of the sofa. 'At least he's still alive!' she said.

'He hasn't regained consciousness?'

'No. There was no point in your going to the hospital first. I'm glad you got my message. As I was coming home, I suddenly panicked and thought I should have made sure Dad told you to go straight to the flat. You and Mum had just gone out when I rang and I told him three times to be sure.'

'He was very good. We were walking Hamish and as soon as we got back, Dad told me. He's getting better in his old age!'

'That,' Lily said, 'is debatable. He told me to watch the doctors all the time because a lot of them don't know what they're doing. It was just what I wanted to hear!'

'He means well,' Annie said. 'He's very keen to look after Milly for you.'

Lily took a gulp of her wine. 'It's all such a mess. I don't know what to do. William might never come out of his coma. He might die, he might not die. I can't plan anything at the moment.'

'You don't have to. Just take each day as it comes.'

Lily gave a slight smile. 'Play it by ear.'

'Exactly. Let tomorrow take care of itself.'

'And every cloud has a silver lining.' Lily took another gulp. 'I can't face the hospital tomorrow. I've told them I'll keep my mobile on and they can ring me if there's any change. Let's go window-shopping in the morning. We can take a picnic to Regent's Park.' She reached out for her bag and rummaged around for her cigarettes. 'I have always hated hospitals. I hate the smell of boiled cabbage, I hate all the sick people and I hate the grime everywhere. I can hardly see out of the windows, they're so dirty. I'm fed up with going in day after day and I'm fed up with looking at William who just lies there like a big, sleeping whale. I'm fed up with talking about William and I'm fed up with thinking about William.'

Annie picked up the bottle of wine and refilled their glasses. 'I think,' she said gently, 'the fish pie will be ready by now.'

It was a dark and airless night. Annie wondered if it was like this every night in London. She kept tossing and turning, trying to get comfortable but her sheets were sticking to her limbs and eventually she threw back the bedclothes and got out of bed.

The light was on in the sitting room. Lily sat on the sofa, silent and still like an elegant statue, her back to Annie. If I was a painter, Annie thought, I would make a wonderful painting of the shiny blonde hair and the pale pinks, blues and greens of the kimono against the grey upholstery. She went over to her sister and stopped, unsure what to do or say. This was a Lily she had never seen before. Her face was red and blotchy, her eyes were puffy and tears were coursing down her cheeks. In front of her was the coffee table, a transparent slab of glass, its great weight supported by at least a hundred back copies of *Vogue*. Usually bare, it was now littered with used tissues and an ashtray brimming with cigarette butts.

Annie sat down beside her and took her hand. 'Lily?' she said softly.

Lily turned, as if from a deep sleep. 'Hello,' she said. 'Did I wake you?'

'I couldn't sleep. How long have you been sitting here?'

'I don't know. I try not to think of him and I keep seeing him lying there, the great big whale. What will I do if he never wakes up?'

'He will. I'm sure he will.'

'The doctors don't think he will. They don't say that to me but I know they think it's hopeless.'

'You don't know that.'

'I do and the trouble is, I don't know how I can go on without him.'

'Lily!' Annie exclaimed, shocked into tactlessness. 'You love him!'

Lily withdrew her hand from Annie's and lit a cigarette with trembling fingers. 'I don't do love, Annie, you know that. We just seem to gel together, we always have. He never gets shocked by anything I say or do, he knows what I mean, he understands how I work. It's *easy* to be with him. I suppose that's why I married him. I know I offend people sometimes. I never offend William. And he makes me laugh, he even makes me laugh when I'm cross with him. How can I look after Luke and Gabriel without William? He holds us all together. I'm hopeless with children. How can I manage them without him?'

'Listen to me,' Annie said. 'Ever since you moved to Somerset, you've been managing without him. William lives in London during the week and he comes home . . . he has been coming home at weekends. William is a part-time father, a superb part-time father, but a part-time father nonetheless and you are a full-time mother. Do you know why I don't come and see you as often as I could?'

Lily gave a short laugh. 'Because you're a lousy sister?'

'Because the only time it still hurts that I have no children of my own is when I'm with you and your boys. They are wonderful children. And that's because of you. I never thought you would be a good mother but you are. You are a brilliant mother. Luke and Gabriel are funny and kind and articulate and opinionated and that's because of you. So don't tell me you can't bring up your boys without William because you've been looking after them on your own for years. And don't tell me it's all over for William because I don't believe it. He's made of sterner stuff. It isn't all over until the fat lady sings!'

'Keep on going till the end of the road.'

'You bet! William's a fighter and so are you. I don't believe the doctors would operate if there was no chance of recovery. Hang on to that! If the worst comes to the worst, we'll send Dad to the hospital and he can talk and talk to William and eventually he'll make William so crazy he'll wake up!'

'Even William doesn't deserve that.'

'We'll see. Can I make you a drink? Would you like a cup of tea or some hot chocolate?'

Lily stubbed out her cigarette. 'We don't have any hot chocolate. I've got some water by my bed.' She stood up. 'I'll be all right tomorrow. It's just . . . I had some stupid idea that after the operation he'd wake up and smile at me and apologize for being such an idiot. Stupid!'

'He'll still do that.'

'Perhaps.' Lily walked to her bedroom and stopped by the door. 'I'm glad you're here,' she said. 'Don't tell Mum I've been like this.'

'Of course I won't. Now go to bed.'

Annie waited until Lily had closed the door behind her and then went through to the kitchen to make herself some tea. As a definition of love, 'we just seem to gel together' was hard to beat. It was funny to think that the hard-headed, materialistic Lily was the only one of the three sisters who had proved successful in forging a loving, enduring marriage. How ironic, Annie thought, that she herself had spent her teenage years obsessed with the pursuit of romance and had ended up leading a life with no strong emotional ties at all. For a moment Ben came to her mind. Annie did a couple of well-executed stamps and put on the kettle.

It was a glorious day, one of those days that tease out the good humour in everyone. Annie and Lily sat on a bench in front of the Serpentine, watching the sun glinting on the water. They had taken off their sandals and pulled up their skirts, enjoying the sensation of the sun on their bare skin. They sat, eating their prawn sandwiches and swigging wine from Lily's stainless-steel tumblers.

Two women raced along the path in front of them, wiry as whippets and just as thin, their faces puce from their exertion.

'Why do people run?' Lily wondered. 'It makes them look

so very unattractive and they can get perfectly adequate exercise by walking briskly.'

Annie yawned. Behind her, she could hear a mother calling to her son. 'Elliot? Elliot, you come back this minute! Elliot, if you don't come back right now, I am going to be very, very angry! Elliot?' Annie yawned again and finished the last mouthful of her sandwich. She could feel a delicious drowsiness creeping over her limbs.

'What are you doing for the rest of your holiday?' Lily asked.

Annie yawned again and pushed her hair back from her face. 'Well,' she said, 'after leaving Josephine, I will spend a couple of days at home and then I'm going to Totnes in Devon. Do you remember my friend Deirdre? She was a teacher at my school in Falmouth. She and her husband moved to Totnes last year. Her husband's a fanatical sailor.'

'Isn't she the sister of the man you nearly married?'

'Lily, do you ever listen to anything I say? Robbie never asked me to marry him. He wanted me to go and live in Australia with him.'

'Actually,' said Lily thoughtfully, 'I'm glad you didn't marry him.'

'Are you? Why?'

'You wouldn't be here now.'

'Oh well, in that case, I'm glad I made the right choice.'

'I'm not saying you made the right choice, I'm saying you made the right choice *for me*.'

'Isn't that the same?'

Sarcasm was lost on Lily. 'Not necessarily,' she said. 'About Ben . . .'

'I don't want to talk about Ben.'

'You have to talk about Ben. You're supposed to be helping me to take my mind off William.'

'This,' Annie said, 'is emotional blackmail.'

'Yup!'

Annie sat back against the bench and stretched out her legs. 'What about Ben?'

'Did I ever tell you I had a long talk with him about your marriage to Jean-Pierre?'

'I don't know anyone called Jean-Pierre.'

'You remember you told Mum to tell Ben you had married a Frenchman? I was there when she did it. Mum is the most useless liar. You wouldn't believe how unconvincing she sounded. So I took the phone from her. I told Ben that you'd been wandering along the Seine—'

'The Seine is nowhere near Abbeville.'

'Ben didn't seem to notice. So I said you were wandering along the Seine and you decided to kill yourself and throw yourself into the river!'

The soft coat of drowsiness that had settled so cosily around Annie disappeared in a second. 'You did what? Lily, I can't believe you said that! You mean to say that all these years he's thought I wanted to kill myself because of *him*? That is terrible! He must think I'm so *wet*!'

Lily giggled. 'Only if you jumped in the water!'

'That isn't funny.'

'You should have heard me, I was so convincing. I told him that just as you were about to hurl yourself into the rapids below—'

'The Seine doesn't have any rapids.'

'Never mind. I told him that at that very moment, a gorgeous Frenchman came up to you and pulled you back. He told you that only ten months earlier he too had been about to end his life after his faithless fiancée had left him for his best friend. He said he realized just in time that his death would destroy his family. Then he took you out to dinner and by the end of the evening you knew you were meant for each other. I told him he had a house near the Eiffel Tower and a villa in Provence and he owned a huge vineyard and you planned to start a family as soon as you could.'

'What on earth did Ben say?'

'He couldn't believe it.'

'I'm not surprised,' Annie said drily.

'And then I told him you told me that you were very grateful to him for jilting you because otherwise you'd never have known that Jean-Pierre was your destiny.'

'I would *never* have said anything as yucky as that!'

'Ben seemed to think you were perfectly capable of saying something like that. He was very upset. I almost felt sorry for him. I told him you'd moved to Provence and he asked for your address.'

'You didn't give it to him!'

'Well, actually, Annie, since there *was* no villa in Provence, no I didn't. I said that although you were pleased he had jilted you, you were still adamant that you never wanted to hear from him again.'

'What did he say to that?'

'He said that sounded just like you and then he rang off.'

'Oh.'

'What was he like when he saw you again?'

'Confused. Now I understand why. He was obviously expecting some Gallic sex-god to be just round the corner. He kept saying he thought I was married.'

'Is *he* married? Does he have a family? Does he look at you longingly when you're talking to someone else?'

'I don't know. I don't look at Ben when I'm talking to someone else. I certainly don't think he's married *now*.'

'I wonder why he *did* leave you. Perhaps he had a hereditary illness and knew he was going to die young.'

'That would be an excellent theory if it weren't for the fact that he is still alive and very obviously in good health.'

'I can't believe you didn't ask him. If I were you I'd go up to him and demand an explanation!'

'Yes,' Annie sighed, 'but then no one would ever dare jilt you.'

'No,' Lily said, undoing another button on her sleeveless blouse. 'That's true.'

'I wish you hadn't told Ben I wanted to kill myself.'

'Well,' yawned Lily, 'it's history now.'

Annie sighed. Of course it was history. Of course she didn't care what Ben thought but nonetheless . . .

'The thing is,' she said at last, 'I don't like Ben thinking I wanted to die because of him. Not that I care what he thinks but I don't like the idea of him having a false history. Do you know what I mean? Lily?'

Lily had fallen asleep. She really was very irritating. Annie shut her eyes but every time she felt glorious sloth approaching, she found herself thinking about the different ways in which she could let Ben know, very carelessly, that she had never once and never would think about throwing herself into the rapids of the Seine. Especially since there weren't any rapids anyway. Perhaps she could meet up with him and mention carelessly as if she'd just thought about it that she would never ever consider suicide and then Ben would say that he'd been told that she had once considered it and she would say that Lily always loved to exaggerate and then *he* would say he had been so jealous of Jean-Pierre and. . . . She opened her eyes and reached for the last of the wine. Having imaginary conversations with Ben was almost as dangerous as having real conversations with Ben.

CHAPTER TWELVE

*Black Book Entry, 1 August: Cressida for being a devious,
manipulative little toad.*

Josephine lived in south London in what Lily called the
'grot end' of the capital. This, like many of Lily's pronounce-
ments, was unfair. Herne Hill was a pleasant enough suburb
with solid Victorian and Edwardian housing and tree-lined
avenues. It had a variety of bars, wine bars, bistros and
restaurants, good basic shops and it boasted an excellent park.
One of its main problems, according to Josephine, who had
owned the same car for almost two decades, was the huge
number of four-wheel drives that ploughed through it to get
to the more up-market Dulwich.

Josephine lived in a Victorian terrace. She and Clement had
bought it when Beattie was five; since Josephine had neither
the time nor the inclination for home improvements it had
barely changed in the intervening years. The Chinese lantern
shades had gone in and out of fashion and were currently in
again, the beige wallpaper had presumably once been popular
and the swirling colours of the hall carpet might once have

been regarded as psychedelic. The patchwork curtains in the sitting room had been made by Clement's grandmother and always made Annie think of *The Little House on the Prairie*. When she said this to Lily, Lily had replied it was a pity some Red Indians couldn't come along and set fire to them. Posters of Bob Dylan and Che Guevara in black plastic frames dominated the hall and the cork tiles in the kitchen had long since lost their golden sheen.

Annie was welcomed by Beattie who kissed her warmly and said she was staying in *especially* for her.

'Thank you, Beattie,' Annie said. 'I'm overwhelmed by such an honour.'

'You should be,' Beattie said. 'I wouldn't spend an evening here for anyone else.'

Annie grinned and put her bag down beneath Bob Dylan. 'It can't be that bad,' she said.

'You have *no* idea! Come to the kitchen and I'll make some tea.'

Annie followed meekly. Beattie was her only niece and she loved her dearly but she did find her self-assurance a little intimidating. Beattie looked and behaved much older than her seventeen years. She had inherited Josephine's bone structure and astonishing eyelashes but had none of her mother's almost puritanical indifference to current trends. From the tips of her immaculately painted nails to the toes peeping out from her high-heeled sandals, it was apparent that Beattie knew everything about looking good. Her blonde hair was tied back in a loose and fashionably baggy bun with the ends splayed out like a halo. She wore a flimsy chiffon mini-dress over stonewashed jeans and she smelt divine. Annie would

180

have liked to ask the name of the scent but couldn't help feeling that for a thirty-seven-year-old aunt to buy the same perfume as her seventeen-year-old niece was one symptom of sadness too far.

Annie sat down at the kitchen table while Beattie slammed doors and opened drawers in an attempt to find what she called 'normal' tea bags. 'Mum *will* inflict her weird fads on us,' she complained. 'She's the only one who likes green tea and yet she puts it in the tea caddy!' She pulled out a Tupperware box from the back of a cupboard and smiled. 'Here they are! Do you want anything to eat? We have some biscuits if Sidney hasn't eaten them all.'

'A cup of tea is all I need!' Annie assured her. 'Where's everyone else?'

'Mum's delivering a baby. It's got stuck or something so she said to say she'll be home as soon as she's unstuck it. Mark is collecting Cressida from the drama club, a place she had no interest in until she discovered the end-of-course show was bang in the middle of our French holiday. But there you go!'

'But, Beattie, didn't Cressida want to go to France?'

'Not with us, she didn't. She's a complete cow. She told Mum her breath smelt the other day. I could tell Mum was mortified and later I made her breathe on me and she didn't have bad breath at all. She knew Cressida was just being vile but even so she's spent twice as long cleaning her teeth ever since. Cressida's vile to Sidney as well but if she thinks she can treat me like that she's in for a big shock. I came back at lunch today and—'

'I thought you had a full-time holiday job?'

'I do but I foiled a shoplifter today and they said I could have the afternoon off as a reward.'

'You foiled a shoplifter! How very dramatic!'

'It was. This girl had come in with a big carrier bag full of coat and I thought that was odd because it was a lovely day and why would anyone carry a coat around. Then she disappeared into the changing booth with loads of clothes and came out wearing her coat and with the carrier bag still full. She'd managed to get all the security tags off. So I waited until she got outside the shop and then I stopped her.'

'Did she try to get away?'

'Oh yes, but I've got a pretty strong grip.'

Annie smiled. 'Has anyone ever told you you're very like your Aunt Lily?'

'Yes. Mum says that all the time but . . .' Beattie stopped at the sound of voices in the hall and hissed, 'Mark and Cressida are here!' She called out in heavily honeyed tones, 'Hello! We're in here!'

Annie wasn't sure what she'd been expecting – a red-eyed child who could swivel her head 180 degrees perhaps – but she certainly hadn't anticipated the smiling, sweet-faced girl who bounded into the kitchen with her father. She had brown shoulder-length hair with a fringe that stopped just before her big, sparkling hazel eyes. She looked like any other modish young teenager in her designer trainers, grey tracksuit bottoms and skimpy pink T-shirt. She held out her hand to Annie. 'Hello,' she said. 'I'm Cressida. You must be Josephine's sister.'

Annie stood up and grasped her hand. 'It's very nice to meet you,' she said.

'Annie, it's lovely to see you!' Mark came over and kissed her on both cheeks. 'We'd have been here earlier but I remembered I told Josephine I'd do supper tonight and so we've done a quick shop. I hope you like kedgeree and spinach?'

'And I'm making the pudding!' Cressida crowed. 'I'm doing baked bananas and we've bought some ice cream as well! *And* we bought some chocolates!' She darted an anxious look at Annie. 'I hope you like truffles!'

'I *love* truffles,' Annie assured her. 'As soon as I've finished my tea, I shall go down to the off-licence and buy wine fit for such a feast! Where am I sleeping, by the way?'

'On the sofa bed in the study,' Beattie said. 'Now that Cressida's here, we don't have a spare room. I hope you'll be comfortable.'

'I shall be fine!' Annie said. She hoped she was the only one who could detect the slight edge to Beattie's voice. 'So, Cressida, tell me about your drama course.'

Cressida proceeded to chat happily about the forthcoming production of *Grease*. Annie saw Beattie roll her eyes and slip away and couldn't help wondering if she and Sidney weren't being unfair to their new stepsister.

By the time she'd returned from the off-licence, Josephine was home. 'Annie, I'm sorry I wasn't here when you arrived! I had a patient who was determined to give birth naturally but we had to perform a Caesarean in the end. How *are* you? You've bought *two* bottles! That's so generous of you!'

'Not at all,' said Annie who knew from bitter experience that Josephine's kitchen was woefully bereft of alcohol.

She had forgotten the influence of Mark who had already opened a bottle. There were enticing smells emanating from the oven, Beattie was preparing a salad and, judging by the sounds from the sitting room, Cressida was watching *The Simpsons*. Annie saw Mark and Josephine clasp hands for a moment and she felt the little knot of anxiety engendered by Beattie's earlier comments begin to unwind. It dawned on her that perhaps the antipathy Beattie and Sidney felt towards Cressida was motivated by jealousy. After all, they had had their mother to themselves for the last two years. Unwilling to direct their ire at a man who made such efforts to get on with them, they had perhaps targeted all their feelings of exclusion against his daughter.

Mark handed Annie a glass of wine. 'Have you been to see William?' he asked. 'How is he?'

'I went with Lily yesterday afternoon,' Annie said. 'It's horrible. Lily sat talking to him about the boys and I tried to say a few words but there is no response, none at all. The doctors say he's stable and there's nothing more they can do for him in intensive care. They talked about sending him to a hospital for long-term coma patients and Lily just exploded. She said it was far too early to give up on him, she said . . . Well, she said lots of things and in the end they agreed to move him to another ward in the same hospital. I got the feeling they were only going to do that so Lily could get used to the idea that he was never going to wake up.'

Josephine sighed. 'I think they're probably right.'

'It's so *unfair*!' Beattie said. 'You couldn't get a nicer person than William. Has Lily tried playing his favourite music to him? I read about a woman who was awakened by a tape of Cliff Richard. Apparently she'd always adored him and her husband wrote and asked him to tape a personal message for her and he did and she woke up. I think it was Cliff Richard. It might have been Robbie Williams.'

'I know William likes Nancy Sinatra,' Annie said doubtfully. 'I remember he wanted the organist to play "These Boots Are Made for Walking" at the end of their wedding service. He couldn't understand why Lily wouldn't consider it.'

'He likes Dolly Parton too,' Josephine said. 'He told me that "Jolene" was a hundred times more moving than a Mozart symphony. He knew all the words too. He sang the whole song to me once.' She bit her lip. 'I can't bear all this.'

The gloom that fell on the room was lifted by the noisy arrival of Sidney who greeted Annie with an enthusiastic hug and announced he was starving.

'Supper's in ten minutes,' Mark said. 'There's a beer in the fridge.'

'Thanks,' said Sidney. 'I have carried so many suitcases up to people's rooms today. The bigger the suitcase the less the tip I get. You have no idea how hard the work is!'

'Huh!' snorted Beattie.

'It's true,' Sidney protested. 'I feel like I'll never walk again!'

'Welcome to the real world!' Josephine said. 'Some time you might even come home after a full day's work and still find the energy to cook a meal for the family like poor old Mark is doing!'

Annie laughed. 'The day that Sidney learns to cook like Mark is the day I'll invite him to come and stay indefinitely. Incidentally, I know you both said you didn't want any wedding presents but I want to do something and I couldn't help noticing a rather scrummy-looking Indian restaurant when I went to the off-licence. So I booked a table for the three of us tomorrow night.'

'I *love* Indian food!' a voice said. Cressida appeared in the doorway.

'I hope you don't mind,' Annie said, giving Cressida an apologetic smile, 'but I thought that tomorrow we'd keep it to grown-ups only. Next time I promise we'll take Beattie and Sidney and you!'

'Don't make promises like that,' Josephine laughed. 'Do you have any idea how much Sidney eats?'

'I do,' Annie said. 'My fridge is only just beginning to recover!' Her eyes flickered towards Cressida. A moment ago, the girl had looked at her with what, had Annie been of a melodramatic disposition, she might have described as hatred. She saw Cressida take a sip from her father's glass and then giggle at his simulated fury. Annie was chastened. Clearly, she *was* showing signs of a melodramatic disposition.

Supper began well with everyone praising Mark on his culinary expertise. Annie then asked Beattie about her future plans. Beattie reeled them off: brilliant A Level results next year, trail-blazing three years at Cambridge, stellar career in publishing. Sidney then disclosed *his* future plans: possibly dodgy A Level results, hotel porter work for as long as he could stick it, lotus-eating travel in Australia, three years doing as little as possible in Hull, possible career as a computer genius. Annie then asked Mark and Josephine about their careers which led to a discussion on the state of the NHS after which, realizing they were perilously close to discussing William again, Annie reverted abruptly to praise of the kedgeree.

It was during the baked bananas that the trouble began.

Cressida was describing a difficult dance she had tried to learn on the course that day. Josephine said, 'You ought to go over it with Annie. She might be able to help. She teaches English and drama, you know.'

Cressida laughed. 'Mummy says teachers are people who can't think of anything else to do.'

'Really?' Annie said. 'Is that what *you* think?'

Cressida wrinkled her nose. 'I suppose so. *Was* there anything else you could do?'

'Actually,' Josephine said sharply, 'Annie could have done all sorts of things. Originally, she worked for the BBC. She chose to switch to teaching because she knew it was one of the most important jobs in the country.'

'Well,' said Annie, torn between gratitude to her sister for coming to her defence and an uneasy awareness that Josephine was bestowing on her a high-mindedness that wasn't strictly warranted, 'it wasn't quite like that . . .'

'So remind me, Cressida,' Sidney asked, 'what is it your mother does?'

Cressida regarded him with justifiable suspicion. 'She's an estate agent.'

'An estate agent,' repeated Sidney. He nodded knowledgeably at Annie. '*That's* what you should have been!'

Cressida's lower lip wobbled. 'You're making fun of me,' she said accusingly. She looked at her father. 'Sidney's making fun of me!'

'Sidney—' Mark began.

'I think we should change the subject,' Beattie interrupted, showing hitherto unimagined skills in diplomacy. 'Let me tell you about my shoplifter!'

For the second time that evening, Beattie recounted her tale, adding new details that displayed either a particularly acute memory or a highly fertile imagination. Annie couldn't help wondering why, for example, only Beattie had noticed there might be something odd about a girl whose eyes kept darting from one side to the other and whose face was drenched in sweat.

'. . . And so,' Beattie finished, 'I was allowed to come home at lunchtime and take the rest of the day off!'

'Quite right!' approved Josephine. 'How very clever of you!'

'And so,' Beattie continued, 'I decided to spend the time looking for the silver chain I lost last week. And I'm very glad I did because I found it! And, you'll never guess, Mum, I found the bracelet Mark gave you as well!'

'Oh that's wonderful!' said Josephine. 'I've looked everywhere for it! I began to think I was going mad! Where did you find it?'

It was then that Annie understood the reason for Beattie's extraordinary display of diplomacy. Beattie gave a steely smile and said, 'Cressida will probably know the answer to that.'

Everyone looked at Cressida. A dark flush transformed her complexion. 'I didn't steal them!' she croaked. 'I borrowed them! I always meant to give them back! And what were you doing, poking around in my room anyway?' She pushed her chair back, shouted, 'I hate you all!' and ran out of the room. The sound of noisy sobs could be heard trailing up the stairs.

For a few moments, no one said anything. Then Mark stood up, said quietly, 'I think, Beattie, you could have handled that with more compassion,' and followed his daughter out of the room.

Beattie reddened but looked at her mother defiantly. 'I can just imagine asking Cressida tactfully if she had seen my necklace: "Yes, Beattie, I stole it and I'll get it for you right away!" She had no intention of returning them! They were hidden at the back of her drawer under a pile of socks! And don't give me that sorrowing look, Mum; if I hadn't gone and searched for them, you'd never have seen your bracelet again!'

Josephine pushed away her pudding bowl and put her hands together as if she were praying. 'Beattie, you are a clever, confident seventeen-year-old. Cressida is a confused, naive young teenager—'

'Excuse me,' Beattie said sharply, 'but she's not *that* naive. She asked Sidney if he minded being the only eighteen-year-old virgin left in London.'

Josephine's jaw dropped. 'She said *what*?'

'Beattie!' Sidney protested.

'I'm sorry, Sidney, I didn't mean to eavesdrop, I was passing your room when I heard her. And for your information, I know at least three other eighteen-year-olds who are virgins, so you shouldn't worry about it!'

Sidney blushed furiously. 'I *wasn't* worried!'

'I should think not!' said Josephine hotly. 'Do you realize that the rates of sexually transmitted infections have trebled among men and women over the last ten years? In the last year chlamydia has risen by eight per cent and diagnoses of syphilis have gone up by twenty-eight per cent! In the circumstances, Sidney, you show great sense in choosing to abstain!'

'Thanks,' Sidney muttered, staring fixedly at his pudding bowl.

'Chlamydia, gonorrhoea and genital warts are all rife

amongst your age group,' pursued Josephine. 'We are talking about an epidemic here—'

'Mum!' protested Sidney, pushing away his bananas. 'Do we have to talk about genital warts? I know about genital warts! You're always talking about genital warts!'

'I'm sorry. It's a subject I feel very strongly about.' Josephine sighed deeply. 'What I was *trying* to say before I got sidetracked was that Cressida is an unhappy, insecure child. It was unkind to show her up in front of everyone. It was unkind and it was cruel. We all have to make allowances for her—'

'I am *so* fed up with making allowances for Cressida!' Beattie exclaimed. 'Has it occurred to you to wonder why your son and your daughter don't actually like being at home any more? I don't even feel this *is* my home now!' She pulled out her mobile from her pocket like a cowboy reaching for his gun. 'I'm going out! And don't worry, Mum, you'll soon have all the time you need to cherish poor, sweet little Cressida because I tell you something: Sidney and I are leaving home as soon as we possibly can and we won't bother coming back!'

Beattie strode out of the room. There was an awkward silence. The front door slammed and Josephine bit her lip. She said quietly, 'She's gone out without her jacket, Sidney. There's a nasty wind tonight. Go after her and give it to her, will you?'

Sidney left without a word. Glancing round the table, Annie noticed that everyone had left the bananas. They looked like slugs stuck in glue. Annie knew she would never want to eat baked bananas again.

Josephine rubbed the sides of her forehead with her index fingers. 'I'm sorry,' she murmured. 'You mustn't think it's like this every night.'

'I'm sure it isn't. And I'm sure Beattie didn't mean the things she said.'

'No.' Josephine reached over for Beattie's bowl and forked the bananas onto her half-empty one. 'She was angry. She gets angry sometimes. Would you like a coffee or some tea?'

'Not at the moment.' Annie saw Josephine glance anxiously in the direction of the stairs. 'Look, do you want to go up and talk to Cressida? I'll do the clearing up.'

'You shouldn't. You're the guest.'

'For goodness sake, I'm your sister. Go on upstairs! Go!'

By the time Josephine came down again, Annie had cleared the table, loaded the dishwasher and tackled most of the pans. Josephine picked up a tea towel and began to dry the casserole dish. 'Mark's decided,' she said carefully, 'that he won't come out with us tomorrow night. I said that we'd eat at home together in that case but he thinks it's better if we go so that he can have a quiet evening on his own with Cressida. Do you mind if it's just me?'

'Of course not!' Annie said warmly. 'I'm sorry Mark feels he can't come. Would it help if I invited Cressida to come with us?'

'I don't think so,' Josephine said. 'They both seem to think they want some time on their own.'

'Right. That's probably a good idea. Never mind! We'll have a great time together! It will be fun!'

'Yes,' said Josephine without much conviction. She looked like she had long since forgotten what that word meant.

When Josephine asked Annie the next morning what she was going to do with her day, Annie said she thought she might visit Tate Modern and check-out the new Hopper exhibition. In fact, as soon as she set foot on the pavement, she decided that what she needed after the dramas of the last few days was retail therapy.

Ever since she had bought and kitted out her present flat, her idea of retail thereapy had, through financial necessity, taken on a slightly different meaning to that of most people. So this morning she headed for Harrods and spent a happy couple of hours trying on a variety of outfits, the combined total of which, she noted happily, amounted to seven thousand, five hundred and sixty-four pounds.

Having handed them back with a wistful sigh, she then went to Piccadilly, stopping only for an overpriced sandwich and cappuccino. She spent half an hour in a bookshop and after much deliberation bought a book for twelve pounds, ninety-nine pence and escaped with her purchase before she could succumb to further temptation.

Having exhausted all consumerist desires, she decided that since she had told Josephine she was going to Tate Modern, it might be a good idea if she *did* go. By the time she got there via the underground and a brisk walk along the Thames, she decided she had better go straight to the Hopper exhibition before she went to sleep.

She was not overly impressed by the collection. The pictures seemed to be full of hard-faced, heavy-jawed women with the bodies of swimming champions who gazed out of windows with blank faces. Eventually she stopped in front of a sinister-looking painting of a mismatched couple outside a house near a dark wood. Annie decided that Edward Hopper must have been a very gloomy man indeed. Perhaps he'd had problems with evil stepdaughters.

Annie sat on a bench and continued to look vacantly at the painting. She tried to focus on the dark forest and the glowering sky but an image of Cressida's crumpling face came into her mind. Annie wasn't sure if it was the influence of Hopper or the exhaustion of travelling round London but she was suddenly attacked by a nasty bout of guilt. Was *she* responsible for last night's disastrous dinner? If she had agreed to take Cressida to the restaurant, then perhaps Cressida would not have been driven to make disparaging remarks about the teaching profession and then Beattie might have refrained from revealing Cressida's jewellery-lifting antics. Annie sighed and focused again on the canvas in front of her. Had Hopper deliberately drawn the house to make it look like the one in *Psycho*? She shut her eyes for a moment and at once had a fearful vision of a demented Cressida sticking a knife in her shoulder.

Back at Herne Hill, Britney Spears and 'Oops, I've done It Again' was battling out with Radiohead and the Scissor Sisters. Presumably all three teenagers were skulking in their rooms. Annie thought for a moment of her calm, tranquil flat and gave herself a mental memo to remember this moment next time she got the baby blues.

Mark and Josephine were in the kitchen and the atmosphere

was thick with tension. Annie's automatic reaction was to gabble her way through the minefield. 'Hi, you two, I'm sorry I'm so late, I should have been back hours ago but I went to Tate Modern and I saw the Edward Hopper exhibition and every picture seemed to be full of unhappy couples . . .' *Red Alert! Don't mention unhappy couples! One mine detonated! Get back on track, you gibbering fool!* 'And anyway then I walked towards the bus stop and I got talking to this homeless girl and she told me she ran away from home after her stepfather beat her up and . . .' *Red alert! Another detonation! Don't mention step-parents!* 'And then I bought her a sandwich, which I freely admit I wouldn't have done had I not been coming here and wanting to impress my big sister! Then I went to the wrong bus stop and so here I am now better late than never and I'll go and freshen up and then we'll get off to our restaurant so I'll see you in a minute, all right?'

She disappeared off to the study before either of her listeners could respond, which was just as well. It could have been worse, Annie thought, kneeling down to reach for her make-up bag which had fallen under Josephine's swivelling chair. She could have revealed a further revelation from the homeless girl, namely that 'our family were fine until my stepdad joined us'.

By the time she returned to the kitchen, Mark was on his own there, gazing at the screen of his laptop. He looked up when she came in and said politely, 'Josephine will be down in a moment.'

'Thanks.' Annie hesitated; she was unsure whether Mark's statement implied dismissal or welcome. 'You're working. I'll get out of your way.'

'No, that's fine.' *Which meant, of course, it wasn't.*

'Mark, I'm sorry about last night. I feel it was my fault. I should have invited Cressida to come with us.'

'There's no reason for you to blame yourself.' *You are one hundred per cent responsible.*

'I just wanted you to know I'm sorry. And I'm sorry you won't be coming out with us tonight.'

'I'm sure you and Josephine will have a much better time without me.'

Oh God, Annie thought, he was seriously angry. 'I don't think that's true at all,' she said awkwardly. 'In fact I suspect any pleasure Josephine might have had went out of the window the moment you said you wouldn't come.'

'Are you saying I've spoilt your evening?'

'I think it's a pity we're having an Indian meal without you, that's all.'

'Well you needn't worry about that. Cressida and I are going to have an Indian takeaway.'

Game, set and match to Cressida. Annie saw Mark give a meaningful glance at his computer screen and was about to leave when Josephine came in. She had changed out of her work clothes into a Laura Ashley dress that had first seen the light of day when she had been pregnant with Beattie. 'Right then! I'm ready to go!' she announced in breezy tones that could have fooled no one. 'Mark, I've checked with Sidney and Beattie and they're both going out so you needn't worry about feeding them.'

'I wasn't worried,' Mark said tonelessly. 'Have a good time.'

One reason why Annie had adored *Dallas* too many years ago was because despite the fact that the oil-rich Texan family was famously dysfunctional, it did at least communicate: often with cruelty, always with passion. Annie had often in her own life felt constrained and frustrated by a very English reserve which in her view was too often mistaken for politeness. Lily didn't have it and neither did her father. Their bluntness could offend and their tactlessness was legendary but at least it was easier to tackle than the dense fog of repressed rage. If Annie had been Lily, she would probably have told Mark to stop being such a kill-joy and get his coat on. But if Annie had been Lily she would not be here because Josephine could only cope with Lily when her life was going well.

So Annie turned her back on Sue Ellen and J.R. and instead said brightly, 'We will! We'll see you later!' and waltzed out of the house as if nothing was even slightly wrong.

Josephine remained relentlessly cheerful as they walked down the road, assuming a huge interest in Annie's trip to Harrods despite the fact that Annie knew it was a shop that Josephine would never choose to enter. By the time they got to the restaurant, Annie was gasping for some alcohol and horrified her sister by ordering a bottle of red immediately.

'Annie!' Josephine murmured. 'We'll never drink a bottle between us!'

'Watch me!' said Annie. Knowing that Josephine would ask for the cheapest item on the menu, she ruthlessly took charge and ordered poppadoms, chicken biriani, pilau rice, a couple of samosas and some aubergine bhaji. She filled both their glasses and listened to her sister tell her what a long time it had been since she had come out for a really good meal and what fun this all was.

Josephine was a lousy liar. Annie looked into her sister's strained eyes and knew she couldn't face a whole evening of this. Come back, J.R. and Sue Ellen, she thought, I need you now. She took a deep breath and went into action.

'Josephine,' she said, 'what are you going to do about Cressida?'

Josephine blinked. 'I know she has problems—' she began defensively.

'She doesn't *have* problems! She *is* a problem. Last time I saw you, you and Mark were blissfully happy and now . . . Now, you're not. You have to do something!'

'I *am* doing something. I'm trying to make Cressida feel at home.'

'And in the process you're driving out your own children!'

'I'm not doing anything of the sort. I'm . . .' Josephine stopped to smile politely at the waiter as he brought their poppadoms. After he left, she looked earnestly at her sister. 'Cressida's had a difficult time. She's an only child and for most of her life her parents have not got on. Mark left home three years ago when he found out that Amanda had been having an affair. It had been going on for five years! Can you believe it? The lover left Amanda as soon as she said she was free and so Amanda decided she wanted Mark back. Mark couldn't tell Cressida *why* he had left home so—'

'Why couldn't he?'

'Because he didn't want Cressida to think badly of her mother.'

'Right, so now she thinks badly of him instead and he spends his time trying to make up to her for something he was never guilty of in the first place! Brilliant!'

'No, he spends his time trying to make her happy. This is a girl whose mother has had to choose between her new boyfriend and her daughter and who chose her new boyfriend. Imagine what that must do to a girl.'

'I don't care about that. I see an unpleasant child who's splitting *your* family apart and you're just letting it happen!'

Josephine split her poppadom, dipped a piece into the tomato relish and ate it. She poured herself some water but it was her wine glass that she raised to her lips.

'You do see that, don't you?' Annie demanded.

Josephine put her glass down. 'Life's so simple for you. It always has been. Everything's black or white, either people are good or they're bad. If people do something terrible then that's it, they're out, they're one hundred per cent bad. Look at you and Ben and I'm sorry, I know you don't like talking about Ben, but I don't particularly like you telling me after one evening what I'm doing wrong with my family, so we're quits. Ben does something bad so that's it, you cut him out of your life! There's no room in your life for compassion or understanding or for error.'

'I think,' Annie said stiffly, 'that you're being a little unfair. The man left me at the altar! He didn't even have the decency to let me know so we could at least stop all the guests arriving! You don't need any understanding to know that's about the most cowardly and cruel behaviour you could find!'

'He did try to let you know.'

'What? What do you mean?'

'He did try to let you know.' Josephine moved her cutlery to accommodate the waiter who had returned with a trolley full of food. He set the dishes on the table and explained carefully the ingredients of each. After he left, Josephine picked up a serving spoon. 'Do you want me to serve you?' she asked.

'No, help yourself. What did you mean when you said he tried to let me know?'

'When you were in France, he came to see me. I was working at St Thomas's. He wanted to know where you were. I said I couldn't tell him. He said he'd rung you twice on the evening before the wedding. He'd got Dad both times and had given him a number and asked him to ask you to ring it.'

'So what did you say? Poor old Ben, we've misunderstood you?'

'No, I told him he was a fool. He knew Dad well enough to know that he never takes in anything that isn't work-related during a crisis. But the fact is at least he tried to—'

'He *tried*? He rang twice and spoke to a man who was obviously preoccupied and who is notorious for forgetting to pass on messages! Did Ben try to ring me the next morning?'

'I don't know.'

'It doesn't matter if he did. He knew, he *knew* that he was setting me up for the biggest humiliation ever and he didn't stop it. It doesn't matter what people *say*, it matters what they actually *do*. Ben might have told you he tried to talk to me but the fact remains that he did not talk to me and at one o'clock the next day he had still not talked to me. It doesn't matter that Cressida acts the way she does because she's upset, what matters is that her behaviour is driving your children away. I have never heard Beattie speak to you like that before.'

'You can't blame that on Cressida. Beattie and Sidney are at the age where people start being difficult. If you had children of your own, you'd know what I mean!' Josephine flushed. 'I'm sorry. I didn't mean . . . Look, I really don't want to talk about any of this any more.'

'Fine,' Annie said. She took a mouthful of aubergine.

'It's very good,' Josephine said. 'I do love Indian food.'

'I'm sorry if you thought I was interfering,' Annie said stiffly. 'Obviously you know far more than I do about teen-agers. You're a mother. I'm sorry.'

'I'm sorry too. I shouldn't have mentioned Ben. And I wasn't saying that—'

'That as a childless woman I should stop pontificating about your offspring? It's all right, I quite agree. I won't do it again.' She forced another mouthful of aubergine into her mouth, kicked J.R. into the corner and proceeded to ask her sister about the one subject that could restore her equilibrium. 'Tell me,' she said, 'is it true that genital warts are on the increase?'

Josephine's mouth twitched and for the first time that evening a genuine twinkle lit her eyes. 'If you don't stop hogging that aubergine dish,' she said, 'I might just tell you.'

CHAPTER THIRTEEN

Black Book Entry, 3 August: Ben Seymour for not growing fat and bald and smelly.

The flat was silent as a church and hot as hell. The first thing Annie did after kicking off her shoes was to open the big sash windows in her bedroom and the sitting room. Then she threw herself onto her sofa and stretched her limbs.

How lucky she was! It was mid-afternoon and all she had to do before bedtime was to buy some provisions, have a shower and relax. She thought of Josephine who had endured years of unremitting drudgery with a husband who had never learnt how to use the washing machine and two further years of full-time work and rearing of teenagers without even *his* support, feeble though it was. She had had a short glimpse of Nirvana and was now back to looking pinched and tense. Annie had sensed an almost fatalistic attitude in her sister, as if she felt that unhappiness was a natural component of her life. And then there was Lily who was probably sitting in the hospital ward right now, watching the man she loved drift ever closer to death.

It was ironic that for all these years her family had pitied *her* and now it appeared that, unencumbered by messy attachments, she had by far the easiest existence. Annie stood up, slipped on her shoes, gathered up her bag, went out into the afternoon sun and vowed she would never feel sorry for herself again.

Her food shop did not take long since she was off to Totnes the next day. She bought bread, cheese and milk and decided to walk back via Henrietta Park and the Garden of Remembrance. The Garden of Remembrance was her most favourite place in Bath. It was an enclosed garden with a rectangular pond, surrounded by a variety of bowers within each of which was a bench donated in memory of a previous inhabitant of the city. Annie liked to think that one day someone would donate a bench in honour of *her* memory. The way things were going, she'd probably have to donate it herself.

Although the park was full of people, the garden was miraculously empty. Annie wandered over to the bench at the far end of the pond and sat down. It was surrounded by lavender and she breathed in the fragrance, shut her eyes and listened to the birdsong emanating from the trees behind her. It was good to be back in Bath, good to be away from the horrors of green-haired muggers and malevolent stepchildren.

When she opened her eyes, she found she was no longer alone. An elderly couple sat holding hands on one of the benches nearest the gate. They were chatting quietly and every now and again the woman would chuckle and smile at her companion. Then the man leant towards the woman and kissed her cheek.

Annie stood up and walked towards the gate. She smiled at the couple and said, 'It's a lovely day!'

The man responded fervently: 'It's a *perfect* day!'

Annie nodded in agreement and walked away without looking back, although she longed to look back because she was enthralled. He had sounded *ecstatic*! What had happened to produce such an exalted condition? Perhaps he had loved her for years but she had been married to a man who burped and farted and picked his nose and perhaps she had loved him but had been stuck with the nose-picker and perhaps a few months ago the nose-picker died and he had plucked up his courage to tell her shyly, hesitatingly, this very morning, that he loved her and she had told him shyly and hesitatingly that she loved him too. Or perhaps, just perhaps, they were one of that almost extinct species, a happily married couple. Whatever they were, a bit of that ecstasy had settled like stardust on Annie and she walked home with a lightness of spirit that bubbled like champagne.

She had planned a lazy cup of tea in front of afternoon television but happiness, even when it was second-hand, proved to be a strong stimulant. So instead, she unpacked, did some washing, had a shower and spent a deliberately frivolous twenty minutes applying make-up and putting on her favourite summer dress, a pale lemon number held up by the narrowest of straps. She *should* ring Lily and possibly Josephine but she couldn't face either of them at the moment. She wanted to hang on to that stardust for as long as possible. 'I am happy,' she told her mirror. 'I am free and I look good and I am ready to go!'

The only problem was she had nowhere to go *to*. She

glanced at her watch. It was ten past seven. She could have a glass of wine, make her toasted cheese sandwich, ring a friend and talk about her sisters, which would make her feel marginally less guilty about not ringing them. It was just her bad luck that her two best friends, Grace and Hannah, the women whose advice she would most value, were both on holiday in, respectively, Portugal and Jersey.

Annie could feel the stardust evaporating around her. 'I'm happy,' she reminded herself doggedly, 'I'm free, I am a woman without complications . . .'

The buzzer sprang into life, providing a welcome termination to Annie's catechism. She strode across the flat and picked up the door phone.

'Annie?' The voice was cautious. 'Are you there? Can I come up for a moment?'

Annie's first, instinctive reaction was to be grateful for the happy synchronicity that had led Ben to her door on one of the few evenings when she looked presentable. Her second reaction was to be revolted by her first reaction and to tell him to go away. Her third reaction was to remember that the last time she had seen him, he had driven all the way to Lily's house in order to make her lunch.

She said, 'I'll let you in.'

When she opened the door, he was standing on the bottom step as if ready for flight. 'You look good,' he told her. 'Are you on your way out?'

Ben looked pretty good too. He wore dark trousers, a casual grey pinstriped jacket and a white shirt.

Annie said, 'No, I got back this afternoon from a rather

gruelling time in London. What you see here is some hastily executed repair work.'

'Then it's very successful.'

'Thank you.'

'I was passing and I rang on the off chance you'd be free to come out and have that supper we missed a few weeks ago.'

Ben's golden hair gleamed in the evening sun and his blue eyes seemed especially bright. 'I don't think that's a good idea,' Annie said.

'The thing is I saw Frances the other week and she was asking about how we met. I managed to change the subject but I know it will come up again and I need to know what it is you want me to say.'

Annie glanced at him suspiciously. 'It's very good of you to be so concerned about what I want.'

She saw Ben shrug modestly. If she refused to go out she would be facing a solitary evening with a toasted cheese sandwich. And it was true that they did have to sort out a sanitized history to satisfy the curiosity of her friends. She said abruptly, 'All right. Wait there while I get my bag.'

She turned and ran upstairs. She picked up her cardigan and bag and checked her appearance in the mirror. She was aware that the stardust was hovering again . . . funny how the prospect of a good meal could alter a mood! She closed the door behind her, ran back down the stairs and into the hall.

Mrs Bartlett who lived in the ground-floor flat was chatting on the doorstep to Ben. She smiled sweetly at Annie and said, 'I've told your young man that I'm glad he's found you at last!'

Annie was startled into silence. By the time she was ready to assure Mrs Bartlett that Ben was neither young nor her man, the old lady had returned to her flat. Annie raised her eyebrows. 'What *did* she mean by that?'

'I have no idea. Is she a bit –' Ben cast a significant glance in Mrs Bartlett's direction – 'funny?'

'Not that I've noticed.' Annie slipped on her cardigan. 'Shall we go?'

Ben fell into place beside her. 'I thought we could try the French restaurant again.'

'I doubt if you'll get in. The tourist season is in full swing now.'

'We can try. Tell me: how's your brother-in-law?'

Annie sighed. 'No improvement. He lies there like he's dead.'

'Your nephews told me about a game he plays with them and their friends. They called it Monsters and Victims. They say he has to chase them all around the garden. He must be pretty fit if he does that on a regular basis.'

Annie gave a grim laugh. 'Every time he plays that game, Lily thinks he's going to have a heart attack. He's grossly over-weight. He's a lovely man. You'd like him.'

'I'm sure I would. It's funny though. I always thought Lily would end up marrying someone tall, dark, handsome and rich.'

'William is certainly rich but even his best friends wouldn't call him handsome. What's really funny is that she loves him and I've only just realized it. She goes to the hospital every day, battles with the doctors, looks a million dollars and, inside, her heart is breaking. It's rotten.'

They had arrived at the restaurant and, as Annie had forecast, it did indeed look heavily occupied. Ben, however, charged in and was greeted like a long-lost brother by a man who, judging by his age and his bearing, was the proprietor.

'Hello, Marcel,' Ben said. 'Do you perhaps have a table for two?'

'But of course, Monsieur Seymour. Come this way!'

Annie found herself being shepherded to a table by the window set apart from the rest of the dining room. She saw Marcel whip away a reserved notice and hoped that they would not be interrupted later by some irate couple.

Marcel handed out menus and looked enquiringly at Ben. 'Would you like a drink while you wait? I can recommend a bottle of the Grand Mayne.'

Ben looked at Annie. 'Are you happy with that?'

'Very happy,' Annie said. She waited until Marcel had gone and then hissed, 'How come he knows who you are?'

'I got chatting to him when I was waiting for you last time. And I think he recognizes me from the television. Now, what are you going to eat? And forget the one-course thing. Everyone says you have to eat the starters here, they're brilliant.'

'Who is everyone?' Annie demanded. 'This is not a cheap restaurant.'

'I doubt you'll ever let me take you out again,' Ben said, 'so this is on me.'

'All right.' Annie picked up the menu and didn't even bother to look at the prices. If he wanted to flash his money around like the celebrity he *wasn't* then she was happy to help him.

By the time Marcel had returned with the wine, she and Ben were both ready to give their order. Annie chose French onion soup and coq au vin while Ben went for pâté and duck.

'An excellent choice, Monsieur Seymour,' Marcel told him. He filled their glasses, smiled benevolently at them both and left them with an exhortation to enjoy their wine.

Ben settled back in his chair. 'Tell me about London. Were you with Lily all the time?'

'No. I stayed two nights with Josephine. It was terrible.'

'Why?'

Annie had planned to stick rigidly to the agreed agenda but Ben looked interested and she was keen to offload the experience and discuss her possible responsibility for the recent rows and recriminations. She told Ben about Clement, about Mark, about Beattie's revelation and the ensuing scene and concluded with a confused assessment of Cressida. 'The thing is I know Josephine is right on one level. Cressida has had a hard time and is obviously unhappy and sees Sidney and Beattie as possible rivals for her father's affections. But on the other hand Sidney and Beattie are right too. There is something downright sinister about the way she acts *in front* of her father and the way she behaves when he's not around. I'm convinced she's determined to get rid of Josephine and Josephine's incapable of fighting back. Fighting Josephine is like stabbing a pillow with a knife. Cressida can't lose. And what's so tragic is that Josephine was so happy with Mark! They were so good together! And there's absolutely nothing I can do!'

The waiter arrived with their first course. Annie eyed Ben's plate with interest and told him a little smugly that she was glad she had chosen the soup.

'The thing is,' Ben said, 'I can make a perfectly good French onion soup myself.'

'Since when did you learn to cook so well?'

'I lived for four years with a woman who couldn't cook. It was a case of either starving or learning how to do it.'

'I see.' Annie picked up her spoon and dipped it into her bowl. She wished she hadn't asked him now.

'I've thought of something you could do,' Ben said.

Annie, unaccountably preoccupied by thoughts of the four-year girlfriend, stared blankly at him.

'About Cressida,' Ben said. 'You say she wants to get rid of Josephine and have her father to herself. You could go and stay and pretend you want to get rid of Josephine too and move in on him for yourself. You can make it clear you are a true femme fatale and—'

'What?'

'You're a femme fatale and Mark is to be your next victim. You must make her think that Snow White's stepmother was like Mary Poppins in comparison with you. After that, she'll be desperate to keep Josephine with her father. It's a brilliant idea!' He picked up the bottle of wine and topped up Annie's glass. 'What do you think?'

Annie's mouth twitched. 'Do you really want to know?'

'I certainly do.'

'For a start, Mark is barely talking to me and has never shown any sign that he even knows I'm a woman. And secondly, I do not exactly look like a femme fatale.'

'I disagree. You're the most attractive woman I've ever known.'

She stared at him, startled. 'Don't say that.'

'I'm just stating a fact.'

'That's rubbish!' She directed a challenging glare at him. He met her gaze squarely without any apparent awareness that he had said anything out of the ordinary. She was the first to look away.

He cleared his throat. 'Annie—'

'Don't!'

'You don't know what I'm about to say.'

'You want to talk about the past.'

'Of course I do. The past informs the present. It's impossible to sit here with you and *not* talk about the past.'

'If you start talking about the past then I'm walking out. I can't have a rational conversation with you about the past. I can't even have an *irrational* conversation with you about the past.' She took a gulp of her wine and groped for safe ground. 'Anyway the femme fatale idea is stupid. I can't see Josephine, let alone Mark, inviting me again in a hurry. The whole thing is hopeless.' She was diverted by the sight of Ben refilling his glass. 'If you're driving back to Bristol tonight,' she said severely, 'you shouldn't be drinking a second glass.'

'I thought I'd stay in Bath tonight.'

'Really?' Annie asked with a smile of steel. 'Were you planning to stay at my place?'

'That's very kind of you but I thought I'd stay in my own house.'

'I thought your house wasn't going to be ready for ages!'

'It isn't, but I camp out there sometimes. I'm hoping to move in properly at the end of August.'

'I see. And by the way, you know very well that I wasn't

210

inviting you to stay with me. I'd rather die than invite you to stay with me.'

'How was the soup?'

Annie bit her tongue and muttered that it was very nice. She was glad that the waiter arrived to collect their dishes. She reminded herself of the reason she had come out with him and said abruptly, 'Shall we sort out our story for Frances and the others? What exactly have you told everyone so far?'

'What *we* have told everyone,' Ben corrected her. 'We met at the BBC and then for some peculiar reason I went out with both of your sisters in no particular order. So how did I meet them? Perhaps they both came to see you and I was talking to you at the time and they were both immediately smitten with me.'

'Definitely not,' Annie said. 'That's just not credible.'

'I think it's highly credible.'

'You *would* think that.'

'Some of your friends,' Ben said significantly, 'wouldn't find that incredible at all.'

'Yes they would,' Annie said. Her eyes narrowed suspiciously. 'Are you thinking of anyone in particular?'

'My lips are sealed.'

'It's Carla, isn't it? Is it? It is! Why on earth do you think she wants to go out with you?'

'She invited me to go to the theatre with her.'

'Did you go?'

'Unfortunately, I was otherwise engaged.'

Some previously unknown devil in her brain instantly wanted Annie to find out what the other engagement was. Her resident angel thumped the devil in the stomach and

211

encouraged her to respond sardonically, 'I'm sure you and Carla have a lot in common.'

'That's very kind of you.'

'I didn't mean it as a compliment.' Perhaps it was as well for Annie's temper that Marcel interrupted them to bring their main course and discuss the next bottle of wine. Ben settled for a Chateau Berliquet.

Annie looked at her coq au vin and smiled. 'Last night,' she told Ben, 'I took my elder sister out to dinner and ordered a bottle of wine and she said we would never manage a whole bottle and now you and I are already on our second!'

'We need it,' Ben assured her. 'The thought of going out with both Lily and Josephine makes me feel quite faint.'

Marcel poured the Chateau Berliquet. Annie downed the rest of her white wine while Ben tasted the red and pronounced it perfect. After Marcel had left them, Annie leant forward. 'You went out with Josephine for a couple of months. Then, when she realized you were her intellectual inferior, she dumped you. By this time you were very fond of all my family. So you asked Lily out—'

'Why didn't I ask you out?'

'Because I found you physically repellent.'

'Excuse me,' Ben said, 'but I'm not going to tell anyone you found me physically repellent.'

'That's all right,' Annie said ruthlessly, 'I'll do that! So you go out with Lily for a little while and then . . .' She paused to take a mouthful of chicken.

'Let me guess,' Ben said. 'Lily decides that she finds me physically repellent too. After which you are so embarrassed by my humiliation that you and I no longer talk to each other.'

212

'You've got it!'

'And meanwhile, what no one realizes is that even while I am seeing Josephine and Lily, my heart in fact belongs to you.'

'I think,' Annie said reprovingly, 'that would make the story far more complicated than it needs to be.'

'Excuse me?'

A middle-aged woman with an American accent smiled apologetically at them. 'I'm sorry to break in on your dinner but –' she nodded at Ben – 'I had you in my hotel room last night!'

Annie laughed. 'Really?'

'Unfortunately only on the TV screen! Would you mind if I had your autograph? Would you sign my guidebook?'

'Of course.' Ben took out his pen and signed with a flourish.

The lady had been joined by her companion, a distinguished-looking man with a superb mane of grey hair. 'Come along, Amy,' he said. 'Leave these good people alone! I have to tell you, sir, that you've given me a lot of trouble tonight. My wife has been watching you and she keeps asking me why I don't look at her the way you look at this young lady here! Goodbye now!'

After the couple had left, Ben and Annie both concentrated on their food for a few seconds. Then Ben said carelessly, 'Nice people.'

'Very.' Annie agreed. She said conversationaily, 'Do you often get people coming up to you like that?'

'Not really. As I think you once pointed out, I am hardly a celebrity.'

'Would you like to be?'

213

'God, no. My worst nightmare would be to have my private life picked over by people who have never met me. I wouldn't like my private life to be picked over by people who *do* know me. And nowadays if you go into the spotlight you have to make this Faustian pact which involves telling everybody about everything. Definitely not for me. Imagine what it must be like to be Julia Roberts or Tom Cruise knowing that every time they venture out people are speculating about what they're doing.'

'Yes,' Annie said, 'the poor things are reduced to visiting uninhabited islands for their holidays while the rest of us are free to visit far more interesting places like Totnes.'

'Is that where you're off to next?'

Annie nodded. Actually, Totnes seemed a million miles away at the moment. She was surprised by a gentle hiccup and a few seconds later by a less gentle one.

'Have some water,' Ben advised. 'Drink it quickly.'

'I'm not drunk,' Annie assured him.

'I didn't think you were.'

Annie took a sip of water and then followed it with a gulp of wine. 'I do have a tendency to get hiccups,' she said. 'I got terrible hiccups at Lily's wedding reception. Then Sidney jumped from the table onto my shoulders and that worked.'

'How clever of Sidney,' Ben said gravely. 'I'm sure you were grateful.'

'I was actually,' said Annie. 'It was a pity he broke three plates while he was doing it but I was certainly grateful. Usually, though, if I drink a glass of water very quickly, they go.'

This time the water failed to help. Annie was still hiccuping as they walked back along Great Pulteney Street. They stopped outside Annie's front door and Ben thanked her for a lovely evening.

'I've just remembered,' Annie said. 'I have something for you. Do you mind coming upstairs with me?'

'No,' Ben said. 'I don't mind at all.'

She left him in the sitting room while she went to her bedroom. When she returned he was staring at the photo of her parents on the mantelpiece. 'When you get old,' he said, 'you'll look just like your mother.'

'Is that good?'

'That's very good.'

Annie gave him the book she had bought in London. 'It's a biography of Cary Grant,' she said. 'It's essential reading. It mentions Gary Cooper quite a few times. Apparently he was very rude and snubbed Cary Grant the first time he met him.' She hiccuped again. 'Damn!'

Ben put the book down on the desk and went over to her. Then he kissed her. He framed her face with his hands and he kissed her. And Annie was so surprised she just stood there and let him. He withdrew his hands and said, 'Did that work?'

'I'm sorry?'

'I was doing a Sidney. Shock therapy.'

'It was certainly a shock,' Annie said. 'I'm not sure it's worked.'

And so he kissed her again. And this time it was less of a shock and even more enjoyable. She felt him pull off her cardigan and now his mouth was skimming the back of her neck and her first reaction was one of divine pleasure and her second reaction was to wonder *how* he knew exactly where to

215

touch her and her third reaction was to remember *why* he knew exactly where to touch her and her fourth reaction was to raise protesting hands to his chest.

He stepped back at once. 'If things were different,' he murmured, 'I'd ask you if I could stay.'

'If things were different,' Annie whispered, 'I'd let you.'

The left strap of her dress had fallen off her shoulder. Ben pushed it back up again. 'I'd better go,' he said. 'Thank you for the evening.'

'Thank you for my dinner.'

She showed him out of the flat and watched him go down the stairs. 'Ben!' she called. 'Stop!'

He looked up.

'You've forgotten your book! I'll get it!' She dashed back into the sitting room, picked up the book and went out onto the landing where Ben was now waiting. He took it without speaking and went back down the stairs.

'Ben!' she said again. 'Stop!'

Ben looked up.

'I wanted to tell you something,' she said. 'Way back then, after you know what, I want you to know I never thought about it. Not for a second. I just wanted you to know.'

Ben shook his head. 'I haven't a clue what you're going on about,' he said. 'But I have to tell you your strap has fallen off your shoulder again and if you stop me one more time I'm going to find it intensely difficult to leave you alone. Goodbye, Annie.'

She heard the front door slam and went back into her flat. She could still feel the sensation of his lips on her neck. Even the gorgeous Robbie had never had the power over her neck that Ben had enjoyed. He had always known that he had only to touch her neck and she would melt.

The devil in Annie's mind was going berserk, demanding that she go after him and drag him back to her bed. Annie took a deep breath. She knew what she had to do.

The cold shower did not work. Eventually she got out of bed and went to the sitting room and turned on the television. She tried to concentrate on the horror film in front of her and realized too late that vampires had a thing about necks too.

CHAPTER FOURTEEN

Black Book Entry, 5 August: Ben Seymour for jilting me . . . just to remind myself.

It was the alcohol. The throbbing in her temples the next morning proved it was the alcohol. Unfortunately, alcohol did not produce amnesia. When she woke the next morning, her first thought was of the way she'd felt when Ben kissed her.

It was her own fault. In trying to detach Ben Present from Ben Past and regard him as an acquaintance and no more, she had failed to take into account the fact that Ben Present continued, against all the laws of justice, to be just as physically attractive as Ben Past.

Now, driving down to Devon, Annie was barely aware of the changing landscape. She felt she was on the brink of a huge revelation, like that tantalizing moment just before orgasm when one knows one is about to achieve total bliss . . . She was doing it again, she was thinking about sex, even with a hangover she was thinking about sex. Could anything be sadder than to have a kiss from Ben and react by turning into one of those pathetic souls who can drive past the starkly beautiful Glastonbury Tor and its dramatic fifteenth-century tower and see only a phallic symbol?

She directed her eyes firmly towards the road in front of her and for the next few minutes concentrated on negotiating Glastonbury's one-way system. She switched on the radio. Mick Jagger was singing 'Let's Spend the Night Together'. Annie switched off the radio. This was ridiculous. *She* was ridiculous. How could she have kissed Ben of all people? How could she have enjoyed kissing Ben? If he had not gone home when he did and if he had made the same suggestion as Mick Jagger, would she have remained steadfast and told him to go? And if not, why not?

Because I fancy him, she thought. And that was it. That was the answer. That was the revelation. She was like Henry the Eighth who destroyed all the monasteries simply because he fancied Anne Boleyn. She was like Mark Antony who threw away a brilliant career just because he desired Cleopatra. How could he love Cleopatra? They had nothing in common, they probably couldn't even speak each other's language: he just fancied her. And she, Annie May, was exactly the same. Her feelings for Ben Seymour, the great love of her life, had always been powered by sex. Forget the perfect life-partner rubbish; she had fallen for Ben and had probably wanted to marry Ben because she had wanted a lifetime of great sex. If she was right – and Annie was convinced now she *was* right, the evidence was clear, her behaviour last night only proved her thesis – then liberation from Ben Past and Present was definitely possible.

She thought back to the first time she met Ben. She had gone to the cinema with some friends from work and in the queue they had met up with some other colleagues. Annie had ended up sitting next to Ben and during one particularly blood-curdling bit – it was *The Fly* and Jeff Goldblum had turned into the eponymous creature and made horrible noises and looked disgusting and was trying to kill poor Geena Davis – she had gripped his thigh. It was a very nice thigh, thick and solid and its attraction had been enough to distract her from the blood and gore on the screen. It was true that in the pub afterwards they had talked with an ease and a familiarity that had seemed extraordinary but, with the benefit of hindsight, Annie realized that physical attraction could make any conversation seem fascinating.

All she had to do was to find someone with whom she could enjoy some first-class sex or, since her life was depressingly free of any candidates at present, at the very least understand that her recent tendency to spend so much time thinking about Ben was based purely on sexual desire. In fact, now she thought about it, she had always been attracted to men of dubious character. In *Gladiator* she had fallen for the mad emperor rather than the brave general. In *North by Northwest* she had preferred the charms of the villainous James Mason to those of the hero, even though the hero was Cary Grant. Was it therefore any surprise that she was attracted to a rotter like Ben? It was just as well that she was spending a few days in Devon. She needed to do some serious thinking.

Totnes was a town beloved by homeopaths, artists, writers and disillusioned emigrants from the world of business. It boasted a lazy river, a bona fide Norman castle, stunning views and a host of little shops that offered such delights as organic, chemical-free skincare, handmade jewellery, old-fashioned sweets, crystals, pendants and books that covered all things spiritual.

Deirdre and Phil lived in a pink terraced cottage off the main street in Totnes. They had married three months after Annie had left Falmouth and moved to Totnes a year later. The cottage had small rooms with walls that weren't quite straight and stairs that creaked with every footstep.

Having initially regarded Phil as dull, Annie had grown to appreciate his kindness and his gravity. He lived his life according to a simple tenet: he tried to be good. Annie had at various times made serious efforts to emulate him and could only admire a man who, unlike her, refused to be deflected every time someone proved to be seriously annoying.

Marriage and motherhood suited Deirdre. She had three-year-old twins and twelve-week-old Andrew. Deirdre had developed a softness and serenity now, as if everything about her had been smudged with an inefficient rubber. It was hard to believe that a woman who could fell a cheeky smirk at two hundred paces and whose flat had always looked like an advert for household cleaners could be the same woman who greeted Annie with a milk stain on her jumper and a laughing apology for the mess everywhere.

The old efficiency was still there though. Deirdre had made scones and flapjacks for tea and she dealt effortlessly with Matthew's querulous demands for juice and Jane's attempts to flick crumbs, while simultaneously feeding Andrew and pouring tea for Annie.

Afterwards, Annie settled herself on the sitting-room floor and played with the twins while Deirdre took Andrew off for a much-needed bath after a Vesuvius-like eruption from his nether regions. Matthew, a carbon copy of his father, took life and his Duplo extremely seriously. Jane, on the other hand, was just like her Uncle Robbie. While Matthew sat solidly constructing a garage for his toy tractor, Jane first tried to build a palace, then decided to make a boat and then happily occupied herself by repeatedly sabotaging Annie's own pathetic attempts to make an aeroplane.

Later, after helping Deirdre with bathing and bedtime stories, Annie sat in the kitchen, chopping mushrooms and sipping wine. 'How do you do it?' she asked Deirdre. 'I think your children are wonderful but if I had to look after them for more than a few hours I'd be flat on my back! How do you cope?'

Deirdre grinned. 'By letting things go. I haven't dusted in months, I don't buy anything that needs ironing and I don't cook anything complicated any more. Hence the stir-fry for dinner. Which reminds me, would you like to cut up the carrots?'

'Hand them over. Do you remember Jessica? She used to make such a big deal about her one child and make out she was some Earth Mother . . . She had to be the most annoying pregnant woman ever.'

'She got divorced last year.'

'Really? That's sad.'

Deirdre grinned. 'Try to sound at least a little sympathetic.'

'I would do but she was such a pain. What about Cherry? Have you heard from her lately?'

'I knew I had something to tell you. Cherry and her husband have moved to Egypt. They're helping to set up this school in Cairo and they're looking for English teachers. I had a letter from her a few weeks ago and she asked me to let her know if I knew any people who'd be interested. She wanted to know what you were doing now.'

'She can't stand me!'

'That's not true! She made a couple of tactless remarks.'

'She said she thought she ought to tell me the children thought I was going out with that PE teacher.'

'Terry Maclean, I remember. You *did* go out with him!'

'No, I didn't. I slept with him twice, that's all. She also told me that my bra was showing through my shirt.'

'She was trying to be helpful! She has an unfortunate way of expressing herself, that's all. Anyway if you fancy a job in Cairo, let me know.'

'I shall never,' Annie assured her friend, 'want to work in Cairo with Cherry.'

Any further thoughts of Cherry were forgotten by the appearance of Phil whose huge frame made the small kitchen seem even tinier. He gave Annie an awkward kiss on the cheek and apologized for being late.

'That's all right,' Deirdre said, 'we've got all the gossip out of the way.'

'And the bitching!' added Annie.

Phil gave a slow smile. 'I don't believe that.'

'No, honestly,' Annie said, 'there'll be no more bitching tonight!'

Nor was there. Over supper, conversation meandered comfortably over a variety of topics: Phil's boat; Andrew's birth ('I had to prise Deirdre away from the vacuum cleaner,' Phil said fondly. 'She wanted to finish tidying before my mother arrived and Andrew arrived five minutes after we got to the hospital!'); Phil's mother's unexpected new relationship with her next-door neighbour despite her concerns about his feet; and finally Deirdre's plans for the following day which involved a trip to the seaside.

When Annie climbed into bed she switched off the light and realized gratefully that she hadn't thought of Ben for at least three hours.

The seaside proved to be a very good idea. There was a seductively soft breeze which tickled the waves, making them arch their backs before toppling forward onto the sand. The beach was full of people, but not unpleasantly so. Annie was particularly impressed by a woman on their left who sat on her towel, issuing a string of calm commands to her gaggle of children. 'Josh, get out of the water, you've been in far too long. Stephen, stop throwing sand at Crystal . . . Crystal if you don't want Stephen to throw sand at you, then you shouldn't throw seaweed at him . . . Angus, we do not want to see your bare bottom, thank you very much . . .'

Annie felt she was developing a good rapport with Deirdre's children. She had impressed the twins with a brilliantly executed dam, they had all enjoyed the picnic and now Deirdre sat feeding Andrew while his siblings sat nearby, making a sandcastle. Phil had rung Deirdre's mobile to say he would join them shortly.

The peace was broken by Jane who decided her mother had spent quite enough time with the baby. 'Mummy!' she said. 'I want to go into the sea!'

Deirdre lifted Andrew to her shoulder and began to stroke

his back gently. 'Daddy will be here soon,' she said. 'He'll go in with you.'

Jane threw down her spade. 'I want to go with *you*!'

Annie raised herself onto her elbows. 'I'll go in with you, Jane.'

Jane's lip trembled. 'I want to go with *Mummy*!'

'I think,' Deirdre murmured to Annie, 'there's a certain amount of J-E-A-L-O-U-S-Y from a certain party. Do you mind taking Andrew? If he starts to whimper, just pat his back. He's such a greedy little thing and he hasn't brought his wind up yet.'

Annie took Andrew gingerly and watched Deirdre take the twins to the water. She felt the baby's body stiffen and she shifted him onto her shoulder. He started to cry and Annie sat up very straight and began to rub his back fiercely. After what seemed an age, she heard a huge burp. She pulled up her knees and brought him to rest against her thighs. 'You clever boy!' she told him delightedly. 'You are such a clever boy!'

Andrew stared at her blankly and then he gave her a huge, toothless grin. His little hand reached out and curled itself round her index finger.

'Andrew,' Annie told him, 'you are one beautiful baby!'

She could swear he understood her. He gave a satisfied gurgle and nodded approvingly as if he was telling her he held her in as much esteem as she held him. Annie swallowed and she felt her eyes fill with tears.

'Annie?'

Phil stood looking down at her. 'Hi,' he said. He cleared his throat. 'Annie, are you all right?'

Annie dashed a hand to her face. 'I'm fine,' she said. 'I had something in my eye. It's gone now.'

'Do you want me to take Andrew?'

'No, go and join the others in the sea. I love holding Andrew.'

'If you're sure.' Phil took off his T-shirt and walked down to the water.

'Andrew,' Annie said, 'I am a very silly woman and if your father doesn't believe me he must think I'm a total fruit cake.' She saw Phil confer with Deirdre who immediately began to walk purposefully out of the sea. 'Andrew,' Annie mused, 'your father thinks I'm a fruit cake.'

Deirdre picked up her towel, wrapped it round herself and sat next to Annie. She took Andrew, settled him in his baby chair, slipped on his sun-hat and moved the chair so he had his back to the sun. 'Right,' she said, 'don't you try to tell me you had something in your eye. What's wrong?'

Annie rubbed her face with her hands and sniffed. She could tell Deirdre she envied the woman with the huge family, which was true. She could tell her she envied *her*, which was also true. But then Annie had envied Deirdre ever since she'd had the twins and it had never made her cry before.

One of Deirdre's many qualities was that she didn't do sympathy. When Robbie went to Australia, she had persuaded Annie to take up jogging with her which had proved to be an excellent therapy. Deirdre had maintained that she needed to lose weight but Annie wasn't deceived. She was pretty sure that as soon as she left Falmouth, Deirdre stopped jogging.

Annie gave a long sigh, scooped up a handful of sand and watched it slip through her fingers. 'Seventeen years ago,' she said, 'I was going to be married. A few minutes before we were going to the church, my boyfriend's mother rang to say that he had decided he didn't want to go through with it. I found the whole experience . . . unpleasant. A few months ago, he turned up in Bath and although I know he's selfish, thoughtless, cruel, despicable and the scum of the earth, he is also, unfortunately, very attractive.' She looked hopefully at her friend. 'Does that make sense?'

'Not really,' Deirdre said, 'but carry on.'

'I keep bumping into him and so . . . sometimes . . . I find it impossible not to think about what life might have been like if he hadn't jilted me.'

'Is he interested in you?'

'Yes, but only because he wants to get rid of the guilt thing. He keeps trying to explain things so I'll forgive him. He hasn't the first idea about how long it took me to stop thinking about it all and so he wants me to rake it all up again and I bloody well won't. But what makes it so difficult is that, despite everything, I do find him so bloody attractive. What I need is a totally basic, utterly physical relationship with someone else so I could stop fixating on Ben! It's a great pity your brother is on the other side of the world, he'd be perfect!' She gave a wry smile and waited for Deirdre to make a fitting response.

Deirdre frowned and began to dry her feet with her towel. 'Actually,' she said slowly, 'he isn't on the other side of the world. He's in Hungary.'

'Hungary? Why? How? Since when?'

'He's been there a year now.'

'A year? Why didn't you tell me?'

'Because if you remember, as a result of my brother, you

gave up a perfectly good job and a flat and decided to start all over again somewhere else. I told Robbie if he ever tried to get in touch with you . . .'

'You mean he *wanted* to get in touch? What about his family?'

'They're in Australia. Things didn't work out. Things never do with Robbie.'

'Poor old Robbie!'

Deirdre raised her eyebrows. 'I wouldn't feel sorry for Robbie. He's not the most reliable of men. I do know he'd be more than happy to occupy your mind, let alone your body, though I have to say that I'm not at all convinced that the way to get over one bastard is to take up with another but . . .'

'You are so horrid about your brother! He is not a bastard!'

Matthew and Jane were racing towards them and Deirdre leant over to grab their towels. She glanced enquiringly at Annie. 'I can give him your number if you like. But are you sure it's a good idea?'

'Yes,' Annie said. 'It's a very good idea. Give him my number.'

They were walking round the castle the next morning when Annie's mobile rang. Annie delved into her bag, pulled it out and checked the small screen.

'Lily!' she said. 'How are you?'

'You'll never guess!' Lily had a rather languorous tone of voice, low, deliberate, melodic. Not this time though. This time she sounded as if she'd run up a mountain and was about to charge all the way down again. 'We've had a miracle! We've got him back! I still can't believe it, no one can believe it, I can tell the doctors and nurses are completely staggered by it, it's like Lazarus rising from the dead, it's incredible—'

'Lily, slow down, I don't understand. What's happened?'

'William's happened! A few days ago, he opened his eyes and looked at me. I asked him to close his eyes and he did so and I asked him to open them again and he did that too! I called to the nurse and she didn't believe me so I told William to do it again and then the nurse ran, she actually ran, out of the ward and got the doctor and the doctor actually *ran* back in with her and then he saw it happen too! And then yesterday William started moving his hands and his arms. And then today I gave him a notebook and a pen and he wrote a word on the notebook and as soon as I saw it I knew he wasn't going to be brain-damaged or anything like that, I knew I'd got William back properly, I've got him back, Annie!'

'Oh my God!' Annie breathed. 'Oh Lily, I am so, so happy! But what was the word? What did he write?'

She could hear Lily laughing down the phone. 'He wrote *Bollocks*!' she said.

CHAPTER FIFTEEN

Black Book Entry, 17 September: Henry for being unkind, unfair and untruthful.

Sidney rang Annie to say he'd just got back from France and wanted to thank her for having him to stay in July.

'It was a pleasure,' Annie assured him. 'In fact you were a godsend. You were brilliant with Luke and Gabriel. I wish you could have stayed longer. It's very nice of you to ring. I'm sure you thanked me when I saw you in London. How are you? Did you have a good holiday in France?'

'It was all right,' Sidney conceded. 'Beattie met a French boy on our first day and we hardly saw her for the rest of the fortnight. The weather wasn't very good. Mum was very depressed and kept trying to pretend she wasn't. She and I had supper on our own every night and we had lots of talks about my gap year. Mum wants me to go out to Uganda and help Dad in his clinic.'

'That would be interesting.'

'If you were working as a hotel porter for the next six months so you could afford to travel, would you rather go backpacking round South America with your friends or work in a clinic in Uganda for your father and his girlfriend?'

Annie, mindful of Josephine's fury at her previous efforts to involve herself in her sister's family affairs, said diplomatically, 'I don't know.'

'Anyway,' Sidney said, 'Mum was only going on about it because she couldn't think of anything else to talk about.' He paused. 'How are you? Have you seen anything of Bella lately?'

The last question was spoken with such studied careless-ness that Annie immediately understood the reason for the call. 'No, I haven't,' she said. 'Funnily enough, Bella doesn't have lessons with me in the holidays.'

'Right.'

'Haven't you tried to contact her? You two seemed to be getting on very well when you were in Bath.'

'The thing is,' Sidney confided, 'I talked to Beattie. She says the reason why I never do well with girls is because I show my feelings. She says girls like a challenge. She says I should wait for Bella to ring *me*.'

'I see.'

'What do *you* think?'

'I think,' Annie said slowly, 'that if Bella were like most girls, Beattie would be right. But Bella is like *you*. You are both attractive and interesting people who have no idea that you *are* attractive and interesting. The reason why Bella liked you so much was because she found it easy to talk to you. And you were easy to talk to because you weren't worry-ing the whole time about being cool. I would think she's feeling pretty bad at the moment. She was friendly to you and now you've made no effort to contact her. And she's far too unsure of herself to ring you!'

'That's terrible!' Sidney cried.

'Of course there is a slight chance that I'm wrong but I think you should take a gamble and ring her and let her know you've been thinking of her. And if you do that and she makes it clear she's not interested, feel free to ring and tell me I don't know what I'm talking about!'

'I'll ring her now,' Sidney said. 'Thanks, Annie! I knew you'd know what to do!'

Annie put the phone down and sighed. It was nice that Sidney had such faith in her wisdom in all matters emotional. If he knew that she was considering revisiting one ex-boyfriend in order to get over another, he might not feel so confident. And had she given him the right advice? Supposing Bella wasn't interested in him? Annie couldn't bear the thought of Sidney receiving another rejection. But she didn't like the idea of Bella thinking Sidney didn't like her. Really, Annie thought, she was in no position to advise Sidney about anything.

Thirty minutes later, Sidney rang again. 'Annie,' he began.

'Sidney,' Annie responded.

'I spoke to Bella. I wasn't cool at all. Beattie would have been horrified.'

Annie swallowed. 'What happened?'

'She wasn't cool either. She was lovely. I have to get back to work. Thanks, Annie, you were absolutely right. Now you *are* cool!'

'Thank you, Sidney,' Annie said gravely. 'I try.'

★

William continued to make progress. Sometimes his notes were confused, 'Nancy Sinatra came to visit me this morning', at other times they were lucid, 'If I die tonight, ring Harry at work. He knows all about our finances.'

Annie, who had planned to spend the rest of her holiday repainting her windows and reorganizing her kitchen was only too happy to delay these tasks and help Lily instead. She spent a night with her parents after delivering Milly to them and then went straight up to London where she was able to report that Hamish, after a sticky beginning, had fully accepted the new visitor and that David and Rosemary were happy to keep her for as long as was necessary. Luke and Gabriel, back from their sojourn in Italy, were now ensconced in the flat and had spent the time since their return in watching the television at the hospital or roaming round the wards.

Once Annie arrived, they settled into a far more satisfactory timetable. Lily went to the hospital every morning. If William was having a good day, she would ring Annie who would follow along later with the boys. On other days, Annie took them out. By the end of the fortnight, they had visited the Tower of London, the London Eye, Madame Tussauds and, best of all as far as the boys were concerned, the disgustingly nasty London Dungeon.

On Annie's last night, she and the boys were watching TV after an enjoyable but tiring day at the zoo. Lily came in and brandished a bottle of champagne. William had spoken at last! 'Absolutely typical,' she laughed. 'After all these weeks do you know what was most on his mind? "Who's looking after Milly?" he asked!'

Driving back to Bath the next day, Annie felt she had learnt a valuable lesson. It was one she had learnt before but had forgotten far too quickly. Her own pathetic concerns about Ben were trivial in the extreme in comparison with William's experience. From now on, she would appreciate all she had: her health, her job, a lovely flat. After ten nights on Lily's London sofa, her lovely flat and her even lovelier bed were particularly enticing.

At home a pile of letters and half a dozen postcards awaited her, including a rather cryptic one from Josephine offering a modest olive branch: *Hope we will see you before too long. Brittany very warm, love Josephine.*

The answerphone disgorged a long message from the headmaster reminding Annie that the in-training day before the start of term was to start at half past eight and not nine and confessing that Annie would have to lose one of her free periods due to the fact that the new English teacher for Year Seven was unable to start work until the beginning of October.

The final message was from Grace announcing her return from Portugal. 'Hope to see you soon. Ben has told me about William. I am so very sorry. Ben asked me to ask you how he's doing, so ring me soon . . .'

Why had Ben not rung himself? Why had he asked Grace to find out about William's condition? Was it possible that he had at last realized that Annie truly did not want to have contact with him? If so, Annie thought severely, that was good. It *was* good. In fact she should be very pleased. Without Ben's disruptive presence, she could throw herself into her work and not waste valuable time thinking about him. From now on, she would remember William's misfortune, concentrate on all the good things about her life and not dwell on anything negative.

A memory, unbidden, rose nevertheless to the surface of her mind. Many years ago, she had been pushing her sprouts around her plate. Her mother, increasingly irritated, had shown her a picture of a starving child. 'Imagine you've eaten nothing but a bowl of rice in the last four days,' she said severly. 'Then look at your sprouts and eat them with gratitude!'

Annie had been struck by the photograph and had tried very had to imagine what it must be like to be so deprived of food. Then she looked at her sprouts, stuck her fork in one of them and took it to her mouth.

'Well,' Rosemary had demanded. 'Aren't you going to eat it? Don't you realize how lucky you are in contrast to that poor little child in the photo?'

'Yes,' the young Annie had said sadly. 'But I still don't like sprouts!'

Annie did not ring Grace back. As always at this time of the year, she had huge amounts of work and she kept telling herself she would ring Grace when she had a moment. The truth was it was always difficult to find a moment when one didn't really want to find a moment. The truth was it annoyed her that Grace had apparently appropriated Ben. He was obviously in constant contact with Grace, he wanted Grace to find out about William, he wanted Grace to tell him about William, he was Grace's friend. Such feelings were petty, irrational, childish and unfair – all of which Annie knew but none of which stopped her from having them.

So when, one Saturday morning in mid-September, Grace dropped in unexpectedly, Annie's mind was a confusion of guilt and constraint. 'I'm sorry I haven't been in touch,' she said (more or less honestly), 'but I've been up to my ears in work and I haven't spoken to a soul outside school' (not at all honestly).

Grace took the proffered coffee and looked anxiously at Annie. 'Are you sure I'm not holding you up? I was on my way to the library and it's so long since I've seen you but—'

'It's great to see you. Really. Do you want a biscuit?'

'Definitely not. The coffee is good! Now what's all this about William? It sounds ghastly!'

As always, Grace listened with complete attention. When Annie had finished, she sighed and said, 'I feel so ashamed.'

'Why on earth should *you* feel ashamed?'

'All these weeks you've been trying to help Lily, you've been worried sick about William and all this time do you know what I've been thinking about? My bikini!'

'I'm sorry,' Annie said, 'you've lost me.'

'Do you remember the bikini I bought in June? On the first day of our holiday, I put it on and came out to the swimming pool and Henry took one look at me and said, "You aren't seriously going to wear that?" and he told me my tummy was too big and I was too old.'

'You're forty-three! You don't *have* a big tummy! *Henry* has a big tummy!'

'I went back upstairs,' Grace said, 'I looked at myself in the mirror and I saw this horrible white, old, flabby body wearing a ridiculous yellow-spotted bikini and I burst into tears! Henry was right! I looked horrible!'

'I've never heard anything so ridiculous,' Annie said robustly.

'I know! It's silly and self-indulgent and—'

'No, I mean *Henry* is ridiculous! It's not true! Henry doesn't know what he's talking about!'

'It wasn't just Henry. The children thought so too. Jake said he was glad none of his friends had seen me. Anyway it doesn't matter. When Ben told me about William, it put everything into perspective.'

'How *is* Ben?'

Grace gave a slight smile. 'Your friend Ben is very funny. I like him hugely and he's being so kind about my ball. He's going to do an item on the Refugee Council on his programme. I always find myself talking to him about me and my problems but he never gives anything away about himself.'

It was extraordinary how one small possessive pronoun could realign an entire relationship and haul it back instantly from precarious rocks! Grace had called him '*your* friend' and at once the shameful feelings of hurt, betrayal and infantile jealousy dissolved, leaving nothing in Annie's heart but well-deserved self-disgust.

'He's so friendly,' Grace mused, 'and so easy to talk to. And yet there's something about him that makes it almost impossible for me to ask him questions about his own life. He's a bit like you really.'

'I'm not like that!'

'You are a bit.' Grace finished her coffee and reached over to put the mug on to Annie's desk. 'I don't know, I'm probably talking rubbish. I'm a bit down at the moment. Henry's going to some drug conference in the Cotswolds tonight and won't be back until tomorrow afternoon. He only told me last night and the kids are both going out and I'd bought us some salmon.' She looked at Annie hopefully. 'I don't suppose you fancy joining me for dinner?'

'I'd love to,' Annie said.

The telephone rang and Annie went through to the bedroom and picked up the handset. 'Hello?' she said.

A voice said, 'Hiya, Annie.'

Annie, midway between bedroom and sitting room, froze. 'Robbie?' She swallowed hard. 'Is that you?'

'I think so. How are you?'

'I am *extremely* well! It's so nice to hear you!' She saw Grace reach for her bag and stand up and said quickly, 'Don't go away, Robbie, I'm just saying goodbye to a friend . . .' She smiled at Grace. 'I'll come round at half past seven, shall I?'

Grace nodded. 'See you tonight,' she said and disappeared quickly.

'So,' Annie said, settling herself into the seat vacated by Grace. 'This is amazing! To what do I owe this unexpected call?'

'One: my censorious sister found out you were unattached and decided I could not therefore sabotage any promising relationship. Although, since you are going out at half past seven this evening—'

'I'm meeting a girlfriend,' Annie interjected quickly. 'I'm having supper with her. I like having supper with friends. You should try it some time.'

Robbie gave a throaty chuckle. 'Oh Annie! Sarcastic and stroppy as ever! I have missed you!'

'And you've tried so hard to get in touch with me,' Annie

responded drily. 'What's the second reason for your phone call?'

'I want to invite you to Budapest! When can you come?'

'Oh right away! I'll forget about work, shall I?'

'Come for a weekend.'

'I'm busy at weekends. I have homework to mark and lessons to prepare.'

'Come at half-term.'

'It would cost a fortune.'

'No, it wouldn't. Flights are very cheap if you book in advance. And you wouldn't have to pay anything when you get here. You can stay with me.'

'How very kind. In your own one-bed flat, I suppose?'

'Not at all. I'm staying in a very pleasant house in a most desirable area on one of the hills above the city. It has three bedrooms. You can choose the one you want. You can even share mine with me if you like.'

Robbie had never been one to waste time. Annie, who, ever since her conversation with Deirdre, had envisaged just such an offer, was unaccountably panic-stricken, like an overconfident lion-trainer who wanders into a cage and is surprised when the lion roars.

'It's a very tempting invitation,' Annie said cautiously.

'Then accept it.'

'The thing is I've made a few tentative arrangements. I'll have to see if I can get out of them.'

'If they're tentative,' Robbie said confidently, 'you can change them. Have you ever been to Budapest?'

'No, but—'

'It's beautiful. You'll love it. I need to know soon because

239

I get very booked up. I'll ring you at the same time tomorrow and you can tell me then. I've gotta go!'

'Yes, but—'

Robbie had gone. Annie sat looking at the phone. Robbie hadn't changed. Prevarication, compromise, careful cogitation, none of these was part of his DNA. He was like a whirlwind. You either gave yourself up to his energy and enjoyed. the ride or you found yourself stranded, wistfully watching the speck in the sky.

Last time she had chosen to be stranded and had bitterly regretted her choice. This time was different. If she went to Budapest it was for only one reason. Did she really want to go out to Budapest just to get laid?

'All right,' said Grace, 'are you going to tell me who Robbie is?'

They were sitting in her kitchen, drinking one of Henry's best bottles of Chablis. Annie's more modest offering waited patiently in the fridge. Annie had arrived just as Jake was going out. 'Cool skirt,' he had said. Normally Annie would have suspected him of sarcasm. Today, armed with the knowledge that Robbie wanted to see her, she had replied genuinely, 'Thank you, Jake.'

Did other people have such changeable views of themselves? Some days, she thought she was Ms Average Incarnate with a nondescript figure, a non-hairstyle and a forgettable face. At other times, like today, she could look at herself in the mirror, strike a Marilyn Monroe .pose and feel she could seduce George Clooney.

Annie had decided that she didn't need to go to Budapest.

Robbie's phone call had been enough to show her she could run her life quite successfully despite the proximity of Ben Seymour. Ben had clearly got the message. They would see each other occasionally, engage in politely sterile conversation and in time she would cease to think of him at all.

Now, sitting in Grace's house, pleasantly empty of Grace's irritating husband and children, Annie felt content. She stretched her arms and grinned. 'Robbie is an old flame,' she said. 'I nearly followed him to Australia seven years ago. He lives in Hungary now.'

'And?'

'He rang for a chat.'

'Does he often ring for a chat?'

'Not really. Actually, I haven't spoken to him for . . . for seven years.'

'And?'

'And what?'

'Honestly, Annie, getting information out of you is like trying to extract the bones from a kipper! An old flame rings you after seven years and simply wants to have a *chat*?'

'He also invited me out to Budapest.'

'Wow! Are you going?'

Annie laughed. 'I have a million and one things to do at half-term and I certainly won't have time to . . .' She stopped. 'Someone's knocking at your door.'

'Our doorbell's stopped working,' Grace muttered, rising from her seat. 'The trouble is my mind isn't programmed to hear door-knocking.'

She ran upstairs and Annie leant forward to look at the book lying on the table. Blazoned across the cover was the title, *From Fat to Thin in Twenty-Four Weeks*. Annie shook her head and murmured, 'Bloody Henry.'

She could hear Grace and her visitor coming down the stairs. A familiar voice was saying, 'I'm sorry, this is the last time I borrow anything from you . . .' and then Grace appeared in the kitchen, closely followed by Ben. He stopped abruptly when he saw Annie.

'Hello, Ben,' she said.

'Will you join us for a drink?' Grace asked.

'No,' Ben said quickly. 'Thank you. I can't. I have someone waiting . . . I have to go.'

'I'll get the soy sauce for you,' Grace said. 'It's in the larder. I'll be right back.'

Annie studied her wine carefully and extracted a minute cork crumb from the side of her glass.

'How's William?' Ben asked.

She glanced up at him as if she had suddenly remembered he was in the room. 'He's conscious!' she said. 'He's talking, he's coherent. We're keeping our fingers crossed but at the moment things are looking good.'

'That's wonderful.'

'Yes, it is.'

Grace returned, brandishing a bottle. 'There's not much in here but it should be enough. I hope you have a good meal!'

'Thanks! You're a star! Don't bother to see me out. Nice to see you, Annie.'

They both listened to him run up the stairs and only when the front door closed behind him did Grace speak. 'You see what I mean? "*I have someone waiting . . .*" I wonder who he's

242

cooking dinner for. With anyone else I'd have asked who it was!' She sat down opposite Annie and put her elbows on the table. 'So: you were telling me about the flame! You're not going to accept his invitation?'

Annie finished her glass of wine. 'Of course I am,' she said. 'I've always wanted to visit Hungary. I can't wait to go.'

As often happened to Annie when she made an important decision and acted on it quickly, something occurred almost immediately to make her regret her impulsiveness.

A week after Annie had rung an annoyingly unsurprised Robbie to tell him she would come to Budapest, Lily made one of her late-night calls. 'Annie, what are you doing on the weekend of October the twenty-second?'

'I'm busy. Why?'

'Make yourself un-busy. It's the boys' half-term, so I'm coming back to Somerset. Most important of all, Josephine will be there too.'

'On her own?'

'Yes. She'll spend the weekend with me and then she's driving on to Taunton for a week of pain-free childbirth.'

'I beg your pardon?'

'You know what I mean. She's presenting a paper or something. On the one hand, it's a pity because Cressida is spending that week with her mother and Josephine's missing the chance to have some time on her own with Mark. On the other hand, it does mean we can talk some sense into her.'

'You don't need me to do that. Josephine will be far more likely to listen to you than to me.'

'That's not true. If we both tackle her, she'll have to listen.

243

Things are getting very serious. You obviously haven't heard the news. Beattie's moved out!'

'She's left home? Why?'

'Guess! Cressida, the devil-child has been weaving her Machiavellian wiles. I must say I thought Beattie was made of stronger stuff. Josephine is distraught, Mark is all stiff lips and stony expressions, Sidney is hardly ever around. I went round to dinner the other night and in the midst of all this gloom and misery, Cressida glowed like a radioactive dagger.'

'Where's Beattie gone?'

'To her best friend who clearly has a very accommodating mother. So you see, you have to come over when Josephine is here.'

'I'd love to but I can't. I've already bought my plane ticket.'

'Where are you going?'

'To Budapest. I'm seeing a friend.'

'Annie, that is incredibly bad timing. We have to do something. Did you know she intends to come and spend Christmas with us but without Mark and Cressida?'

'No, I didn't. Poor Josephine!'

'I tell you something. If Josephine doesn't do something soon, she's going to lose her children as well as her husband. We need to think of a cunning plan. How long are you going away for? When do you get back? Annie? Do you hear me?'

'Yes,' said Annie slowly. 'I was thinking of a cunning plan.' She propped up her pillows behind her back and leant against them. 'Did you tell Josephine you were going to invite me over?'

'No, I don't think so. Why?'

'Don't tell her. Don't let her know *I* know that she's going to be away at half-term.'

'Why? Annie, is this a serious plan?'

'It's all I can think of. I'll ring up and say I need somewhere to stay for a couple of days when I get back from Budapest. I'll express sadness that I'll be missing Josephine—'

'And then you'll bend Mark's ear while I bend Josephine's! Brilliant! In that case you can go to Budapest with my blessing. Who is it you're going out to see?'

Annie hesitated for only a second. 'No one special,' she said.

Bella was having a good term. The unhappy girl who had first appeared at Annie's flat in a state of such intense self-consciousness had disappeared along with the baggy tracksuit. These days, she turned up in floaty skirts and velvety jackets, all of which she assured Annie had been found in Bath's very best charity shops. The long curtain of hair that had covered half her face had been replaced by a spiky fringe and gentle layers which revealed a fine pair of sparkling brown eyes.

Annie would have liked to take the credit for the transformation but was ruefully aware that the credit should go to Miss Appleby and possibly Sidney. Rehearsals for *Romeo and Juliet* were going well and Miss Appleby had belatedly realized she had a true star in her cast.

The evening before her trip to Hungary, Annie gave Bella an extra lesson in preparation for her LAMDA exam the following week. Bella's face shone with enthusiasm. 'I've worked out what I'm going to do,' she said. 'I haven't told my dad about the exam and I won't tell him until after the play. Miss Appleby says I have to go to drama school, she thinks I should try for RADA! Once Dad's seen the play and heard about my exam result, he'll let me apply. He'll have to.'

'You haven't *done* your exam yet, Bella! Anything can happen. And as far as your long-term future is concerned, you don't need to make any plans yet, you've still got lots of time. Are you still applying for university?'

'Oh yes, but I won't go!' She smiled happily at Annie. 'Don't look so worried. I know what I'm going to do.'

But Annie was worried. After Bella left, she started to pack her case but found it difficult to concentrate. Bella had allowed no room in her programme for failure. She was happy, too happy at the moment. In Annie's experience, it was never a good idea to be too happy.

The phone interrupted her thoughts and Annie moved the case, sat on the bed and picked up the handset.

'Annie? It's Carla here. How are you?'

'I'm very—'

'Good. Annie, I want to ask you rather an odd question. Are you and Ben an item?'

Annie gave a laugh that was a little too protracted. 'Why on earth should you think that?'

'It was something Hannah said.'

'You must have misunderstood. Anyway, I haven't spoken to Hannah for ages. I've hardly spoken to *Ben* for ages! Why are you so concerned?'

'I want to ask him to dinner,' Carla said, 'but not if he's keen on you.'

'He's not keen on me. And I'm not keen on him. In fact,'

Annie added carelessly, 'I'm off to Hungary tomorrow to see a rather gorgeous old boyfriend.'

'Really?' Carla breathed. 'Lucky you!' She hesitated and Annie could almost hear her thought processes whirring busily. 'Is this classified information,' she asked, 'or can anyone know?'

Annie gave a shorter laugh this time. 'Anyone at all,' she said.

CHAPTER SIXTEEN

Black Book Entry. 29 October. Ben Seymour for everything. Again.

'Well?' Robbie demanded. 'What do you think?'

Same shock of curls, same body that looked like it was made of matchsticks, same broad grin. Annie put down her bag. 'You are just the same!'

'Not me, stupid! The city! What do you think of Budapest?'

'I've only just got off the plane! From what I could see from the window, the Danube was long and grey. The rest of the place looked pretty grim.'

Robbie took her bag and threw it into the boot of his car. 'You can't see the good stuff from the sky. You have to remember the Communists were in power here for forty years and they were never known for their artistic taste. All the concrete blocks you see were built in the last sixty years. However,' he added, opening the passenger door for her, 'even the Communists couldn't destroy everything. I'll take you for a drive round the place and then we'll go and have some lunch.'

She had forgotten his capacity for enthusiasm. From the moment he put the key in the ignition he fired facts at her. The history of Hungary seemed to be a long road of autocratic rulers, violent revolts and terrifying executions, including one which she would definitely relate to her younger nephews since it involved someone being fried alive on a red-hot iron throne.

Robbie stopped the car by a vast square with a pale blue surface that looked like marble and gleamed in the sun. At one end there was a row of statues, in the middle of which soared a tall column with what looked like an angel on top.

'This is the Heroes' Square,' Robbie said. 'In the middle is the Archangel Gabriel. They put that up to celebrate the millennium. The statues below are all heroes from the past. They look like they've walked out of *Lord of the Rings*, don't you think?'

They got out of the car and Annie whistled. 'It makes Trafalgar Square look pretty tame,' she said. 'I feel like I'm walking on an ice-rink. It's so clean and smooth.'

'This is one of my favourite places,' Robbie said. 'It's uncluttered and simple and elegant. There's nothing else like it here. Think what happened in this country: four hundred thousand Jews were deported to Auschwitz in 1944 . . . *four hundred thousand*! Three-quarters of Budapest's buildings were damaged or destroyed in 1945, two thousand people were executed after the uprising in 1956. All that horror and that terror and that cruelty and yet here we are today standing in this beautiful square under a blue sky in a country that's part of the European Union! Aren't human beings amazing?

We do these terrible things to each other and yet somehow we recover and grow and move on—'

'And do terrible things all over again!' Annie laughed. 'You are still such an optimist, Robbie. You see, I would say that human beings aren't amazing at all. I would say that human beings are fundamentally nasty, brutish and good at finding inventive ways to kill each other.'

'Remind me to take you to the statue of Raoul Wallenberg. He was at the Swedish embassy here in the war and saved about thirty-odd thousand Jews.'

'I know all about Raoul Wallenberg. He was a good, brave man. And for every good, brave man there are at least a thousand horrid, bullying ones and I bet I know which category most of these heroes fell into.'

'Yes, but the point is that in the final analysis there *are* far more good people in the world than there are bad people. That's what gets me about the media. It reports all the terrible things we do but it never shows all the good things that go on so we come to believe the world's full of murderers and rapists and terrorists when in actual fact they are the minority! How many bad people *do* you know?'

'You forget I'm a teacher. I know a lot of bad people.'

'Seriously, are you telling me you know more bad people than good people?'

'No, but the trouble is the bad people break the rules and the good people don't, so the bad people always win. Look at Ghenghis Khan!'

'Even Ghenghis Khan died in the end.'

'Robbie, everyone dies in the end!'

'I'd forgotten how we used to argue,' Robbie said.

'I hadn't,' Annie said. She grinned. 'Are you sorry you invited me out here?'

'No,' Robbie said. 'I like arguing with you. Shall we carry on with the tour?'

Robbie was an excellent guide, not least because it was evident he loved the place. As they drove along, he maintained a constant flow of information. 'Look over there . . . Do you see the waterfall? That's where a bishop was thrown to his death in a spiked barrel. And further up you can see the Independence Monument. It's fourteen metres high and I can see it from my house, I'll show you tonight . . . That's the Gellert Hotel – if you were staying longer I'd take you to the thermal baths there . . . There's the Royal Palace, we'll see that tomorrow, it has fantastic views. *Now* do you think Budapest is grim?'

They had lunch at a little restaurant, set in the renovated Karoli Palace. It had its own garden courtyard and they sat out in the sun and ate pancakes stuffed with goulash.

'This is so weird,' Annie said. 'I haven't seen you for seven years and you haven't changed at all. You still enthuse about everything and you still talk and talk!'

'You've changed,' Robbie said. 'Your hair's longer which is nice, you've lost weight which is bad and you have a wrinkle between your eyes. You've obviously been frowning too much.'

'Well, at least my hair isn't going grey.'

'You said I hadn't changed.'

'That was before you pointed out my wrinkle.'

'It's a nice wrinkle.' He reached into his jacket and pulled out a dog-eared photo. 'Do you want to see a photo of my daughter?'

251

A little girl with dark curls and serious eyes stared out at Annie. 'She's lovely,' Annie said. 'She doesn't look like you.'

'She resembles her mother.'

'You must miss her.'

'I went over in the summer. What about you? Do you want children?'

Annie shrugged. 'I did. But it's a Catch 22. I don't want to bring up a child on my own and I don't want to have a permanent partner. I like living on my own.'

'So do I.' Robbie grinned. 'Most of the time.'

'Me too,' Annie confessed. 'You and I seem to be worryingly alike. Except I couldn't leave my daughter on the other side of the world.'

'I ring her every week. Kate's a happy little girl. I'm not worried about her. Her mother has married an upright, all-Australian guy who loves them both and has a steady income. I've never had a steady income in my life.'

'What about now?'

'Especially not now. I'm working for a charming Australian guy who's letting me stay in his house and everything's great. But he's also very impulsive and he could call me back tomorrow. And after that, anything might happen.'

Annie smiled. 'Just as well that I didn't go to Australia with you.'

'We might both be very different people if you had done.'

'We certainly would,' Annie agreed. 'I'd be an embittered harridan, demanding you send me some money for our ten children.'

Robbie shook his head. 'No,' he said. 'I just can't see you as an embittered harridan.'

'That only goes to show,' Annie retorted, 'how little you know me.'

After lunch, Robbie drove them out of the capital. He said he was taking her to a park. They arrived at a small suburb whose greatest mark of distinction was a lofty electric pylon.

The park turned out to be a small field. They bought their tickets at a red-brick kiosk, manned by a very fat old gentleman who looked as if he'd had trouble getting into it. Robbie had given Annie no idea as to what she should expect and so she was unprepared for the sight that awaited her: a collection of vast stone men who had apparently been brought together and dumped at random. One of them, a flag-bearing soldier, was at least four times the size of Robbie. Nearby there was another great statue of a bespectacled civilian who looked as though he suffered from constipation. Over in one corner there were three huge soldiers with thighs like those of Arnold Schwarzenegger in his prime. A few feet away, a giant Lenin gesticulated furiously in the direction of the electric pylon.

'Incredible,' Annie murmured. 'What is this place?'

'Statue Park. Every town in the country used to have monuments like these.'

Annie shook her head. 'I know they should be awe-inspiring, but in this place they just look . . .'

'Silly?' Robbie suggested. 'Most of this stuff was destroyed after the Iron Curtain fell. Whoever decided to put these here was a genius. They provide the perfect warning to all those who take themselves too seriously.'

'There's a poem that Shelley wrote,' Annie said. 'It might have been written for this place.'

Robbie nodded.

> ' "My name is Ozymandias, king of kings:
> Look on my works, ye Mighty, and despair!'
> Nothing beside remains. Round the decay
> Of that colossal wreck, boundless and bare
> The lone and level sands stretch far away." '

Annie was impressed. 'Robbie, that was beautifully spoken.'

'I happen to be an expert on Shelley. He's a hero of mine. And I like that poem. It's what I was saying to you earlier. Everything passes.'

'I suppose so,' Annie said. 'Eventually.' She bit her lip and pushed her hair back from her face. She was *not* going to think of Ben. 'Tell me,' she said abruptly, 'seeing as you're the great Shelley expert, did he ever write anything cheerful?'

' "If Winter comes," ' said Robbie instantly, ' "Can Spring be far behind?" ' What do you think of that, Miss Brilliant English Teacher?' He grinned. 'I do enjoy surprising you.'

Annie stared at him for a moment. Then she put her hands to his face and reached up to kiss him.

Robbie blinked. 'What was that for?'

Annie smiled sweetly. 'I rather like surprising you too,' she said.

It was bliss to sit in a bath full of soft, scented water, sipping a mug of tea and contemplating the evening ahead. They were going to walk down the hill to what Robbie had promised was a superb restaurant and enjoy caviar and Hungarian champagne. Robbie had said they could eat themselves stupid since the walk back up the hill afterwards would soon make them thin again. Annie was still not sure what would happen after that. Robbie had made no sign that he anticipated a night of passion and it was quite probable that he no longer fancied her. He had shown her into her own room with its own en-suite bathroom and had not even hinted that she might like to consider alternative arrangements.

If he didn't fancy her, it didn't matter too much. If he did, that didn't matter either. One of the reasons why she had originally fallen for Robbie was the knowledge that he possessed a sort of weightlessness that precluded any lasting commitment on his part. Robbie would never be a Triffid.

Annie shut her eyes and slid further into the water. She was not going to worry about anything. She was about to spend an evening with a man she still found attractive and of whom she expected nothing at all. What more could a girl want?

The restaurant was large and opulent with gold-flaked wallpaper, starched white tablecloths and napkins, shining glasses, and a generous number of dignified waiters in black-and-yellow-striped waistcoats who buzzed around the tables with unremitting courtesy.

It was a great place for people-watching. On their right was a large family party with what looked like at least an eighty-year age gap between the oldest and the youngest members. All were dressed smartly, even the little boy, who sported a vast red bow tie. Annie was glad she had packed her black dress and silver earrings. At the table behind Robbie sat a young couple who listened to each other with the rapt intensity peculiar to those in love. At the back of the room, a group of elderly musicians played discreetly.

It was only when their waiter brought them a silver platter of caviar and crudités that a thought struck Annie. 'Robbie,' she murmured, 'this is going to cost a fortune!'

'Don't worry about that,' Robbie said airily, 'I'm doing this on expenses. Don can afford it.'

'Who *is* this mysterious Don?'

'He's my father-in-law. Or rather, he's my ex-father-in-law.'

'So he's your charming employer? And all those photos in your house are of his family? What about the one of the two pretty girls in my room? Are they his daughters?'

'The dark-haired one is Beth, my ex-wife. The blonde one –' Robbie paused while he filled Annie's glass – 'is her sister.'

'I see. So why are you working for him? And why are you here? Start at the beginning!'

Robbie laughed. 'Is this how you talk to your pupils?' He raised his glass. 'I haven't told you how lovely you look tonight.'

'Thank you.' Annie was pretty certain that the compliment was designed to change the conversation but it still succeeded in confusing her. She raised her own glass and took a hefty gulp. 'All right. Now tell me your life story from when you arrived in Australia.'

'I met Beth, which was very nice. Beth got pregnant and I married her. Beth had a baby, which was not so nice.'

'Why? Were there complications?'

'Yes. She went off sex.'

'For ever?'

'It seemed like for ever.'

'Even you,' Annie told him severely, 'would go off sex if you were woken every few hours by a squawking, defecating infant.'

'I *did* wake up every few hours.'

'Did you feed the baby? Did you change her nappy?'

'No, but—'

'I rest my case.'

'Anyway,' Robbie said, 'I was very responsible. I realized I had made my extremely unexciting bed and I was prepared to lie in it.'

'I bet it didn't stop you sneaking into other beds.'

'Do you want me to tell you my life story or not?'

'Sorry,' Annie said, 'please continue.'

'In the end, Beth left me. She fell in love with someone, I was very understanding and my father-in-law rewarded me by offering me a job out here. He's half-Hungarian and he owns properties and a couple of clubs out here. Until recently, he spent half his time in Budapest. Now his girls have grown up, his wife wants him to stay at home with her. So he's given me eighteen months to see how I shape up and he lets me have the run of his house. So there you are. That's why I'm here.' He stared innocently at Annie. 'Why are you looking at me like that?'

Annie's eyes narrowed. 'It doesn't add up. If you're all such good friends, why on earth would your father-in-law want to send you out of the country and deprive his granddaughter of her father?' She studied him suspiciously. 'What's Beth's sister like?'

'Andrea? She's nice.'

'She looked more than nice in the photograph in my room. Is she married?'

'Yes.' Robbie shifted in his seat. 'Yes, she is.'

'You had an affair with her! You did! And now you've been sent into exile! Robbie, you are appalling! I take it all back. You and I are not alike at all. I would *never* have an affair with a married man!'

'That's probably because you've never fallen in love with one.'

'I wouldn't let myself fall in love with one! And I'd certainly never let myself fall in love with a brother-in-law! I have to say that . . .'

To Robbie's obvious relief, Annie was diverted from any further high-minded observations by their walrus-moustached waiter who had arrived at their table with a very full trolley and proceeded to flambé their meat with a gravity and professionalism that demanded their admiring attention.

After that, Annie found it difficult to remain censorious. The food was delicious, the wine was plentiful and by the end of the meal Annie had difficulty in remembering why she was supposed to be censorious in the first place.

It was while they were drinking their coffee that Annie suddenly grabbed Robbie's arm. 'Robbie!' she hissed. 'Look behind you!'

Robbie turned immediately. The young man behind him had risen from his chair and fallen to his knees in front of his girlfriend. He uttered a few urgent words, the girl smiled radiantly – oh how well Annie remembered that rapture, that all-conquering feeling of total joy and confident love! – then the man rose to his feet, the girl nodded and said something, the man enveloped her in his arms and the restaurant erupted with cheers and applause. One of the violinists stepped forward and the room went silent. He must have been at least seventy but the sounds he conjured from his instrument were as sweet and strong and joyous as the couple he played for. When he finally finished, he accepted the noisy approbation of his audience with a little bow and stepped back to join his fellow musicians.

'Hey!' Robbie said. 'You're crying.'

Annie reached for her napkin and wiped her face. 'I have to confess something to you,' she said.

'In that case,' Robbie advised, 'you'd better have some more wine. Here!'

Annie waited while he filled her glass and then took a restorative sip. 'I came to Budapest for a reason,' she said, 'and that was –' she stopped to take another three sips – 'that was to have sex with you.'

Robbie, who had been helping himself to the cheese on Annie's plate, choked. Annie immediately poured him some water and fixed him with an anxious scrutiny.

'Excuse me,' Robbie said at last, 'but did you say what I thought you said?'

'I did and I'm sorry! I just wanted to make use of your body! I'm sorry!'

Robbie took a long swig of his wine, pushed his plate aside and sighed heavily. 'I don't know what to say,' he said at last.

'I know! I know!' Annie wrung her hands in anguish. 'Of course I see now it was quite wrong! You don't have to worry!

259

It was a silly, selfish idea and of course I won't come near you now, I promise I won't—'

'Hang on a moment.' Robbie squared his shoulders and smiled bravely at her. 'I can't pretend I'm not hurt by your admission—'

'I know! Please believe me—'

'But,' Robbie continued, 'on the other hand I also feel very strongly that if you want to use my body then the least I can do is let you avail yourself of it freely and without hesitation.'

'That's very sweet of you but—'

'I know. In actual fact,' Robbie added nobly, 'I'd be *glad* to have sex with you.'

'The thing is,' Annie said sadly, 'I don't think it would work. You don't know *why* I want to have sex with you.'

'To be perfectly honest,' Robbie said, 'I don't really mind.' He caught sight of her stricken face and said quickly, 'Tell me all about it.'

Annie took a deep breath. 'There's a man in Bath. When I was twenty, we were going to be married. Just before the wedding he got his mother to ring, *he* didn't ring, his *mother* rang and she said he didn't want to marry me.'

Robbie took her hand. 'What a coward! What a bastard!'

'I know. It was terrible. It was the most terrible moment of my life. And now he's come to Bath and he wants to be friends and he's not married and I hate him and I find him very attractive and I feel very confused and I thought if I had sex with you then I wouldn't want to have sex with him and I know that's very stupid—'

'It's not stupid at all,' Robbie assured her earnestly. 'Actually, it's amazingly intelligent and perceptive and wise.

It's very wise. It always works for me. Whenever I try to get over someone I love and lose I find that all I have to do is sleep with someone else and I'm all right again.'

'Yes,' Annie frowned, 'but I think perhaps you get over people quite quickly anyway.'

'Not at all,' Robbie promised. 'I think we should get home right away so I can do my best to help you.'

'I can't ask this of you. It's treating you like a prostitute.'

'I don't mind.'

'Well, I do!'

'In that case,' Robbie murmured, leaning forward to brush her mouth with his lips, 'you can regard the night ahead as therapy. I will be your therapist.'

'I suppose if you put it like that . . .'

'I think,' Robbie said, 'I'd better call for a taxi.'

Annie frowned again. 'I thought we were going to walk back.'

Robbie raised an arm, nodded at the waiter and smiled sweetly at her. 'I've changed my mind,' he said.

When Annie awoke the next morning, she groaned and put her hands to her throbbing temples. She opened her eyes. Someone had forgotten to close the curtains last night and the sun directed its rays directly at Annie. She shut her eyes again. She could remember thanking Robbie for agreeing to have sex with her. She groaned again. She could remember lying naked in his bed, pulling his face down to her breasts and instructing him to do whatever he wanted. She could remember wrapping her legs round his bottom while he sucked one of her nipples and she could remember shouting she was in heaven. She groaned again. She remembered that long after what must have been one of the noisiest climaxes in their joint sexual history she had stared at the moon while Robbie snored gently beside her and had known that the therapy hadn't worked. Annie groaned one more time and put her pillow over her head.

It was taken from her a few minutes later by Robbie. He wore blue pyjama bottoms and held a long glass full of dark red liquid. 'Hair of the dog!' he said. 'Drink it up!'

Annie sat up gingerly and took the glass. 'Robbie,' she murmured, 'I want you to forget everything I said last night.'

Robbie sat down beside her and brushed her face with his hand. 'It's forgotten already.'

'Also,' Annie said, 'I want you to forget everything we *did* last night.'

Robbie's hand had strayed to her shoulder. 'That might be more difficult.'

'Robbie,' Annie said, 'do you remember that I explained that there might be a reason why new mothers don't want sex?'

'I do,' Robbie said.

'Well,' Annie said, 'the same goes for women with hangovers.'

Robbie removed his hand and stood up. 'I'm making scrambled eggs,' he said. 'You'll feel fine in half an hour!'

As always, Robbie was over-optimistic. They finally left the house in the early afternoon by which time Annie, with the help of her sunglasses, felt ready to face the world. Robbie took her to the Statue of Independence and to the Royal Palace, both of which Annie admired but neither of which she enjoyed as much as their final destination in a quiet little spot near the Hungarian Parliament. They sat on a bench and gazed at the stone likeness of Imre Nagy, the reformist Communist Prime Minister who had stood up to the Russian invaders in 1956 and was executed in 1958. The sculptor had put him on a stone bridge. He stood looking out towards the Parliament; behind him a gossamer-like tree swayed gently in the breeze and under the bridge a small pond reflected his gentle face. It seemed to Annie that the entire creation had been made with huge affection and respect and was a million times more affecting than the bombastic monsters of the day before.

At home they had an early supper. Annie told Robbie she had had a wonderful time and that if he ever wished to visit Bath she would try to return his hospitality. Robbie made her promise that if ever she felt lonely and unhappy, or required more therapy, she would ring him. She kissed him on the cheek and went to bed. Later, he came into her room and slipped into bed beside her. She did not turn him away.

On the plane going home, Annie's book remained unopened on her lap. She sat, staring out of the window, endlessly reminding herself of Robbie's dictum: Everything passes. However often she soundlessly repeated those words, the big concrete fact remained stubbornly lodged in the centre of her mind: she was in love with a man she could never forgive.

CHAPTER SEVENTEEN

Black Book Entry, 1 November: Carla for being irritating, annoying, unpleasant and stupid.

Josephine's front door was opened by the last person Annie expected or indeed wanted to see. 'Cressida!' she exclaimed. 'How lovely to see you! I thought you were staying with your mother this week?'

'I was,' said Cressida. She fixed Annie with a challenging eye. 'When I heard you were staying the night, I decided to go tomorrow instead.'

Perhaps it was the unhappy plane journey she had just endured and the snail-like drive along the M25, or more possibly it was the smug glint in the teenager's eye and Annie's realization that Josephine faced an adversary who was leaving nothing to chance. The fact that Cressida was wearing a scarlet T-shirt that Annie had seen on Beattie in the summer did not help either. For whatever reason, Annie instantly dropped her cunning plan and decided instead to carry out an even more cunning one, devised by the very man she had been trying with such spectacular failure not to think about.

'What a pleasant surprise!' Annie cooed. 'Though I must confess I was rather looking forward to having your gorgeous father to myself for a little while!'

Cressida made a face. 'Dad's not gorgeous!'

'You'd better believe it,' Annie laughed. 'Is he still at work?'

'Yes. He'll be back soon.'

'Good!' Annie pushed past Cressida who would probably have kept her on the doorstep for ever. She put down her suitcase, took off her jacket and clapped her hands together. 'I could kill for a cup of tea!' She strode through to the kitchen without looking behind her and made straight for the kettle.

Cressida stood in the doorway with her arms folded. 'Sidney won't be here for dinner. He's going to the cinema.'

'Oh what a pity!' said Annie who knew very well that Lily had instructed him to keep out of the way. 'I do love Sidney! Now, I remember where the tea bags are but I don't know about your cups and saucers.'

Cressida stalked over to the cupboard next to the dish-washer, pulled out a mug and set it with a thud on the table in front of Annie.

'If you want to get on,' Annie said, 'please don't feel you have to keep me company. I have a lovely book to read!'

As she had expected, this was sufficient motivation for Cressida to pull out a chair and sit down. The girl narrowed her eyes. 'Why have you never married?' she asked abruptly. 'I'd hate to be a sad old spinster.'

'Ah!' exclaimed Annie archly – she had never quite under-stood the meaning of the adverb but at the moment she was pretty sure it accurately described her present style of speech.

'Up until very recently, I never wanted a husband of my own. I've always found I preferred to borrow them.'

Cressida's mouth dropped open. 'What did you say?'

'The great advantage of borrowing husbands is that you can always give them back when you get bored with them!' Annie dropped a tea bag into her mug and cocked her head sideways. 'Are you sure you don't want a drink?'

'I'll have some juice.' Cressida went to the fridge and pulled out a carton.

'Quite recently,' Annie mused, 'I started to think that it would be nice to have a little baby and a nice, steady man to look after me, someone who knows about children and who will always be there for me, someone kind and caring, some- one –' Annie paused to stare dreamily at the tap over the sink, which was definitely in need of a new washer – 'someone like your father.'

Cressida sucked in oxygen through flaring nostrils. 'My father,' she pointed out stiffly, 'is married.'

'But not,' Annie responded gently, 'for much longer. I think we both know that, don't we?'

Two raspberries expanded on either side of Cressida's nose. 'I don't know what you mean!'

'It's for the best,' Annie assured her. 'Josephine was far happier before she married Mark. She's a great worrier, you see. Before Mark, she only had to worry about Beattie and Sidney. Now she's got you. She spends a ridiculous amount of time worrying about you, whether you're happy living here, whether you're happy at school; honestly she worries for England! I think Josephine will be far happier on her own.'

'I don't believe this!' Cressida gasped.

Annie did wonder if she was overdoing the wicked sister act. She said cheerfully, 'Did you know I'm planning to move to London next year?'

Cressida cast smouldering eyes at her. 'Why?'

Annie gave a little shrug. 'I'm bored with Bath. Also, I got a little too friendly with my headmaster and he's beginning to irritate me. So I thought I'd come up here! I have even started looking at properties in Herne Hill. The internet is full of them. You can get virtual tours. Wouldn't it be funny if I was your neighbour?'

The front door slammed and Mark's voice could be heard in the hall. 'Hello! Anyone at home?' He came through to the kitchen and beamed at them both. 'Annie! You look very well. You know my little girl has stayed on specially to see you?'

Annie reached out for Cressida's hand. 'I can't tell you how much that means to me,' she said.

'It's so kind of you to entertain me like this,' Annie said, 'I couldn't face driving all the way back to Bath from Gatwick tonight.'

If Mark knew that the journey from Gatwick to Bath was only an hour or so longer and certainly less stressful than the drive from Gatwick to Herne Hill, he was too polite to say so. 'It's a pleasure. I'm only sorry Josephine isn't here and it's a pity Sidney won't be back till late.'

'Oh that doesn't matter. I know how important a teenager's social life is.' Annie sipped her wine and wandered over to the chopping board. 'Can I do anything to help? You're working so hard!'

Mark laughed. 'Cooking is my hobby. We're nearly ready to eat.'

'You make me feel so guilty!' Annie returned to her chair and sat down. She could see a glimpse of scarlet in the crack in the door. 'Josephine is so lucky to have you! I love good food but I'm a hopeless cook. When I'm on my own I eat bread and cheese.'

'You ought to look after yourself better. It's important to eat properly.'

'I know.' Annie sighed and bit her lip. 'The trouble is when I'm on my own I can't be bothered. It can be quite lonely sometimes.' She sighed again.

'Are you all right?' Mark asked gently. 'You seem a bit low.'

'I'm fine, it's only . . .' Annie covered her face with her hands.

'Annie? What is it?'

Annie sniffed and discreetly dropped the sliver of onion she had stolen from the chopping board. 'It's silly! Please don't worry!'

'Annie?' Mark came over and put a hand on her shoulder. 'What is it? Please tell me! I want to help!'

Annie turned and with a little sob flung herself at Mark's diminutive chest.

'There, there,' Mark said, patting her back awkwardly. 'There, there.'

'You're so kind! And I'm so stupid! I'm fine most of the time but every now and then I'm aware of how alone I am in the world and I get a little sad, knowing I'll never find a partner of my own.'

'Annie,' Mark assured her earnestly, 'you are a very attractive woman! You are warm and funny and intelligent and—'

'What's going on?' Cressida entered the kitchen with the ferocity of a Hercule Poirot about to forestall a murder.

'Nothing at all,' said Mark briskly, gently disengaging himself from Annie. 'Annie had something in her eye.' He tore off a piece of kitchen paper and handed it to Annie. 'Are you all right now?'

Annie nodded gratefully and wiped her face with the paper. 'Shall I lay the table?' she asked.

'Certainly not. You stay there. Cressida, get the cutlery out, will you?'

'So,' Annie said, squaring her shoulders and smiling bravely. 'How are you enjoying school, Cressida?'

'I'm not,' Cressida said shortly.

'Oh dear, that's a pity! I must say I often wonder if boarding schools aren't the answer for teenagers.'

Mark chuckled. 'Don't let Josephine hear you say that! She disapproves of private schools!' He set a plate in front of her on which lay buttery new potatoes, garlic-flecked spinach and roasted trout sprinkled with thyme and lemon.

'Wow!' enthused Annie. 'That looks divine!' She reached for the salt. 'There's a very good state boarding school in Somerset.'

Mark served out Cressida's food. 'Josephine disapproves of boarding schools too!'

Cressida helped herself to another potato and took her place at the table. 'My education,' she said flatly, 'is nothing to do with Josephine.'

'Hear, hear!' Annie agreed. 'If you want to go to boarding school—'

'I didn't say I *did* want to go and it's none of your business either!'

'Cressida!' Mark said sharply. 'There is no need for such rudeness. This isn't like you!'

'Oh please don't tell her off,' Annie said quickly, 'Cressida's quite right. As she told me herself I'm just a sad old spinster. What do I know?'

'Cressida!' Mark said again. 'I can't believe you could be so rude!'

'I wasn't being rude. Annie is a spinster. It's a fact.'

'The term is out-dated and gratuitously offensive, as you know very well.'

'Mark, please,' Annie murmured, 'I'm sure Cressida didn't mean to upset me. I've forgotten already!'

Mark raised his glass to her. 'You are a kind woman, Annie.'

'Nonsense,' Annie smiled. 'I can't tell you what fun it is to be here with you.' She smiled sweetly at Cressida. 'And with you, Cressida.'

Annie had breakfast with Mark and Cressida the next morning and left after subjecting both of them to long and lingering hugs. She drove off in an extremely good mood which only evaporated as she approached Bath.

The rest of the half-term was taken up with rehearsals for the Christmas concert, which for some reason known only to the headmaster was being held in November, and an in-training day of mind-numbing boredom on the mechanics of electronic registration.

On Saturday, Annie went for a power walk with Grace. 'Right,' said Grace as they crossed into Cleveland Walk, 'tell me everything about Budapest.'

Annie, striving to keep up with her arm-swinging, foot-striding friend, protested breathlessly, 'Do we have to walk quite so fast?'

'If we don't, we're not getting proper exercise. So tell me: did you have loads of hot sex?'

'Lots and lots,' Annie said and was pleased to see that Grace's hands stopped swinging and slipped into the pockets of her jacket instead.

'Annie!' Grace exclaimed. 'You didn't!'

'I did. We did other things too. We went to Statue Park and saw the Royal Palace and we—'

'Never mind about the tourist stuff! What happens *now*? Will you go out there again? Will he come and see you here?'

'I doubt it. I do like Robbie. Seven years ago I was in love with him. But *now*, it's a bit like hearing the echo of someone's voice: you know it's someone familiar but you don't know where it's coming from and you know it's only an echo, it's not the voice itself.'

'Is he serious about you?'

'Not in the slightest. We got on very well. And Budapest is a marvellous city. You should take Henry off for a romantic break there.'

'Chance would be a fine thing.' Grace turned onto the footpath that led to North Road. 'Henry's working so hard at the moment. He wants to take on another partner. I might actually see something of him when he does.'

'So I take it your half-term has been less than exciting?'

'Jake and Fizzie are not being easy. Jake has decided he's made all the wrong university choices. Fizzie has been dumped by her boyfriend and is in a foul mood, though I have to say that Fizzie in a foul mood isn't that different from Fizzie in a good mood.'

'Poor Grace!'

Grace grimaced. 'It's her age! I see her look at me sometimes. Everything I do or say seems to irritate her and she makes me feel I am utterly boring. Perhaps I am boring.'

'Grace!'

'I know, I know! I mean I read all these articles about how important it is for teenagers to break the umbilical cord. But Fizzie seems to be taking an axe to our one.' She stopped for a moment to take a breath. 'Let's go straight up the hill, no messing, then we'll take a break at the top.'

Annie was too busy trying to keep up with Grace to raise any protest. They crossed the road and climbed over the stile. Annie was quite relived that the steepness of the hill and the speed of their progress precluded conversation. Grace rarely moaned about her children but whenever she did so, Annie was restrained from voicing an opinion by her determination not to reveal that she thought both Fizzie and Jake were over-indulged and under-employed.

By the time they reached the top, both women reached for the bench like long-distance swimmers striving for dry land. They sat back in silence, recovering their breath while looking out at the Bath skyline. This view never failed to remind Annie of her love for her adopted home; the graceful hills surrounding the city were like friendly giants, guarding the pale buildings that clustered round the noble and magisterial presence of the Abbey.

Grace took off her jacket and stretched her arms above her head. 'How's William?' she asked.

'Not so bad.' Annie had rung Lily a few days ago in order to confess her appalling behaviour at Herne Hill. Annie preferred to confess crimes to those she knew would be sympathetic. Grace, for example, would be horrified to know that Annie had displayed such malevolence towards a thirteen-year-old girl whereas Lily had been delighted and was only cross that she hadn't devised such a plan herself. 'The good news,' Annie said, 'is that William has been moved to a re-habilitation unit. They think he might be home by Christmas.' She paused and then, prefacing her change of topic with a small light laugh, said, 'I had a funny phone call from Carla before I left. She wanted to know if there was anything going on between me and Ben Seymour.'

'Really? What did you say?'

'What do you think? I had no idea what she was talking about. She admitted she wanted to move in on him.'

Grace chuckled. 'She's certainly done that!'

'Already? What's happened?'

'Frances told me she and Ted went to supper with Carla on Saturday. The only other guest was Ben. They all had a very jolly time and when Frances and Ted got up to go, Ben said he would order himself a taxi since he had drunk too much to drive home. Frances says that Carla said, and I quote, "*Don't bother to get a taxi, Ben, I'm sure we can sort something out!*" And then the next morning Ted went to the gym in Weston and saw Ben coming out of Carla's house. What do you think of that?'

Annie's thought processes were blocked by a graphic vision of Ben and Carla writhing about on Carla's shiny brown sofa. 'Good for Carla!' she said tonelessly. She stood up abruptly. 'Shall we go on? I thought this was meant to be a power walk!'

Annie opens her front door and looks warily at Ben. 'Hello,' she says.

'Annie,' Ben says, 'I have to talk to you, I can't take this any longer. Please don't say anything. Just listen. The night before our wedding, I was knocked over by a bus. I got up again and I thought I was all right but I wasn't. I wandered round the streets and finally found a bus shelter. When I awoke I thought I was a schoolboy again. I thought I had an exam that morning. It sounds crazy but I suppose I had concussion. So I rang home and told Mum I couldn't go through with it. She thought I meant the wedding. I met up with some people and stayed in their place for a few days. By the time I got my memory back, you were gone.'

Annie raises an eyebrow. 'And what about Carla?'

'Carla?' Ben frowns. 'What about Carla? We're just friends. I stayed on her sofa a few weeks ago. I'm not interested in Carla!'

Annie opens her front door and looks warily at Ben.

'Annie!' Ben says. 'Do you remember Jenny Evans in marketing at the BBC? The night before our wedding I went out with some mates and Jenny said she'd give me a lift home. But instead she drove me to her home and she locked me in her cellar. She said she couldn't bear to think of me marrying anyone but her. The next morning she rang my mother and told her I didn't want to marry you. Luckily I found an axe under some newspapers and I broke the door down but by the time I got home you were gone.'

Annie raises an eyebrow. 'And what about Carla?'

'Carla?' Ben gives an incredulous laugh. 'Carla disgusts me! She has a laugh like chalk scraped against a blackboard, her dress sense is appalling and her new hairstyle is a big mistake. If you paid me a million pounds I wouldn't sleep with Carla.'

When Annie wasn't devising ever more improbable revelations from Ben, she was besieged by soft-focus pictures of him and Carla making love. She was sleeping badly, she was eating too little and drinking too much. Every time the telephone rang, she hoped and feared it might be Ben. Floundering in the Sea of Despond, other anxieties attached themselves to her like limpets. She worried about Josephine, she worried about William and most of all she worried about Bella.

Bella was convinced her drama exam had gone swimmingly and every time she talked about her future plans, Annie felt a niggling sense of danger and foreboding.

'Bella,' Annie said gently, 'I'm sure you did really well in the exam but—'

'I'll get honours. You see if I don't!'

'Even if you do, that doesn't necessarily mean you should dismiss university out of hand—'

'When my family sees the play, they'll agree with me. I don't want to mess around with gap years. Miss Appleby says when you're an actress, you're considered past it at twenty-five!'

'Bella, you're still very young! When's your birthday?'

'Fifteenth of July.'

'That's my mother's birthday! Well, there you are, you'll only be eighteen then. Why not keep any deferred university places, try for drama school in your gap year and then you have far more time to convince your family you are really serious. But you never know, you might very well feel different next year.'

'I won't. I'd die if I couldn't act. And I know I can do it! You will come and see the play, won't you? I can introduce you to Miss Appleby. You'll like her.'

Annie nodded but she didn't say anything. She was pretty sure she wouldn't like Miss Appleby at all.

Driving back from school, Annie made a momentous decision. For months she had refused to let Ben mention the past for fear that it would reawaken the old misery. The truth was that she was miserable anyway. The only solution was to tell Ben she wanted to hear his story after all and hope it would extinguish her preoccupation with him. She would ring him after supper. She remembered there wasn't actually any supper to eat and she pulled up outside the little grocery store on Bathwick Hill.

She took her bag from the passenger set, locked the car and turned in time to see Ben walk out of the shop.

'Annie!' he said. 'How are you?'

Why did you jilt me? She was on the verge of asking him but a couple of schoolchildren were trying to get into the shop and a woman with too much lipstick was trying to get out and now was definitely not the right time. 'I'm very well,' she said.

'I hear you've been to Budapest.'

'Carla must have told you. Yes, I had a terrific time. How *is* Carla?'

'Last time I spoke to her she was very well.'

'Good.' It was no good, she was doing her best to press the lid on all the bile and jealousy and venom welling up inside her but the task was beyond her. She gave a brittle smile. 'I think you make an excellent couple.'

'Knowing that she's a friend of yours,' Ben said gently, 'I'll take that as a compliment.' He glanced at his watch. 'I have to dash. Goodbye.'

Damn! Damn, damn, damn! Why had she made such a crass remark? Why had she sounded such a bitch? Probably, she told herself despairingly, because she was a bitch. Worse, how could she ask him to go over the past at the very moment when he had made it very clear he had followed her instructions and had indeed moved on? He had moved on into the grasping arms of Carla and she was stuck in the mire and there was nothing she could do about it.

CHAPTER EIGHTEEN

*Black Book Entry, **9** December: Ben Seymour for ever and ever.*

Two beacons of light penetrated the dull misery that had enveloped Annie like a shroud. Both came in the form of phone calls, the first from Lily.

'Guess what!' As usual, Lily dispensed with any form of greeting or identification. 'William will be home for Christmas! It's official! He walked down half the corridor on his own yesterday. I've promised the boys they can stop boarding at the end of term and Mum and Dad will bring Milly home with them on Christmas Eve. I never thought I would say this but I am so looking forward to leaving London.'

'I bet you are! Lily, that's fantastic! Have you heard any news about the green-haired assassin? What's happening to him?'

'He's on remand in a secure unit.'

'Let's hope he's extremely uncomfortable!'

'I shouldn't think he'd notice either way. I gather he's taken enough drugs to fill Wembley Stadium and they've scrambled his brain. He's nineteen and has no future. You can't help feeling sorry for him.'

'I can,' Annie said. 'The fact that he nearly murdered your husband makes it very easy for me not to feel sorry for him.'

'I felt like that before I met his mother. I imagined he was a terrifying *Clockwork Orange* type of thug. But he's not. He's just a pathetic teenage drug addict. And his mother is nice. She's visited William twice. Even *you* would feel sorry for *her*. In the last few years he's stolen virtually everything she had. He even took his sister's engagement ring. She showed me a photo of him when he was twelve. He had dimples. She said he had a passion for cinema and wanted to be a film director when he grew up. Now he keeps hearing that dead man from Nirvana in his head, telling him to kill himself.'

'And I suppose he'll say that *he* told him to attack William.'

'I don't know. At least he's getting some treatment now and he's not out on the streets attacking anyone else. To be perfectly honest, I want to start thinking about something nice for a change. I'm thinking I might take down our beech hedge when I get home and build a ha-ha instead. What do you think?'

'I'm not even sure what a ha-ha is. And I think you're very forgiving. I'm not so sure I'd be as understanding.'

'Of course you wouldn't,' Lily agreed. 'You're like one of those terrifying goddesses from Ancient Greece who go around killing their children in order to get revenge on their father.'

'I think,' Annie said loftily, 'you are referring to Medea and she was not a Greek goddess.'

'You know what I mean. You're like the Elephant Who

Never Forgets. How is Ben by the way? You haven't killed him yet?'

'He's going out with a friend of mine.'

'Really? What's she like?'

'She's the sort of woman who looks over your shoulder when she's talking to you just in case she's missed someone more interesting. She's fixated on finding a man and she's not too fussy. She has a laugh like a battering ram.'

'Gosh, Annie,' Lily said admiringly, 'if that's how you talk about your friends, I'd hate to be your enemy!'

The second shaft of light came courtesy of Josephine. Annie, mindful of the empty bottles littering her kitchen floor, had just poured herself a half glass of wine. On hearing Josephine's voice she carried on pouring. 'How are you?' she said, hoping she didn't sound like a woman who could be plausibly accused of trying to steal her sister's husband.

'I'm very well,' Josephine said. 'Isn't it wonderful about William?'.

'It certainly is.'

'He's even started making jokes again. He told me one yesterday when I went to visit him.'

'Was it a good one?'

'I don't know, I didn't understand it, but then I never *do* understand William's jokes. Of course Daddy's convinced that he's responsible for William's progress. Did you know he sent him some porridge oats and told him that if he ate nothing but porridge, he'd be kicking a ball in no time?'

'When has William ever kicked a ball?'

'Dear Daddy. He means well.' Josephine paused as if

recharging her batteries before launching into possible re-criminations or accusations or remonstrations. 'Actually,' she continued, 'I was really ringing to find out how *you* are. How are you?'

'Me?' Annie breathed a sigh of relief. Josephine was not angry. 'I'm fine.'

'You don't have to be brave with me,' Josephine assured her. 'Mark is very worried about you. He said you seemed very depressed. And lonely.'

'Oh. Yes. I was. I mean I am.' Annie sighed loudly into the handset. 'I'm sure I'll feel better soon.'

'Of course you will. Mark and I've been talking and we thought it would be lovely if you could come and stay for a proper weekend when neither of us is on call. We could throw a dinner party for you. I was still married to Clement the last time you came to a dinner party!'

Annie remembered it well. She had been set up – with an obviousness that still made her cringe – with an anaesthetist who had clearly been affected by the mechanics of his job since he spoke so slowly that Annie had found it impossible not to finish his sentences for him. He had started explaining why he had never married and Annie had responded by nodding sympathetically every few minutes while in fact listening to a rather interesting conversation at the other end of the table about some doctor's kleptomaniac daughter. At the end of the evening the anaesthetist had grasped her hand between both of his, told her he was delighted that he had at last found someone who shared his radical views on child-rearing and implored her to give him her phone number. It was only by inventing an ardent new boyfriend that she had been able to retrieve her hand from his extremely clammy palms.

'Thank you,' Annie said, 'I'm sure that's just what I need. Unfortunately, all my weekends up to Christmas are full of rehearsals and school concerts.'

'Well, we'll do it in January! It will be such fun! Bring your diary to Lily's at Christmas and we'll sort something out.'

'I will,' Annie promised. After all, a dinner party at Josephine's was a small price to pay for not being found out and at least Mark would be cooking.

'There's something else,' said Josephine. 'It's about Cressida.'

'Oh yes?' *Oh God.*

'I wanted to thank you. Cressida said she had a chat with you. She said you told her how much I liked her. You made a great impression. She's been trying so hard to get on with us all in the last few weeks. Even Sidney's noticed an improvement. And the other wonderful news is that Mark went over to see Beattie and he's persuaded her to come home. Of course we still have our ups and downs. Cressida's a fragile little flower really. But things are definitely better. Thank you, Annie.'

Perhaps Josephine was right. Perhaps all Cressida needed to know was that Josephine really cared about her. Perhaps Cressida was indeed a fragile little flower who had at last responded to the innate goodness of her stepmother. Perhaps Annie was being a cynical cow to imagine that Cressida had in fact responded to the innate nastiness of her stepmother's sister. Annie decided she was indeed a cynical cow

282

since there was no way she could see Cressida as a fragile little flower.

'Everything passes,' Robbie had said. Annie had taken to muttering it like a mantra and on some days she almost felt it was true. She tried to visualize herself climbing slowly but surely out of a deep and dismal pit. She told herself that eventually she'd be back on firm ground. Then she had an evening with Grace and was thrown back down to the bottom.

With Henry away at yet another drug conference, Grace had suggested a supper and DVD. Duly ensconced in the sitting room with lasagne and red wine, Annie was happy to simulate approval when Grace produced *The Wedding Singer*.

Grace's laughter was infectious. The lasagne was excellent and the wine was plentiful and Annie began to enjoy herself. She had forgotten how funny the film was. In the penultimate scene she watched again as Adam Chandler walked over to Drew Barrymore, looked into her eyes and sang that he wanted to grow old with her.

Grace, a hopeless romantic, began to sniff. Annie felt an unexpected lump in her throat. She swallowed. She blinked rapidly. She swallowed again. This was ridiculous. This was soppiness to end all soppiness. She could feel the tears coursing down her cheeks and wiped her eyes fiercely with her hands. It was then that she understood the full enormity of what had happened to her.

Annie May, fully-paid-up cynic and fierce debunker of all things sentimental, had become a Triffid.

She could not blame Ben for this appalling metamorphosis. Why had she allowed him to come to Lily's house? Why had she gone to dinner with him? Why had she stepped inside his new house? She should have had nothing to do with him. This was all her fault. Meanwhile Ben had, after all, done as she asked and was leaving her alone.

After this, Annie knew she had to do something. The solution, like so many good solutions, came when she least expected it.

She had not been looking forward to Hannah's hen night. In her present mood she was not sure she could cope with Carla's smug satisfaction at having at last nabbed her very own Mr Perfect. Annie was also frightened that she might reveal herself to be too nasty and self-centred not to begrudge Hannah her current happiness.

In fact, the party was fun. She was relieved to find out that she was not totally irredeemable. One look at Hannah's shining eyes gladdened her heart. Also, Carla was, unusually for her, reticent about her own affairs and seemed happy to let Hannah be centre stage.

Subjects of discussion had included: a debate about Frances's anniversary present to her husband and the reasons why he might not have been unduly grateful to receive a nasal hair-trimmer and an oral-hygiene kit; Annie's recent trip to Budapest and a subsequent analysis of Annie's peculiarly masculine ability to separate sex from romance; and a stirring, if slightly slurred, speech from Hannah on the joys of finding a soul-mate.

It was this last peroration that led Frances to ask Carla how her relationship with Ben was progressing.

Carla shrugged. 'It's not,' she said flatly. 'I finished it on Wednesday.'

'But, Carla!' Frances protested. 'It's only been going a few weeks. You were all over each other at your dinner party!'

'And since then I have been the one to instigate every single meeting. He has never *ever* rung me! So I thought I would wait for him to ring me for a change and so I waited and I waited and after seven days I gave up and rang him myself!'

'And what did he say?' asked Hannah.

'He said it was good to hear from me.'

'Well,' said Hannah encouragingly, 'that's nice.'

'No, it was not nice, Hannah, it's what he always says when I ring him. So I said to him that in my ignorance I assumed that we were having a relationship and that in my experience if a man is in a relationship with a woman he does occasionally want to speak to her.'

'And what did *he* say?' asked Frances.

'He said he was very busy at work.'

'Perhaps,' said Hannah, 'he *was* busy at work.'

'So busy that he couldn't pick up the phone once in seven days? So I said to him that he seemed to place a higher priority on his professional life than he did on his private life. And *he* said I was a very perceptive woman.'

There was a thoughtful silence for a few seconds and then Hannah said hopefully, 'You can't say that isn't a compliment.'

'Of course it isn't a compliment, it just means that Ben agrees with what I said. So I said to him I wasn't prepared to go on seeing a man who couldn't be bothered to make any effort.'

'And what did he say to that?'

'He said he quite understood.'

'And then what did he say?'

'And then I hung up on him.'

'It seems to me,' Frances said wisely, 'that he is a classic commitment-phobe. He's never married, has he? Given that he's not gay, there's something odd about that. What do *you* think, Annie? You knew him years ago.'

Annie, suddenly overwhelmed with the urge to cheer poor Carla who, she had just realized, was indeed a good friend, nodded her head sagely. 'You mustn't take it personally,' she told her. 'He's like that with all his girlfriends. He behaved in exactly the same way to both my sisters.'

Grace frowned. 'I thought you said they gave *him* up.'

'That's true,' agreed Annie, 'but only because he never rang them up! He told Lily he got nightmares about waking up and finding himself married and he told Josephine that he could never endure the thought of sharing his home with anyone else. Josephine always reckoned he needed to see a psychiatrist.'

'I must say,' Frances said, 'he doesn't look like someone who needs to see a psychiatrist.'

'That,' Annie said darkly, 'doesn't mean anything!'

Later, as Grace and Annie meandered back along the canal, Annie linked arms with Grace and said she thought she might buy a new dress for Hannah's wedding on the following Saturday, something stunning and sexy and very expensive.

Grace laughed. 'You're in an exceptionally good mood,' she said.

It was true. Annie was in a wonderful mood because the solution had finally presented itself. She was fed up with trying not to think about Ben. She was fed up with pretending she wasn't interested in him. Ben was free. She was free. She could never forgive what he'd done to her so she would refuse to think about it. She would see him at Hannah's wedding next week. She would tell him there was no need for explanations about the past. The past would be ignored, erased and obliterated. The future was what mattered and she couldn't wait for it to begin.

The sun continued to shine on Annie. On Monday, she raced back from school, dashed into town and found her perfect dress for the wedding within twenty minutes: calf-length, grey flecked with pink, it somehow gave her a waistline she knew for a fact she did not possess.

On Tuesday, her post brought joyful tidings. Bella had secured her honours. Annie rushed to the phone and remembered that Bella would still be at school. She had cancelled her usual lesson with Annie because she had a dress rehearsal. Annie decided it would be far better to give her the news when she saw her at the play on Friday. If the play was a disaster, the news would console her and if the play was a success, Bella could revel in the dual glory.

On Thursday, Lily rang with the excellent news that Mark was now coming down for Christmas with Josephine. The downside was that Cressida was coming too which meant that, as Lily informed her with great relish, Annie would have to remember to cast predatory eyes in Mark's direction whenever Cressida was about.

On Friday evening, Annie was on her way out of the flat when the telephone rang. She dashed back in, picked up the phone and interrupted her nephew's effusive greeting. 'Sidney, I'd love to chat but I'm in a hurry. It's Bella's play and—'

'I know,' said Sidney. 'I want you to buy some flowers for me. I'll pay you back but—'

'Sidney, I do not have time to buy flowers—'

'Go in the interval! There must be a garage somewhere nearby! I'm working through the weekend and I can't come down to see the play. I promised Bella I'd buy her flowers and I've only just remembered it was her first night last night! *Please*, Annie!'

'All right, I'll try! Now I have to go!'

All term, Annie had felt an inexplicable anxiety about Bella. Despite the exam success, the sense of foreboding continued to linger like a bad smell. In the last few weeks, she and Bella had held long discussions about the character of Nurse. Now, as she drove to the school, she was plagued by doubts. Had they over-analyzed the role? Would all the hard work only exacerbate Bella's awareness of the smallness of her part?

She slipped into a seat at the back of the hall just as the curtains opened. She was tense and stiff for the first few scenes and then allowed herself to relax and enjoy the play. Romeo was good, Juliet less so. She looked pretty but was far too knowing and coy. Abby, as a calm, confident and blithely insensitive Lady Capulet was excellent. And Bella . . . Bella was superb! Seeing her on the stage was a revelation. Swathed in vast amounts of padding and a horrendous grey wig, patting her hair smugly in front of the mirror and ogling every available man with a knowing smile, she proved to be a natural comedienne. She was the star of the show.

There was one particularly superb moment after Juliet

asked her nurse for advice after hearing that her new young husband, Romeo, had killed her cousin, Tybalt. Bella had successfully led the audience to believe that she was, despite her absurd preening, a true source of support and wisdom. Now Bella's nurse appeared to be about to offer some sound and sage advice:

> *'Then, since the case so stands as now it does,*
> *I think it best you married with the County.*
> *O, he's a lovely gentleman,*
> *Romeo's a dishclout to him . . .'*

The enthusiasm with which Bella suggested a course of bigamy to her young charge was as much a surprise to the audience as it was to Juliet. Best of all was the jolly smile with which Bella accompanied her extraordinary suggestion.

No doubt about it, Bella was a star. Such was Annie's relief that she felt duty bound to repay the fates with a noble action. She therefore raced out to the car at the beginning of the interval in order to carry out Sidney's request. She crept into the hall half an hour later clutching a cellophane-wrapped bouquet of tired red roses and a bottle of water for herself. Once she had recovered her breath, she watched the play with a critical eye. Some of the actors were inaudible, most of them moved stiffly. In the final scene the dead Juliet could be seen rearranging her dress. Bella's excellence had been achieved, Annie was certain, in spite of Miss Appleby's direction and not because of it.

If Annie had any doubts that she might be blinded by proprietorial affection, they were dispelled by the curtain call.

When Bella came on for her curtain call, she received the loudest applause of the evening.

Miss Appleby, a tall, thin woman in a long black dress and violet boots, came onto the stage and announced she would only talk for a few moments. She proceeded to speak for what seemed like an eternity and finally, with a dramatic flourish of her arms, turned to her cast and told them to go and meet their fans.

By the time Annie was able to reach Bella, she could see her talking animatedly to a bald-headed man and a laughing woman in a grey wool dress that Annie instantly coveted. This must be Bella's mother, the woman who had once been in Annie's favourite television serial. She had the same blonde hair and trim figure but otherwise bore little resemblance to the glamorous girl of Annie's memory.

Annie was touched by Bella's welcome. 'Annie! Thank you so much for coming!' She turned to her companions and said, 'Annie's my drama teacher! She's wonderful!'

Annie laughed and said, 'I can't take any credit for tonight! You were superb!' She held out the flowers. 'These are from Sidney!'

'He's so thoughtful!' Bella breathed. 'He's so kind!'

'He is,' said Annie. 'I shall tell him how good you were tonight. And there's one other thing. I have received your exam results. Very annoying!'

'Why?' Bella demanded. 'How badly did I do?'

'You were so sure you would get honours,' Annie said. She smiled. 'And you were absolutely right!'

Bella's eyes widened and she flung her arms round Annie. Then, with equal abruptness, she released her and said, 'Oh

Annie, here's my father! I'm so glad you can meet him!'

Annie turned with a ready smile that settled like concrete on her face. Bella said, 'Daddy, I want you to meet my drama teacher,' and then Annie reached out and took the hand of Ben Seymour.

CHAPTER NINETEEN

Black Book Entry. 13 December. Me for being so feeble, so pathetic, so wet.

It was Annie who spoke first. 'We've met already!' she said. Gathering up every last drop of dramatic talent, she managed a small, tight smile. 'Hello, Ben. I had no idea you were Bella's father. You should be very proud of her.' She was good. She was very good. She sounded cool, calm and confident, the epitome of a cool, calm and confident drama teacher.

Ben stared at her for a few agonizing moments and then said stiffly, 'Thank you.' He had no talent at all.

'I must go,' Annie said as if she had just remembered something terribly important and interesting she had to do right away. 'Well done again, Bella!'

A speedy but dignified exit was made impossible by the hordes of chattering relatives and excited pupils. Annie, jostling her way through them, felt as though she was wading through treacle; it seemed to take a lifetime to get away from that hall and out into the cold night air. He had a daughter!

Bella was his daughter! They even shared the same slow, slightly crooked smile. Why hadn't she noticed? Why *should* she have noticed? She told herself, don't think, just get in the car and start the engine. Impossible not to think, impossible not to remember that Bella's birthday . . . her eighteenth birthday . . . was on 15 July, the same day as her mother's birthday. Ben's daughter had entered the world five months after the wedding he chose not to attend. *Ben's daughter!* She gripped the driving wheel as if it were a lifebelt. All the agonizing she had done, the questions she had asked herself, the grieving she had done for the loss of her great love and all that time her great love had been behaving with the sordid predictability of every love-rat since time immemorial. It was enough to make her want to turn back, go straight into that hall and punch him in the face, and if Bella hadn't been there she probably would have done.

At home, she took off her coat, went through to the kitchen and poured herself a drink. She put it down on the breakfast bar and walked back to the sitting room. She picked up a cushion from the sofa, beat it into shape and put it back again. Then she walked over to her bedroom and pulled back the white coverlet. She returned to the sitting room and lit the gas fire. She went back to the kitchen and had a gulp of her wine. Then she was off again, raging round the small flat, furious with herself for crying, furious with Ben for everything. She went to the bathroom and splashed her face with water. She looked at herself in the mirror with disgust. Her eyes looked like cold sores.

The buzzer went and Annie made straight for it. She hesitated for only a moment before picking up the door phone. His voice sounded measured and grave. 'Annie, it's me. I wondered if you wanted to talk.'

She went downstairs and opened the front door. 'Come on up,' she said curtly and walked back upstairs without looking back. He followed her into her flat and stood looking at her but saying nothing.

She folded her arms. 'Why didn't you tell me you were Bella's father?'

He looked tired and crumpled and unhappy. 'Annie –' he paused to rub his forehead with his hand – 'I didn't even know you *knew* Bella until tonight. And I did try to tell you everything. More than once I tried to tell you and you stopped me. You said you didn't want to know.'

The fact that this was indisputably true only fuelled Annie's fury. Keep control, she told herself, keep control. 'Can I get you a drink?' she asked icily.

'I'd love a glass of water.'

'I'll be right back. Do sit down.' She went through to the kitchen and made a series of V-signs in his direction which she knew was childish but which was deeply satisfying. Then she filled two tumblers with water. How could she have ever thought she could have gone on seeing him without wanting to know why he'd left her? She must have been crazy. Did other people pursue actions that suddenly seemed incomprehensible to them? She had spent seventeen years, wasted seventeen years trying to learn not to think about what had happened. And now here she was back in the same dank hole into which he had originally thrown her. Seventeen years on and she was back in the hole! She had learnt nothing! She had gained nothing! She swallowed, picked up the tray and went back to the sitting room.

Ben had taken off his mac and was sitting on the sofa. He rose when she came in and watched as she put the tray down on the coffee table. She took her glass of water and placed herself in front of the fireplace. 'Sit down,' she said. 'You say you wanted to tell me everything. I'm listening.'

He sat down again, stared for a few seconds at the water in front of him and then put his hands together. 'I met Bella's mother at a party. You and I had split up. I was feeling angry, mostly with myself and with you as well. I wanted to stop thinking about you and I couldn't. I was twenty-four, I felt I'd been pressured into settling down and—'

'Excuse me, but when did I ever insist that I wanted us to "settle down"?'

'Annie, I'm not trying to justify my actions or my thoughts, I'm trying to explain what happened.'

'All right.' The fire, along with Ben's self-serving explanation, was making her hot. She went over to the armchair, sat down and crossed her legs tightly together. 'Do continue.'

Ben took a sip of his water. 'A friend of mine had been working on a TV drama and he invited me to the post-production party. Angelina Partridge was there. We got talking, we drank a lot, she seemed to like me. I was flattered. She was six years older than me, she was a glamorous actress—'

'And so you fucked her.'

He met her stare without flinching. 'And so I fucked her. The next morning we said goodbye and I walked home and I wished I hadn't slept with her. And after that, I did a lot of thinking and I thought there was not much point in being free to have loads of one-night stands with random women when all I really wanted was to be with you. And then I panicked and thought I'd lose you if I didn't show you how serious I was. So I asked you to marry me.'

'Are you saying you didn't really want to marry me?'

'I did want to marry you, of course I did. And then, two weeks before the wedding, I went over to my parents for Sunday lunch. When I got there it was clear they'd been rowing. There was a bad atmosphere. I was used to bad atmospheres, I'd grown up with them and I did what I always did in those circumstances. I talked a lot and I talked about me because if I talked about me they stopped being angry with each other. I told them I was nervous about living so close to your parents, I told them I wasn't sure I wanted to move out of London.'

'You never said any of this to me! I thought you loved Pixie Cottage as much as I did! I remember you saying how lovely it was!'

'It was a fantastic offer: a pretty little place with a garden, rent-free. And you adored it. Everything happened so quickly. It seemed churlish to have reservations. And most of the time I was fine about everything. As I say, I talked too much. I expressed doubts that most of the time I hadn't even known I'd felt.'

'If you'd wanted to stay in London, I'd have stayed with you.'

'I know that now. I wasn't thinking clearly.' He sighed and pushed his hair back from his forehead. 'A few days before the wedding, my father rang and wanted to take me out to lunch.

I didn't want to go. I'd had my stag night the evening before and was feeling pretty rough. But I went and he told me he'd been very disturbed by the things I'd said. And then he told me he was gay.'

'Your father is *gay*?' Annie had met Ben's father twice. He had been debonair, witty and charming, a man who knew how to talk to women. Ben looked very like him.

'I found it hard to believe too. My mother's girlfriends all adored him. She was always worried he was having affairs with other women. In retrospect, I suppose she got it half right. He said he hadn't been sure at first. He thought if he married, he'd stay straight. He began to have second thoughts but his future father-in-law had offered him a job and given them a flat and he'd felt trapped and unable to get out of it. He said he was worried I might make the same mistake. He said it was seeing me so worried that made him decide he had to leave my mother. He couldn't live a lie any longer. He asked me if I really wanted to settle in Surrey. He said he thought I was too young.'

'And you agreed with him?'

'Annie, my father had just told me that he was gay, that his marriage to my mother was a sham and that I was responsible for making him decide to break it up. I don't think after that I was capable of thinking anything coherent at all. I mean, I knew I was different from him. I wasn't gay, I did love you, but everything else . . . the wedding, the house in Surrey . . . all that suddenly seemed very scary. And I couldn't talk to you about it: you were so confident, so happy, so sure.'

'So you decided to run away instead?'

'No, I didn't decide that. I told myself I had pre-wedding

nerves and I'd be all right once the ceremony was over. The day before the wedding, I was about to leave work when I got a message from Angelina asking me to ring her. I was in a hurry, I had to collect my stuff from my flat before the new tenant arrived. When I got to my parent's house, I rang her and she said she had to talk to me. I met her in a pub in Fulham. She told me she was pregnant and that I was the father. She said she wanted to keep the baby. She'd met an American producer over Christmas and she was going to the States with him. If things worked out I'd never hear from her again. But she wanted me to know what was happening in case she needed financial help in the future. I gave her my parents' number and told her to get in touch at any time and then I left. I think I went a little mad. It felt like all these walls were closing in on me and every time I found a door, it disappeared. I went to a bar and had some drinks. I tried to ring you but your phone was engaged. I went round to see a friend and rang you again. I got your father and he said you'd gone to bed. I got stoned with my friend and ended up on the sofa. I woke up at eleven the next morning and knew I couldn't walk up the aisle.'

'And you didn't think to let me know about this?'

Ben drank some water and put the glass back on the tray. 'Annie, I rang and rang. Your phone was engaged the whole time. I should have got in the car and driven over and told you face to face. I couldn't bear to hurt you.'

'Quite right,' Annie said. 'Far more sensible to wait until the wedding was about to start. Far more sensible to get someone else to tell me. Far more sensible to give me no idea at all what was going on. Great decision, Ben.'

'I didn't want someone else to tell you. When I couldn't get through myself I rang my mother. She was horrified and hysterical. It turned out my father had left the night before. She said lots of things about Dad and then she said lots of things about me. None of them were very nice. She told me not to contact you, she said I'd make things even worse if I tried to talk to you myself.'

'And you believed her?'

'I suppose if I'm honest I wanted to believe her. She said she'd ring you. She said she didn't want to see me or my father ever again. Then she rang off and I drove to Brighton.'

'Why did you go to Brighton?'

'I don't know. I just got in the car and ended up there. I checked into a bed and breakfast. I don't remember much about the next few days. Then one morning I was sitting on the beach. It was raining and a couple of children walked past me. I could see them laughing at me. They thought I was mad. I realized if I stayed in Brighton any longer I probably would go mad. I rang your home and your mother refused to talk to me so I got in the car and drove over to you. You'd gone away and no one would tell me where you'd gone. When I got back to work they told me you'd left and I knew I'd made the biggest mistake of my life.'

'Are you asking me to feel sorry for you?'

'No. I behaved appallingly. I did a terrible thing to you. I wanted to see you. I wanted you to be angry with me. I wanted to sort things out. At first I thought we *would* sort things out. Then I heard you were getting married and I thought we never would and I was stuck with the guilt. I've been stuck with it ever since.'

'I am very glad to hear it.'

For the first time that evening, Ben gave a faint smile. 'I can imagine you would be.'

'And so now you're here and you're the father of one of my pupils. How very weird.' Annie hesitated. 'She's a very talented actress.'

Ben picked up his glass and finished his water. 'I don't want to talk about Bella.'

Annie gripped her hands together and swallowed. 'Your relationship with your daughter is of course nothing to do with me. I do think I'm entitled to a little more information about you and Angelina. Did she decide to stay with you after all?'

'I never asked her to stay with me and she never wanted me to ask her. She did go to the States. Her boyfriend had got her a small part in a horror film but it ended up on the cutting-room floor. Apparently she told him he was the father of her baby. She said Bella was premature but he must have wondered when the premature baby turned out to be a strapping great infant of eight and a half pounds. Anyway, he left when Bella was only a few months old. Angelina's sister went out to see her. Meg and her husband couldn't have children of their own. They lived in a nice house in Bath and had a comfortable income. Meg persuaded Angelina to let them have Bella.

'So the woman I saw at Bella's play was Angelina's sister?'

'Yes. She was there with her husband.'

'So what happened to Angelina?'

'She stayed on in the States. She did thousands of auditions and got the occasional small part. Then she met some millionaire lawyer and married him. I was walking down Oxford Street one day when she came up to me. I didn't recognize her at first. We had lunch and she told me all about Bella. Meg's husband had died in a car crash a few weeks earlier and Angelina had come over for the funeral. She thought it might help Meg and Bella if I got in touch and I was only too happy to do so. Meg was very kind. She let me come down whenever I could and I gradually got to know my daughter. She started coming to stay with me at half-term and I'd take her on holiday in the summer. A couple of years ago, Meg married again. Chris is a decent man but it's been difficult for Bella. She had adored Meg's first husband and then after his death she had got used to having Meg to herself. There were arguments. I decided it was time to move down here and provide Bella with a bolt hole when things got difficult. When the chance of the Bristol job came up, I grabbed it. Now Bella stays with me most weekends.'

'I see.' Annie stood up. 'Thank you for clarifying the situation.'

'Annie . . .'

'It's very late and I'm pretty tired.'

'Is that all you have to say?'

'What do you want me to say?'

'Look, I know how upset you are. I know you've been crying. I know I hurt you.'

'Yes,' said Annie. 'You hurt me. And now I don't want to talk about it any more. Just now, I'd really like you to leave my home.'

'Of course.' Ben reached out for his mac and stood up. 'Can I say one more thing? I have never stopped regretting what I did on the day of our wedding. I made a terrible mistake. I fully accept that. I'd just like you to consider the fact that the actions we take don't always define the people we are. On a particular morning a long time ago I behaved like a jerk. That doesn't necessarily mean I'm a jerk now. Annie? Will you please at least think about that?'

'I don't know. I might. Now I'd be very grateful if you'd go.'

He paused. 'Annie, I screwed up. When I saw you again I thought I might have the chance to make things right.'

'How can you make things right again? Everything's different. You have a daughter who you don't want to talk about. That's fine. She's nothing to do with me. She is *nothing* to do with me. And you don't have anything to do with *me*. I wasn't the one who made that decision. I wasn't the one who decided to leave you thirty minutes before our wedding. I wasn't the one who felt sick at the thought of marrying you. Now I really, really want you to please go downstairs and leave my flat.'

Ben went to the door and paused. 'What I said about Bella. I didn't mean that I—'

'Please, Ben,' Annie said fiercely, 'just go!'

Ben nodded and then went out of the room. She waited until she heard his footsteps on the pavement and then she went through to the kitchen, replenished her wine glass and returned to the sitting room. She sat down on the sofa and almost immediately, a great wailing sob pushed its way up through her throat, pulling at her insides and emerging into the air like a newborn infant. She had always wanted children, she had wanted Ben's children and she had none. And Ben had Bella. Angelina Partridge and Ben had Bella.

302

She took a gulp of her wine but it was no use; another gut-wrenching sob tore itself from her and she cried and cried and cried for the marriage she should have had and the child that should have been hers.

When Annie awoke the next morning, a man was beating drums inside her head and her eyes felt like they'd fallen to the back of her skull. For a while she lay without moving but the drummer wouldn't go away. She rang Grace and asked her to give her apologies to Hannah: she had a crippling bout of . . . she panicked for a moment while she tried to think of something sufficiently horrible . . . gastro-enteritis and would have to miss the wedding. She promised to ring again soon and rang off, and then she buried herself under the duvet.

On Tuesday Bella came round for her last lesson of the year. Still high on the success of her play, Bella launched into an in-depth analysis of the production's strengths and weaknesses after which Annie suggested a little awkwardly that Bella might decide now was the time to stop having private lessons. Bella said of course she wanted to continue her lessons and that if it was a question of money she hadn't forgotten their bargain and she had indeed brought with her the full money for this very lesson. Annie assured her it was nothing to do with the money and Bella asked in a tone of injured bewilderment why Annie didn't want to teach her any more and Annie assured her she did and that indeed she was very proud of her and Bella smiled radiantly and said well that was all right then and wasn't it funny that Annie knew her father?

Annie said it certainly was.

Then Bella asked Annie if she'd talk to her father about the advantages of drama school and Annie said she was sorry but she could not interfere in the family dispute and that Bella and her father must sort out their disagreement on their own.

And after Bella left, Annie lay down on the floor and did thirty press-ups. Annie had discovered the day before that it was virtually impossible to cry while doing press-ups and press-ups would make her look good while crying very definitely made her ugly.

CHAPTER TWENTY

Black Book Entry, 27 December: Ben Seymour again and again and again.

Lily was an expert at Christmas. She was also a Superwoman. She had brought William home only three weeks ago and the boys had broken up ten days after that. Somehow she had managed to stock the larder, make the beds and turn the house into a seasonal wonder. A vast Christmas tree, dressed in gold and white, stood in the hail and soared through the stairwell. Christmas cards cascaded down walls. Mistletoe hung from doorways. Swathes of ivy decorated the mantelpiece, wove round the banisters and garlanded paintings. And everywhere there were candles filling the house with the scent of cinnamon.

Best of all there was William, a little shaky and not able to lead the customary Christmas expeditions over the fields, but still gloriously, indefatigably William, laughing at his own jokes, sitting spellbound in front of the Christmas films and an enthusiastic participant in every board game. Milly, restored to the family home, remained glued to his side.

Truth to tell, despite Lily's brilliant organization and William's larger than life presence, Annie found Christmas this year a considerable strain. She was like a very bad juggler who has limited success in keeping one ball in the air and is suddenly presented with a further three. First, there were her parents, always worried that Annie, being single and childless, must necessarily be severely depressed. As always when in their presence, Annie felt obliged to project the image of a successful and satisfied singleton. However, Mark and Josephine were expecting a sad and wistful woman looking for love. Worse still, when Cressida was around – and Cressida was one of those girls who always seem to be around when least expected – Annie was supposed to be a single-minded temptress, determined to catch Mark in her web. Trying to project all these disparate persons into one seamless whole was exhausting and not helped by the fact that at all times Annie was aware of an underlying rage that made her feel like an inefficient pressure cooker.

A related concern was Sidney's relationship with Bella which Annie, for reasons she knew were illogical, could not help regarding as incestuous. So far as she could ascertain, their relationship appeared to be conducted mainly through cyberspace but Bella had apparently met up with him twice in London and when Sidney told Annie cheerfully that he would want to come and stay as soon as he could get some holiday, she could barely suppress a shudder. She couldn't resist asking Sidney if he knew anything about her family. Sidney said he didn't which shouldn't have surprised Annie since he would be far more interested in finding out if Bella agreed that Kasabian was the best new band of the moment than in discussing her parents' complicated private lives.

Annie's parents went home on the morning of the twenty-seventh, it being a cardinal rule of Rosemary never to inflict parental company on any of her daughters for more than three days. As they were about to drive off, David wound down his car window in order to tell Annie he and her mother both thought she looked peaky. 'Go and join that gym!' he urged. 'Get some fun in your life! And some exercise!' He then drove off quickly before a smouldering Annie could respond.

Josephine and Mark left with their three in the afternoon and Annie kissed them all, even Cressida, and said she couldn't wait to visit Herne Hill at the end of January. 'Don't worry about any dinner parties,' she assured her sister, 'I'm coming to see *you* not your friends.'

Josephine smiled. 'It will be no trouble! We'll enjoy planning it! I have a couple of very interesting guests in mind already! Goodbye now!'

After this exchange, Annie returned to the house and played a very aggressive game of Cluedo with Luke and Gabriel. She had agreed to stay on for one more night in order to have a post-mortem about Mark, Josephine and Cressida.

In fact, Annie surprised herself as much as she did William and Lily during supper by asking them if they minded if she told them about Ben.

The boys were watching a film in the playroom. Lily directed a triumphant glance at her husband. 'You *see*?' she demanded. She turned to Annie. 'William said I shouldn't ask you about Ben. He said you wouldn't want to talk about him!'

'I haven't wanted to talk about him for seventeen years,'

Annie said, 'and a fat lot of good it's done me. The thing is: it's happened all over again!'

Lily's eyes widened. 'You mean he's jilted you again?'

'It feels like he has. I found out a few days before Christmas that one of my private pupils is his daughter!'

'Oh my God!' Lily exclaimed. 'That's so spooky! It's like Kismet! It's like Fate is trying to tell you something!'

'Fate did tell me something,' Annie said shortly. 'Bella is eighteen next July!' She gave Lily a significant look. Lily looked back at her blankly. 'Don't you see? Bella will be eighteen next July which means that Bella was conceived a few weeks before Ben asked me to marry him!'

'Now that *is* wrong,' William said as if everything else Ben had done had been all right. 'What a bounder! To have a mistress even before he's married! Not that I'm saying you should have a mistress *after* you marry, it just seems pretty rich to have one *before*!'

'It wasn't quite like that,' Annie conceded grudgingly. 'He says he had a one-night stand with Bella's mother when we split up for a few weeks. She told him she was pregnant the night before the wedding.'

William whistled. 'Poor bugger!' he said. 'What rotten luck!'

'William!' Annie protested. 'You just called him a bounder!'

'I didn't realize he saw this other woman during a break in your relationship. As I say, poor bugger!'

'To be fair to Ben,' Lily said, adopting a magisterial manner, 'you can't blame him for sleeping with another woman when he wasn't even seeing you at the time. What I

308

don't understand is why he didn't tell you about the baby.
I mean he obviously loved you or he wouldn't have tried so
hard to find out where you went after the wedding.'

William shook his head. 'Poor bugger!'

Annie glanced irritably at her brother-in-law. 'Will you stop
saying that?' she asked. 'Just remember he got his mother to
tell me the wedding was off.'

Lily rested her chin on her hands. 'That was very bad. Why
did he do that?'

'He says now he wasn't thinking straight. His parents were
on the verge of splitting up and his father said Ben was signing
his life away before it had started and then the pregnancy
news happened. Ben said he got smashed the night before the
wedding and the next morning he couldn't face it. He *said*
he tried to ring me.'

'He probably did,' Lily said. 'If you remember, Daddy was
on the phone the entire morning!'

'Anyway he says he rang his mother and she said she'd
tell me.'

'An action he clearly regretted,' Lily said quickly, 'judging
by his behaviour afterwards.'

'Poor bugger!' William murmured.

'William!' Annie exploded. 'What about me? What about
my humiliation? What about my life being ruined? What
about the fact that he was a great big coward?'

'Absolutely,' William agreed, 'but then we all do things we
regret later. I once stole the goldfish from my neighbour's
pond and put them in the big pond on the village green. I only
did it because my neighbour told my mother she'd seen me
smoking. But I felt very bad afterwards. The poor fish didn't

like their new home. They obviously found the move very traumatic and most of them died.'

'William, that is completely different. You didn't ruin anyone's life!'

'Well I did, as a matter of fact. I pretty well ruined the lives of six fish.'

'Oh for goodness sake,' Annie said, impaling the Stilton with the cheese knife, 'you can't compare me with six gold-fish! It took years for me to recover from what he did.'

'Does Ben want to get back with you?' Lily asked.

'Possibly,' Annie said, 'if only so he can stop feeling guilty. He doesn't like me talking about his daughter though. When I told him Bella was a very good actress, he more or less told me to mind my own business. And then he has the nerve to say he wants to make everything right again!'

At the other end of the table William shook his head again. 'Poor bugger,' he said.

When Annie left the next morning, William handed her a bag with a video inside it. 'I've got the DVD now,' he said, 'so you can have the video. Watch it when you feel low; it's a great film with a great last line. Let me know what you think.'

Annie drove home feeling scratchy and ill-tempered. After all these years of silence she had decided to talk to William and Lily about Ben. And all they had done was to make excuses for him! The more she thought of it, the more partisan their opinions seemed. It was almost as if they were trying to find excuses for him. As if anything at all could excuse what he did! It was inexcusable. It was. She had no reason to be rattled by anyone who might suggest otherwise.

310

Nevertheless, it would be good to get support from someone else, someone who would reinforce her conviction that Lily and William had no right to feel even slightly sympathetic towards Ben. After all these years of trying to erase the past, she now felt an almost obsessive need to pick over the facts with someone who would fully appreciate the enormity of the wrong that had been done to her.

She was *not* the Annie of seventeen years ago, she would not suffer in silence this time, she would behave like the mature woman she was sure she could be and calmly and sensibly analyze the situation, reflect and move on. Grace would understand! She would talk to Grace!

Annie arrived home at midday and rang her friend immediately. Grace suggested a walk but, 'It can't be a long one. I shouldn't be going out at all but I'm fed up with being on the phone all day. It hasn't stopped going all morning!'

Annie kicked off her shoes and settled back on her bed. 'Why?'

'Have you forgotten? My ball is tomorrow! You can't have forgotten!'

'No of course not,' said Annie, uncomfortably aware that her brain was only able to focus on the one subject at present. 'Are you sure you have time for a walk?'

'I'll meet you in front of the Holbourne Museum in eight minutes,' Grace said. 'Don't be late!'

Annie put the phone down, stood up and eased herself back into her shoes. Grace's peremptory tone made her smile. She had a glimpse of an alternative Grace in a parallel universe, a Grace who had no demanding children or husband, a Grace who was ambitious, decisive and focused. Supposing in that alternative world, it was *she* who had the husband and children. What would *she* be like? She sighed and then checked her watch. Fortunately she had no time for such hypothetical fantasies. She had to get to the Holbourne Museum in six minutes and twenty seconds.

She and Grace converged on the museum at the same time. Grace kissed Annie warmly and said, 'Let's go through Sydney Gardens and out by the canal. I have a box of Hannah's wedding cake for you on my kitchen table. I'm so sorry I forgot it! My brain has too much information in it!'

Annie smiled. 'Are we confident this ball is going to be a success?'

Grace shuddered. 'Don't even joke about it. I had a phone call on Christmas Eve to say the lead singer of the band I've booked had developed laryngitis! I was reduced to begging Jake's friends to step in if necessary and that would have been a true disaster, they all think they're Eric Clapton and insist on doing guitar solos which are tedious enough when Eric Clapton does them. Fortunately, the lead singer turns out to be a hypochondriac who didn't have laryngitis at all. We had my sister-in-law – you know, Amy, the barrister? – and her family staying over Christmas. I was tearing around, preparing Brussels sprouts and trying to locate missing tombola prizes and I heard Amy ask Fizzie what she wanted to do after university and do you know what Fizzie said?'

'Something bad,' said Annie perceptively.

'She said she thought she might be like me and find a man to support her so she could do nothing all day!'

'I'd have made her make the Christmas dinner,' Annie mused.

'Amy was very nice. She said that in that case Fizzie had better learn to cook and clean and drive and be able to keep her temper! Fortunately I didn't have time to worry about losing my temper. And to be fair to Fizzie, she's still nursing a broken heart. And then Ben did an item on his programme just before Christmas and we sold a lot more tickets after that, which is wonderful of course but it's made me even more jittery about the whole thing. I must say, Ben's been wonderful!'

'Has he indeed?' Annie asked with enough vitriol in her voice to destroy an army.

'Annie?' Grace eyed her curiously. 'Why are you always so dismissive about Ben?'

Annie opened the gate and they joined the towpath. 'It's a long story,' she said. 'I'll tell you when you have more time.'

Grace put her arm through Annie's. 'Hang the ball,' she said, 'I can't do any more before tomorrow anyway. Tell me the long story.'

So Annie did. She told her about the wedding day that wasn't, her flight to France and her abrupt resignation from the BBC, her discovery about Bella's parentage and Ben's attempt to excuse the inexcusable.

It was difficult to gauge Grace's reaction since she had wound her scarf round most of her face in response to the sharp breeze. When Annie had finally finished, she did however respond in tones of suitable disgust. 'It must have been a nightmare! How could Ben be so cowardly and so cruel? He must have been horribly embarrassed when he saw you that evening at Frances's party! How could he have left you to hang on a question mark for the rest of your life?

He must have known you needed to hear some explanation!'

Annie hugged her arms to her chest. 'Actually,' she said stiffly, 'I didn't want an explanation. I had had the most humiliating day of my life because of him. Why on earth should I want to speak to him after that?'

'Well –' Grace paused to step aside for a couple of elderly cyclists – 'I can quite see you'd be too proud to go after him but if he got in touch with you and wanted to speak to you. . . . Annie, he *did* seek you out, didn't he? Annie, how could you not want to hear why he'd jilted you?'

Annie stared at a family of ducks proceeding sedately along the edge of the canal. Grace was proving to be just as unsatisfactory as Lily and William. She said defensively, 'I never wanted to see him again. There are some things you can never forgive.'

'Sometimes,' Grace said, 'your intransigence is truly scary. What happened after you met him again? Did you still refuse to speak to him?'

'No of course I didn't. I simply refused to let him talk about the past. It was only when Bella "introduced" me to her father that I decided it was time to know what had happened. And now Ben expects me to forgive him so we can be jolly friends and I can forget what he did even though that might be a little difficult since I teach his daughter drama every week. I find his attitude incredible!'

Grace looked at her watch. 'We'd better turn back,' she said.

'Of course.' They turned and began to retrace their steps. Annie glanced impatiently at Grace. 'Don't you think I'm right?' she asked.

314

'Ben did something very wrong,' Grace said slowly, 'but he's obviously wanted to say he's sorry for a very long time. Isn't it time you accepted his apology?'

Annie picked up a stick and hurled it into the canal. 'Because of Ben,' she said, 'I left my family and my friends, I gave up my job, I changed my entire life.'

'Exactly!' Grace exclaimed. '*You* changed your whole life, *you* decided to give up your job and go to France; you can't blame Ben for *your* choices!'

'I took those choices because Ben jilted me! I did what I did because he did what he did!'

'I know but what I'm saying is you didn't have to do what you did just because he did what he did. You could have made different choices.'

Grace's scarf had uncoiled itself and Grace wrapped it round her neck and chin again. For a minute or so they trudged along in silence and then Annie sniffed. 'You realize what you're saying? You're telling me that it was my fault and not Ben's that I was unhappy for so long.'

Grace pulled down her scarf. 'I'm not saying that at all—'

'Yes, you are. And actually,' Annie jammed her hands into the pockets of her coat, 'I'm beginning to think you might be right.'

That evening, Annie sat in her sitting room, contemplating the bleak conclusion she had reached. She alone had chosen to leave the job she loved, she alone had chosen to cut herself off from friends and family, she alone had chosen not to go to Australia with Robbie – though, actually, that was a decision that had probably been very sensible – and she alone had chosen to steer clear of emotional commitment in the last seventeen years. She had chosen to let Ben's desertion poison her life. She pushed her hair back from her face and groaned. She remembered William's video and went through to her room and fished it out of her bag. If ever she needed cheering up it was now. She glanced at her watch. It was half past seven. She was not going to spend the rest of the evening whipping herself into a quivering heap of self-loathing.

Grosse Pointe Blank proved to be a brilliant film. There were several reasons:

1: It had John Cusack in it.
2: It had a superb soundtrack.
3: It was very funny.
4: It was very successful in making Annie forget her self-lacerations.

Indeed it was so successful that the shock she received at the end of the film was all the more extreme. When Minnie Driver made the final voice-over statement, Annie froze. Then she grabbed the control and rewound so she could hear it again. She rewound again and played it one more time. Then she switched off the video and switched off the television.

She felt like God must have felt after seven days of creating mountains and volcanoes and rivers and stars and suns and wondering if He'd ever get it right and wondering what on earth He was doing and then finally discovering He'd made something rather wonderful ... if indeed He had spent seven days making the world, which He hadn't since Annie didn't believe He even existed. The God analogy was getting complicated. What she really felt like was the producer of a play with forty children of whom only seven could act and then watching it in performance and seeing that a miracle had happened and everyone had produced something glorious. What she felt was like the sun breaking through after days of grey clouds and even greyer rain. And best of all, she could see there was nothing wrong in having doubts about a lifelong way of thinking, in fact having doubts about a lifelong way of thinking was healthy and mature and sensible.

The phone went and Annie reached out for the handset.

'Annie?'

Annie was too shocked to respond. If she had believed in God she would have thought He was trying to tell her something.

'Annie, I know you don't want to speak to me but—'

'No, that's all right.' Annie swallowed. 'Hello, Ben.'

'I won't keep you,' Ben said. 'I only wanted to know if you were going to Grace's ball tomorrow and if you knew . . . The thing is, I bought a ticket from Grace but it occurred to me that you'd rather I didn't go and—'

Annie leant back against the cushions. 'I'm going and I'm very happy for you to go.'

There was a long pause and then Ben said, 'You're not planning to murder me with the tombola bucket, are you?'

Annie smiled. 'Why on earth should I do that?'

'The last time I saw you, you did make it pretty clear you never wanted to talk to me again.'

'Oh that!' Annie said airily. 'I've forgotten all that!'

There was an even longer pause. 'You're like an elephant, Annie. You never forget things.'

'Didn't you say that people can change?'

'Yes, but . . . Are you *sure* you don't mind me being at the ball?'

'Not at all. I look forward to seeing you.'

'Now you're really worrying me,' Ben said. 'Goodnight, Annie.'

Annie laughed and switched off the phone. Immediately it rang again. This time it was Grace.

'Annie, I've been thinking and thinking and I feel really bad. I was monumentally tactless this afternoon and I had no right to say what I did. I have no idea what it must have been like for you and I'm so—'

'Grace!' Annie said. 'Don't worry! You weren't tactless, you were very sensible and I found your comments very helpful.'

'You're very kind but I feel terrible. And then I realized that I've put Ben on our table tomorrow night and I know you won't want to sit near him—'

'Actually,' said Annie, 'I do.'

'You do what?'

'I want to sit near him. I want to talk to him. You were right. I want to sort things out. I'm fed up with being bitter and angry. I want to have a good time tomorrow night and I intend to have a good time!'

'Wow!' Grace exclaimed. 'I don't know what to say. That's great! Now I can go back to just worrying about the ball itself.'

'Don't be silly, the ball will be a great success!' Annie laughed. 'You've spent months organizing this and you've left nothing to chance. What can possibly go wrong?'

★

318

That evening, Annie took out her Black Book and read through her life's catalogue of petty grievances, serious wrongs, disappointments both trivial and huge. What was it Minnie Driver had said? Forget about forgiving and just accept? In other words, don't forget, don't obliterate but accept that people can make mistakes, accept that people can change. She stared at the book. It was a bad book, full of silly memories and stupid things that people had once done or said. She had always regarded it as her refuge and her shield when in fact it was really a great, heavy, rusty, grim anchor, keeping her tied to a festering boulder of resentment and misery. It was time to let it go.

She stood up, went through to the kitchen and found a supermarket bag. She put the book inside it, grabbed her keys, put on her coat and walked out of the flat.

It was a beautiful night, cool and still with a large, creamy moon in the sky. She walked down the road to Laura Place and stopped in front of her destination: a large civic litter bin. She stood in front of it with a beating heart and then, before she could change her mind, thrust the Black Book into the bin where it fell with soft thud.

Annie blinked, took a deep breath and walked back home.

CHAPTER TWENTY-ONE

It was not often that Annie felt satisfied with her appearance. Tonight, she was almost tempted to find her camera and take a picture of her reflection. Her black dress might be ten years old but its empire line was as flattering as ever and its cleavage-celebrating front made her feel sexy. She had showered and washed her hair and her fringe, which generally insisted on following its own agenda, now lay demurely across her forehead. She spent ages making up her face but it was worth it: usually when she tried to smoulder at the mirror she looked like she had toothache. Tonight, she looked like she was a genuine smoulderer. When her taxi called for her, she sprayed herself generously with the expensive perfume Lily had given her for Christmas and flew down the stairs. She could have had a lift with Grace and Henry but that would have meant leaving an hour ago and there was no way that Annie wanted to hurry over her preparation.

The Assembly Rooms had been built in 1771 and the Ball Room was the largest eighteenth-century room in Bath. When Annie walked into it, she stood for a moment and gazed at the sparkling, intricate chandeliers, the high ceiling and the elevated windows (deliberately positioned in order to make it impossible for prying eyes from outside to look in).

She saw Edward detach himself from a group and walk purposefully towards her. 'Annie!' he exclaimed, kissing her on both cheeks. 'You look wonderful!'

'And you look . . . very smart,' Annie said. Edward did not look wonderful. His trousers and dinner jacket were too tight and his cummerbund, a red and white spotted affair only served to accentuate his generous waistline.

'The place is full,' Edward said. 'Grace has done a great job, hasn't she? She's given us some tasks to do. You and I and Frances have to sell raffle tickets before dinner starts. Grace says we can't sit down unless we sell them all.'

'I'd better go and get them, then,' Annie said. 'Where *is* Grace?'

'She's in the Octagon Room, I think. Last time I saw her, she was sorting out the raffle prizes. The band is coming on after dinner. Will you dance with me later on?'

'Yes,' Annie said, 'as long as you stop looking at my cleavage.'

Edward looked hurt. 'I wasn't! And even if I was, you couldn't blame me. If you women insist on wearing provocative . . .'

Annie wasn't listening. She had seen Ben and he had seen her. She saw him stride towards her. He looked beautiful.

Edward greeted Ben warmly. 'Saw you on the telly last night! How are you? Don't you think Annie looks wonderful?'

'She looks lovely,' Ben agreed. 'I've been charged to give you a message, Edward. Carla wants you. She's been looking for you all over the place.'

'Oh dear,' Edward said. 'It doesn't do to keep Carla waiting. I'll see you both later.'

'Tell me,' Annie murmured, 'was Carla really looking for him?'

'I'm sure she'll be very happy to see him.'

'Poor Edward. You're a ruthless man, Ben.'

His blue eyes looked intently at her. 'Only where you're concerned.'

She swallowed. She couldn't wait. The epiphany she had experienced the night before was too great, too wonderful. She needed to share it at once. 'I saw a film last night,' she said. 'It was very good. It was called *Grosse Pointe Blank*.'

'A great film,' Ben said, 'with a great gun-fight at the end.'

'Yes. Well, anyway, Minnie Driver says at the end, "Forget about forgiveness, just accept he's a jerk." Or something like that.'

Ben frowned. 'I don't think she says anything about jerks.'

'I don't care,' Annie said. 'The point is—'

She was unable to tell Ben what the point was because Frances chose this moment to join them. 'Hey! I'm glad you're both here. I can kill two birds with one stone. How are you, Ben? Annie, we have to get to work. Grace wants us to sell these tickets. And she wants to see you, Ben, right away. She thought it would be nice if you could say a few things about the Refugee Council before the raffle tickets are drawn.' She handed Annie four books of tickets. 'Let's split up. I'll do this room. You go and do the Octagon Room.'

'Right,' Annie said, resisting the urge to ask Frances to

322

go away and come back in twenty minutes. She gave Ben a light smile and set out to sell tickets. She would resume her conversation with him later.

Except everyone seemed to be conspiring against her. No sooner had she sold her tickets – which she did in record time, being ruthless in her determination to finish the job as soon as she could – than Grace appeared and gave her some more, mollifying Annie slightly with the promise that she had put Ben next to her at dinner.

After Annie had sold her second batch, she went off in search of Ben. She could see him sitting near the door with Carla who was gesticulating wildly. Annie began to walk towards them when she was intercepted by Ted.

'Annie!' he beamed. 'Just the woman I want to see! I need your advice. It's about Frances's birthday present!'

'Really?' Annie asked.

'I've been to Boots,' Ted said. 'And I looked at all the make-up stuff and I didn't understand any of it. You have no idea how many odd-sounding things there are with words on them I've never heard before. Do *you* know what *antioxidants* are? And what's a *re-plumping emulsion*? And *dermo-contractions*! Have you ever heard of them?'

'No, I haven't,' Annie said, 'but—'

'You could spend a fortune in there! You can get body-lifting creams and clarifying creams and creams that make moisture surge and scrub creams and comfort creams and—'

'My gosh, Ted,' Annie said, torn between irritation and admiration, 'you've certainly done your homework!'

'I found it quite interesting actually. Except when the beauty woman behind the counter came over. She was terrifying.

Looked like a china doll. She asked me what sort of complexion Frances had and when I said it was pink, she looked at me as if I was mad. Anyway, I decided it was safer to give the beauty counter a miss!'

'Very sensible,' Annie agreed. 'Well, I think I ought to—'

'So then,' Ted continued inexorably, 'I thought I'd get her a hairdryer. Do you know how many different sorts of hairdryers there are?'

'No,' Annie sighed.

'Hair-diffusing machines, hair-sculpting machines, hair—'

'Listen, Ted,' Annie said desperately, having just seen Ben and Carla leave the Ball Room, 'if I were you, I'd buy Frances a gift voucher from a health and beauty clinic. There are loads of them in Bath and it would do Frances good to have a lovely, self-indulgent facial or massage. She could even have some foot treatment. And now I must go and find Carla. Apparently she was looking for me.'

She got as far as the Octagon Room when she was stopped again by Ted. 'There was something else I wanted to talk to you about,' he said. 'I need your advice again.'

'Really?' Annie said, surreptitiously scanning the room for signs of Ben.

'The thing is, Josh was a bit low over Christmas. He was hoping to go to Edinburgh to read history but he's been rejected. He says he doesn't want to go to anywhere else. So now he's thinking he might have a gap year and then apply again to read Scottish ethnology.'

'Is he interested in Scottish ethnology?'

'No but he doesn't think anyone else will be either so he reckons he'll have a good chance of getting in. You're a teacher. Do you think Scottish ethnology would be a good subject to study?'

Annie sighed. 'I don't really know a lot about Scottish ethnology. In fact, if I'm honest I don't know anything about it at all . . .' She could see Ben in the doorway. She smiled at him. He smiled at her. He was coming over! 'But knowing Josh, he'll do really well at it and Edinburgh is a very good university. Oh look, here's Ben!'

'Ted!' Ben said. 'Carla's in the bar. She asked me to find you. I've no idea why but she's very keen to speak to you.'

'Oh dear!' Ted raised his eyebrows. 'I'd better go.' He smiled at them both. 'I'll be right back!'

'And I suppose,' Annie murmured, 'that Carla really does want to see Ted?'

'I'm sure she will,' Ben said. He took her arm. 'Annie, I like your friends, but it would be nice to talk to you for five minutes without being interrupted. Would you like to step outside for a moment and get some fresh air?'

No sooner had Annie agreed that it was a little hot than Grace swept down on them looking, to Annie's jaundiced eye, like a seagull diving towards its prey.

'Annie,' Grace said, 'can you go and tell everyone at the bar that dinner is ready? Tell them the seating plan is by the door. Ben, you stay with me, you're doing the speech, remember?'

Annie locked eyes briefly with Ben and then went obediently to the bar.

By the time she got to her table, most of her dinner companions were there. 'Annie!' Henry cried. 'You're sitting between Edward and me, you lucky girl!'

'Actually,' Annie said, 'I think Grace wanted me to sit next to Ben.'

Henry squeezed her arm and whispered conspiratorially, 'I've changed the seating plans. Grace had put me next to Carla and while I love her dearly when she's sober . . .' He left the sentence hanging in the air and raised his eyebrows significantly. Annie felt like slapping him.

Ben came to the microphone. 'Good evening!' he said. 'Grace asked me to say a few words before dinner about the charity we are all supporting tonight. She is under the mistaken impression that I am more articulate than she is. In fact the real reason I agreed to speak is because Grace was so passionate and persuasive about the value of the Refugee Council that she turned me into an instant convert.'

'He's very pleased with himself,' Henry muttered in Annie's ear.

'Shut up, Henry!' Annie murmured.

Ben wasn't pleased with himself. He was terrific. He made a few self-deprecatory jokes, he dropped in a few interesting facts – Annie had not known, for example, that fish and chips, the Mini and Marks and Spencer were all created or invented by refugees who came to Britain – and flattered the audience by suggesting that they had come here in order to support a charity rather than to have a good time. He made it very clear that it was Grace who was responsible for the entire evening and ended by suggesting that everyone should thank her for all she had done.

The applause was deafening. Ben took Grace's hand and Grace, with shining eyes and very pink cheeks, nodded her thanks. Impulsively, Annie touched Henry's arm. 'You must be very proud,' she whispered.

'I am,' Henry said. 'The girl's done well!' Which, coming from Henry, was a compliment indeed.

After the raffle, came the dinner. Annie, stirred by Ben's speech and Grace's happiness, forgave Henry his interference with the place settings. Every now and then she glanced surreptitiously at Ben who was monopolized by Carla. Their conversation was intense and conducted in low whispers and if Annie had been inclined to eavesdrop, which of course she wasn't, she would have been able to hear little or nothing.

It was at the end of the meal, when the band was already tuning its instruments that Carla suddenly spoke up. 'Don't you think,' she said in a loud rasping voice, 'that a man who can break a woman's heart and show no remorse, no remorse *at all*, is a cad of the first order?'

The question was clearly rhetorical but since her dinner-table companions were all aware of Carla's volatility, most of them made soothing sounds of agreement.

'I do!' Carla said. 'I think a man who says one thing and does another, who knows he's wrecked a woman's life and doesn't give a damn, I think that . . .' She paused to shake off a restraining hand from Ben. 'Fuck you, Ben, I'm going to speak! I'm going to speak!'

Annie glanced at Ben and felt a shiver of disbelief. His eyes were fixed with grim intensity on Carla and he pulled again at Carla's hand.

'I will not be silenced!' Carla pulled her hand away and stamped her fist on the table. 'It's not fair! It's not fair to me, it's not fair to Grace, it's not fair to all the other women! Did you have no idea, Grace, that your husband has, to my certain knowledge, slept with at least ten women in this room? No of course you didn't. And you didn't know either that I've been sleeping with your husband on and off for about a year? Funnily enough, when I started talking about a future together he started feeling guilty about you. So he finished it. Which was fine, Grace, except that as soon as he heard I was interested in Ben, he started ringing me again and telling me he loved me again. And I was stupid enough to believe him. So then yesterday he tells me what fun we've had and by the way he's finishing it again. This from a man who told me I gave the best blow jobs in the world and—'

'That's enough!' Ben's tone was low but furious. 'You've ruined Grace's night. Now be quiet!'

Carla's face crumpled and she began to sob. 'I'm sorry, I'm sorry, I'm just so unhappy and now I'll go home. Ben, will you take me home?'

Ben stood up and helped Carla to her feet. He put an arm round her and ushered her out of the room.

There was an appalled silence. Carla's tirade had reached most of the tables and everyone's eyes were on the departing Ben and Carla. Annie, whose first guilty reaction had been one of relief that Ben was innocent of any wrongdoing, looked across at Grace who sat drained of colour and as still as a statue.

Annie went over to Grace and put a gentle hand on her shoulder. 'I think that now might be the time to get the band playing.'

Grace stirred and said, 'Yes, yes of course. I'll go and tell them to start.' She rose from the table and hurried across to the podium.

Henry cleared his throat. 'How very embarrassing!' he said with a ghastly attempt at joviality. 'Looks like Carla's finally flipped! She appears to be living in a fantasy world!' He glanced restlessly at each of his remaining dinner companions and waited for someone to say something. 'You surely don't believe this rubbish, do you?' A dull red colour suffused his cheeks. His eyes darted round the nearby tables. He muttered, 'I'm not staying here to be gawped at.' He pushed his chair back. 'Tell Grace I'll see her at home.'

On the podium, the lead singer bounded up to the microphone. 'Hi, folks, let's get this party moving! This first song is for all those of you who can't . . . "Get No Satisfaction"!' He clapped his hands together and the band swung into action.

Frances glanced questioningly at her husband who had pushed his chair back abruptly. 'Where are you off to?' she asked.

Ted straightened his jacket. 'I'm going to dance with Grace,' he said. He marched across to the podium, said a few words to Grace and took her onto the dance floor.

'Well done, Ted,' Annie said softly.

Frances nodded. 'It's at times like this,' she said, 'that I remember why I married him.'

Later, in the taxi with Grace, Annie took her hand.

Grace gave a long, shuddering sigh. 'Do you mind if I stay with you?' she asked. 'Just for tonight, I don't think I can bear to stay in the same house as Henry's penis.'

★

As soon as they got into the flat, Grace asked Annie if she could have a shower.

'Of course,' Annie said. 'I'll get you a towel. And some pyjamas.'

After Grace had shut the bathroom door behind her, Annie took off her shoes and unfurled the futon. She made up the bed and went through to her bedroom. She had no idea what she should say to Grace. She had no time for Henry. Grace was a hundred times too good for him but . . . Annie sighed. She noticed her answerphone was flashing and pressed the button.

– Annie, it's just after midnight. I did intend to come back but I didn't feel I could leave Carla until she'd gone to sleep. She was sick three times, once over me which is another reason why I've come home. If you see Grace tomorrow, tell her Carla was very sorry. Tell her I'm sure Carla made half that stuff up. I'll speak to you soon. Goodnight. –

'Funny how men stick together.' Grace was standing in the doorway. She was wearing Annie's pyjamas and her face was scrubbed and shiny. 'What's a little infidelity between friends?'

Annie sighed. 'That's not fair. Ben was only trying to help. –

'I know. But I know Carla a lot better than Ben does. The only time she tells the truth is when she's drunk.'

The phone rang and Grace stepped forward. 'I can't speak to him. Not tonight.'

Annie picked up the receiver. 'Hello, Henry.'

He did not bother with a greeting. 'Is Grace with you?'

'Yes, she is.'

330

'Put her on, will you?'

Annie paused and looked at Grace who shook her head violently. 'She doesn't want to speak to you.'

'Perhaps you'd be good enough to let her tell me that herself.'

Annie pushed back her hair and sat on the bed. 'I don't think you understand, Henry. She doesn't want to speak to you at all. She'll talk to you tomorrow. She's staying here tonight.'

'Why the fuck is she staying with you? What have you been saying to her?'

Annie strove to keep her temper. 'I haven't said anything to her. It was Carla who said something to her.'

'Look, this is ridiculous. I'll come round.'

'If you come round, I won't let you in. You can see Grace tomorrow.'

There was a long pause. 'If that's what Grace really wants. Annie?'

'Yes, Henry?'

'You haven't told her about us, have you?'

'There's nothing to tell.'

'Annie? There's something else.'

'I'm listening.'

'I can't find the drinking chocolate.'

Annie looked across at Grace. 'He can't find the drinking chocolate.'

Grace folded her arms. 'Tell him it's in the middle drawer on the left of the sink.'

Annie relayed the information to Henry.

'Thank you.' There was another pause and then Henry

exploded. 'This is bloody inconvenient. Jake's rampaging round the house with all his friends and one of them has just been sick. Fizzie's watching some appalling film in the sitting room and snarls whenever I enter. And Grace is supposed to be collecting Chloe from her boyfriend's home in Salisbury tomorrow morning.'

'You'll have to do that,' Annie said.

'Bloody hell!'

'Goodnight, Henry.' Annie put down the phone. 'That's fine,' she said. 'Henry is collecting Chloe in the morning so you can have a lie-in.'

'I've been so stupid!' Grace said. 'All those weekends at drug conferences. Those meetings with potential partners. I should have realized. At least once a year he talks about getting a new partner. It never comes to anything. He just recycles the same tired old alibis. I've been so stupid.'

'No you haven't. Why should it have occurred to you that Henry was lying?' Annie glanced uncertainly at Grace. 'Perhaps he wasn't lying. Not all the time. He does sound very upset.'

'I'm going to leave him.'

'Listen,' said Annie, 'you're feeling mad right now and I don't blame you. But you don't want to make any hasty decisions. You need to talk things through with him, hear his side of the story.'

'Oh right,' Grace said fiercely, 'just like you did after Ben jilted you! I can't believe you of all people are saying this!'

Annie bit her lip. 'That's exactly why you should listen to me. I did refuse to talk to Ben and now . . . now, I wish I *had* talked to him. What I did was like locking the door and refusing to let him in and then discovering that all I'd done was to imprison myself. You might find that—'

'That I can live with a man who's slept with half the women in Bath? I don't think so!' She gave a little shake of her head. 'I'm going to bed. I'm sorry I snapped at you.' She turned and walked across to the futon in the sitting room. Then she called out, 'Annie? Did Henry ever try anything on with you?'

'No,' Annie said. 'He didn't.'

Four weeks after Grace and Annie had met, Grace invited Annie to supper with her family. When Annie was bemoaning the fact that she couldn't afford a computer, Henry made a suggestion. He had just bought a laptop, he said. He'd be happy to give her his old computer. Would she like him to bring it over and set it up for her?

He had delivered it the very next evening. He had been kind and patient, explaining how it worked and where she could buy a printer for it. She'd been very grateful and had asked if she could pay for it. That was when he had looked at her with a suggestive smile, lunged forward and stuck his tongue down her throat. She had slapped him and invited him to take his computer and himself out of her flat.

He had told her stiffly that of course she should keep the computer. She had responded with equal coldness that that was very kind of him. He had assured her he wasn't being kind. If he took it back with him, Grace would only suspect something.

CHAPTER TWENTY-TWO

Grace left late the next morning, wearing Annie's green corduroys and grey sweatshirt and carrying her ballgown in a Waitrose bag. Annie made herself a cup of coffee and contemplated the day ahead. She thought about Ben and resisted the temptation to ring him. The poor man was probably still sleeping after all the exertions of the night before. She had planned to visit the sales this afternoon but it didn't seem right to enjoy such frivolity when Grace's heart was breaking. She decided to do her seasonal spring clean instead. Perhaps she would persuade Grace to come out with her tomorrow.

She had just started clearing away Grace's bedding when the buzzer went. Annie picked up the door phone and heard Ben's voice ask, 'Can I come up?'

Her heart leapt like an overexcited kangaroo. 'I'll be right down!' she promised and flew down the stairs.

Ben hadn't shaved. He must have woken late and come straight over. 'Hi!' Annie smiled. 'Come on up!' She shut the door behind him and followed him up the stairs. 'You'll have to forgive the mess. Grace stayed the night with me and she only went a little while ago. Can I get you a drink? I suppose it's a bit early for alcohol but . . .'

'I don't want anything to drink,' Ben said. He stepped round the futon and positioned himself in front of the fireplace. He stood stiffly with his hands behind his back. 'I can't stay long. I came round to ask you a favour.'

'I'm intrigued,' Annie said. She gathered up the pillows from the floor and threw them onto the sofa. 'What can I do for you?'

Ben's face was inscrutable. 'I understand from Bella,' he said, 'that you've been setting yourself up as a career advisor.'

Annie made a face and laughed. 'I wouldn't say that! What's she been telling you? Look, are you sure I can't get you something? You look exhausted . . . I'm sorry you had such a bad time with Carla.'

'I don't want anything.' The voice was quiet and deliberate. 'I understand you think Bella should ignore my advice about her future.'

Annie sat down on the arm of the sofa and frowned. 'Ben, I'm sorry, I haven't got a clue what you're talking about.'

'Do you have any idea,' he said, 'how stupid you've been?' The question was voiced in the same low, measured tones that somehow made it all the more insulting. 'It's obvious that you've been pursuing your vendetta against me but did you have to use Bella to get at me? Do you have any idea how vulnerable and impressionable she is?'

'Hang on a moment!' Annie stood up and walked over to look straight into Ben's eyes. What she saw in them caused a dull flush of mortification to spread over her cheeks. 'What exactly are you accusing me of? Because so far none of what you've said has made any sense at all!'

'I know,' Ben said heavily, 'that a long time ago you suffered a disappointment at my hands and—'

'Excuse me!' Annie said. 'I suffered a *disappointment*? Is that what you call it? You are responsible for *disappointing* me?' She looked at his cold eyes in mounting disbelief and seventeen years of suppressed rage swept over her with all the force of a tidal wave. 'You really are incredible! You have no idea at all! When you got your mother to do your dirty work, I was about to go to the church. I was the happiest girl in the world! So your mother rings and my family points out to me that most of the guests are already at the church. The marquee is up, food for one hundred and eighty-five people is prepared, the champagne's on ice. Some of the guests, a lot of them being your relatives incidentally, have travelled a considerable distance, so we can't send them away without any refreshment. So my father goes to the church and explains that the groom has belatedly decided he doesn't want to marry me after all. He tells everyone to come home and we'll have a party anyway. I get out of my wedding dress and into something sensible and I spend the afternoon talking to people who don't know what to say to me and then when they all leave at last, taking their wedding presents with them, I go upstairs and I hear my family talking about me in hushed whispers as if I'm some sort of freak, which of course I am now. And all I can think of is that the person I trusted most in the whole world has ruined my life and I will never be the same again. I leave my job, I leave my friends, I leave my family because I can't bear to be anywhere that reminds me of you! I change my entire life because of you! So, yes, I suppose you could say that was a disappointment!'

Ben pushed back his hair. 'I don't have time for this. If you have any idea where Bella is, I'd be very grateful if you could tell me.'

'Well, of course I don't know! Don't you know where your daughter is?'

'As it happens, I don't.' Ben pulled out a letter from his pocket. 'Meg rang me early this morning. Bella is missing. She's run away. She left a note on her pillow. Perhaps you'd like to see it.'

Annie snatched it from his hand and read it through once, then frowned and read it again.

Dear Meg,

I'm sorry I can't live here any more. No one here understands what I want to do or takes me seriously. I thought after you'd seen the play you'd at least think about me applying for drama school. You said a few months ago that if I had a gap year, you'd consider drama school and now you say you'll consider it after university! It's not fair and you wouldn't have changed your mind if you hadn't listened to Dad and Dad doesn't know anything about acting. My drama teacher says I am born to act and I should fight for what I want. She says I should listen to no one but myself. She told me to follow my dream and that's what I'm going to do. Don't worry about me.

Love,
Bella

Annie handed the note back to Ben who put it back in his pocket.

'I wanted to ask you,' he said, 'if, along with all your other advice, you might have given her any suggestions as to where she should go when she left home?'

Annie shook her head. 'I said nothing,' she said. 'I said nothing at all.'

'In that case,' Ben said, 'I'll get out of your way. Goodbye, Annie.'

She heard him go down the stairs, she heard the door shut and she heard his footsteps on the pavement. Annie went to the window and watched him disappear up Pulteney Street. He had pulled out his mobile and was talking into it. What was he saying? Was he telling Meg that the bitch had refused to help? How dare he think she could be so evil, so calculating, so ruthless! As soon as Bella came back, she . . . A rush of fear, like a freezing draught, paralyzed her thoughts. Bella had told her more than once that if she couldn't act she would die. She was passionate and impulsive and quite capable of doing something stupid. In her mind's eye she saw the body of Bella floating in the canal like Millais's Ophelia. She wouldn't. She couldn't. She must be with a friend. But Ben had said they'd rung all her friends. Where was she? Where could she have gone?

Annie packed away the bedding and folded up the futon and all the time her mind was racing. There was something Bella had told her, they had talked about favourite places, Annie had said something stupid about using favourite places as positive memories and Bella had said . . . What had Bella said? Annie prowled round and round the flat like a caged animal, biting her nails and cursing her inefficient memory. She stopped suddenly by the bedroom window. Westward Ho, Dartmouth Row! The place where a kind family friend had decorated a bedroom just for Bella with a poster of Audrey Hepburn on the wall. *That* was where Bella would be.

She threw a few things together and was on the motorway within forty minutes. Her mind continued to throw up different images: Bella opening the door and refusing to come home; Bella jumping off London Bridge; Bella jumping off the top of the National Theatre. She switched on the radio and heard Slade singing, 'So here it is, Merry Christmas, Everybody's Having Fun!' She switched it off and shouted, 'No, I'm not, you stupid people!' and then switched it on again because the silence was even worse. At least the roads were relatively clear. She reached Blackheath within three hours.

Dartmouth Row was quite easy to find and Westward Ho, a moderately sized Victorian house, was near the top. A Christmas tree sparkled in the window of the front room. Annie swallowed, walked up the path and rang the bell.

The door was flung open by an attractive woman, probably a few years older than Annie, with short blonde curls, black trousers and a big, dark green jumper. The woman had a smile on her face that faded as soon as she saw Annie. 'I'm sorry,' she said. 'I thought you might be—'

'Bella?' Annie finished for her. 'I thought she'd be with you.' The disappointment was crushing.

The woman shook her head apologetically. 'I wish she was. Please, come in.' She led Annie through to the brightly lit sitting room. It was dominated by a vast painting of Fred

Astaire and Ginger Rogers dancing in a hall, empty apart from a little old man sitting in the corner. The woman saw Annie looking at it and smiled faintly. 'The little old man is Degas. I call it "Dancing for Degas".'

'You did it?' Annie asked. 'It's wonderful.'

'Thank you.' The woman gestured towards a gold-coloured sofa on which was draped a chocolate-coloured rug. 'My name is Rachel. And you are . . .?'

'Annie May. I've been giving Bella private drama lessons for a few months. I'm sorry to burst in on you like this. Ben – Bella's father – told me this morning that Bella had run away. I remembered her telling me this was her favourite place and I thought . . . I hoped . . .'

'Meg rang this morning. She had the same idea as you. I think you both might be right. Every time the bell rings I think it must be Bella.' She pushed a rogue curl back from her forehead. 'I'm very fond of her. I always wanted a daughter and instead I have two lovely sons who are both sports mad like their father. The three of them are all in Switzerland at the moment rushing up and down mountains on skis, which I'm sure is very exhilarating but it all seems such a lot of effort, don't you think? So of course I love it when Bella comes to stay and we all go to the theatre and visit the shops and her eyes don't glaze over when I talk about Harrison Ford! Have you come from Bath? You've had a long journey. Can I make you a cup of tea? I was going to make a pot anyway.'

'That would be very kind.' Annie waited until Rachel had left the room and then she sat back against the sofa and closed her eyes. It had been crazy to zoom up here without a thought. It was obvious that Meg and Ben would have considered every possibility. She opened her eyes. There was a fire crackling in the grate and the light from the amber-coloured standard lamp washed the room in a warm and friendly glow. She could see why Bella liked this place so much. There was a good atmosphere here. The Christmas tree stood slightly askew in its red bucket and looked as if it had been to one party too many. This was a room designed for comfort rather than style. She yawned again and closed her eyes.

'Hello? Who are you?'

Annie opened her eyes. At first she thought she was dreaming but the vision was quite definitely real. Annie swallowed and sat up straight. 'I'm a friend of Bella. My name is Annie.'

The vision spoke again. 'I'm Angelina. I'm Bella's mother.'

Bella's mother did not look like Bella's mother. She did not look like anyone's mother. Bella's mother looked like a Lady Penelope puppet spookily Pinocchioed into life. Her age was impossible to imagine. The most cursory glance might suggest she was in her twenties but no twenty-something looked like she did. Her bee-stung lips looked like they'd been stuck onto her face with glue. Her complexion was shiny and stretched as if someone had crept up behind her and thrown a piece of cling film over her features. She had a long, wispy fringe and blonde ringlets tumbled over her shoulders. Dynamic breasts battled against a tight pink cardigan tucked into a wide leather belt that emphasized the tiniest of waists. Black leather trousers, revealing tight buttocks and slender thighs, completed the picture. She looked like nothing on earth. She looked *literally* like nothing on earth.

'So you have joined in the search,' Angelina said. She went and stood by the fire. 'How very kind of you.'

341

'Bella's father told me the news this morning,' Annie said. 'After he'd gone, I remembered Bella saying how much she loved this house. So I leapt in my car and came up here. It was stupid! I didn't stop to think.'

'It's not stupid at all. This is where Bella will come. Rachel is my best friend. Whenever I'm in England, I stay here and my daughter always comes to see me. This is a second home to both of us. Bella was supposed to be coming up here for New Year. She knows I'm here. We have a very special relationship. She tells me everything!'

'She didn't tell you she was running away,' Annie pointed out.

'She will do,' Angelina said serenely. 'She'll turn up here today or tomorrow. I know Meg says they've rung up all her friends but there must be some they don't know about. I was always doing things like this when I was Bella's age. Children love to be the centre of attention. I know I did!'

Annie stared at her in disbelief. The woman was behaving as if Bella had just slipped out for an hour or two. Controlling her temper with difficulty, she murmured, 'I don't think that's why Bella has run away. Your daughter seems to feel things very *intensely*. I wonder if . . .' She stopped and stood up as Rachel came back into the room bearing a tray loaded with mugs and sugar and Christmas cake.

'Sit down, sit down.' Rachel set the tray on the coffee table in front of Annie. 'Please help yourself to cake. It's bought, not made, but it's very good!'

It was only then that Annie realized how hungry she was. 'Thank you,' she said. She helped herself to a slice and ate it greedily.

Angelina helped herself to a mug and went and sat in the armchair to the left of the fire. 'Meg says they all had a silly quarrel on Boxing Day. It sounds as if Ben was as tactless as ever. Apparently he told her she had as much chance of being a successful actress as she did of flying to Jupiter. Meg said Bella was upset and continued to be sulky for a few days but eventually returned to her normal self. Meg and her husband went out last night and when they got back, Bella's door was shut and they presumed she was asleep. When Meg got up this morning she went to see if Bella wanted a cup of tea and found the note from her on her pillow. I blame Ben! He is quite impossible. He hasn't the least idea how to talk to her. He has this silly prejudice against the acting profession. He wants Bella to be a teacher. A teacher! Every teacher I know – though admittedly I know only two – are both quite batty. One of them had a breakdown and the other looks as though she's going to cry all the time. I wouldn't want a daughter of mine to be a teacher!'

'Angelina,' Rachel protested, 'Annie is a teacher!'

'Are you really?' Angelina asked. 'Oh Annie, I'm so sorry! You don't look mad at all!'

'Thank you,' Annie said. 'But appearances can be deceptive. I don't think Bella should be a teacher either. I don't think Bella should be anything she doesn't want to be. And if Bella's determined to be an actress, there's not a lot Ben can do about it. Bella can apply to drama school and, if necessary, work her way through college. Other people do that after all.'

Angelina gave a shrug. 'She loves her father. Of course at the moment she hates him as well. He has handled the whole business extremely badly! A couple of years ago, I could have asked Marshall – that's my husband – to help Bella but he's very tedious about money these days. You know how mean men can be!' She smiled, revealing a range of flawlessly white teeth.

Annie wondered quite how much money Marshall had spent on his wife's appearance. She finished her tea. 'I should be getting back,' she said. 'If Bella turns up, could you possibly let me know?' She took her diary from her bag, ripped out a page and scribbled down her number.

'If you give me your notebook,' Rachel said, 'I'll write down my number. You might hear something. If she contacts you, tell her we're longing to see her.'

Annie passed it over and stood up. 'Thank you for your hospitality,' she said.

Angelina gave a languid wave. 'Goodbye, Annie. Thank you for trying so hard to help my little girl.'

Rachel scribbled a number and passed back the book. 'I'll see you to the door,' she said.

It was dark now, with a slight smattering of rain. Rachel stood on the pavement with Annie and said softly, 'I don't know how well acquainted you are with Bella's father but he's not quite the ogre Angelina makes him out to be. He's brought Bella here a few times and he loves her very much. He's never really got used to Angelina's appearance. I think he thinks she had all her surgery done in order to further her career. I suspect he's terrified that Bella might go the same way. Of course he's wrong. Bella is a very different character. Angelina's my best friend and I love her but her appearance was always important to her. Bella's not like that. You might try telling Ben that.'

Annie gave a short laugh. 'I think you'd better tell him yourself,' she said. 'I don't expect to be talking to Ben any more.'

Annie got into her car and sighed. She had been impulsive and silly. The thought of driving all the way back to Bath seemed unutterably depressing. She could always call on Josephine and beg a bed for the night. Herne Hill was only a twenty-minute drive away. She clapped her hands suddenly. 'You are a fool, Annie May!' she told herself. She grabbed her bag and pulled out her mobile. Then she rang Josephine and was relieved when her sister answered.

'Josephine,' she said quickly, 'this is very important. Is Sidney with you?'

'He's in the bath. Can I get him to ring you back?'

'No, I'm coming over. I'm only in Blackheath. Tell him I'll be there as soon as I can.'

She switched off the phone, chucked it into her bag and turned on the ignition. The roads were blissfully empty and she arrived outside Josephine's house in fifteen minutes.

Cressida answered the door and Annie gave her the briefest of salutations before spying a wet-haired Sidney at the top of the stairs. Josephine came out of the kitchen and presented a bewildered face to her sister. 'Annie, it's lovely to see you. Are you here to stay? We're supposed to be going out but—'

'This is a very fleeting visit, I'm afraid,' Annie said briskly. She was already halfway up the stairs. 'I need to have a word with Sidney and then I'll say goodbye. All right, Sidney? Shall we go into your room?'

She had half expected Bella to be hiding in Sidney's

wardrobe but its doors were gaping open and showed nothing more interesting than a tangle of clothes. There was a copy of *The Hitchhiker's Guide to the Galaxy* on the bed and a mass of CDs on the floor. Of Bella there was no sign.

Annie threw the book onto the pillow and sat down on the bed. 'Bella's run away,' she said. 'Her family are in a terrible state. As it happens so am I. That's why I'm here. She left either in the middle of the night or very early this morning. She's not with any of her friends in Bath. If you know anything at all, you have to tell me. I've driven up from Bath and I am feeling very tired and dangerously emotional. I need some help, Sidney. We're all imagining death and destruction.'

Sidney's mouth twisted and he went very red in the face. 'Did she leave a note?' he asked awkwardly. 'Did she say what she was doing?'

'She left a note but she gave no idea of where she was going. Sidney, did you know what she was going to do?'

Sidney bit his lip. 'I can't—'

'Sidney, if you know anything at all, you have to tell me. Her family is worried sick about her. She might be living rough on the streets or staying with some white slave traders or shooting cocaine.'

'You don't shoot cocaine, Annie!'

'Well, whatever it is you do shoot. Sidney, I know you don't want to betray any confidences but you have to tell me what you know. Nothing can be resolved by Bella running away. Except her exams, of course. I mean if she doesn't come back to school this term, she can kiss goodbye to her A Levels. Will you please tell me where she is?'

'I don't know,' Sidney said. 'I honestly don't know. She

had an argument with her family a few days ago and she rang me. She said she couldn't bear to live at home any more. I didn't take it seriously. We all feel like that sometimes. I told her that at least she didn't have a patronizing younger sister and an irritating stepsister.'

Annie smiled faintly. 'I bet that went down well.'

'Actually it didn't. She said I didn't understand and rang off.'

'And that was the last time you spoke to her?'

'Yes. I tried to ring this afternoon but her mobile's switched off.' He glanced anxiously at his aunt. 'You do think she's all right, don't you?'

'Can you think of anyone she might have gone to? Has she told you about any friends or relations she really likes?'

Sidney pressed his index fingers against either side of his nose. 'I don't know,' he began, 'this is probably nothing.' He stood up and went to his desk. He opened one of the drawers and pulled out a very fat envelope. 'I had a letter from Bella at half-term. She and a friend went to stay with her great-grandmother in Scotland. They haven't got a phone there and mobiles don't work so she wrote to me. She thinks her great-grandmother is wonderful. But Bella wouldn't have gone all the way up there on her own. It's in the Highlands!'

'Sidney,' Annie beamed, 'you are brilliant! I remember Bella telling me about it! Did she put the address on the letter?'

'Yes, but there's no telephone. You're not thinking of going all the way up to Scotland? She might not even be there! Why don't you ring her family and let *them* go?'

That would be the sensible thing to do. She should ring Meg. But if she rang Meg, she might get Ben and nothing would make her have a conversation with him.

CHAPTER TWENTY-THREE

Annie arrived at Tigh Begh the following afternoon. The tiny, white-washed cottage was at the very end of the glen, just a few yards from the loch. It sat at the bottom of one hill and between two others. It looked like a jewel in the palm of a giant.

Annie had parked her car at the top and had half stumbled, half walked down the track, aware that her pink lace-ups and thin jacket were not ideally suited for travel in the Highlands. At least there were lights on in the cottage and a thin spiral of smoke from the chimney.

The door was opened by Bella who looked at Annie in the same way one might regard a flying pig.

'Hi,' Annie said cheerfully, 'I was just passing and I thought I'd drop by!'

An elderly woman with short white hair and a small, thin frame, appeared in the kitchen. 'Let the lady come through,' she told Bella. 'You're letting all the cold in!'

There was a blazing log fire in the small sitting room; it made shadows dance on the walls and filled the place with the scent of pine cones. Annie, seeing the half-completed game of Scrabble on the table, apologized for interrupting it.

The lady laughed. 'Bella was thrashing me! I'm glad you came! Have you come a long way? Did you have trouble finding us?'

'I've checked into a bed and breakfast in Oban. The lady there gave me very good directions.' Annie glanced at Bella who was clearly stunned by her presence and temporarily incapable of doing introductions. 'I'm Annie May,' she said. 'I'm Bella's drama teacher and—'

'I knew I recognized you!' the lady crowed. 'You were going to marry Ben! I came down for your wedding! You and I had a very nice chat about Fort William!'

'Did we?' Annie, hearing Bella's sudden intake of breath, could feel a dull flush suffuse her features. 'And you came all the way from Scotland for the wedding? What a terrible waste of time for you!' She was aware of Bella looking at her as if she were an entire herd of flying pigs and murmured apologetically. 'It's a long story.'

'Do sit down,' the lady said. 'Take the armchair by the fire. You must be cold.' She took a seat opposite Annie and motioned to Bella to join her on the sofa. 'I thought you were magnificent!' she said. 'I'm Ben's grandmother. Please call me Elizabeth. You were so composed and calm and your heart must have been breaking!'

'Excuse me,' Bella stared at first one woman and then the other. 'I don't understand any of this! Will someone please tell me what you're both talking about?'

'I'm sorry,' Annie said. 'All this must seem very odd!' She sat up very straight and forced herself to smile. 'A long time ago, I was going to marry Ben. Then he decided he didn't want to marry me and I didn't see him again until a few months ago. I had no idea he was your father until I saw him at your play.'

Bella's eyes widened. 'Wow!' she said.

'And how did you come to be here?' Elizabeth asked. 'This is all very interesting!'

Annie relaxed a little, enjoying the fire's warmth on her legs. 'Ben came to see me yesterday.'

'So you two are friends again?'

'No, we are not. As a matter of fact,' Annie gave a light laugh, 'he was very rude to me. He was also very upset. He was worried sick about Bella.'

'I'm not going home!' Bella said quickly. 'He doesn't care about me. If he cared about me, he'd try to understand why I want to be an actress.'

'Your father's problem,' Annie said, 'is that he cares too much. He's so busy worrying about all the heartbreaks you'd face in a competitive career, he doesn't have time to worry about the heartbreaks he's causing you now. If he loved you a little less he wouldn't be so difficult.'

Bella bit her lip and stared at the fire. Elizabeth and Annie exchanged glances but said nothing. Bella turned abruptly and frowned at Annie. 'Why was Dad rude to you?'

'It was because of the things you said in your note. He thought I'd encouraged you to pay no attention to him and—'

'He's so silly! I was talking about Miss Appleby!'

'He didn't realize that. I don't think he was thinking very clearly at all. He and Meg are in a terrible state. Then I went to see Sidney and now *he's* in a terrible state. He was the one who thought you might be in Scotland. I have to tell you I think it would be cruel to put your family through another sleepless night. They do have a right to know you are safe.'

'The trouble is,' said Elizabeth, 'I have no phone here

and mobiles don't work. And I don't like driving at night.'

'I quite understand.' Annie sat forward and fixed Bella with an earnest gaze. 'I'm staying in Oban tonight. Will you let me ring Rachel and Angelina and ask them to pass on the news that you're here and you're all right? I was in Blackheath last night and—'

'Why did you go *there*?' Bella asked.

'I remembered you said how much you liked staying there.'

'I'm sorry.' Bella had gone very red. 'I didn't mean to cause so much trouble. I couldn't bear being at home any more, I was so angry and then I heard Abby's brother was driving up to Oban after his final shift at the pub and it seemed such an amazing opportunity to come up here and talk things through with Great-Gran. I knew she'd understand how I feel.'

'I may understand,' the old lady said, 'but it doesn't mean I approve of what you've done. It's high time your poor family knows where you are.' She smiled at Annie. 'You've been very kind. When you ring, perhaps you could suggest that Ben comes up to collect Bella. Tell him there's no hurry. I'm more than happy to keep her as long as he wants. And tell him it's high time he visited his aged gran anyway! Now you must be hungry and thirsty. Will you stay for supper?'

'Thank you,' said Annie, rising from her chair, 'but if you don't mind, I won't. I'm feeling rather tired and if I stay in front of your lovely fire any longer I'll fall asleep. I'll see you when term starts, Bella. And no more running away. Take it from one who knows: running away never solves anything!'

She was halfway up the hill when she heard her name being shouted and turned to see Bella racing up towards her. She waited and was gratified when Bella impulsively took her hand. 'I wanted to thank you for coming all this way to find me. But I still don't understand why you did!'

'I'm not sure either,' Annie admitted. 'I think I felt a little responsible.'

'Why? You hadn't done anything.'

'Exactly. I knew how important acting was to you. I suppose I felt I should have spent more time talking things over with you. And then when your father visited me, it was obvious he was so frightened that something terrible might happen – and though I hate to speak well of him, he obviously loves you very much . . . After he left, I found *I* kept imagining terrible things were happening to you. In the circumstances, I couldn't stay at home and do nothing.' She smiled. 'It's freezing out here. You must go back.'

Bella gave Annie a quick, impulsive hug. She said, 'I wish Dad *had* married you!' and ran back down the hill, leaving Annie to grope for a tissue and stumble up towards her car.

It was bliss to climb into bed at last. The bed and breakfast lady had been very kind and had insisted on making her sandwiches and a cup of tea. Annie had rung first Sidney and then Rachel and had asked her to relay all the news to Meg and to Ben. Now she rested her head on her hands and thought about her evening. Elizabeth was one of those rare souls who spoke as they thought. She had spoken directly and without embarrassment about the wedding that wasn't and had assumed that Annie would be similarly forthright. And so Annie had been. In the last few months, Annie had talked about that incident more times than she had in the preceding seventeen years and she had discovered in the process that each time she referred to it, the horror of it diminished. She had not yet reached the stage when she could tell all and sundry but it no longer seemed like the shameful secret it had been. As for Ben . . . she would think about Ben tomorrow. She yawned, turned over and surrendered gratefully to sleep.

Annie spent most of New Year's Eve in the car and most of New Year's Day in bed asleep. In the afternoon, she dressed and went over to see Grace.

Fizzie answered the door and said, 'Thank God it's you! Come in!'

With a beating heart and a mind racing with various scenarios, Annie followed Fizzie downstairs and was led straight to the utility room. Two laundry baskets belching dirty clothes stood in the middle of the room. Fizzie gestured hopelessly at them. 'How do I work the frigging washing machine?'

'Annie?' Henry's voice called from the kitchen. 'Is that you?'

'Wait a moment,' Annie said and went through to the kitchen.

She stood and stared at the mayhem. It was hard to believe this was the same room in which she had spent so many hours, a room which was always scrubbed and clean, which always smelt good and which always had flowers on the dresser. Now, the sink was full of dirty saucepans. Every available surface was covered with the detritus of meals. The table held cereal packets, empty beer bottles, newspapers and the battered remains of a holly arrangement. Amongst this, Jake was trying to hack turkey from an enormous carcass. The place smelt of stale cooking and stale beer.

Henry was wearing tracksuit bottoms and a stained jumper. He was unshaven and his complexion was pallid. The entire scenario reminded Annie of one of those Hogarth cartoons depicting the evils of gin. 'Where's Grace?' she asked.

'She's gone to her parents,' Henry said. 'Chloe's gone with her. The thing is we don't know how anything works. We can't use the dishwasher or the washing machine. I keep trying to ring her but she won't speak to any of us.'

Jake put down his carving knife. 'It's so unfair!' he said. 'I can see why she won't speak to Dad but I have my A Levels in June and all this is very difficult for me. And it's Christmas! Mum should be here! I can't believe she could be so selfish!'

'*What* did you say?' Annie demanded incredulously. She looked at Henry and at Jake and at Fizzie who had come in and made straight for the turkey. Annie put her hands on her hips and her eyes narrowed. 'Let me tell you what's selfish, Jake. Selfish is thinking about your own spoilt self all the time, even when you know that your mother is desperately miserable. Selfish is not lifting a finger to help a woman who spends every spare moment looking after all of you. Selfish is letting this house become a pigsty while she's away and expecting she'll clear up when she gets back, *if* she gets back. Look at you all! Grace goes away and you're as helpless as newborn kittens! None of you deserves Grace! Certainly you don't, Fizzie: you do your best to belittle your mother at every opportunity. You're greedy and you're self-centred! And, Jake, you're just as bad: you seem to get particular pleasure out of making her look stupid. But I suppose you're only copying your father because that's just what he's always doing as well. Not one of you ever bothers to think about what she feels or thinks. The three of you make me utterly sick, and don't look as though you're going to cry, Fizzie, because you have some work to do. Now I tell you what I am going to do. I will show you all how to use the washing machine. I will show you all how to use the dishwasher. And then I think you should all spend the rest of the day cleaning up this pigsty because if I were Grace and I came home and I saw all this I would turn on my heel and I would walk straight out again and I would never come back! And by the way, you will have to rinse all these dirty plates first, because if you put these filth-encrusted things in the machine, they will stay filth-encrusted. Now, Fizzie, Jake, Henry, gather round for your first lesson and pay attention!'

When she thought about it later, she couldn't help smiling but at the time she was so furious that she could only speak in her most terrifying Miss May-like tones, making each one of them show her that they had understood her instructions. When she finished, she surveyed them severely and folded her arms. 'Let me tell you something: I have decided it's time to change my life and I think it's time you decided to do the same. Grace has been the most unselfish wife and mother I know. Her only fault is that she's been so unselfish that she's turned you all into useless, self-centred parasites. It's time that all three of you grew up.' At which point she swept out with her head high.

When she got home, she threw off her coat, went straight to the computer and switched it on. Then she rang Deirdre and had a long conversation with her. Then she sat down at the computer and sent off a flurry of emails. And then she sat and gazed into space and wondered if she wasn't making a terrible mistake.

CHAPTER TWENTY-FOUR

An extraordinary fact about Annie's job was that no matter how dramatic her holidays were, within days of the beginning of a new term, school always threw up problems that had the power to intrigue or irritate and always divert. She had only been back for three weeks and already the holidays seemed like a distant memory in the face of new and puzzling pre-occupations. Why had Kylie Adams and Amber Barnard in 7F fallen out after a two-year friendship? How could she make Billy Walker and Matthew Hinchcliffe understand that improvised plays should not comprise one long simulated, or in their case not so simulated, fight scene? How could she stop the head of English from appropriating drama lessons for extra SATs preparation? It was odd that even now, after making such recent life-shattering decisions, the community of her school continued to absorb her.

Today had been particularly difficult with a bruising interview with the Head who had done his best to make Annie change her mind. She got home, picked up her mail, went through to her bedroom and switched on the answerphone. There was a message from Frances asking her to ring back any time after eight. There was also the usual one from Ben: 'Hi, Annie, this is to tell you again that I know I am a toad but I love you, I want to marry you and most of all I want to talk to you. So please ring me!'

Annie deleted his words and took off her jacket. She went through to the kitchen and made herself a cup of tea. What she would like to do was to sit in front of the television and watch mindless drivel for a couple of hours. But she had essays to mark before Bella arrived for her second lesson of the term.

She sat down at her desk and moved the vase of yellow roses in order to make room for Year Seven's homework. The florist had called three times in the last three weeks. Her initial impulse had been to bin every last leaf but she loved flowers and it seemed silly to waste them. She had contented herself with tearing up the notes that had accompanied them.

Grace rang when Annie was on her tenth essay – *Skellig is a story about a smelly angel. I hope angels aren't really smelly* – and Annie was only too happy to be distracted. She had not spoken to her friend since the morning after the fateful ball, partly because she felt Grace might not want to be contacted and partly because she had spent most of the intervening period on the motorway. 'Grace, it's lovely to hear you!' she exclaimed. 'How are *you*? How are your parents? Is Chloe still with you?'

'Never mind all that,' Grace said. She sounded uncharacteristically bolshy. 'Frances rang me this afternoon. She'd been looking through the Property Section of the *Chronicle*. She said your flat was for sale.'

Annie pushed back her chair, crossed her legs and threw down her pen. 'Ah,' she said.

'Well?' Grace demanded. 'Is it true? Is it on the market?'

'Yes, it is actually'

'I thought you loved your flat?'

'I did. I do. The thing is –' Annie paused – 'I'm moving to Egypt in April.'

'What?' The word burst from the phone like a firecracker. 'Why on earth are you moving to Egypt? When did you decide this? Were you ever going to tell me? What's so special about Egypt?'

'I have this friend called Cherry . . . Well, she's not a friend at all, actually, in fact she's very annoying but she used to teach with me in Falmouth. She's opened a college in Egypt and is looking for English teachers.'

'I see.' There was an ominous silence at the end of the line.

'I was going to tell you,' Annie said feebly.

'When? The end of March? After you left? You have a funny idea of friendship, Annie, you really do. Why are you doing this?'

'It's a challenge. I thought it was time for a change'

'What's happened between you and Ben?'

Annie hesitated. She didn't want to go into all that had happened and she had to crush the weariness that almost prevented her from doing so. 'Bella ran away. She left a note saying her drama teacher had told her not to listen to her father. Ben accused me of trying to hurt him by getting at her. He muddled me up with Bella's school teacher. Anyway, Bella's home now and—'

'Has he apologized?'

'Oh yes. He sends me flowers and messages.'

'Which you disregard. You are unbelievable. You are following exactly the same stupid path you trod seventeen years ago!'

'You see,' Annie said. 'That's why I didn't want to have this conversation! I knew you'd say that!'

'Because it's true!'

'It is *not* true. Seventeen years ago, he ruined my life. Seventeen years later, I finally decided to accept what had happened. I even decided I wanted to give us a second chance. It was like pushing back a huge boulder and emerging from my safe little cave. And what does Ben do? As soon as I venture out, he throws a load of manure over me and now it's gone into my safe little cave so I can't even stay there any more.'

'So you're running away again.'

'I am not running away, I am starting a new life.'

'Oh I see,' said Grace. 'I can't believe you can be so stupid! Well. At least you've made me see what I've been doing. I don't want to be like you. I don't want to run away when the going gets tough. I am coming home!'

'You're coming home to Henry?'

'I'm coming home to divorce Henry! At least *I* have some courage!'

'Now look here—' Annie began and then stopped as she realized Grace had rung off. Annie sat and stared at the receiver. She was glad that Grace had found some strength and anger at last. She was glad the worm had turned. It just seemed rather unfair that the worm should turn against *her*.

*

After the drubbing she had received from Grace, she was ill-prepared to accept another onslaught, particularly from Bella. At her first lesson last week, Bella had appeared awkward and tense and had only relaxed when Annie announced briskly that they must sort out festival entries.

This week, Bella had not even sat down before she glanced accusingly at Annie and said, 'My dad is really sorry, you know!'

Annie collected her box of play scripts from under her desk and came and sat down by the fire. 'I'm sure he is. Now about the Mid-Somerset Drama Festival—'

'When he came up to Scotland to get me,' Bella said eagerly, 'I told him what you'd done. And I told him you had said you wouldn't interfere between me and him, and you wouldn't give me advice about my future. I told him it was Miss Appleby and not you who said those things in my letter. He was so upset, Annie! He went out to the loch and threw stones in the water for over an hour!'

'And I'm sure that made him feel much better. Now—'

'And then Great-Gran told him she could understand him making a mess of his life once, but that to do it twice was a sign of monumental stupidity. And he agreed! He was so sad! And he's going to let me try for drama school! He wants to marry you, Annie! And I want him to! I'd like to have you as a mother!'

'You have quite enough mothers already. Now, I really think—'

'He loves you! Won't you forgive him?'

'Bella,' Annie said, 'I'll say one thing and then I don't want to talk about your father any more. A long time ago, he hurt me very much. A few weeks ago, he hurt me all over again. I am not going to let it happen a third time. Now let's talk about this festival!'

On Saturday morning, Annie's first viewers, a confident young couple in their twenties, came to see the flat. They spent twenty minutes checking the windows, opening cupboards, conferring in local whispers. Then they stared at each other, nodded and smiled. The woman said, 'We like it! When could you move out?'

Annie gaped at them. Aware that she must resemble a goldfish, she cleared her throat. 'A week before Easter is the earliest I could manage.'

The woman hoisted her bag onto her shoulder. 'That would be perfect. Give us a couple of days and we'll be in touch.' A quick smile and they were gone.

Annie stood in the middle of her flat and tried to quell the rising surge of panic. This was all happening far too quickly. She felt a sudden impulse to get out of the flat and grabbed her bag.

The sky was blue and the sun was cool but bright. She bought herself a sandwich and a small bottle of wine. She needed to rid herself of the feeling that she was swimming towards a deep bottomless hole. Walking briskly towards the park, her attention was drawn to the billboard: 'TV Reporter opens His Heart to the Chronicle! *See Page Two!*' Annie walked on and then turned back towards the kiosk. She bought a paper and felt her stomach turn over. Above the headlines about the soaring costs of the Bath Spa project, there was a photograph of Ben.

She made straight for her favourite bench at the Garden of Remembrance. There was a couple at the other end of the garden and Annie recognized them as the happy pair she had seen in the summer. She smiled and they waved.

Annie took out the paper and turned to page two. There was a huge photograph of Ben looking soulfully towards the Abbey. Above it was the title, *Ben Seymour Reveals His Broken Heart!*

In the few months since his arrival here, local news reporter, Ben Seymour, has established himself as one of our most popular local faces. Armed with good looks and a ready smile, he always makes us feel better.

Appearances, however, can be deceptive. For Ben is nursing a broken heart.

'A long time ago,' he tells me, 'I met the love of my life. I was young and stupid and scared of commitment and I lost her.

'When I moved here a few months ago, a miracle happened. She was here! I had a second chance to find happiness! But a few weeks ago we had a misunderstanding for which I had only myself to blame. I said some terrible things and I messed it up all over again.

'Now she refuses to speak to me. I know there will never be anyone else. I can't believe I was such an idiot!'

Ben says he's telling his story in the hope that others will learn from his mistakes. 'If you have a chance of happiness,' he says, 'don't throw it away like I did!'

Now, Ben plans to throw himself into his work. He says he is very lucky to live in a beautiful city like Bath and, despite his heartbreak, he has no plans to move.

That was it. Annie re-read the article and gazed at the photo of Ben. She took the bottle from her bag and awarded herself a hefty swig. Then she took out her mobile.

'Grace? Did you tell Ben I was going to Egypt?'

'Yes,' Grace did not sound in the least contrite, 'I certainly did.'

'You had no right to do that, no right at all—'

'I think I did. I think it's right that Ben should know you're leaving the country as a consequence of his actions.'

'Well, as a consequence of *your* action, he's gone and made a fool of himself in The *Bath Chronicle*! I did not want something like this to happen! He'll be a laughing stock! He's a very private person! He'll absolutely hate all this. I'm very angry, Grace! Very angry indeed.'

'Where are you? Are you at home?'

'No, I'm sitting in the Garden of Remembrance where I'd planned to have a nice, tranquil picnic and now I'm—'

'Well, stay there. I'm leaving now. I'll be with you in a few minutes.'

Annie put the phone back in her bag. She couldn't believe Ben had done this. She couldn't believe Grace had told Ben. She took out her cheese and tomato sandwich and ate it furiously. Then she reached for the bottle and had three big gulps of wine. She should have told Grace not to come here. She did not want to sit around for ten minutes with Ben's mournful face staring up at her. She took the paper and turned the page. She tried to concentrate on an article on a golden-wedding-anniversary couple and then another on a new anti-litter campaign.

She was on the letters page when she heard the gate click

and glanced up. A man in dark glasses and a black beret and a jacket with a turned-up collar was proceeding shiftily towards her. He looked like someone out of a *Pink Panther* movie. Annie stared blankly at him and then, as incomprehension gave way to recognition, her mouth twitched. It was impossible not to smile.

'Can I join you?' he murmured. 'It's me!'

'I would never have guessed.' Annie said tartly. 'Do you have any idea how ridiculous you look?'

'A little,' Ben said apologetically. 'I was trying to disguise myself. I'm worried people will look at me.'

'Of course they'll look at you, dressed like that!' She stared at him suspiciously. 'What are you doing here anyway?' She paused and answered her own question. 'Of course. How silly of me. Grace told you I was here. I take it Grace is not coming down here?'

'Grace thought—'

'I don't care what Grace thinks. It seems to me Grace is doing far too much thinking at the moment . . .' She bit her lip and tried to compose herself. 'Anyway, since you are here, I can at least tell you . . .' She stopped again and regarded him with exasperation. 'I can't talk to you seriously when you're looking like that!'

'You don't think I look a little dashing?' Ben asked hopefully.

'No, I do not.'

Ben took off his hat and his glasses, sat down next to her and smiled sheepishly. 'Hello,' he said.

'Never mind that. I want to get one thing clear. I presume you did this ridiculous interview in order to please me. If you think I would want you to pull a silly stunt like this, then you must think I am a very nasty, vengeful woman!' Annie sniffed. 'But then of course you *do* think I'm a nasty, vengeful woman, don't you?'

'I think you're many things,' Ben said, 'but never nasty and never vengeful. The last time I saw you, I was scared and desperate and I lashed out at you. I'd seen Bella hug you after the play and she introduced you to me as her drama teacher. It never occurred to me she wasn't talking about you but I should have known . . . I was stupid! When Bella told me she had been referring to her drama teacher at school and not you, I knew at once it would never have been you. I did not do the interview with the paper because I thought you would like to see me squirm. I did the article for two reasons. The first was panic. As soon as Grace told me you were planning to move to Egypt, I had to think of something that would make you at least agree to talk to me again. And secondly . . .'

'Well?'

'Well, it's all a bit like Henry the Second really.'

'What does Henry the Second have to do with the *Bath Chronicle*?'

'Well,' Ben said, 'a long time ago King Henry the Second lost his temper and declared he'd reward any knight who'd kill Thomas Becket. When Thomas was murdered, Henry was appalled and filled with remorse. For the rest of his life, he wore a hair shirt next to his skin and he ordered some monks to flog him. I don't know any monks and I'm not sure where I could find a hair shirt.'

Annie bit her bottom lip in an effort to repress a smile. 'And now I'm supposed to forgive you?'

'I behaved abominably.'

'Yes, you did. Did you really think I would tell Bella to *follow her dream*? I would never tell anyone, least of all Bella, to follow a dream! And you virtually told me I was responsible for luring her to her doom! You treated me like I was a pantomime villain! As if I'd do anything to hurt Bella!'

'I know. I know! I was scared and I felt guilty and I took it out on you. When I realized what I'd done, I wanted to pull my tongue out.'

'But you resisted the temptation.'

'If I had done, I wouldn't have been able to tell you that in seventeen years there hasn't been a day when I didn't think of you.'

'You were really vile,' Annie told him.

'I was horrible. Will you marry me?'

'And that's another thing! I resent this view you seem to have of me, this belief that I can only be happy if you ask me to marry you! I know this might be difficult for you to believe. And that's another thing I've been wanting to tell you for ages. I did not try to kill myself after I went to France! I only found out a few months ago that Lily told you that and it was a complete fabrication. Funnily enough, I have managed to be quite content without you. And I haven't pined for a husband. In fact I have spent the last seventeen years actively avoiding any lasting relationships. It is not sad to be single! *I* am not sad to be single! A lot of the married women I know would love to be in my shoes! So, I accept that you are sorry for jilting me seventeen years ago and I accept you are sorry for thinking I was the most evil woman since Lucrezia Borgia and now you can relax. You do not need to do any more acts of grovelling. I do not need you to marry me!'

Ben rubbed his eyes with his hands and sighed. 'Annie,' he said wearily, 'I'm not asking you to marry me because I think it would be a fitting penance on my part or because I think you need me. I am asking you to marry me because *I* need *you*! I've never married either. I've had some good relationships but you're the only woman I wanted to spend my life with. When I saw you drop that glass at Frances's party, I knew right away that I loved you. Why do you think I bought the house in Sydney Buildings?'

Annie faltered. 'You bought that because of me? You knew I'd like it?'

'Of course I did. You always wanted a house with water at the bottom of the garden. I was all set to buy a place down the road from Meg. And do you remember that evening I took you out to dinner? I'd spent the last few days, coming round on the off chance you might be in. Each night, I reserved a table. Marcel thought I was a very sad case. So did your neighbour on the ground floor. When I heard you'd gone to Hungary to see an old boyfriend, I thought I'd lost you again.'

'So you started going out with Carla.'

'So I stumbled into bed with Carla and wasn't quite sure how to stumble out again. Annie, I love you. I want you to be my wife. I want—' Ben froze suddenly.

The elderly couple had left their bench at the other end of the garden and were standing in front of them. The man smiled encouragingly at Ben. 'I saw your interview in the paper,' he said. 'Glad to see you're making it up with the young lady!'

His companion beamed approvingly. 'You looked so sad in

the photograph!' she said. 'Let me give you some advice if I may. Never go to sleep on a quarrel!' She linked arms with her partner and they walked out of the gate.

'That's what my grandmother used to say,' Annie murmured.

Ben picked up his beret and his glasses. He jammed the beret over his forehead and put on his glasses.

'Ben!' Annie's eyes were alight with laughter. 'Take them off!'

'Not in a million years,' Ben said.

'If you take them off,' Annie said graciously, 'I will at least consider your proposal of marriage.'

'It's tempting,' Ben conceded. 'But no.'

'I *can* think of two good reasons for marrying you,' Annie said.

'Really?' Ben murmured.

'The first is that I seriously like your house.'

Ben nodded. 'That's a pretty compelling reason.'

'And the second is that I could then avoid going to see Josephine next weekend. She wants to fix me up with one of her doctor friends.'

Ben nodded again. 'That's an even more compelling reason.'

'Unfortunately,' Annie said severely, 'I can't think of any others. Apart from the not entirely irrelevant fact that the last time you asked me to marry you, you had second thoughts at the worst moment possible and apart from the other not entirely irrelevant fact that only a few weeks ago you considered me capable of deliberately trying to ruin your daughter's life . . . apart from those facts, I have also agreed to go and teach in Egypt and I have handed in my resignation to my headmaster and he might not agree to take me back. Given all these circumstances, you can see why I have to think about it all.'

'I do see that,' Ben said generously.

Annie looked at him. 'I do wish you'd take those silly things off,' she said.

'Nothing,' Ben said, folding his arms, 'will make me take them off in public ever again.'

'You can't go round looking like that!' Annie protested. 'You'll be a laughing stock.'

'I already *am* a laughing stock,' Ben pointed out sadly.

'Oh for heaven's sake!' Annie exploded. 'I'll marry you! All right? I'll marry you if you take those ridiculous things off!'

Ben unfolded his arms and took off his beret. For a moment Annie felt a twinge of panic. But it was all right. He took off his sunglasses and his eyes were warm and loving. He was a Triffid too.

POCKET
BOOKS

Debby Holt
The Ex-Wife's Survival Guide

*'You've been a great friend to me as well as a wife –
and I hope we'll always be friends.'*

Sarah Stagg thought she had it all: a lovely husband, twin
teenage sons, a cottage in the country. Then her husband,
a keen amateur thespian, leaves her for his leading lady,
her sons go off to India, and for the first time in twenty
years, Sarah is very alone and very single.

The path of a discarded wife is strewn with hazards
and humiliations - and Sarah needs to acquire skills
for survival . . . fast!

Help (and hindrance) is at hand in the form of
well-meaning neighbours, a psychopathic mongrel, an
unassuming plumber - and an unwelcome role as Mrs
De Winter in the forthcoming Ambercross Players'
production of *Rebecca*.

Warm, witty and utterly beguiling, this sharply observed
comedy of (anything but) peaceful village life will appeal
to anyone who has lost the love of their life and had to
start over again.

ISBN 1 4165 0246 7
PRICE £6.99